D1633878

The '86 Fix
By Keith A Pearson

For more information about the author and to receive updates on his new releases, visit…

www.keithapearson.co.uk

PART ONE

1

They say you should never google your symptoms if you're unwell. I knew this, and it was sage advice. While suffering from a fever last year, I developed a particularly unattractive rash. Of course I googled my symptoms, and I had Ebola, obviously. A doctor corrected my ludicrous self-diagnosis and sent me home with some antibiotics, and a warning not to do it again.

I did it again.

The stakes were lower on the second occasion because there was nothing physically wrong with me, and I was thrilled to discover I was suffering from a condition called hyperacusis. I initially thought it was just one of those things that happened when you hit middle-age, like haemorrhoids or gout, but my intolerance of everyday sounds was recognised as a legitimate medical condition, my constant complaining validated. However, my thrill was short-lived once the doctor told me there was no magic pill to cure it. If I wanted to overcome my condition, I had to undertake a three-month course of therapy. That would be far too much effort for a man like me, so I never bothered.

My hyperacusis is at its worst in the morning when I first wake up. Lying in bed with no distractions, my ears torment me by picking up every sound within a sixty yard radius of our bedroom. It starts with the neighbour's dog barking. Next, thumping music from a car cruising slowly up our road. A young child wailing incessantly from a bedroom somewhere. Finally, Steve from next door, stood in his garden and coughing through his first cigarette of the day. So many irritating sounds, each one spiking anxiety.

Then there's Megan's breathing.

I've spent an unhealthy amount of time analysing Megan's guttural breathing, trying to identify a comparable sound that might explain to her why it's so annoying. Sucking lumpy gravy through a straw was the best I could do. She replied that it didn't matter because she was asleep and therefore it was my problem, not hers. That single statement nicely sums up the state of our relationship after twenty-five years of marriage.

The clock beside our bed squeals an alarm. 7.30am; time to rise and begin another god-forsaken day. I sit up, grimacing at the random aches and pains my forty-six-year old body has bestowed upon me this morning. I stare at my sleeping wife as she lies on her back beside me, every breath nudging her closer to a throttling. Her blonde hair is splattered across the pillow, and her once-pert breasts now hang like the ears of a springer spaniel. Her nightdress has the word 'Dreamy' emblazoned across the front — it's a delusional statement. I know I'm being harsh, and if I'm honest, the years have been equally unkind to me. I'm at least five stone overweight and my once thick mop of sandy hair is now beating a hasty retreat from my forehead, while simultaneously turning grey.

Couple our aesthetic issues with the contempt we now harbour for one another and it doesn't make for a happy marriage. What we have is a loveless marriage of habit, filled with so much apathy that neither of us can even muster enough enthusiasm to end it. It's a pitiful existence.

"Megan, it's seven thirty," I mumble while prodding her shoulder.

No response, just the sustained guttural breathing. I try again with a little more volume.

"Megan, wake up."

A slight break in her breathing suggests she might have heard me, but still no answer.

"Megan, get up," I shout.

"Shut the fuck up, Craig. I heard you the first time."

Megan is apparently awake now. I don my dressing gown and scuttle out of the bedroom.

I pad across the landing to the bathroom and position myself in front of the toilet, my bladder screaming to be emptied for the third time since I went to bed last night. I wash my hands and head downstairs to put the coffee on while Megan readies herself for work. She'll take a two-minute shower, throw on some random items of clothing, and drag a brush through her tangled hair. Minimal makeup is then applied before she douses herself in far too much perfume. This routine is usually accompanied by a series of screamed profanities and the sound of doors being slammed. My wife is not a morning person.

Downstairs, the percolator finally deposits sufficient coffee into the pot. I fill two mugs and drop one teaspoon of sugar in mine, three in Megan's. Despite consuming the output of a small sugar plantation each week, Megan has somehow maintained a reasonably slim figure, and that annoys me immensely. As I stand in our small kitchen sipping my coffee, Megan storms in. Any attempt at conversation would be futile, so I offer a faint smile which isn't reciprocated. She grabs her mug from the kitchen side and stomps off to the sitting room. I glance at the clock on the wall which suggests I need to get my arse in gear. I gulp down the rest of my coffee, drop the mug in the sink and head upstairs to conduct my morning ablutions.

Shaved, showered, and dressed in a neatly pressed pair of grey trousers and a light blue shirt, I grab my mobile phone, wallet, and keys from my bedside table. I traipse back downstairs to find Megan in the kitchen washing up our coffee mugs.

"Would it kill you to rinse your mug?" she asks in a tone that suggests she's spoiling for an argument.

"Sorry," I timidly respond.

She slams the clean mugs onto the draining board and pulls a tea towel from a drawer.

"We're going out for drinks after work so don't bother with dinner," she says.

Megan is the manager of a call centre. Her job is to supervise a team of enthusiastic irritants as they plague the nation with telephone calls to sell services nobody needs and products nobody wants. Despite being at least twenty years older than most of her colleagues, Megan is under the misguided illusion that working with a group of immature idiots keeps her spirit young. Based on previous experience, she'll probably stumble home after midnight, moderately drunk and convinced she's had a good time. At least that leaves me in charge of the TV remote control for the evening. It's the small victories that make life with Megan sufferable.

She departs for work without saying goodbye. I take a few minutes to sift through the spam emails on my phone and leave the house. I lock the front door and squint at the bright morning sun as it climbs through a cloudless blue sky. I almost appreciate the moment until our neighbour's bastard dog starts yapping again. Wishing the damn thing would drop dead, I lumber the thirty yards to a bay where my car is parked. I pause for a second to look back at the only thing in my life of any real value — our small, two-bedroom terraced house.

We bought it in 1992 when home ownership didn't require a mortgage comparable to the national debt of Greece. It sits on a street of equally unattractive properties that were all constructed in the mid-70s. After forty-odd years, most of the homes now look tired, neglected and in urgent need of maintenance. That irony isn't lost on me.

I haul my backside into the car and turn the engine over. My ten-year-old Mazda is one of the ugliest cars ever to have graced British roads, but it's reliable and cheap to run. On cue, the engine spits into life. I drag the seat belt across my bulging stomach and hit the power button on the stereo. The sound of Rockwell's 'Somebody's Watching Me' rings out from the speakers. I swing the car out of the parking bay and embark on the short journey to work, accompanied by Mr Rockwell's paranoid delusions.

For the last twenty-six years, I've worked at the local branch of RolpheTech. The company was founded in 1983 as a small chain of five stores that just sold computers. RolpheTech now has over two hundred branches and we sell an array of electrical paraphernalia from toasters to tablets, cameras to coffee machines. We occasionally still sell the odd computer.

Ten minutes later I pull into the staff car park behind the store; an architectural eyesore situated in a small retail park on the outskirts of town. Even on this bright, sunny morning, the grey concrete facade retains a depressive quality. I began working here as a sales assistant in 1990 and climbed the greasy pole to become branch manager twelve years ago. I have no idea where the last twenty-six years have gone, but I do know this isn't how I saw my future panning out when I was a bright, ambitious teenager.

My plan was to pass my O-level exams and secure a position at a decent college. I'd then go on to university to study computer sciences before embarking on a career as a distinguished programmer. I envisaged spending my days cracking codes for the government, or developing software for a multi-national company.

My grand plans patently never came to fruition. I don't know whether to blame fate, bad luck, or my incompetent decision making. It's probably a combination of the three, but as I can't control fate or bad luck, I have to accept that my decision making is the most likely reason I now live such an underwhelming life.

So here I am.

I fiddle with the multitude of locks at the rear doors of the store. There are two padlocks to undo plus a rusty mortice lock. I've done this so many times now, I'm almost Houdini-like with my unlocking duties. I turn the final key just as a white BMW enters the car park, squealing to a halt a few spaces away from my Mazda. The BMW belongs to our recently appointed sales director, Marcus Morrison.

Sometimes life deals you a hand so appallingly bad, it beggars belief. Six weeks ago I was dealt such a hand. My new boss and I were not strangers. We had history.

Thirty years ago, Marcus and I were pupils at Heathland Secondary School. Although we happened to be in the same building at the same time, we rarely mixed in the same circles. Marcus was one of the cool kids. I was a social leper. Marcus was handsome and possessed the physique of an athlete. I was gawky and possessed the physique of a malnourished trainspotter.

We also both lived on the same housing estate, although the term 'estate' was highly contentious amongst its residents. Those who had delusions of grandeur insisted on calling it a 'development' while those of us from a working-class background always called it 'the estate'. Regardless of the label, it was a badly-planned smorgasbord of three hundred boxes, scattered in a seemingly random manner across the various roads, avenues and cul-de-sacs. A box for everyone and everyone in a box.

My family lived in a modest semi-detached house while Marcus's family lived in one of the expensive executive homes on the other side of the estate. Despite coming from very different homes and mingling in very different peer groups, for one hour every week Marcus and I shared a single interest — the school computer club.

Computer club was run by Mr Scott, a stout, fifty-something career teacher who patently lost a straw-pulling contest. His forfeit was to oversee computer club. He would appear at 3.15pm to open the computer lab so we could pay homage to the dozen BBC Microcomputers, then return at 4.15pm to usher us out, and ensure that nobody had the school's one-and-only floppy disk drive stuffed in their Parker jacket.

That hour was by far my favourite of the school week. I was obsessed with computers and desperately wanted to be part of the technological revolution they promised. In the mid-80s, it was becoming increasingly obvious that those who controlled the computers would eventually control the world. The potential was intoxicating. In reality, our hour in computer club was typically spent listening to the high-pitched screeching of a cassette player as it took an age to load a blocky hangman game.

While the cassette player screeched away, Marcus would chat with me, but there was always an ulterior motive. We both owned the same model of computer at home and he would regularly ask to *borrow* one of my games. He could be the model of consummate charm, but if that didn't work, he'd drop the mask and resort to a series of subtle threats. Never of a physical nature, he was too clever for that and preferred to use psychological means to achieve his objective. He was a devious little shit.

Despite all the blessings that both his wealthy parents and Mother Nature had bestowed upon Marcus, I subsequently learnt that his life after Heathland Secondary School was somewhat chequered. He went through college and attended university, only to drop out after just four months. An equally brief stint working for his father's company followed before he left under a cloud. He then spent the next few years travelling and generally doing very little.

Then in the early 1990s, Marcus got his big break.

He took a job as a sales assistant with a startup company in the fledgling mobile phone industry. He could not have been in a better place at a better time. The industry was on the verge of unprecedented growth as the demand for mobile phones rocketed. The company prospered and carried Marcus along on their wave of success.

Then six weeks ago, during what I assumed would be a routine RolpheTech management meeting, I sat, mouth agape, as Marcus was introduced as our new sales director. After a thirty-year break, Marcus Morrison is back in my life, and today we're scheduled to have our first official meeting.

2

Marcus strides across the RolpheTech car park towards me, carrying a leather briefcase and immaculately dressed. His tailored charcoal suit precisely fits his tall, athletic frame. His insincere smile reveals platinum-white teeth and his dark brown hair is meticulously coiffured. In the bright sunshine his hair colour looks synthetic, suspiciously free from even a single strand of grey hair.

"Morning Pelling," he chimes.

Using my surname is a throwback to our schooldays, and a reminder that the dynamics of our relationship are no different. Marcus is still in control.

"Morning Marcus," I reply a little nervously.

"Beautiful day, isn't it?"

"Yep, another day in paradise," I mutter quietly enough for him not to hear.

Pleasantries over, he barges past me and through the door at the rear of the building. I pull the heavy door shut behind us, enter the alarm code and guide Marcus up the stairs towards my office on the first floor. Although this is his second visit to our branch since he joined RolpheTech, he was escorted by our managing director the first time. He was fairly aloof that day, and we barely spoke, but judging by his demeanour this morning, I've got a feeling the Marcus Morrison I remember from school has turned up.

We enter the poky confines of my office and Marcus surveys the room with a look of disdain plastered across his face. He places his briefcase on my desk and clicks the catches open.

"Coffee with one sugar would be nice," he says as he sits himself down in my chair on the opposite side of the desk.

He opens his briefcase, withdraws a wad of paperwork and slaps it on the desk. I stand motionless with my hands in my pockets, silent and seething.

"Quarterly sales figures for this branch. We'll go through them when I've got that coffee. Chop chop Pelling," he says with a thin smile, almost willing me to defy his instructions.

He's obviously assumed that I haven't changed and I'll be just as subservient as I was at school. I don't disappoint him. I exhale a quiet sigh and slope out of the office. I trudge down the corridor to the staff room and put the kettle on. I grab a couple of mugs from the draining board and dump two large scoops of instant coffee and then sugar into both, resisting the overwhelming urge to spit in Marcus's mug.

As the kettle boils, the first of my colleagues arrives.

"Morning," grunts Geoff Waddock.

Geoff joined RolpheTech four years ago after his insurance business went bust. He lost his big house, the expensive cars, and the luxury holidays, followed by his wife, his career prospects, and what remained of his hair. He's become a bitter man who now views life through a grey lens of pessimism. Despite his sullen attitude, I like having Geoff around as he makes me feel slightly better about myself. As crap as my life is, at least it isn't as bad as Geoff's.

"Morning Geoff. Coffee?"

He nods and lowers his plump, fifty-nine-year old frame onto a chair which creaks in complaint.

"Who owns the BMW in the car park?" he snaps.

"Marcus, our new sales director," I reply while grabbing another mug from the drainer.

"He's parked in my bloody space. Typical BMW driver, no consideration."

"I'll be sure to point that out to him."

I stir Geoff's coffee and leave before he has the chance to complain about it.

I shuffle back into my office and place the mugs of steaming coffee on the desk. I take a seat while Marcus sits back in my chair studying our branch sales report. He lifts the nearest mug with his free hand and blows across it. No thanks are offered as he sips the coffee, almost oblivious to my presence. Minutes pass before he finally drops the report on the desk and begins his lecture.

"Disappointing quarterly sales figures again, Pelling. 17% below target and the board of directors are not happy. You are aware this is the third quarter in a row your branch has failed to meet target?"

I feel myself becoming riled.

"As I've already told the board, the targets are unrealistic. Our sales have been declining since a new supermarket opened in the town. They stock almost everything we do: phones, cameras, tablets, kitchen appliances. It's no surprise we're losing sales."

"So what are you going to do about it?"

"What can I do about it? Frankly, I'm surprised we're only 17% down."

"You're the manager, Pelling, and therefore it's your responsibility to find the answers. You need to come up with something more constructive than blaming the competition, because the board won't want to hear that."

"Whether they want to hear it or not, it's a fact, Marcus, and ignoring it won't make it go away," I offer in defence.

Marcus places his mug on the desk and sits forward.

"Your branch is bringing down the figures for the whole region and it's unacceptable. Things are in the offing at head office, so I need this branch back on target or there will be consequences."

I sit forward in my chair.

"What exactly do you mean by *consequences*?"

Marcus drums his fingers on the desk. He appears to be contemplating whether to expand on his threat. The urge to demonstrate his authority is too much, and he eventually decides to unveil his thoughts.

"Given the fact that this branch is an embarrassment to the company, my view is that it should be shut down."

I feel the blood drain from my face. Of all the things I could have predicted when I left the house this morning, this would not have been one of them.

"What? Why would you think that when we're still making a profit? It doesn't make sense," I splutter.

"Your profits are minimal, and let's face it, this branch is an utter shit hole. It's situated in a poor location and needs a fortune spending on it to bring it up to standard. If, as you say, competition has increased, then it makes little sense to invest in improvements. It's had its day, so I think it would be better if we cut our losses and close it."

Crap. My defence has only given him more ammunition. I need to try another tactic, a more human approach.

"What about the staff? Some of them have worked here for years."

"There might be a few positions in other branches, but your prospects aren't looking so good. How long is it you've been with the company? Twenty-odd years, isn't it?"

"Twenty-six," I mumble.

"Look on the bright side, Pelling, you'll receive a decent redundancy package. You'll be out of a job, but you won't be skint, least not for a few months anyway."

His last blow is delivered with a smile I'd love to punch from his face.

Marcus puts the paperwork back in his briefcase before he takes a final sip of his coffee and stands to leave. It appears our meeting is now over. For once in my pitiful life, I need to do something, say something, anything.

"You're unbelievable, Marcus. Six bloody weeks you've been here. You're deluded if you think the board of directors are going to close our branch on your say-so."

"Oh Pelling, if only you knew the truth," he laughs.

"What truth? What are you on about?" I bark.

"You'll find out in time, but I can assure you that the board will take my recommendations seriously. We've got a meeting planned for next week and I'll submit my recommendations then. I'm confident I'll get my way, Pelling."

My aggressive approach has clearly failed. All I can do is revert to type.

"Please Marcus, don't do this, I'm begging you."

"You always were a whiney little shit, Pelling. Truth be told, I never liked you at school, and I like you even less now. Maybe fate has brought us back together so you can reassess your pathetic excuse for a career, and I can put a few things to bed once and for all."

"What's that supposed to mean?"

"Consequences, Pelling. What goes around, comes around."

Without offering me a chance to respond to his cryptic statement, Marcus waltzes out of the office. Twenty-six years of employment — all but wiped away in a five-minute conversation.

I remain seated on the wrong side of my desk although it doesn't look like it'll be my desk much longer. I slap my cheeks, hoping that this is a bad dream and I can wake myself up. It's not and I can't. Contrasting thoughts run through my mind. As mundane and unfulfilling as this job is, I don't want to lose it, possibly because I'm too comfortable and too set in my ways now. It's a habit that fits me. While this wouldn't be my career of choice, the thought of starting again fills me with dread.

Geoff raps his knuckles on the office door, waking me from my trance.

"You coming down to the shop floor at some point this morning?" he asks.

I gaze up at the clock on the wall. It's 9.15am. I realise that I've been staring at nothing for the last fifteen minutes, drowning in a pool of morose thoughts.

"Give me a minute," I sigh.

"It's dead down there, so I wouldn't be in too much of a rush," he adds before waddling off.

I need to get my head together, but then I think about what Megan will say, and my parents who have enough problems of their own to deal with. I tell myself it's just a job. Nobody has died, and at least I'm not Geoff. Suddenly a wave of guilt crashes over me. While I've been wallowing in self-pity, I've overlooked the fact my colleagues will be out of work too if Marcus gets his way. I think about Geoff, who is blissfully unaware that his perception of rock-bottom is just about to shift again. I think about Lucy, my assistant manager, a single parent bringing up a teenage daughter. I think about Alan, our young stockroom assistant, who was out of work for over a year before we hired him. None of them deserve this.

Now carrying the weight of the world on my shoulders, I reluctantly rise from the chair and try to regain my composure. As I mentally prepare myself to go downstairs to the shop floor, my phone rings in my pocket. I pull it out to see the name 'Dave Wright' on the screen. Dave and I have known one another since infant school and he's the nearest thing I have to a best friend.

I swipe the screen to accept his call and lift the phone to my ear.

"Morning chubs," he says playfully.

"Dave, it's not a good time, mate. Can I call you back later?"

"No worries, I was only calling to remind you about Saturday."

"I've told you, I'm not going," I snap.

"Somebody piss on your cornflakes this morning? Look, meet me at the Fox & Hounds later and we'll talk about it. I know something that might change your mind."

I'm still reeling from Marcus's bombshell and in no mood to argue with Dave.

"Fine. I'll see you there at six," I sigh.

"Nice one, see you then."

With his mission accomplished, Dave ends the call.

This year is the 30th anniversary of the year we left Heathland Secondary School, and somebody with too much time on their hands has decided that we should mark the occasion with a reunion. Saturday is the date for the reunion, and I can't be arsed to attend. The prospect of spending an evening in the company of random strangers who I have nothing in common with, other than we shared a few years in the same dreary school, is not my idea of fun. Whatever Dave thinks will change my mind, I think he's underestimated my resolve.

I take a deep breath and head downstairs to the shop floor. I wander across to the customer service desk where Lucy is having an animated conversation with an elderly man. Between them sits an antiquated toaster which I assume is the subject of that conversation. I take a seat at the other end of the desk and gaze at the security monitor which displays monotone views from the six cameras dotted around the shop floor. Besides the elderly man there are only half-a-dozen customers milling around. I wonder how many of them are killing time until the furniture store next door opens.

I look up from the low resolution view and stare across the real world space that has become my second home. It's funny how you stop noticing things when you see them every day. The grubby carpet peppered with dark spots of dried chewing gum. The once-white walls that are now mottled grey and splintered with veiny cracks. The polystyrene ceiling tiles which bear the scars of numerous water leaks and no longer snugly sit in their frame. There's no doubt that our branch is looking tired, but like an old pair of fraying underpants, the aesthetics are less important than the comfort born from familiarity. I hate Marcus for threatening to take this away from me.

Freed from her encounter with the elderly gentleman, Lucy wheels her office chair across the space between us. Noticing the vacant expression on my face, she goes straight into concerned mode.

"Geoff told me you had a meeting with our new sales director. Is there a problem?" she asks, perceptive as ever.

Lucy and I have worked together for almost ten years and in that time, she's learnt how to read every one of my expressions. I have to admit I initially gave her a job because I fancied her. But over the years we've developed a genuine friendship. That's not to say she isn't still an attractive woman, with her auburn hair, lightly freckled complexion and opal-green eyes, but beyond the aesthetics she's a decent human being. Telling Lucy about Marcus's plan would be the conversation I'd dread the most. It would wait.

"Nothing serious, Lucy, just going over the sales targets," I reply.

"Did you tell him about the supermarket?" she asks, her expression troubled.

"I did, and the board are aware of it," I reply, trying to offer reassurance.

Lucy isn't an idiot though, and she knows our branch has been struggling.

"So you think everything will be okay, Craig?"

I've never been a good liar, but this wasn't the time to share anything with anyone. I had no idea if Marcus's threat had any credibility. I offer her a smile, and with something approaching a passable look of sincerity, I tell her that everything will be fine. Lucy returns the smile, and seemingly satisfied with my answer, she wheels herself back to the other end of the desk where another customer has appeared.

The rest of the day passes in the same banal manner that most days at RolpheTech do. Pensioners asking for help with technology nobody has the patience to explain. Parents allowing their unruly offspring to charge around the store unsupervised. Middle-aged couples wanting to discuss the merits of overpriced coffee machines they'll buy and use only once. Everyone gets on with their job just the way they usually do. I can almost pretend this is a normal day, so in my usual head-burying manner, that's exactly what I do.

Closing time eventually arrives and we go through the end-of-day routine. One by one my colleagues say their goodbyes and leave for the day. I'm left alone in an empty store with just the faint hum of the fluorescent lights for company. I head for my office, grab my car keys from my desk, and switch off all the lights. The alarm is set and I go through a reversal of the padlock routine on the back door. Another day, done.

The Fox & Hounds is only a five-minute drive away so there is no doubt I'll be at the bar before the perpetually late Dave arrives. My round first I guess. My resolve to skip the reunion remains steadfast, but I have to admit I'm a little intrigued how Dave thinks he'll change my mind.

3

I pull into the car park at the Fox & Hounds a few minutes before six o'clock. The only other parked vehicles are a battered van and the landlord's car. I make my way through the small beer garden which is cluttered with rickety picnic tables, all weathered to a stony shade of grey.

I push open a door which grants access to a dated saloon bar. The sun has moved to the rear of the building, heating the air in the room to an oppressive level. The smell of stale beer and fried food hangs heavy in the air. A solitary guy in dark red overalls is sat at the far end of the bar, looking lost in his thoughts as he nurtures a half-empty pint glass. I approach the bar and perch myself on a stool.

I sit for a minute in an uncomfortable, sweaty silence. Sean, the landlord, eventually wanders in from the other bar.

"Sorry Craig, you been waiting long?" he asks.

"Two days," I reply, for no particular reason other than I'm hot, bothered and in need of a pint.

Sean offers me a forced smile as he reaches up to grab a pint glass from the shelf above the bar.

"Usual?"

I nod, pull out my wallet, and drop a tenner on the bar while Sean pulls my pint. As he tops the glass with a frothy head, the door swings open and Dave strides in. He's wearing shorts and a tight-fitting black t-shirt which perfectly displays his muscular physique. Inspired by a midlife crisis, Dave has become a regular in the gym for the last few years, transforming his once-plump body. While I'm deeply envious of Dave's physique, I'm not so envious of the countless hours he spends in the gym maintaining it.

Sean looks up and greets Dave with a nod.

"Usual Dave?"

"Please. Your round is it, Craig?" Dave asks as he notices the tenner on the bar.

"It looks that way, doesn't it?"

Sean grabs another pint glass from the shelf and starts filling it. I pay for our beers and we leave the heat of the saloon bar for the garden. We select a table that looks least likely to collapse and sit across from one another, both taking welcome gulps of our cold beer.

Thirst sated, Dave opens the conversation.

"I assume from our brief conversation earlier you've had a shit day?"

I spend the next ten minutes explaining the day's events and what Marcus has in plan for our store. Dave frowns and delivers his considered analysis of the situation.

"I think you're fucked, mate. Marcus might be a complete arsehole, but you know he always gets his own way. Always has, always will."

"Thanks for the positive words of encouragement, Dave. I feel so much better now."

"Just telling it as it is, mate."

He takes another large gulp of beer before continuing to depress me.

"Do you remember in primary school we were allowed to bring a toy in on the last day of term?"

I nod, unsure where Dave is going with this random question.

"Well, I must have been about seven or eight years of age, and I took my Big Trak in. Do you remember it?"

"The programmable truck?"

"That's the one. Anyway, loads of kids wanted to play with it, and eventually Marcus asked if he could have a go. In my naivety, I said yes. You know what the little bastard did? He took the batteries out and hid them. He said I couldn't have them back until the end of the day because too many kids wanted to play with me and not with him."

"You're kidding?"

"Nope, and it sounds like he hasn't changed one bit. Perhaps you're better off out of it, mate. I'd take the money and run."

Maybe he's right but that would mean letting Marcus have his way again. Thirty years on and I'm still his bitch.

"More beer will make things better," Dave says, and heads back to the bar.

As the early evening sunshine warms my back, I can sense the alcohol taking effect, my mood softening to a more wistful state. I haven't eaten anything since lunchtime, which is a bad idea when meeting up with Dave. Saying that, eating anything cooked in the Fox & Hounds kitchen is an even worse idea, so I vow to fill up on crisps when it's my round.

Dave returns holding two fresh pints and places them on the rickety table.

"So, the reunion on Saturday," he begins.

"I've got three words that will convince you to come along," he adds.

"Marcus. Stabbed. Repeatedly?"

"Better than that mate. Tessa. Lawrence. Coming," he says smugly.

I almost choke on my beer.

"How do you know?" I ask with some scepticism.

"Remember Wayne Russell from geography class?"

"Vaguely."

I don't.

"Wayne's younger brother, Stuart, works for the same company as Tessa. She told Stuart she was coming along. I spoke to Wayne at football yesterday, and he told me."

I'm not sure I quite follow the series of events that led to this revelation, but if true, it does put an entirely new complexion on my possible attendance.

"Okay, I might be persuaded," I say.

"I thought you might have a change of heart when you heard about Tessa."

"Almost. Do you know if Marcus is going?"

"No idea, mate," Dave shrugs.

The prospect of spending an evening in the same room as Marcus was one of the main reasons I didn't want to attend in the first place. There is no way he'd miss the opportunity to lord it over his former schoolmates one more time. School reunions were a dream for people like Marcus. People who'd actually achieved something in life and wanted to gloat. However, the prospect of seeing Tessa again was far too compelling. Fuck Marcus.

Tessa Lawrence was my first love. I was sixteen when she stole my virginity, and with it, my dreams.

We were in the same form group throughout secondary school and I had lusted after her from day one. By the time we'd reached our final year, my mild crush had developed into a full blown obsession as Tessa flowered into a stunning young woman. She was petite, but curvaceous, with a bob of shiny black hair and caramel eyes. Coupled with her playful, flirtatious character, Tessa was everything that boys my age desired, and she knew it. But I was so far down her list of potential boyfriends that I might as well have been invisible.

That was until one Friday afternoon in May, 1986.

I was walking home from school and stopped outside Patels' Newsagent, in two minds if I fancied a can of Coke or not. The shop was always packed with schoolkids, which inevitably meant a queue for those who had chosen to pay for, rather than shoplift, their post-school refreshments. I gazed at the queue through the window and considered whether I could be bothered to wait in line. I decided I was thirsty enough, so I entered the shop, grabbed a can of Coke from the fridge, and plodded up the aisle. As I approached the back of the queue, my heart skipped a beat as Tessa stepped out of nowhere and joined the line in front of me.

I shuffled up and stood a few feet behind her. Apart from the fleeting moments our paths had crossed in the form room, it was as close as I had ever physically been to Tessa. I stood so close I could smell her perfume, which reminded me of strawberry-flavoured Opal Fruits. I could just make out the straps of her bra below her white polyester blouse. I could see the tight curves of her perfect bottom, framed in her navy skirt. As I stood mesmerised, I prayed the moment would never end.

The queue moved and Tessa took a few steps forward. I shuffled nearer, trying to maintain the socially acceptable distance between us. Just as I inhaled another deep breath of her perfume, she suddenly turned around and glanced in my direction. Our eyes met for a split second, but just as I expected Tessa to turn back to the front of the queue, she did the unthinkable. She held her position and smiled.

"Hello you," she said cheerfully.

I turned around to see if she was speaking to somebody behind me. With nobody there, I turned back to face her.

"Hi Tessa," I replied meekly, wondering if my cheeks were as obviously red as they felt.

For an awkward moment, no further words were exchanged. I dropped my gaze from her face to her folded arms, cradling her purchases: a can of Lilt, a bag of Monster Munch, a Marathon and, surprisingly, a copy of 'Your Computer' magazine. With the sudden realisation it looked like I was staring at her tits, I shifted my eyes back to her face.

"Good magazine. I didn't know you were into computers," I spluttered.

"Oh, I'm not, I don't know the first thing about them. My mum asked me to pick it up as my little brother got a computer for his birthday, but none of us have the faintest idea how to get the damn thing working."

Then I made the first mistake of many.

"I might be able to help," the words leaving my mouth with no authority from my brain.

"Ah right, you go to that computer club thing after school, don't you?"

I nodded sheepishly. Tessa thought for a moment, chewing her bottom lip in a way that took her cuteness to new heights.

"Do you think you could get it working?" she asked hopefully.

"Probably. Do you know what model it is?"

"I think it might be an Amstrad. I try to avoid my brother's bedroom if I can help it," she replied with a giggle.

"Okay, I'm sure I could get him up-and-running in no time," I said confidently.

"Oh Craig, that's sweet of you. Can you come round tomorrow some time?"

I paused for a second, trying to offer the impression my diary was full of meaningful commitments, rather than the reality of playing computer games and masturbating.

"Yeah sure. I've got some free time early afternoon if that works for you?"

"Perfect. Thank you so much for this, Craig. I want to go to a party tomorrow night and need to keep in my parents' good books. Let's say about one o'clock. Have you got a pen? I'll give you my address."

I rummaged in my school bag, found a scrap of paper and a pen, and jotted down Tessa's address. With the queue gone, she turned and dropped her purchases on the counter.

"Sorry, I don't need the magazine now," she said to Mr Patel.

Tessa paid and turned to leave, but not before flashing me another smile. I watched her intently as she sashayed towards the door, capturing and storing every exquisite movement. Then she was gone.

Mr Patel coughed to attract my attention. I paid for my Coke and floated home in a state of hormone-induced euphoria.

Those hormones would prove to be my downfall.

4

I could hardly sleep that night. My mind crashed from wild optimism to cold realism, back and forth, up and down. By the time I got up on Saturday morning, I had settled on accepting the situation for what it was; an opportunity to spend an hour or two in the company of a girl I adored. If nothing else, I could at least show Tessa that I was more than just the quiet geek from computer club she happened to see every morning at registration.

With little else to do, I switched on my computer to drag my thoughts elsewhere for a few hours. The computer, a Commodore 64, had been a gift for my 13th birthday. In the three years I'd owned it, I'd become fairly adept at coding. After initially learning the basics of the computer language, conveniently called BASIC, I started creating my own games. Early attempts were fairly simplistic and comprised just a few hundred lines of code, but as my confidence and skills developed, so did the complexity of the games I created. The project I was working on at the time was a complicated role-playing game I'd titled, 'Afterpath'.

The game centred on a character called Professor Lance Gilgrip. While on holiday in Mexico, the unfortunate professor's wife was kidnapped, and subsequently killed in a bungled rescue operation by the local police. The heart-broken professor channeled his grief into developing a machine that would allow him to travel back in time and undo the decisions that led to his wife's ultimate demise.

The game involved the professor navigating his way through a series of interactions with various characters, hoping to stop either the kidnap, or the bungled police operation. However, if the professor made any incorrect decisions during those interactions, his timeline spun off in a different direction, to an alternative future; usually one where his wife, or the professor himself, ended up dead. It was like cracking a code to a safe — only one sequence of correct interactions would lead the professor to his ultimate aim.

I spent two hours trying to work my way through a major bug with the game, but the complex layers of code made it near-impossible to make any real progress. Growing frustrated that I was no closer to fixing the bug, I turned my attention back to my visit to Tessa's house. I switched the computer off and headed for the bathroom.

I took a long shower and doused myself with an excessive amount of Jazz aftershave I'd received at Christmas. I'd hoped to wear it on occasions where I might come into close contact with girls. The bottle was still full. I put on my best pair of jeans and the only vaguely fashionable shirt I possessed. It was a soft, burgundy material with a button-down collar. Finally, I put on my brand new Nike trainers.

I then went back into the bathroom and styled my hair using liberal amounts of toxic-green hair gel. I brushed my teeth and took one final look at myself in the bathroom mirror. Passable. Definitely passable.

I spent the next fifteen minutes anxiously pacing up and down my bedroom, trying to imagine the things I might say or do to impress Tessa. With no inspiration and my nerves frayed, I gave up and left the house.

It was unusually chilly for late spring and the watery sun struggled to warm the air. I cursed my decision not to wear a jacket. Within five minutes of brisk walking I warmed up a little, only then to panic about sweat stains appearing on my dark shirt. I slowed my pace and walked on.

Bang on time, I arrived at Tessa's house. It was a huge, red-brick building, Victorian or Edwardian I guessed. I crunched across the gravel driveway and approached the front door. I tried to steady my nerves and rapped the brass knocker. Until the moment Tessa opened the door, I had never seen her wearing anything other than school uniform. I think my jaw may have dropped when she stood before me, dressed in white jeans and a cropped yellow t-shirt that displayed her naked midriff. She looked incredible.

"You're the punctual one, aren't you? Come on in," she said with that killer smile.

My bone-dry mouth would only allow me to offer a feeble greeting. I took a few steps across the tiled floor into the large hallway, a broad staircase directly ahead of me. Compared to our bland, boxy house, it felt like a stately home.

"Let's get you upstairs and I'll introduce you to Kevin, my little brother."

I followed Tessa up the stairs, not once taking my eyes from her perfect backside. At the top of the stairs, we turned along a bright, airy landing. Tessa rapped on the second door along before opening it. The familiar smell of a teenage boy's bedroom drifted across the landing and hit me like a stinking brick. A combination of cheap deodorant, sweaty socks and that indescribable odour that can't quite be placed, or you'd want to analyse too deeply. We entered the room to find the stick-thin figure of Kevin, sat at a desk across the room. He was wearing a baggy blue tracksuit and looked more like a child than a fourteen-year-old adolescent. There was dirty laundry strewn across the floor and an unmade bed, positioned against the wall opposite the desk.

"Kevin, this is Craig, he'll help you with your computer," Tessa said gently.

Kevin remained transfixed to the blue screen which displayed very little.

Tessa turned back to me.

"He's quite shy," she said apologetically.

"Hi Kevin," I said.

He didn't answer, but prodded a few random keys on the computer keyboard.

"Can I leave you boys to it?" Tessa asked, aiming the question at me rather than Kevin.

"Um, sure," I replied.

Tessa smiled and left the room, closing the door behind her.

So there I was, abandoned in a stinking bedroom with just Kevin the mute for company. It wasn't quite the afternoon I had hoped for.

I approached Kevin's desk and looked over his shoulder. The computer was an Amstrad CPC 464, a hugely popular machine with a combined keyboard and tape recorder, plus a colour monitor. Kevin continued to stare blankly at the screen, fingers poised over the keyboard but remaining motionless.

"Okay Kevin, Tessa says the computer doesn't work. Can you tell me what the problem is?"

After what seemed like an eternity, Kevin eventually spoke.

"Can't get games to load," he quietly replied.

"Can you show me what you do to load games?"

Without replying, Kevin typed a command and hit the enter key. An error message appeared.

"Have you got the operating manual, Kevin?"

He reached down below the desk and retrieved the manual, dropping it onto the desk next to the keyboard. I scanned the manual until I came to the section about loading software. I studied what Kevin had typed on the screen and compared it to the instructions on the page. According to the manual, you had to simply type the word 'CLOAD', followed by a single speech mark. I bent down to get a closer look at what Kevin had typed and immediately saw the problem — he'd added two apostrophes rather than a single speech mark.

I moved the cursor to the end of the line, deleting the apostrophes and adding the single speech mark. I pressed 'Enter' and a further instruction appeared — 'Press PLAY then any key'.

Kevin suddenly sat bolt upright, moving closer to study the new words that had appeared on the screen before him. I hit the play button on the tape recorder and then the 'Enter' key again. The silence was pierced by the familiar, high-pitched screeching from the tape. The screen changed from blue to a vibrant shade of red and then, line by line, a loading graphic slowly appeared. A huge grin spread across Kevin's face, and just to make me feel a shade more uncomfortable, he began clapping and whooping. I was about to explain his mistake, but by that stage he was in such a state of excitement I doubted he would take it in.

The one and only benefit of Kevin's noisy outburst was that it brought Tessa back into the room. She looked at the screen which was displaying a full loading graphic for a game I didn't recognise. Kevin continued to clap and whoop, and then suddenly turned to face Tessa.

"He fixed it! He fixed it!" he shrieked.

Before I could explain just how simple the problem was to fix, Tessa moved in to grab me in an unexpected embrace. She was a good eight or nine inches shorter than me, and with her head pressed tightly against my chest, I inhaled the clean, floral smell of her hair. It was a welcome relief from the stench of Kevin's bedroom. Until that point, the only females to have ever hugged me were my mum and gran. But unlike those maternal hugs, Tessa's hug caused an immediate stirring in my groin. As much as I didn't want her embrace to end, I was becoming increasingly conscious of my erection. It needed little encouragement to make an appearance at the best of times.

I reluctantly broke away from Tessa's embrace, unsure if she'd noticed the bulge in my jeans. She kept a hand locked to my upper-arm and stared up at me.

"Thank you so much for this, Craig. You have no idea what this means to Kevin."

Judging by Kevin's enthusiastic reaction, I guessed it meant a lot. Tessa released her hold on my arm, turned and placed her hands on Kevin's shoulders.

"Mum wants to take you into town now, Kevin. Maybe you can buy more games?" she said in a tone a mother might use with a toddler.

Kevin looked up at me with eyes which were as disturbingly big and brown as Tessa's.

"Will more games work?" he said in a worried voice.

"Yes they will. I'll write some instructions just in case you get stuck again."

Without warning, Kevin leapt from his chair and threw his arms around me.

"Thank you, friend," he said.

I gulped back the sudden surge of an unrecognised emotion that Kevin's gratitude had awoken.

"It's no problem," I replied with a slight croak in my voice.

As Kevin bounced off downstairs, it crossed my mind what a difference that single speech mark had made to him.

With the computer problem solved, I reluctantly accepted my time with Tessa was over. I turned to say goodbye but Tessa got in first.

"Got any plans for the rest of the afternoon?" she asked.

"Nothing important. Why do you ask?"

"Well, seeing as you're now my brother's hero, you could hang around here for the afternoon. Maybe listen to some music or something?"

"Yeah, I'd like that."

"Brilliant. You'll enjoy it, I promise," she added with a playful grin.

5

Once Kevin and his mother had left the house, we moved to the more fragrant surroundings of Tessa's bedroom. It was a huge room with tall windows hidden behind baby pink roller blinds. In fact, the whole bedroom was a picture of pinkness from the poster-clad walls to the thick carpet. The pinkness was only broken by the bulky, black hi-fi system and two speakers sat on top of a chest of drawers.

We sat on her bed, and after maybe twenty minutes of uncomfortable small talk, Tessa got up and sauntered over to the chest of drawers. She rummaged through a box of cassettes, selected one, and dropped it into the slot on the front of the hi-fi. She pressed the play button and a cacophony of electronic chords filled the air, followed by an electric guitar. Then the unmistakable voice of Freddy Mercury boomed out. Even with my limited knowledge of pop music, I knew the track was 'One Vision' by Queen.

"My favourite album, 'That's what I Call Music 6'. It's a bit old now but I still love it," Tessa shouted over Mr Mercury.

The next few moments were as wonderful as they were surreal. Tessa stood in the centre of the room and strutted around, holding an invisible microphone and lip-syncing to the lyrics. She posed and pouted in a Freddy Mercury style, thrusting her hips back and forth. I was mesmerised by her performance.

As the track ended, Tessa stood breathlessly before me.

"Dance with me Craig," she pleaded.

The next track started. I thought the voice sounded like Nik Kershaw, but I wasn't familiar with the tune. Tessa beckoned me to stand, so I hesitantly got up from the bed and moved towards her, feeling more than a little self-conscious. Her arms encircled my waist, pulling my body tight to hers. I placed my hands on her shoulders and let Tessa take the lead. Not for any chivalrous reason, I just couldn't dance to save my life. She slowly circled her hips, grinding against me as she stared into my eyes, with a mildly psychotic look on her face.

Two things then became apparent.

Firstly, the song, which I later learnt to be 'When a Heart Beats', was virtually impossible to dance to, even if you knew how to dance. Secondly, Tessa seemed unconcerned that my penis was fully erect and pressed hard against her stomach.

We continued to sway around in clumsy circles, Tessa's eyes never leaving mine and her hands grasping my buttocks. My hands had fallen from her shoulders to her waist in an effort to control her relentless grinding. As Nik Kershaw wound down, Tessa's hands left my buttocks and climbed to my shoulders. She pulled me closer so our faces were only an inch or two apart. I knew what was about to happen.

I had only kissed one girl before, and that was in the last year of primary school. It was a sloppy, awkward and ultimately brief moment with a girl called Karen O'Donnell. I had grave doubts my single snog experience with Karen would help in that moment.

Tessa moved in, closing her eyes and tilting her head slightly to the left. I mirrored her actions and our mouths met. Within a split second, she had thrust her tongue into my open mouth and began exploring wildly. I attempted to reciprocate, but with no obvious pattern to Tessa's probing tongue, it was impossible to make progress. Instead, I took the opportunity to grope her body.

I began at her waist, where her naked torso was exposed below her cropped t-shirt, and slowly moved north until I reached her shoulder blades. Her tongue became more frantic, and she pressed herself tighter to my body. My hands continued to wander over the smooth skin of her back until suddenly, she pulled her face from mine.

"Get undressed. I'll be back in a minute," she whispered before she turned and left the room.

I distinctly remember thinking that all my Christmases had come at once, but in my excitement I had overlooked one minor issue; I didn't have a clue what to do, or how to do it. This was not a scenario I could have envisaged in even my wildest or wettest dreams. Forget first base, or second, or even third, I was about to try for a home run off the first ball. In reality I was ill-prepared for sex with anyone, let alone with a girl who was obviously more experienced than I. My penis didn't care and led the way.

Keen to get under the duvet before Tessa returned, I undressed like a man possessed. I had grave doubts that the full glory of my skinny, naked body would have been much of a turn on. After fumbling with my shirt buttons for what seemed like an eternity, I stripped off my jeans, considered leaving my socks on, but relented, and slid under the duvet.

The hi-fi was now playing a Eurythmics track called 'There Must be an Angel'. I laid on my back staring at the ceiling, my penis protruding like a stumpy tent pole beneath the pink duvet. I tried to control my heart rate as the anxious seconds turned into minutes. The bedroom door eventually opened and Tessa appeared wearing a silky dressing gown; pink obviously.

Closing the door behind her, Tessa approached the bed. She stopped a few feet short and slowly untied the chord that kept the silky material tight to her curves. The dryness in my mouth returned with a vengeance as I gulped nothing but air. Both ends of the chord dropped vertically, and the dressing gown opened just an inch, providing a tantalising glimpse of the treasure within. Tessa stood for a few seconds before raising her hand to tease the silky material from her left shoulder. With no resistance, it slid down her naked body to the floor.

Her body was every bit as perfect as I'd imagined. I could barely breathe as I lay there staring wide eyed at the first naked female I'd ever seen in the flesh. I had dreamt about this moment so many times, and now I was only seconds away from touching her, having her. I was in heaven. The sensuality of the scene was only slightly marred by Jim Kerr singing 'Alive & Kicking' in the background. I've never liked Simple Minds.

Tessa edged forwards and pulled the duvet back to reveal my naked body, and now painfully erect penis.

"Somebody is pleased to see me. Room in there for another one?"

I shuffled closer to the edge of the bed and Tessa climbed in beside me. She rolled onto her side so we were facing one another, and then she moved in for more aggressive French kissing. To address the awkward angle of her attack, I raised my upper body and propped myself, somewhat uncomfortably, on my right elbow. My contortion seemed to help as Tessa continued her hungry assault on my tonsils.

Our sloppy kissing continued for a few minutes. I didn't have the faintest idea what I was supposed to do, so I continued to run my free hand up and down her body, in the least sexual manner possible — akin to stroking a dying dog. Pins and needles attacked my right hand which was trapped in an impossible position under my hip. Tessa eventually broke for air, and as if she'd read my mind, she whispered instructions.

"Finger me."

To your average sixteen-year-old male, fingering is like gravity — you know it exists but you don't understand how it works. The only research I could call upon was a low-budget VHS porn video I'd watched at Dave's house. I was faced with a dilemma. Did I admit to Tessa that I didn't have a clue what to do, or did I try to busk it? I decided upon the latter option. As Tessa rolled onto her back, the first problem became apparent. I was right handed, but I was leaning on my right arm which meant I had to administer the fingering with my left hand. I foolishly pressed on regardless.

I ran my hand across Tessa's stomach as she mewed gently in anticipation. I slowly moved my hand towards the target area until it was roughly in the correct location. That was the point where my plan, if you could call it that, ended. My knowledge of the terrain was minimal, and with no real idea what I was doing, I poked and prodded my way around like a fat-fingered child experimenting with Play-Doh. This pitiful action continued for only a minute before Tessa decided she'd had enough of my assault on her genitals and pulled my hand away.

I didn't actually know what foreplay was, but I decided it was over, anyway. My penis had been erect for at least fifteen minutes, and my testicles were throbbing. My biology lessons at school never covered exploding testicles, but I wasn't prepared to take any risks.

"Can we have sex now please?" I whimpered.

Tessa smiled, and without saying a word, she turned to her side. She pulled open a drawer in her bedside cabinet and withdrew a condom. This one act substantiated my earlier view that this was not the first time Tessa had done this. I guessed that she probably wasn't a virgin. Any lingering doubts to Tessa's virtuous nature were quickly extinguished as she placed the edge of the condom wrapper in her teeth, tore it away, and pulled the condom out in one fluid motion. Case closed, she had definitely done this before.

She turned back onto her side to face me, and without warning, she grabbed my penis in her right hand. An electric spasm shot through every nerve in my body, my testicles throbbing in complaint. As the spasm subsided, Tessa expertly rolled the condom onto my pulsing member with her left hand.

"Your first time?" she asked, as if the answer was not already obvious.

I nodded, still reeling from having my penis grasped by an actual female.

"Don't worry. I'll be gentle with you," she smiled.

Tessa rolled onto her back and shuffled nearer to the centre of the bed. I took this as an invitation to assume the missionary position above her, arms pressed either side of her head for support, and our genitals in the same approximate neighbourhood. In my blissful ignorance, I was unaware that the docking procedure required some fairly deft navigation. I thrust my hips forward and my penis dug into the mattress, south of the intended target. I repositioned and tried again. I went too high and my penis slid across Tessa's stomach. This went on for several more futile, and increasingly embarrassing attempts, before she became rightfully impatient.

"Just relax," she said, with a detectable hint of frustration in her voice.

She then reached down and held my penis in the correct position. I slowly let my hips relax, and finally, felt myself enter her.

"That's good, now shag me hard," she ordered.

I let my hips rise and fall in stiff, mechanical movements, like the Tin Man in a porn version of The Wizard of Oz. As clumsy as my technique was, I was too excited to care. This was it. I was actually having sex with Tessa Lawrence. Years of waiting, of dreaming, and finally…

Oh dear.

After barely a dozen rusty thrusts I could already feel the pressure mounting. If I was to postpone the fast-approaching conclusion to our love making, I had to focus on a negative stimulus. I recited lines of computer code in my head. I tried to recall elements from the periodic table — and in a final act of desperation, I pictured the ruddy face of Mr Scott from computer club. It was all to no avail. I couldn't hold back the tide any longer. With one final thrust, I exploded into orgasm, almost unaware that there was another person engaged in the act below me.

Forty seconds and it was all over.

As the final waves from the concluding event ebbed away, I opened my eyes and the first thing I saw was the look of disappointment and mild annoyance on Tessa's face.

"I'm sorry," was all I could say.

She let out a sigh.

"Don't worry about it, Craig," she said wearily before turning her head away from me.

The next few seconds were excruciatingly long as Tessa gazed into space, and my arms cramped.

"Shall I get off now?" I asked.

Still gazing away from me, Tessa replied curtly in the affirmative.

I pulled backwards and crabbed my body to the side, so we were lying like two spoons together. Freed from my body on top of her, Tessa visibly shuddered and was out of the bed within a second. She snatched her dressing gown from the floor, and I caught a final glimpse of her naked body before it was hidden beneath her silky dressing gown.

"My mum will be back soon. The bathroom is at the end of the landing so get dressed there. And make sure you flush the condom away," she said flatly as she tied the chord around her waist.

She then stomped across the room and sat down on a cushioned stool next to her dressing table. I watched her for a moment as she brushed her shiny black bob. No further words were exchanged, but I caught her glare reflected at me in the dressing-table mirror. I took this as my prompt to follow Tessa's instructions.

I gingerly crawled from the bed and scanned the floor for my clothes, which were in a crumpled pile six feet away. Trying to avoid any chance that Tessa might catch my naked reflection in the mirror, I shuffled across the space and bent over to scoop up the pile of discarded clothes. Just as I reached for an errant sock, my body let me down again. Several litres of pent-up wind escaped my colon, rasping beyond my clenched buttocks.

I made a bolt for the bathroom, hurriedly dressed and left Tessa's house; the forgotten condom dispatching its contents into my underpants a few hundred yards later.

6

On the Monday after my visit to Tessa's house, she approached me on the way home from school. She told me gently, but firmly, that there would not be a repeat performance. She added that it would be better if we kept what happened just between the two of us — I agreed with some relief. I was utterly heartbroken, but not exactly surprised after my performance. What I wasn't prepared for was the emotional firestorm that awaited me. From the moment I closed the door at Tessa's house, my mind trapped itself in an endless loop, analysing every action and every word, over and over again. The more I tried not to think about it, the more vivid and excruciating the memories came.

To make matters worse, we were reaching the end of the school year and my exams were imminent. As I sat in my bedroom and stared at my textbooks, nothing would bypass my introspection of that afternoon, and revision became impossible. I stupidly purchased a copy of 'Now That's What I Call Music 6', and listened to it on a constant loop, torturing myself further. I was an emotional wreck.

I struggled through my exams and a few weeks later, a brown envelope landed on the doormat at home. I felt sick as I tore the envelope open, knowing deep down that the contents would end my dreams. I wasn't wrong. My grades had fallen off a cliff and there was no way I'd be able to secure a place at college with such poor exam results. As bad as I felt in that moment, I knew worse was to come when my parents arrived home from work, bringing their high expectations with them. It wouldn't be long before I crushed those expectations.

"Oh Craig, what happened?" Mum said with a look of abject disappointment written across her face.

"We had such high hopes for you, didn't we, Colin?"

My dad, sat in his favourite armchair reading the newspaper, looked up with a face of stone.

"This is down to that bloody girl you've been sulking about, isn't it?" he asked, ignoring Mum's question.

I was surprised he'd even noticed my change of mood, such was his general lack of interest in my emotional wellbeing which he'd long-since delegated to my mum.

"I've not been myself, I know that," I offered in defence.

Dad dropped the newspaper to his lap and ran a hand through his thinning hair. I instinctively knew he was about to deliver a lecture.

"Look boy, life is tough and you have to play the hand you're dealt. You can't change anything so you need to pull yourself together and concentrate on what you're going to do next."

"I could re-sit my exams?"

"And you expect us to carry on supporting you? No chance. You had your opportunity, and you blew it because you sat in your bedroom and, rather than revise, you sulked over some bloody girl," he bellowed angrily.

I looked towards Mum in the hope she might interject in my defence. She dropped her gaze from mine and remained silent, ever the loyal wife.

Dad continued his rant.

"If you want to continue your studies, do it in a few years' time when you can afford it. For now, you have to pay your way in life, because I'm sure as hell not going to subsidise you. I'll give you four weeks to get yourself a job and start paying housekeeping."

With that, he picked his paper up to indicate that the conversation was over, as were my hopes for the future. Mum offered me a weak smile of condolence before she bustled off to start dinner.

I barely left my bedroom for the next few days. My head was a complete mess, and I spent those days running the full gamut of emotions. It was too much for a sixteen-year-old boy to cope with. On the fourth day of my self-imposed exile from society, a gentle knock on the door woke me from my trance. The door opened and Mum invited herself into my room, taking a seat on the edge of the bed where I lay.

"Are you okay, love? I'm worried about you," she said softly.

I stared across at her — the woman who had brought me into this world and then dedicated herself to protecting me from it. I suppose it's part of parenthood that at some point, you have to accept you can't protect your child from everything. There's some pain we're all destined to taste, and this was my time.

I looked into her eyes and the dam collapsed. I felt my lips tremble, and my chest heaved gently. My eyes misted with tears, and I couldn't hold back any longer. For the first time in years, I cried. Uncontrollable, deep sobs. My mum didn't say a word as she moved across the bed and held my convulsing body. Through stinging tears and with a broken voice, all I could say were three short words.

"It hurts, Mum."

She waited for a few moments, and slowly released me from her arms, before gently cupping my face in her hands.

"I know it hurts, sweetheart, and it will do for a while yet. But every day it will hurt a little less, and one day the pain will go forever. I promise you."

She smiled and used her thumbs to brush away the tears from my cheeks. I couldn't have loved my mum any more than in that moment. Her simple act of maternal intervention had allowed me to release weeks of pent-up emotion. My problems were still real, but Mum had at least removed the emotional millstone that had been slowly crushing me. It was enough to build upon.

I hugged Mum tightly, not wanting to leave the sanctuary she provided. Eventually, and a little reluctantly I broke the embrace.

"I've ruined everything. What am I going to do now, Mum?"

She smiled and dropped her hand into the front pocket of the apron which she always wore around the house. She pulled out a piece of paper and pressed it into my hand.

"I went shopping with your Aunt Judy before work this morning. On the way back, we passed the video store on Eton Drive. You know the one?"

I nodded in reply. We didn't own a video player, but I'd seen the store countless times on the way to the chip-shop, which was a few doors away.

"They've got a sign in the window. They're looking for a trainee manager and I thought you might be interested."

Compared to my revised career prospects which were long-term unemployment or a low-paid youth training scheme, it actually seemed a preferable option.

"The phone number is on that piece of paper. Have a think about it, and if you feel ready, give them a ring. Nothing ventured, eh?"

She ran her hand through my hair, and with a final assurance that everything would be okay, she went back downstairs.

I sat and stared at the piece of paper for some time, like it was a ticket for a journey I didn't want to take. But faced with few other options, and a father threatening to make me homeless, I thought it might be a short-term solution. Mum was right; nothing ventured.

I traipsed downstairs and took a seat on the fake mahogany telephone bench, which was too big for our small hallway. I placed the piece of paper down, lifted the receiver and carefully dialled the number. It rang nine or ten times, and just as I was about to hang up, a breathy voice answered.

"Hello, Video City," he said tersely.

"Hello. I'm ringing about the job you're advertising in the window, the trainee manager position. I'd like to apply, please," I said in my best telephone manner.

"Hold on," he replied.

I heard the sound of the telephone receiver being dropped onto a hard surface, followed by some coughing and other assorted noises I couldn't identify. This continued for a minute until he picked up the receiver again.

"You still there?" said the voice.

"Yes."

"Can you come in tomorrow for an interview, about four o'clock?" he asked.

"Yes I can. Who should I ask for?"

"Me, Malcolm. I'm the owner. I'll be the only person here, but we don't open until five so we can have some privacy," he replied as his heavy breathing seemed to intensify.

Malcolm asked my name, my age, and a few other basic questions, which he seemed to note down judging by the long pause after every answer. When he finished, I politely said goodbye and put the receiver down, thinking to myself that Malcolm sounded more like a predatory paedophile than a legitimate businessman. Still, beggars couldn't be choosers, so I headed to the kitchen to give Mum the good news.

7

I awoke the next morning, and for the first time in a long while, I wasn't immediately greeted by bleak thoughts. My actual first thoughts concerned my one-and-only suit, and whether it still fitted me. Mum had accompanied me to Dunn & Co the previous year to acquire a suit for my cousin's wedding. After an hour of trying on various suits that made me look like either an accountant or a geography teacher, we settled on a compromise; a silvery-grey number with wide lapels, grey flecks and a slight sheen to it.

I pulled open the doors to my wardrobe and scoured the rail in search of the suit. As mild panic rose, I found it hidden amongst a section of clothes that even somebody as unfashionable as me wouldn't dare be seen in. I laid the suit on the bed and stripped off my pyjamas. I slipped into the jacket, deliberately avoiding eye contact with the mirror on the inside of the wardrobe door. The cuffs were about half-an-inch short of my wrists, but apart from that, it still seemed a respectable fit.

Next, and of greater concern, the trousers. I pulled them on, and to my utter relief, I could still button them up around the waist. I dared to face the mirror, and even without a shirt, I thought I looked like a man in a suit should. That was until my eyes dropped south and I realised the hems of both trouser legs hung a good inch above my ankles. Shit. I had no back-up plan, but assuming that Malcolm and I would be separated by a desk, I thought I could get away with it.

With the suit issue resolved, I got dressed, left the house and walked to the bus stop. My plan for the day was to head into town and visit the library so I could scan a few books on interview techniques; something our school curriculum had failed to furnish us with. The bus arrived, and fifteen minutes later, I stood in the reference section of our local library. I spent the next two hours studying the library's meagre selection of relevant books, jotting the most important nuggets of information into a small notepad. I knew that I had to give a firm handshake, look the interviewer in the eye, and ask lots of questions about the business. I knew I had to speak enthusiastically, but I should also listen carefully. Not one book covered the subject of ill-fitting trousers.

I returned home and went straight to my bedroom to get ready for the interview. I put on the best of my old school shirts, and a tie pilfered from my dad's wardrobe. Finally, on went the trousers, the jacket, and my black leather school shoes. I took a final look in the mirror, and happy that I looked smart enough, headed downstairs. After Mum had given me a positive second opinion on my attire, she kissed me on the cheek and wished me good luck.

The last of the summer sunshine broke through the choppy clouds as I ambled my way to Video City. Even though it was my first job interview, I didn't feel particularly nervous. I was well prepared, and I didn't think Malcolm would provide the most challenging of interviews. He hadn't asked for a CV and there was no request for an application form to be completed — most importantly though, he hadn't quizzed me about my qualifications.

I arrived at Video City just before four o'clock and pushed the front door. Locked. There was no doorbell, so I rapped on the glass door and took a step back. While

I waited, I inspected what I hoped would become my place of work. The store had been split into two areas either side of the front door, walls lined with shelves and faced with hundreds of video cases. Handwritten labels were stuck at various intervals, indicating which genre of movie was on each shelf, and a six-foot wide counter sat centrally at the rear, with tatty movie posters stuck to the front. I wasn't sure what to expect of a video store, but I think my first impression was that it looked a bit low rent.

Seconds passed before a figure appeared through an archway behind the counter. I shuffled nervously on the spot as a man waddled towards the door and reached up to unlock a bolt at the top. As he stretched, his brown polo shirt lifted, and his vast gut pressed against the glass. He then bobbed down to unlock another bolt at the bottom of the door and pulled it open.

Judging by his laboured breathing, the unlocking process must have been quite a workout. The man held out a pudgy hand for me to shake.

"You Craig?" he puffed.

"Yes, here to see Malcolm for an interview," I replied, unsure if the man stood in front of me was Malcolm.

"That would be me."

I shook Malcolm's hand firmly, as per the note gleaned from my library session earlier. His palms were clammy, handshake feeble.

"Let's chat in my office," Malcolm said.

He bolted the door again, mercifully with his back to me, and plodded across the store towards the counter. I couldn't determine Malcolm's age, his excessive weight distorting his features. I guessed he was in his fifties, judging by the clumps of greying hair above his ears and unruly strands teased across his bald dome. He left the pungent smell of cigarettes and stale sweat in his wake as I followed with some trepidation.

He led me beyond the counter and through the archway, into a small corridor. Dim light entered through a filthy, glazed door at the rear. I earmarked it as my best option for escape, should the need arise. There were two further doors in the corridor; one to my left and one to the right. Malcolm pushed open the door on the left to reveal a room about ten-feet square. It contained several pieces of mismatched office furniture, including a large oak desk, which Malcolm flopped behind. He nodded at the chair in front of the desk to intimate I should take a seat.

Gaining his breath back after the arduous task of walking thirty feet, Malcolm began the interview.

"Right Craig, let me explain the situation. I've owned this place for a couple of years and built a good business, but I've heard another video store is opening in the town next month so I need to raise my game. I run the place on my own with a bit of help from my niece, but she's due to start at college next month, so she'll only be able to work on Saturdays."

The throwaway comment about his niece starting college summoned an irrational pang of jealousy.

He continued, "I'm too stuck in my ways, so what I need is some new blood. I need somebody with enthusiasm and fresh ideas to help me move the business forward. Does that sound like something you could bring to the job?"

One immediate thought that struck me about Video City was that I hadn't seen a computer anywhere. I asked Malcolm how he coped with the inventory of videos and customer database without a computer.

"I use index cards, like a library," he replied almost shamefully.

That was my opportunity.

"I could help you computerise all of your records. We could create a database for all the videos, and another for all the customers. With some tweaking, I could get the two databases to work together so you could manage everything far more efficiently than with index cards."

Malcolm rubbed one of his bristly chins as he thought about my suggestion.

"You know how to do that?" he asked.

"Sure, it shouldn't be too difficult. I could help you choose some suitable hardware and an off-the-shelf program to manage the two databases. Then it's just a case of adapting it to your specific needs and entering all the data," I replied confidently.

Judging by the shift in his body language, Malcolm appeared keen on the idea.

The rest of the interview was nothing more than a series of mundane questions Malcolm probably felt obliged to ask. He then explained the job hours, which would have been fairly anti-social for anyone with a social life, and the pay which was £100 a week to start, rising to £125 a week after a four-week trial period.

As he concluded the interview, Malcolm asked one final question.

"What's your favourite film, Craig?"

Stupidly, I hadn't given this obvious question any thought. I scanned my mind for something credible.

"Probably one of the Star Wars films. I'd have to say 'Return of The Jedi' shaded it for me."

Malcolm's eyes widened at my answer, and a broad smile spread across his face. He strained to raise his bulky frame from the chair and grabbed a set of keys from his desk.

"Good answer. Follow me," he ordered.

I followed Malcolm back into the corridor. He unlocked the other door and then held it ajar so a sliver of weak light could enter. I couldn't see more than a few feet into the dark room.

"Go on in," Malcolm said.

I paused for a moment. None of the library books had given advice on how to handle sexual molestation in a darkened room. I considered my limited options. I needed this job, but I couldn't think of any way to excuse myself from entering Malcolm's lair without jeopardising my application. With no obvious alternative, I entered the dark room, passing uncomfortably close to Malcolm as he held the door open. I shuffled forward and stood motionless, praying my eyes would quickly adjust to the darkness. All I could hear was Malcolm's raspy breathing behind me. Then I sensed movement.

I squinted as a fluorescent bulb suddenly flickered into life above me. As my eyes readjusted to the light, I absorbed my surroundings. The room was the same size as Malcolm's office, but there was no furniture. Racked shelving covered three of the four walls, every shelf crammed with Star Wars memorabilia. Scores of toy characters stood to attention in their original packaging. There were dozens of boxes printed with pictures of various spacecraft, lined up next to thermos flasks, lunch boxes, masks, jigsaws, books, and a host of other Star Wars branded products. I turned to my left and the fourth wall was covered in framed pictures of the cast, each one with a penned scribble I assumed to be an autograph. Hung in the centre, in pride of place, was a glazed display case containing a light sabre and Darth Vader's infamous black helmet. I didn't know if they were actual set props, but they looked authentic.

"What do you think? It's my pension," Malcolm said proudly.

I turned to face him. "Wow! This is quite a collection, Malcolm. I could spend hours in here."

"I thought you might like it. Oh, and the job — do you fancy starting tomorrow?"

8

Both parents were pleased to hear that I'd found a job, although for slightly different reasons. Mum was happy because I seemed a little more optimistic about life, and Dad was happy because I could pay housekeeping. I knew that it was a fairly menial job, but part of me was quite looking forward to sorting out Malcolm's computer system. It wasn't quite what I had in mind when I dreamt of working with computers, but it was a start.

My first day began with Malcolm and I heading over to the local branch of RolpheTech — an irony that would not become apparent until some years later. We trawled the aisles in search of a suitable computer before settling on an Amstrad business machine. Malcolm's initial enthusiasm for entering the computer age took some testing when we got to the checkout and the bill was over £500. We loaded everything into the boot of Malcolm's turd-coloured Ford Cortina and headed back to the store.

I spent the next few days configuring the system, so it allowed us to cross-reference all the video titles with the customer database. It was a fairly rudimental system, but a world apart from Malcolm's index cards. I then faced the arduous task of entering all the records. I had grossly underestimated how much time, and tedium, it would entail. There were over eight-hundred videos in the store and the customer list contained over eleven-hundred records. With each record taking about three minutes to input, I calculated I would be bored witless for several weeks. Thankfully, Malcolm let me set the computer up in his office so at least I could sit in peace while I slaved away amongst boxes of index cards and lists of videos.

My fourth day fell on a Saturday, and as Malcolm had entrusted me with my own set of keys, I arrived a little early to show willing. I let myself in, took up position in the quiet office and switched the computer on.

Once the computer had finally spluttered into life, I refreshed my mind on where I'd finished the day before and arranged the index cards so I could plough through them as efficiently as possible.

I was about twenty minutes into the task, and in a world of my own, when I heard the back door being opened. Assuming it was Malcolm, I continued to focus my attention on the computer screen and the next index card, methodically entering the information into the computer. A female voice suddenly jolted me to attention.

"Hiya."

My eyes shot straight towards the door. A girl who I assumed to be Malcolm's niece, stood in the doorway — I'd forgotten she worked on Saturdays. She was slim, with tightly permed blonde hair, and dressed in an oversized orange t-shirt that clashed with her striped leggings. While she wasn't in the same league as Tessa, she was attractive in an unconventional way.

"You must be Craig, the computer geek," she said.

"Um, yeah."

I could feel my cheeks redden. I was hopeless at talking to girls.

"How's it going?" she asked.

"Not bad, thanks."

The girl nodded slowly. Her face suggested that she was struggling to think of anything else to say. Her eyes darted around the room as if searching for inspiration to break the uncomfortable silence. Seconds passed before she spoke again.

"Can I get you a cup of tea?"

I would have preferred coffee, but didn't want to appear impolite.

"That would be great. Milk and one sugar please."

She smiled and left without another word.

A few minutes later, she returned holding a white mug and carefully placed it on the desk.

"I hope it's okay. I'm not very good at making tea, more of a coffee girl myself," she said with a nervous smile.

"Thanks. I'm sure it's fine."

I picked up the mug and took a sip of the piss-weak tea.

"It's good," I lied.

"Great, I'll leave you to it then. If you want another one, just come and find me. I'll be out front with Uncle Malcolm."

"Will do. And thanks again, err...," I stumbled, realising I didn't know her name.

She looked at me blankly for a moment before she triggered.

"Oh, sorry. I'm Megan," she chuckled.

9

As I estimated, the new system was ready within two weeks and I set up the computer on the counter at the front of the store. Malcolm beamed like a child on Christmas morning as I explained how to use the system. After fixing a few minor bugs that his training had highlighted, we were good to go. I stood at his shoulder as he served the first dozen customers, and after the occasional prompt, Malcolm eventually got the hang of it.

"This is incredible. You're a bloody genius," he said in a break between customers.

I sheepishly smiled, a little uncomfortable with his praise.

"I'm glad you think it's been worth it."

"Oh, it most definitely has."

Malcolm seemed lost in his thoughts for a moment as he stared at the computer screen.

"Something wrong?" I asked.

"I was thinking about your trial period, Craig. Look, you've more than proved yourself so I think we should make this a more permanent position."

"Really? That would be great."

"And let's forget the trainee manager title. I think you'd make an excellent assistant manager. What do you say?"

I knew it was only a token title, but I felt flattered that Malcolm had such faith in me. Perhaps it wasn't the career of my dreams, but I'd grown to like Malcolm, and the job had proven to be a welcome distraction from the despondency of recent months.

"I'd really like that, Malcolm. Thank you."

"Excellent. You are officially now the assistant manager of Video City, and I'm sure the extra twenty-five quid a week will come in handy."

"I'm sure it will," I replied.

As the weeks and months went by, I drifted into a comfortable routine. Freed from the shackles of the store, Malcolm spent an increasing amount of time scouring the country for Star Wars memorabilia, so I ran the place on my own a few days each week, except on Saturdays when Megan helped out. The more time I spent with her, the more I looked forward to our Saturdays together. Slowly, our relationship developed from one of awkward silences and undrinkable tea to blatant flirtation, but it took almost five months before I plucked up the courage to ask her out on a date.

One date led to another, and then after six or seven further dates, we had the opportunity to spend the night together. My parents were visiting friends for the weekend, so it seemed an ideal opportunity for Megan and I to consummate our relationship, and if I'm honest, for me to draw a line under my last performance in the bedroom. Although Megan was reluctant to go into detail, she admitted it wouldn't be her first time, but hinted that her first sexual encounter hadn't lived up to her expectations. I could only hope those expectations remained low.

The day arrived, and I had the afternoon off to prepare. I tidied my room, changed the bed linen and loaded my stereo with a cassette of suitable music I'd taped from the radio. I put a bottle of Blue Nun wine in the fridge and set the table for our takeaway dinner. Megan arrive bang on six o'clock and she'd clearly made an effort, if you discounted her 'Frankie Says Relax' t-shirt.

The early part of the evening went exactly to plan. The Chinese takeaway arrived, and we sat down to eat, casually chatting and sipping the vinegary wine, just like the proper adults we were. We finished eating, tipped most of the Blue Nun down the kitchen sink, and then indulged in some heavy petting on the sofa.

As things became more heated and the familiar feeling of aching testicles returned, I took Megan by the hand and led her upstairs to my bedroom. I turned on the lamp which I'd already positioned to provide the bare minimum of light, and hit the play button on the cassette player. As Randy Crawford sung about 'Almaz', we slowly undressed one another, and climbed into my single bed.

Half an hour later, and relieved in every sense of the word, we were lying in the standard post-coitus embrace. Megan's head was resting on my chest as I gently stroked her hair. As much as I had wanted Tessa, this was how my first time should have been. Megan then broke the silence with a sledgehammer.

"I think I'm falling in love with you, Craig."

I hadn't seen that coming. While I had developed feelings for Megan, I had no idea if it was love. What I did know was those feelings weren't anywhere near as strong as they'd been for Tessa — but how are you supposed to reply to a statement like that, other than going along with it?

"I think I love you too," I replied, assuming it was what she wanted to hear.

Seemingly satisfied with my response, Megan raised her head and kissed me.

"We're going to be really good together."

And that was that. I was on the relationship roller coaster, and there was no way to get off.

Life continued to roll along in an uneventful, predictable routine for the next eighteen months. Nothing at all changed at Video City, but Megan and I decided to rent a small studio flat and we moved in together. My eighteenth birthday came and went, while Megan left college and took a job as a receptionist. Thoughts of Tessa became less frequent but more poignant. I wondered if Megan held similar thoughts of the guy who took her virginity, but it was never a question asked. Perhaps we rebounded together into our safe little rut, neither of us brave enough to question if there was anything better beyond. But we were comfortable, we were content.

While my relationship might have been in a rut, my career certainly was. Six months into her first job, Megan was promoted, while I was still working at Video City. A year later, she started a better job with another company. I was still working at Video City. Six months on and the company promoted her. I was still working at Video City. It then reached the point where Megan was earning double my salary. After I made several, half-hearted threats to leave, Malcolm had agreed to increase my pay, but we'd reached the stage where the store simply didn't generate enough income to justify any further increases.

As we drifted into the 1990s, I vowed to do something about my stagnant career. Unfortunately, the country was in the middle of a deep recession and decent jobs were hard to find. I applied for every position I could, but my appalling exam results ensured that my CV never reached the top of any pile. With job opportunities dwindling, and a growing collection of rejection letters to my name, I became increasingly despondent. Megan was keen to move out of our tiny flat, but less keen to subsidise the move with her wages. This became the source of many an argument, always ending with a promise from me that things would change. As the pressure mounted and our relationship began to crack under the strain, things did indeed change.

10

A bitter wind stung my face as I walked to work on a frigid February morning. Malcolm was on his travels again, hunting for some elusive Star Wars toy he'd been trying to find for months, so I had agreed to open the store. We always bolted the front door from the inside and let ourselves in through the back door. That door was accessed via a small delivery yard at the rear of the building. As I turned the corner into the yard, I pulled a bunch of keys from my pocket, keeping my head lowered to avoid the cold wind tearing at my face. I sorted through the keys, and with numb fingers, prised the correct key from the bunch. As I looked up to unlock the rear door, I stopped dead in my tracks.

The rear door to the store was slightly ajar, the glazed section gone. I cautiously moved forward, calling Malcolm's name a few times, but there was no response. I pushed the door open with my foot and stared into the dark corridor. No sounds, no movement. With my heart pounding, I slowly stepped across the threshold into the corridor before pausing a few seconds. I called Malcolm's name again. Still no sounds, no movement. I took a couple of wary steps forward, shattered remnants of the window crunching under my feet. I kept my focus on the archway directly ahead of me, and seeing that the computer was still on the counter, I breathed a sigh of relief. That relief lasted barely a second as I turned my head to the left. The door to Malcolm's Star Wars collection was open a few inches, a flare of splinters around the lock.

I nudged the door open and took a step into the doorway. I thumped the light switch. The fluorescent bulb coughed light into the room, confirming my fears. I checked every shelf, but whoever had been in there had done a thorough job. There wasn't a single item remaining. I ran into the front of the store, and with shaky hands, I jabbed 999 into the phone.

Two uniformed officers arrived fifteen minutes later, eventually followed by two detectives from CID. They quickly set about asking questions, taking notes, and dusting anything and everything for fingerprints. An hour later, as I sat on the counter out front, one of the CID detectives approached me.

"I'll be frank, young man, it's not looking good. It seems they were only interested in the memorabilia. Coupled with the lack of physical evidence they left behind, I'd say they were professionals rather than opportunists. I'm afraid I don't hold up much hope of you ever seeing that stuff again," he said grimly.

"I don't understand. Why did they only take the memorabilia and nothing else?"

"I'm no expert, but I'd imagine it's in high demand and easy to shift. Certainly easier than hundreds of videos with limited value."

"God, Malcolm will have a fit when he finds out. It's taken him years to build that collection."

The detective chewed the end of his pen for a second.

"I'm guessing there isn't an alarm system or any security cameras?"

"No, afraid not."

He let out a sigh and shot me a look as if to suggest we almost deserved to be burgled. He gave me the phone number for an emergency glazing company before handing over his business card.

"Get Mr Franklin to call me the moment he returns."

Five minutes later, they all left.

I put a handwritten note in the window to say we'd be closed for the day due to unforeseen circumstances, and then I rang the glazing company. An hour later the glazier arrived and set to work fixing the back door. Making quick work of replacing the single pane of glass, he gave me a hand-written invoice and left. I made myself a coffee and sat on the counter, wondering how I would break the news to Malcolm. That task was prematurely ended by a knock on the front door. It was Malcolm, carrier bag in hand and a puzzled look on his face. I unlocked the door and let him in.

"Why are we closed?" he said with no greeting.

There was no easy way to say it, no way to soften the blow, so I came right out with it.

"I'm sorry Malcolm, we've had a break-in."

A look of horror slowly rose on Malcolm's chubby face. Before I could say another word, he darted past me and through the archway behind the counter. I closed my eyes and waited for the inevitable reaction.

"No! No! No! Dear god, no!" he howled.

I drew a deep breath and followed Malcolm through to the back of the store. He sat slumped against the wall in the now-empty room, head in hands.

"What the hell happened, Craig?" he asked with a tremor in his voice.

I went over the day's events, from the moment I arrived at the store. Malcolm just sat there, not saying a word and probably in shock. Eventually he clambered to his feet and barged past me. He disappeared into his office for a minute and then left through the back door.

"Where are you going? You need to call the detective," I called after him.

"I'm going home. Just leave me alone."

I called Megan at work to give her the bad news and she paid Malcolm a visit to check up on him. One subsequent consolation of the burglary was that Megan suggested I suspend my job search until Malcolm was in a better frame of mind. He eventually appeared at work a few days later. He looked and smelt awful, even by his own low standards. Every day for the next few weeks he'd turn up and shut himself away in his office, barely uttering more than a dozen words. It reminded me of my dark days post-Tessa, but unlike me, Malcolm didn't have a mother to rescue him. I couldn't let the situation continue as it left both of us in a state of limbo.

Almost three weeks after the burglary, I knocked on the door to Malcolm's office and pushed it open. The smell was appalling. Malcolm sat in his chair, staring at a solitary Star Wars figure on his desk, the elusive one he'd finally found on the day of the burglary. I took a seat at the opposite side of the desk, but Malcolm didn't shift his gaze from the figure.

"Malcolm, Megan and I are worried about you. It's been three weeks now and it can't be doing you any good hiding yourself away in here."

I waited a few moments but there was no response.

"Talk to me, Malcolm, please," I pleaded.

His hollow eyes finally moved from the figure.

"It's all over, Craig. When those bastards stole my collection, they stole my future too. Everything I had planned, gone."

"I know it must feel that way and I do understand, but plans can change, and besides, you've still got this place."

"You're a good lad and I appreciate what you're trying to do, but I don't have it in me anymore," he sighed.

I was losing the battle so the only remaining option was to bare my soul.

"Do you remember when I came in for my interview?"

He nodded but said nothing.

"When I walked through that door I didn't have a future. I sat in this chair at absolute rock bottom. But you gave me a chance, you gave me hope — and if you hadn't done that, then I'd never have met Megan. That proves that good things can come from bad situations."

I had nothing else left to say, and we sat in silence for a few moments. Malcolm forced a faint smile.

"You've got a wise head for one so young."

He plucked the figure from his desk and held it in his hand, staring at it intently.

"Maybe there is still some hope. Give me this evening and I'll be okay tomorrow, promise."

With that, he hoisted himself out of the chair, put on his coat and left. I doubted my words of wisdom were the catalyst, but clearly Malcolm found something to motivate him. I didn't care, I just wanted to get on with my life.

When Malcolm arrived for work the next day, his mood was more optimistic, and thankfully he'd had a bath. We had a long chat during which he apologised for shutting himself away and thanked me for showing concern. We settled into our old routine and life bumbled along at work. Alas, the same couldn't be said about life at home. With concerns about Malcolm in the past, Megan made it clear my hiatus from job hunting was over. It wasn't long before I was back to trawling the employment section of the local paper and making frequent, fruitless trips to the job centre.

It was after one of those trips to the job centre I returned home and unexpectedly found Megan sat on the sofa, an hour before she usually got home from work.

"We need to talk," she said solemnly.

Just four little words, but capable of striking fear into any man. I took a seat next to her on the sofa while mentally going through a list of all the things I'd said or done over the previous month that might have annoyed her. I drew a blank.

"What have I done?" I asked defensively.

Her lip trembled.

"I'll tell you what you've done, Craig. You've made me pregnant."

11

The words hit me like a freight train. We were twenty years of age and having a baby was not even on the agenda, let alone a possible reality.

"Are you sure?" I said predictably.

"I've just been to see the doctor, which is why I'm home early. He said it's definite."

Tears welled in her eyes and she flung her arms around me.

"What are we going to do?" she choked through her tears.

There were many ways I could have answered that question, but it would have been a lottery. I played safe and answered her question with one of my own.

"What do you want to do?"

We broke from our embrace and I took her hands in mine. Still sniffling, Megan gave me her answer.

"I don't want an abortion, I could never do something like that."

Megan had patently made up her mind, but felt it necessary to discount the only possible option for me.

"I want to keep her, but only if that's what you want?"

Whether she intended it or not, by referring to the baby as 'her' made it all the more real. Suddenly we weren't discussing a cluster of newly formed cells, but a smiling baby girl. It was impossible not to let that picture dictate my feelings.

"Whatever makes you happy, makes me happy," I smiled.

I held her again and tried to block out the facts of our situation, the most pressing being our living arrangements. Even the rent on our tiny studio flat would be a struggle without Megan's wages. My career at Video City had reached a financial peak, and there were no new job opportunities on the horizon. A baby was the last thing we needed.

We spent the evening concentrating on the positive aspects of our impending parenthood. Then the subject of my career came up. In fairness to Megan, she was more supportive and encouraging than before. I guess she realised that no amount of nagging would change the situation, so a carrot replaced the stick. In return for promising to do everything possible to find a new job, I wanted a few weeks grace before we told anyone about the baby. Despite our predicament, I still had some pride left and didn't want people casting doubts about my ability to provide for my new family.

The first week passed and despite my best efforts, I drew a blank on the job front. As we entered the second week, I was growing more concerned. Then, for the first time in my life, Lady Luck paid me a visit.

I was alone in the store one evening when an unassuming man, wearing jeans and a scruffy sweater, approached the counter. He handed over the movie he'd selected, together with his membership card. As I entered his details into the computer, it crashed. Our computer was due an upgrade and would randomly crash for no apparent reason.

"I'm sorry about this, I need to re-boot the computer. Shouldn't take more than a few minutes."

The man nodded and watched me closely as I went through the re-boot procedure.

"You seem to know your way around a computer," he said casually.

I explained how I'd computerised our system a few years earlier. The man seemed lost in his thoughts for a moment, then threw a question out of the blue.

"I wonder if you might be able to help me with something?" he asked.

"Sure, I'll do my best."

"Have you heard of RolpheTech?"

I chuckled and pointed out that we'd purchased the troublesome computer from the local branch of RolpheTech. The man then held out his hand and introduced himself as Brian Carter, manager of said branch.

"One of our team has just handed in his notice, so we'll be looking to recruit a replacement soon. I wondered if you might know somebody who has experience with computers and might be interested?"

I thought for a few seconds.

"Nobody springs to mind I'm afraid. Sorry."

Brian raised his eyebrows.

"Nobody?"

The penny dropped.

"Um…I might be interested," I replied, hoping I hadn't misread the situation.

Brian smiled and handed me a business card.

"Call me tomorrow and we can arrange for you to pop in for a chat next week. If you like what you hear we can take things from there."

I shook Brian's hand again, and after I booked his video out, he left the shop saying he would look forward to my call.

I locked up at the end of the evening and strolled home, wondering if I should give Megan the good news that evening or wait until I'd had my chat with Brian. I decided on the latter option as I didn't want to raise her hopes. I called Brian first thing in the morning and arranged to see him on the Monday of the following week. With my deadline for telling our families about the baby looming, Megan was losing patience, but I assured her that something positive was on the cards, and not to worry.

Monday arrived, and I was in a determined mood as I approached the RolpheTech store. This was my one-and-only opportunity to appease Megan, so there was no margin for error. I entered the store and strode purposefully towards the service desk, where a genial woman took my name and then called for Brian over the tannoy. A few minutes later he appeared, looking much more like a manager in his pinstripe blue suit. He shook my hand before leading me up to his office on the first floor. I kept the picture of our unborn baby in my head. I had to do this for her, or him.

Brian started the interview in a fairly formal manner, telling me about the company and what the position entailed. As we talked, his passion for technology became apparent, and we were soon chatting enthusiastically about the latest developments in the computer world. Brian was obviously a geek at heart, and our conversation veered off-topic several times as we discussed subjects that had no relevancy to the job.

After an hour of chatting, Brian switched back into manager mode.

"I'll cut to the chase, Craig. I think you'd fit-in really well here. You obviously know your stuff when it comes to the products and you've got plenty of customer service experience. I don't want to put you on the spot, but I need to book a recruitment advert in the paper tomorrow. If you can give me a decision now, I might be able to save a few hundred quid on that advert. The position is yours if you want it. What do you say?"

I gave Brian the most emphatic and positive 'yes' possible.

We spent the next ten minutes going over the employment contract, which included details of a decent basic salary, and potential to increase it with sales-based commission. I did a few sums in my head and worked out that if I hit my targets, we could afford to move to a bigger flat and just about survive without Megan's wages. It would be tight but do-able. The only downside was that I wouldn't be able to start for four weeks but at least it would give Malcolm time to find my replacement.

With everything agreed, I was about to leave when Brian slapped his forehead.

"Sorry Craig, I almost forgot. I have to send some paperwork up to head office so they can add you to the employee database. We usually get an application form before the interview, but in your case it didn't happen that way. If you've got ten minutes, can I be a pain and ask you to complete the form?"

"Sure, no problem," I replied.

Brian handed me a six-page form and a pen, before saying he had a few things to do downstairs.

"I'll only be ten minutes. If you get stuck on anything, just leave it and we'll cover it when I get back."

I nodded and Brian disappeared out the door. I sailed through the form, which was fairly self-explanatory. Then I came to the section about qualifications. Bollocks. If I listed my actual grades, maybe I'd be shooting myself in the foot. Perhaps they had some minimum standards, and when Brian saw my woeful results, he'd revoke the job offer. But if I embellished the grades, would anyone check? I guessed they wouldn't and added my enhanced exam results.

I completed the final section of the form just as Brian returned to the office. He quickly scanned it as my heart began to beat a little faster. Seemingly happy, he dropped it into a tray on his desk. My mild panic subsided — it looked like my decision had been the right one, for a change. Brian shook my hand again and showed me out of the store.

I raced home and called Megan at work, the relief in her voice palpable as we discussed when we would tell our parents about the baby. I ended the call and sat back on our tatty sofa with a self-satisfied grin on my face. Things were finally going my way. Then my thoughts switched to Malcolm, and I immediately felt less optimistic. His state of mind was still fragile after the burglary, and the last thing I wanted to do was send him spiralling back into a depressed state. It would be a difficult conversation, but one I needed to have sooner rather than later. I decided to head over to the store after lunch and get it out of the way.

An hour later I pushed-open the front door at Video City.

"What are you doing here, young man, can't keep away from the place?" Malcolm joked.

I laughed nervously and said we needed to have a chat. His smile instantly faded. He locked the front door and suggested we talk in his office. I followed him in and we took up our familiar positions either side of his desk.

I bit the bullet.

"Malcolm, there's some good news, and some not-so-good news."

I told him about the baby and he seemed genuinely delighted. With a broad smile he reached across the desk and shook my hand.

"I'm so pleased for you both Craig. You and Megan make a smashing couple and I'm sure you'll make great parents," he said warmly.

Now the not-so-good news.

"The thing is Malcolm, there is no way I can afford to support Megan and the baby on what I earn here. I know you've done everything you can but we both know that the money isn't there to increase my pay any further."

Malcolm nodded slowly in agreement.

"There's no easy way to say this, so I'll just spit it out. RolpheTech have offered me a job and I've accepted it. I'm sorry but I'm afraid I'm leaving."

He sat back in his chair and appeared to be letting the implications of my resignation sink in. I felt like a cheating husband who'd just told his wife about an affair.

"You okay, you hear what I said?"

A grin slowly broke across his face and developed into a deep belly laugh. It was not the reaction I'd expected.

"Oh Craig, you have no idea how happy you've just made me," he said with too much joy for my liking.

It crossed my mind that perhaps Malcolm thought I was a complete idiot and had wanted rid of me for months.

"Well I'm glad you're so pleased about it. And there was me fretting about telling you when I needn't have worried," I said bitterly.

"No, no. You misunderstand, let me explain."

"I'm listening."

Malcolm adjusted himself in his chair as if he was about to read the news.

"A few weeks before the break-in I received a letter from some company called Blockbuster. The letter said they were looking to acquire existing video stores as part of their UK expansion program. They wanted to know if I was interested in selling the business, and if I was, it would be worth my while speaking to them."

"You never mentioned anything about it to me," I said indignantly.

"There was no point. I wasn't interested in selling to them or anyone else, but that was before the break-in. You must understand that my head wasn't in a good place after it happened, so I wrote back to them to see what they'd offer for the business."

"And?"

"They made me an offer, a bloody good one too. It was still nowhere near what my collection was worth, but it was enough for me to do something constructive with whatever time I have left on this planet."

"So when were you going to tell me?"

He let out a sigh and continued.

"I didn't accept their offer. A condition of sale was that I had to release all my staff as they wanted to bring in their own people. So if I took their money, you'd be out of a job, but I couldn't do that to you. Truth be told, I'm a sentimental old git, and you've kept me going when few others gave a toss — and if you hadn't been around, then I doubt I'd even have a business to sell."

Malcolm's confession lingered in the air for a moment as my anger turned to guilt.

"Shit, I'm sorry," I said.

Malcolm smiled.

"Don't be. When I declined the offer, they said they'd leave it on the table for three months in case I changed my mind. I've still got time to accept it, hopefully with your blessing?"

"If you think it's the right thing to do, then go for it," I replied with some relief.

I left Malcolm to write his acceptance letter and headed home. Everything was falling into place and as I skipped up the stairs to our flat, I offered a silent prayer that this sudden turn of good fortune would continue.

12

Megan and I attended our first baby scan at the hospital and we sat nervously in a crowded waiting room. Eventually a dumpy nurse called Megan's name. She led us into a room with a treatment table in the centre, next to a trolley laden with medical apparatus and a small monitor. With a reassuring smile, the nurse asked Megan to lie on the table. She then asked Megan to lift her jumper before smearing my girlfriend's tummy with translucent gel as I gripped her hand.

Reaching over to the trolley, the nurse picked up a probe, and pressed it against Megan's tummy. She moved it in slow, deliberate strokes while staring intently at the black-and-white monitor ahead of her. After what felt like an eternity, the strokes stopped, and the nurse smiled.

"Found you," she said to herself.

She made a few subtle changes to the position of the probe, and further checks to the screen, then turned to us.

"Baby is doing fine," she said.

We stared at the black-and-white image on the screen as the nurse pointed out the baby's tiny, but healthy heartbeat. Megan looked at the screen and then back at me.

"It's our baby," she croaked.

I swallowed hard.

"I know."

It was all I could say. Our imaginary baby was now real.

We took the bus home, and Megan sat with her hands perched protectively on our little bump. Countless visits to Mothercare ensued, with Megan fawning over prams and cots we couldn't afford. One unforeseen benefit of Megan's pregnancy was that it gave us a common purpose and galvanised our relationship. Our pre-pregnancy arguments, which had been increasing in frequency, were forgotten, as our entire focus turned to the baby.

We decided on the name Jessica if it was a girl, and Joshua if it was a boy, and both names met with Malcolm's approval as I sat in his office on my final day at Video City. The store was closed, and workmen were already stripping the place bare, so I was there out of sentiment rather than for any practical purpose.

"They don't hang around," I said.

"I know. I only signed the contract two days ago, and the money hit my bank account this morning. Technically, we're squatters now," he chuckled.

I handed my keys over to Malcolm and picked up a carrier bag containing four years' worth of tat I'd left in the store.

"So what's next for Malcolm Franklin then?"

"My options have been compromised, but I'm sure I'll find something to keep myself occupied. Hell, might even rekindle my modelling career," he replied with a broad smile.

We shook hands, and with a promise I'd keep him up-to-date with news of the baby, I left Video City for the last time.

The following Monday was my first day at RolpheTech. Brian greeted me on my arrival and took me up to the staff room, where he introduced me to my new colleagues. Promptly forgetting everyone's name, I then had to sit in Brian's office and watch the company induction video, which featured some wooden acting and questionable production values. Highlights of the hour-long video included a demonstration of how to sell a pen, and role played scenes about objectionable customers. Just when I thought I couldn't be any more bored, Brian handed me a test paper to ensure I'd thoroughly absorbed all the information in the video. I passed on that occasion.

After my morning tea break, Brian partnered me with Clive — a dour man with lank hair, bad skin, and glasses that were too big for his face. What Clive lacked in charisma, he more than made up for with his knowledge of computers. I stood and watched him as he served customer after customer, confidently answering every single question posed. He seemed to know the exact specification of every computer, and I had to admit I was impressed. I spent the rest of the week shadowing Clive, and I soon realised that behind his dull facade, he was actually an exceptional salesman. Rarely did a customer approach Clive and leave the store empty-handed.

At the start of my second week, Brian allocated a section for me to look after and I was allowed to serve customers without supervision. Based on Clive's strategy, I spent every free minute learning about the products to an almost obsessive level. The sales flowed and by the end of the week, even Clive congratulated me with a limp handshake. I was thoroughly enjoying the job and slowly getting to know my new colleagues. Having spent so long working alone with just Malcolm for occasional company, it made a welcome change to be part of a team.

My first payslip arrived, and much to my delight, the sales commission was better than I had expected. That little extra was just enough for Megan and I to put down a sufficient rental deposit on a bigger flat, so we decided to go hunting for a new home that weekend.

Saturday came, and we headed into town to trawl the estate agents. After an hour of dealing with a variety of contemptuous, arrogant suits, we retreated to a cafe with our meagre collection of suitable property details. We listed the pros and cons of each one and whittled our options down to two flats; one converted from a large Edwardian house, and the other in a modern, purpose-built block. Thankfully, both properties were managed by the same estate agent and we returned to their office to book viewings for both properties that afternoon.

At two o'clock we arrived at the modern block of flats, just as a silver BMW pulled up. A stereotypical estate agent in his mid-twenties exited the car and strode towards us with his hand extended.

"Mr Pelling and Miss Franklin I assume?"

We both nodded, and he introduced himself as Simon from Brooks & Co. We shook hands, and he opened the door to the communal hallway. The tiled floor was a grimy shade of grey and the walls were probably once white. Our first impressions weren't particularly positive as Simon unlocked the door to the flat and invited us in. Those first impressions didn't improve once we crossed the threshold, and we toured the flat with dwindling enthusiasm. Every wall was badly decorated with woodchip wallpaper, painted an insipid shade of pale green. The beige carpets were worn and dotted with grubby stains. An overriding smell of cheap air-freshener and piss hung in the air. The thought of our child crawling across those filthy carpets brought our viewing to an end with a polite, "Don't think this one is for us."

We went back outside, and remaining optimistic, Simon promised that the second flat would be more to our liking. We didn't have a car and the second flat was almost a mile away, so I told Simon that we'd get there as quickly as we could, but as Megan was pregnant, we couldn't rush.

"Don't worry about it, take your time," he said with a smile — and then promptly got in his BMW and drove off.

Twenty minutes later, we arrived at the second flat where Simon greeted us outside the grand Edwardian building. Seemingly oblivious to the scowl on my face, he opened the main door which led into a huge hallway that reminded me of Tessa's house. Shaking the memory from my mind, we entered the flat and it couldn't have been more different from the one we'd just viewed.

The enormous sitting room had a high, corniced ceiling and a tall bay window which flooded the room with light. Every room had stripped oak floorboards, the walls painted in warm sandy shades. Both the bedrooms were cavernous, and the kitchen even had enough space for a small dining table. The flat was stunning, and Megan could barely contain her excitement as she soaked up the finer details in the sitting room.

"It's perfect," she cooed.

"I knew you'd like it," Simon replied smugly.

"Oh Craig, don't you just adore this fireplace?"

At that point, I was more concerned that perhaps we'd misread the cost of the rent. Megan ran her hand over the marble mantelpiece and gazed dreamily around the room.

She then turned to Simon, and in her most grown-up voice, she said, "I love the period features. Is that dildo rail original?"

He looked at me as if seeking permission to point out Megan's faux pas. I shrugged and shook my head.

"Um, yes, I believe it is," he replied.

Megan obviously loved the place, but I thought the flat seemed too good to be true at the quoted rent. I broached the subject with Simon.

"Obviously we like the place, but the rent seems a little on the low side for a property of this size. Is there a catch we've overlooked?"

"Ah, well there is a reason the rent is so low. Two reasons if I'm being honest."

"I'm listening."

"Okay, the first issue, which you may have already noticed, is that there isn't any parking."

With precious little chance of us being able to afford a car for the foreseeable future it wasn't a problem for us.

"And the second reason?"

"Cards on table. If the owner doesn't find a tenant within the next two weeks, it's highly likely his mortgage company will repossess the flat. He lost his job and we've been trying to let the place for almost two months at a higher price, but with no luck. We only dropped the rental price this morning as a last resort."

I looked across the room at Megan.

"We'll take it," she said with no consultation.

As we were paying clients, Simon generously offered us a lift back to the offices of Brooks & Co. to complete all the paperwork. It would take a few weeks for all the references to be processed, but with a sizeable deposit cheque in hand, Simon assured us the flat was ours. Megan was ecstatic, and I was relieved. All I had to worry about was paying for the place once Megan's wages dried up. That was a problem for another day, so I put it to the back of my mind.

I got to work on Monday in a determined mood. My previous payslip had demonstrated that if I applied myself, the money would follow. So I approached my section as a man on a mission for commission. Unfortunately, Monday mornings were the quietest part of the week, so my mission was quickly derailed with only a handful of customers venturing near my section. With boredom mounting, I had little else to do other than dust every product and every shelf, twice. I ensured all the price tags were present and correct, then I checked the latest stock list for any new lines due for delivery that week.

The morning dragged-on until my rumbling stomach turned my attention to lunch. I was considering my options when a nasally voice came across the tannoy.

"Staff announcement. Craig Pelling to the manager's office. Thank you."

I was immediately a fifteen year-old again and being summoned to the headmasters' office. The same butterflies and the same desperate rummaging through my mind as I tried to recollect what I might have done wrong. I couldn't think of anything, but that didn't stop the anxiety as I clambered up the stairs to Brian's office. By the time I approached his door, I'd convinced myself that I was about to be fired. I pictured our little family living in a grotty bedsit in an equally grotty neighbourhood.

I knocked on the door and waited for fate to kick me in the nuts again.

13

Brian called me in, and I opened the door to find him stood behind his desk in the process of putting his jacket on.

"Thank god, I was about to come and find you," he said urgently.

"What's wrong?" I gulped.

"I've just taken a call from the head of personnel at your girlfriend's company. He could only give me some brief details, but apparently they found her unconscious in the toilets and she's been taken to hospital," he said anxiously.

I stood frozen, unable to speak.

"I'll run you over there now. You need anything before we go?"

I couldn't process what Brian was saying and remained frozen until he put his hand on my shoulder and spoke again.

"Craig, we've got to go, now," he ordered firmly.

Snapped from my temporary trance, I followed Brian down to the staff car park. We jumped into his car and he sped away before I could put my seat belt on.

We made the two-mile journey to the hospital in less than five minutes. Brian dropped me off at the main entrance and told me not to worry about work, and to call if I needed a lift home later. I was already out of the car as I thanked him. I crashed through the doors into the reception area and approached a po-faced woman sat behind a large desk.

"My girlfriend, Megan Franklin, was brought in this morning, but I don't know anything else. Can you help me?" I gasped.

The receptionist slowly lifted a pair of glasses to her face and studied the computer monitor in front of her. She hit a few keys and looked back up at me.

"Your name sir?" she said flatly.

I gave her my name, and she told me to take a seat while she made some enquiries. I reluctantly found a seat and after ten minutes of impatient waiting, I was about to badger the receptionist again when a tall, forty-something man in brown cords and a white shirt approached the desk. He spoke briefly to the receptionist who nodded in my direction. He turned and walked over, taking a seat next to me.

"Mr Pelling?" he confirmed.

"I'm Dr Renwick. I understand Miss Franklin is your girlfriend. Is that correct?"

I nodded, and before I could get a question out, he stood and suggested we talk in his office.

I followed him along an endless corridor, trying to keep pace with his lanky strides that implied Dr Renwick didn't want to engage in conversation until we reached his office. He eventually stopped and opened a door, holding it ajar for me to enter. The room was claustrophobic, with barely enough space for the desk, a few filing cabinets, and the couple of chairs it housed. Closing the door, the doctor asked me to take a seat in front of his untidy desk. He took a seat opposite me and rifled through some paperwork before sitting back in his chair with a pensive look on his face.

He cleared his throat.

"There really isn't an easy way to tell you what I'm about to say, so I'll get straight to the point. My apologies if it comes across as a little blunt, but I want you to be clear on the situation. Are you okay with that, Mr Pelling?"

I nodded.

"Miss Franklin has suffered a miscarriage. I'm sorry to say she's lost the baby."

A dozen confused questions stormed my mind at once, but my mouth couldn't deliver a single one. Assuming my silence meant I was ready for more bad news, the doctor pressed-on.

"Mr Pelling, I'm afraid the situation doesn't end there. Miss Franklin lost a lot of blood before she arrived here and we had to operate immediately to stem that bleeding. She's in surgery as we speak, and her condition is critical. She's receiving the best of care and we'll do everything we possibly can, but she's a poorly young woman."

"But she'll be all right though?" I croaked.

"As I say, she's receiving the best of care so try to remain positive," he replied with a weak smile.

Just an hour earlier, my biggest problem was what to have for lunch — but within those sixty short minutes, I'd lost my unborn child and been told my girlfriend was critically ill. There was precious little positivity to grasp.

Dr Renwick showed me to a relatives' room and promised to update me the moment he had any further news. Before I could ask any questions, he said he had an urgent matter to attend to and left me to my own devices. I stood and gazed around the room which was furnished like a budget hotel. A faded blue sofa sat against a magnolia wall, below a framed print of a rural scene. There was a small TV sat on a shelf, opposite a compact vending machine for relatives who sought solace in a can of Dr Pepper or a Twix. If the room was supposed to provide comfort, it failed miserably. I slumped down on the sofa and wondered just how much grief that room had seen. It was not a room for good news — just bad news or fragile hope.

Painfully long minutes ticked-by as I tried, and failed, to ignore the needles of anxiety peppering my chest. Now and then, a wave of deep panic would descend on me, dissipating just before the urge to flee the room became overwhelming. To distract myself, I picked up a dog-eared magazine from a coffee table next to the sofa. I scanned the words on the pages, but my mind failed to turn them into coherent sentences. I got up, paced the room in small circles, and then turned on the TV, just in time to catch a chirpy advert for baby food. Jesus.

I wanted to grieve the loss of our baby, but my concern for Megan was overwhelming. I thought back to when she first told me about the pregnancy and a damning memory returned — the last thing we needed was a baby. No god had listened to me before, but maybe he had this time. Was I to blame? Trying to avoid the question, I sought further distraction. I walked over to the window and gazed out upon flat-roofed buildings, set against an opaque sky. It was a dreary, sombre view that perfectly mirrored the way I felt in that moment. I turned away from the window just as the door opened behind me.

Dr Renwick entered the room, clutching a black clipboard. He suggested I sat down, so I dropped back onto the sofa and he perched himself on the arm, studying the notes on his clipboard before speaking.

He picked up in the same blunt manner as before.

"Miss Franklin is no longer on the critical list. We stemmed the bleeding in time and all things being equal, she should make a full recovery."

Before I could let the relief wash over me, the doctor's thin smile disappeared. His body language suggested my fragile hope was about to be fractured.

"While it's a positive outcome regarding her condition, I'm afraid the miscarriage had wider implications than the loss of your baby alone. There was extensive, and potentially life-threatening damage to Miss Franklin's womb. Unfortunately we had no alternative other than to conduct an emergency hysterectomy."

I heard the words, but like those in the magazine, my brain couldn't convert them into anything that made sense.

"I don't understand what you're saying."

"Mr Pelling, a hysterectomy is an operation to remove all, or parts of the womb. There are no long-term health issues relating to the procedure and a woman can lead a perfectly normal life without a womb. However, I'm afraid it means that Miss Franklin can no longer conceive or carry a child."

I stared at the Doctor, trying to absorb the ramifications of his words.

"We can't have kids?" I asked in a low voice.

"In the biological sense, I'm afraid not."

Dr Renwick ensured I understood the situation and handed me a pamphlet to absolve himself of any further questioning. He asked if I wanted to see Megan and led me back along the endless corridor and up a flight of stairs. We entered a ward divided into four individual sections, each containing six beds, occupied by women of differing ages. At the end of the last section were three doors directly ahead of us. The doctor peered through the glazed port hole in the door on the left before ushering me in. With the blinds closed, and the lights off, the room was relatively dark compared to the brightness of the main ward. My unconscious girlfriend was lying on a bed positioned against the back wall, next to a machine with blinking lights and numbers. The urge to run returned.

Dr Renwick left the room, and for while I stood at the end of Megan's bed, trying to comprehend the view. She had an oxygen mask over her face, and there were various wires attached to her thin body. It was a scene I'd viewed many times on TV; ill-preparation for the distressing reality. I tentatively approached a chair to the side of the bed, taking a seat and staring at the mother of my lost child. She didn't look much more than a child herself. Her skin was ashen, and they'd dressed her in a light blue smock that hung from her bony shoulders. Her permed hair looked like a bird's nest, a few unruly strands plastered to her moist forehead.

I sat there for hours, just watching her chest rise and fall in slow, rhythmic breaths. I could hear the faint thrum of activity from the ward beyond the door, but it was otherwise quiet, almost peaceful. My eyelids grew heavier, and just as I was about to rest them for a while, Megan's forehead furrowed and her eyes flickered. I leapt from my chair and leant over her as her eyes blinked to find focus.

"Megan, it's okay, I'm here," I said softly.

Her blue eyes bore a look of confusion as she lifted a weak hand to her oxygen mask, tugging it from her face. Her lips peeled-apart as she tried to talk, but her mouth didn't cooperate. I'd noticed a jug of water and paper cups sat on a small table in the far corner of the room. I sprung from my chair and half-filled a cup with tepid water. I held it to Megan's mouth before she lifted her hand again and held it herself, drawing tiny sips into her dry mouth. She emptied the paper cup with one final tilt and let her hand fall to her chest. Her lips smacked as she prepped her mouth and finally whispered a few weak words.

"What happened, where am I?"

I didn't answer Megan's question. In one of the most shameful acts of my life, I said that we really should get a nurse to check her over, and I left the room. I didn't have the fortitude to inflict so much pain on somebody I cared so much about. I scoured the ward and found a nurse who I hoped could do the job I couldn't. She was in her fifties, and her face was kind, her manner reassuring. In a soft Irish accent she told me her name was Marion, and not to worry, that she would talk to Megan. She patted me on the arm before heading off to devastate my girlfriend. I couldn't even bear to be in the room when it happened. I found a seat in a small reception area and waited like the coward I was.

Minutes passed as I sat staring at my feet with my head in my hands, guilt rising. Megan would be beyond devastated to hear that we'd lost the baby. If that was the extent of the bad news, at least there would still be enough hope to build upon. But for Megan there was no hope of ever being a mother, and that would be unbearable for her to hear. Yet there I sat, forty feet away, while she went through that ordeal with a complete stranger. What a despicable little man I was. I stood up, and dressed in a cloak of shame, I walked back to the room.

I entered to find Nurse Marion sat on the chair I'd occupied earlier, holding Megan's hand. She looked up at me with a smile that I guess was meant to reassure me. Megan looked broken, her cheeks stained by tears, her eyes puffy and red. Marion said she'd give us some time alone, and with a final squeeze of Megan's hand, she left the room. I sat on the edge of the bed and tried to speak, but struggled for words. Every inch of me wanted to scoop Megan up from the bed and hold her tight — her tender, post-op body made that impossible. Instead, I held both her hands, and gently pressed my forehead to hers.

I finally croaked a few words.

"I'm so sorry, honey."

Her body shook, followed by an inevitable explosion of grief. Deep, raw, unadulterated grief. I wrapped my arms behind her shoulders to bring her close, her head buried in my chest. I held her as tight as I dared until she cried herself out, then slowly let her fall back into the pillows. I took her hands again, while trying desperately to keep my own emotions in check. This was a time to be strong, no matter how hard it was.

"I wish there was something I could say, something I could do to make it better."

Megan gazed into my eyes, struggling to keep herself from breaking down again. Her voice weak, she found some words.

"Why us Craig, why me?"

"I don't know honey, god, I wish I did. I'm not going to pretend this will be easy, but I'll be here for you, always, I promise. We'll get through this, you know that?"

Her eyes dropped, and she replied with a faint nod.

"I want my mum," she said quietly.

It hadn't even crossed my mind to tell Megan's parents what had happened. Somewhere, they were going-about their daily business without a care in the world. I now had to tell them their daughter's life had just been torn apart. When I thought it couldn't, the day just got worse.

I promised Megan I would be as quick as I could and darted out of the room. I eventually found a pay phone back on the main corridor. A gaunt man in a red dressing gown was making a call, so I leant against the wall and considered what I would say to Megan's parents. I had to tell them about losing the baby, but was it appropriate to tell them over the phone that their daughter would never bare them a grandchild? I decided it wasn't. The gaunt man finished his call and shuffled back along the corridor. I picked up the receiver, dropped a coin into the slot, and dialled their number. After six rings, Megan's mum picked up the phone.

"Hello Sally, it's Craig."

Before I could say anything else, Sally started wittering-on cheerfully about a cot she'd seen that morning. Without drawing breath, she gave me a full description of the cot and a detailed set of instructions for finding the shop.

I interjected, maybe too bluntly.

"I'm sorry Sally, Megan has lost the baby."

Her verbal onslaught stopped mid-sentence.

"What? No, she can't have," she replied in obvious disbelief.

"I'm at the hospital now, Sally. Megan is asking for you, so please get here as soon as you can."

She said they'd be with us in ten minutes and hung up.

True to her word, Sally, and her husband Martin, arrived ten minutes later. I stood at the back of the room while both parents comforted their daughter. I felt like an outsider, a macabre voyeur watching in real time as a family shared their grief. I made an excuse about going to the toilet and left them to it. They didn't need me there, and I suspected Megan's parents didn't want me there. Somehow the fact I'd also lost my unborn child was inconsequential to them. If I wanted sympathy, I'd have to find it elsewhere. I headed back to the pay phone and called my mum. She listened to me cry again.

Megan would spend ten days in hospital, and with little else to do, we talked a lot. She tried to focus on a new future, one that didn't involve parenthood, but might involve the zealous pursuit of a stellar career and all the associated trappings. Her aspirations seemed unconvincing, but if it gave her something positive to look forward to, I was happy to go along with it. But lurking beneath Megan's resolve, something negative had seeded. A toxic combination of resentment and bitterness that would fester in the years to come, eventually defining her.

We married within a year, the wedding a welcome distraction from the reality of our relationship. We may have looked like any other newly wed husband and wife, but we left the church as two people who had lost a baby and faced a future without children. It would become the only bond holding us together. I never thought about it too deeply, but I suspect guilt and misguided loyalty were the real foundations of our marriage.

It would never be enough.

PART TWO

1

Holding a mug of coffee, I open the door to the spare room where Dave is sprawled across our futon, snoring loudly. The duvet I gave him last night is on the floor, and he's still wearing his shorts and t-shirt.

Our evening at the Fox & Hounds ended early after Dave tried his hand at karaoke. His horrific rendition of 'Karma Chameleon' virtually emptied the bar, and the landlord made it clear it was time for us to leave. Dave claims that since he started his fitness regime, his enhanced metabolism has rendered him unable to handle his drink. It's not uncommon for him to become paralytic after only five or six pints. He had seven pints last night. With Dave in such a mess, and Megan out with her work colleagues, I thought it best to deposit him on the futon in our spare room.

I place the coffee mug on a small table and kick Dave's outstretched leg, in an effort to wake him.

"Oi! Rise and shine Boy George."

Dave slowly comes round, and judging by the look on his face, vague memories of last night gatecrash his first thoughts.

"Fuck, I feel horrendous," he grunts.

I pick up the mug of coffee and hand it to him.

"Cheers. Where's Megan?"

"She left for work five minutes ago, but not before telling me you pissed over the bathroom floor last night. She's not best pleased with you, mate."

Dave rolls his eyes.

"She's a ray of sunshine isn't she? Why do you put up with her constant whinging, mate?"

I don't answer.

Time has hardened the way people think about my wife. Their sympathy has ebbed away, and the reason she is the way she is, long forgotten. It seems a lifetime ago that she was that poor girl who lost a baby and the chance of motherhood. She's now regarded by many of my friends and colleagues as a moody harridan. It's hard to defend her sometimes, but the picture of a young, broken woman in a hospital bed is forever a reminder I'm partly responsible for her being the way she is. I created, and now have to live with, this particular monster.

I tell Dave to lock the front door on his way out. He nods and returns to his coffee. I leave the house and start the journey to work, accompanied by a dull headache and furry mouth. I turn on the radio, just in time to hear the news. Another celebrity, who I assumed was already dead, has died. I change the station hoping to find something a little less depressing. My search only finds a succession of inane breakfast DJs. I turn off the stereo and wallow in the silence.

I arrive at work and head straight for the staff room, in dire need of coffee and painkillers. One-by-one, the staff arrive, and the chatter becomes too much for my aching head. I ask Lucy to open up the store and head for my office, under the ruse I've got some urgent paperwork to attend to. What I'm actually attending to is Marcus's plan to close our branch, or more specifically, an idea that might derail his plan.

My inspiration came last night at the pub, roughly around the fifth pint. Our alcohol-fuelled drivel centered on a question about Arnold Schwarzenegger films, and which one was our favourite. I went for 'Terminator 2' and Dave chose 'Total Recall', which was also the movie of choice for a certain customer at Video City many years ago. That customer got me out of a hole back then, and it struck me that he could do the same again now.

I close the office door and put my coffee on the desk. I rummage through my desk drawer, trying to locate an item that might well hold the key to our collective futures. I eventually find what I'm looking for — a single business card. I hold it out in front of me as if I'd unearthed The Holy Grail. Printed below the RolpheTech logo is the name of our potential saviour. I smile to myself and triumphantly read the name out loud.

"Brian Carter."

This is the same Brian Carter who hired a copy of 'Total Recall' from Video City in 1990 and subsequently offered me a job. A few years after I started at RolpheTech, Brian secured promotion to area manager, and then director. Despite his rise up the corporate ladder, we remained friends, and we'd occasionally meet for a few beers when he was in the area. Although Brian retired from the board several years ago, I know that he retained a small shareholding in RolpheTech, and is still well-connected with many of the current board members.

I grab the phone from my desk and dial Brian's mobile number. He answers almost immediately.

"Hi Brian, it's Craig, Craig Pelling."

"Good morning, young man. How the devil are you?"

We spend ten minutes idly chatting before I get down to the matter in hand.

"I have to be honest Brian, there is an ulterior motive behind my call."

"Okay, I'm listening," he replies hesitantly.

I explain the situation with the branch and give him the lowdown on Marcus.

"Sounds like you've got yourself in a pickle there, young Craig."

"That's putting it mildly. Unless I can get somebody to fight our corner with the other board members, I'm screwed. Is there anyone you can talk to?"

"There might be. I still play golf with two of them, and as luck would have it, we've got a game booked this weekend."

"I'm sorry to ask you, Brian, but I have to do something and you're my best, well, only hope — and you understand it's not just my job at stake? There's a decent bunch of people working here who don't deserve to lose their jobs."

"I've always had a soft-spot for your branch, Craig, and you're a good lad. I can't promise anything, other than to get your points across to people who might listen. Fair enough?"

"Can't ask any more than that, Brian. I appreciate it."

With an assurance he'd call me in a few days' time, Brian ends the call.

Feeling slightly more optimistic about our chances, I gulp the cold dregs of my coffee and head down to the shop floor. While it's far from busy, there are a few dozen customers browsing the aisles. I amble across the shop floor and take up position behind the customer services desk. Geoff is sat at the other end of the desk, staring intently at his phone while jabbing the screen. Judging by his eye-rolling and occasional slaps to the forehead, I assume he's not watching videos of playful kittens. Just as his cheeks turn an interesting shade of mauve, he slams the phone down on the desk.

"Bollocking hell," he mutters under his breath.

He sits and stares at the phone, shaking his head. Strictly speaking, the staff aren't supposed to use their mobile phones on the shop floor, but I don't think Geoff is in the mood for a lecture so I let it pass.

"You okay, Geoff?" I ask.

"No, I'm not," he grunts.

"Anything I can help you with?"

"Not unless you've got a time machine," he mumbles.

"Afraid not. Do you want to elaborate a bit?"

He lets out a deep sigh.

"I was checking the value of some shares I own. Just when I think they can't fall in value any further, they do."

"I thought you were skint?"

"Well I wasn't, but I sure as hell am now. I bought the shares years ago after I received an inheritance. I thought it would be a safe investment to buy shares in a bank. Banks never go bust, do they? Anyway, I accidentally forgot about them when the receivers were liquidating everything I owned, after the company went down. I was hoping they might be a nest-egg for my retirement, but they're almost bloody worthless now."

Before I can offer any hollow words of comfort, Geoff snatches his phone from the desk and storms off towards the far side of the store. I wonder just how much more bad news he can take. All I can do is offer a silent prayer that Brian comes through.

As I check the security monitor to ensure Geoff isn't venting his rage at a helpless customer somewhere, I'm distracted by a middle-aged couple as they approach the desk.

"We're looking for some help to choose a vacuum cleaner."

It's going to be a long day.

Lunchtime eventually arrives, and notwithstanding my ever-expanding waistline, I decide that the only way to cure my hangover is by consuming a couple of bacon rolls with lashings of brown sauce. I stroll to the burger van, which is always pitched on the edge of a trading estate, a few hundred yards from the store. The owner of the van is a ratty-looking man called Vince, and he greets me with a toothless grin. Both the freshness of the fare and Vince's personal hygiene are questionable, but when you fancy a bacon roll, even the threat of listeria isn't a sufficient deterrent. With bacon rolls acquired, I head back to the store.

I sneak up to my office so I can consume them in secret and avoid a sermon about my eating habits from Lucy. I devour the first bacon roll, but just as I'm about to make a start on the second one, my mobile phone rings. I swipe the screen with a greasy finger to accept the call from my dad.

"Hi Dad."

My dad has never been a man to fill a phone call with idle chit-chat. He's from a generation that used to pay for their phone calls by the minute, usually in a public phone box. There was no time to waste on pleasantries.

"Can you come over after work? I need to talk to you," he says stoically.

"Sure, why? Is Mum okay?" I ask apprehensively.

"She's fine. Just come over and we'll talk then."

"Are you not going to give me a clue?"

"For crying out loud, just do as I ask, will you," he snaps, then hangs up.

His rudeness no longer surprises me. My dad is only capable of displaying three emotions: anger, frustration, or apathy. I've long-since stopped trying to understand what goes on in his head. Whatever he needs to see me about, I'll find out later.

I take a bite of my second bacon roll, but my appetite has gone. I put the remaining roll back into the greasy paper bag and drop it into the bin under my desk. Typical of my dad to steal even the smallest pleasure from my life. I often wonder why he took on the responsibility of parenthood, such was his indifference to my presence growing up. I struggle to recall even a single situation where he showed me any warmth or affection. He wasn't and still isn't much of a father.

I head to the toilets to wash the grease from my hands. It's a shame I can't cleanse the guilt for indulging in Vince's coronary-blocking food so easily. As I scrub my hands in the sink, my mind wanders to Saturday and the reunion. I feel a slight flutter of excitement at seeing Tessa again. And while Marcus will undoubtedly be there too, I can at least take comfort that his plan to close our store might not pan-out the way he hopes. I dry my hands and contemplate skiving off for a few hours tomorrow, to go clothes shopping. While I can't do much about my plump, middle-aged physique, I can at least make an effort with what I wear.

I decide to hole up in my office for the afternoon and complete the staff rotas for next month. It's a tedious task, but preferable to proffering the benefits of dull kitchen appliances to dull customers. A few hours into my task, Lucy brings me a coffee. She sniffs the air and immediately detects the lingering smell of bacon from the roll in my bin. I then receive a ten-minute lecture about why I shouldn't be eating processed, fatty foods.

She has a point, so I sit quietly like a naughty schoolboy, listening to her lecture before I end it with a promise I'll start a diet next week. With a sceptical frown, she heads back to the shop floor. I retrieve the roll from the bin and finish it off. I am a weak man.

Closing time arrives and once everyone has left the store, I go through the locking up procedure and jump in the Mazda. It's usually only a ten-minute drive to my parents' house, but the rush hour traffic is a nightmare so I pull up outside their house almost half-an-hour later. I lock the car and stand for a moment to survey the street where I grew up.

A fair few of the properties are now owned by landlords and rented to tenants who patently don't have the same sense of pride as the homeowners in the street. Nothing much else has changed, apart from the amount of cars abandoned along the kerb side. I assume the planners failed to predict the long-term parking needs on the street, so each home only has a single parking space at the front. Back then it was rare for any family to have more than one car, but now every home appears to have three or four. The only house that doesn't have a car on its driveway is the one I'm standing in front of — my childhood home.

I ring the bell and hear my dad cussing as he struggles to move his arthritic body from the sitting room to the front door. I can only imagine the welcome a caller would receive if they were selling double glazing, or offering to share their love of Jesus with the homeowner. Seconds pass before I hear the lock being undone, and my dad opens the door. The brawny father I grew up with is now a near-skeletal wisp of a man. His hair is gone, and he now shuffles through life on legs that are barely fit for purpose. He squints at me through ice-blue eyes, sunk in darkened sockets.

"Expected you twenty minutes ago," he grunts.

The body may be shot, but his mind and manner are as brusque as they've ever been.

"Sorry, traffic," I reply.

Dad doesn't acknowledge my excuse and hobbles back to the sitting room. I close the door and follow him in. Mum is sat in a wing-backed armchair near the window and looks up as I enter, a smile breaking on her lined face.

"Hello sweetheart."

I lean over and give her a kiss on the forehead.

"Hello Mum."

Throughout her life, Mum always had a figure you might describe as 'cuddly'. She was once an avid baker, and our kitchen was never short of a freshly baked cake, pie or pudding, many of which Mum would sample to perfect her recipes. Unfortunately, her long-term fondness for baked goods gradually nudged her body further along the obesity scale. By the time she hit her sixties, the scales tipped and a diagnosis of type-2 diabetes followed. Coupled with a series of other weight-related health issues, Mum's mobility is now limited to shuffling around the house.

I sit down on a chintzy two-seater sofa that was last fashionable decades ago. The old man plants himself in a matching wing-backed armchair in the opposite corner of the room. A carriage clock ticks loudly in the background as I wait for Dad to tell me why I'm here. He sits upright and clears his throat, perhaps savouring his position as head of the house once more.

"Your mother and I have been talking, and we've decided to move home. The house goes on the market next week."

I'm slightly taken aback. I always assumed my parents would live out their days in this house.

"Why now?" I ask.

"This damn arthritis is getting worse, and we're both struggling to get up and down the stairs. Then there's the garden. I resent paying that so-called gardener to come round every few weeks. He's bloody useless, isn't he Janet?"

My mum nods.

"Yes dear."

Their garden has always been Dad's pride and joy, but he can't even mow the lawn now. Somewhat reluctantly, he hired a local gardener although it appears the poor bloke is failing to meet Dad's stringent horticultural standards.

"Where are you going to live?" I ask.

For one fleeting second, I fear he's going to suggest they move in with us.

"We've put a deposit down on one of those new retirement flats in the town centre. It's on the ground floor, so there are no stairs, plus it's handy for the shops and the doctor's surgery. It should be ready in a month or two. The estate agent reckons we'll sell this place by then."

"That sounds perfect," I smile, hoping my outward relief isn't too obvious.

"It'll do us. Anyway, we've got to get the house cleared as there's far too much stuff to put in the flat. I've spoken to a house clearance company, and they'll be taking away the stuff we don't need in a few weeks' time. You need to sort through your bedroom before they arrive and take anything you want to keep."

Such was the precarious nature of my relationship with Megan, Mum half-expected me to return home one day. She's consequently kept my bedroom exactly the same way it was the day I moved out. I say 'expected', but I suspect there was a lot more hope than expectation. Even after all these years, my former bedroom remains a time capsule of my teenage years. Apart from my clothes and a few other odds-and-ends I took when I moved in with Megan, everything I owned as a teenager is still upstairs.

"Okay. I've got the day off next Thursday, so I'll come by in the afternoon and sort it out."

The old man nods, and we sit in an uncomfortable silence before Mum suggests a cup of tea might be in order.

2

I drive into town hoping this shopping expedition will be more successful than my last. I made two mistakes that day. The first was purchasing a shirt from a store that was totally age-inappropriate. The second was not trying it on while in the store. I thought the shirt in question looked fantastic on the mannequin, but when I tried it on at home, it was like trying to squeeze a kingsize duvet into a pillowcase. I took it back the following day and complained to the prepubescent manager that the size label was patently wrong. With almost perceptible glee, he pointed out that the shirt wasn't designed for men with my frame. I will not be returning to that store.

I enter the multistorey car park, located adjacent to our shiny new shopping centre that only opened last month. My first reaction to this new shopping experience is to balk at the exorbitant cost of leaving my car on a patch of tarmac for a few hours. I then spend several frustrating minutes driving around aimlessly before finding a space to park the Mazda. After squeezing out of the inadequate space between my open door and the adjacent car, the next challenge is to find the lifts down to the shops. Several hundred yards of increasingly angry stomping ensue before I spot a sign for the lifts and make my escape.

By the time the lift descends and the doors open to the bright shopping centre, I've already forgotten which floor I parked on. With no clue where the shops I need might be located, I wander along the concourse, and up several escalators to get my bearings. More by luck than judgement, I stumble across a clothes store on my list to visit. The menswear section is on the first floor, so I head up the stairs and into the harshly lit space.

The wall on the left is covered with dozens of rails containing a myriad of shirts and tops, while the wall on the right is equally well stocked with jeans and trousers. I decide to choose the jeans first, so I head over to the right-hand side of the store and scour the rails.

On closer inspection, the choice of jeans won't be as straightforward as I hoped. There was once a time when purchasing jeans required you to decide upon three basic options: waist size, leg length and a few different colours. However, what I'm now faced with is a bewildering range of styles including: *skinny, slim, classic, relaxed, low-rise, boot-cut,* and *straight.* Through a process of deduction, I immediately discount styles which include the words 'slim' or 'skinny'. I can only assume *low-rise* means they'll hang off my arse. As I don't even possess a pair of boots, I also discount *boot-cut.* Down to three options. I decide my best bet is either *relaxed* or *classic*, so I search both rails, and choose a dark blue pair of each style, in my size.

With jeans in hand, I wander over to the other side of the store and browse through the range of shirts. Unlike the jeans, the shirts are all the same cut, so my choice will really boil down to colour. I avoid any lighter colours that will accentuate my flabby midriff, and I don't want anything with a garish pattern that Megan might choose. I finally decide upon a black shirt which looks stylish, but suitably understated.

I locate the dressing rooms and step into a vacant booth. Thankfully, the booth has a proper door with a lock rather than just an ill-fitting curtain to protect my modesty. I strip down to my pants and socks so I can see the full impact of my new ensemble. It's a decision I immediately regret as I turn and face the mirrored wall in front of me. The harsh spotlights cast damning shadows from every ripple of fat on my body. If that wasn't bad enough, the booth also has mirrored walls on both sides, so a slight turn to the left offers me a rarely seen view of my lardy back and sagging arse, repeated to infinity. Like a rubbernecker who can't help staring at a car crash, I inspect my multiple reflections for a few depressing minutes.

Disgusted enough, I turn away from my chubby reflection and grab the first pair of jeans from the peg on the door. I try on the *classic* style jeans first. It doesn't go well. I manage to pull the jeans over my backside and up to my waist, but it's obvious the top button will never stretch across to the opposing flap. I peel myself out of the jeans and throw them in the corner. I remove the *relaxed* style jeans from the hanger, and with some trepidation, slide my left leg in. I pull the left leg over my foot and switch my balance before sliding my right leg in. So far, so good. I pull them up, expecting to meet resistance from either my chubby thighs, or chubbier backside, but they eventually reach my waist. I tug the two flaps together, and after sucking-in a little, I manage to fasten the top button. Relief.

With my upper body still exposed, I daren't turn around and face the mirrors just yet. I unbutton the black shirt, pull it from the hanger, and slip it on. I fasten the buttons from the top, and all is well, until I reach the buttons nearer my stomach. These take some effort to fasten, but I force them into place.

Now fully dressed, I turn to face the mirror. The jeans look okay, albeit they're a tad snug around the groin. A larger size would remedy that issue, but that would take me into a realm of sizing I vowed never to reach, so I'll live with it. However, what I can't live with is the shirt. The material is stretched to bursting point across my gut, and the buttons look like they could detach at any second. With the arms already a tad too long, going up a size is not an option. Back to the drawing board.

I try on a few more shirts but none of them fit, so I'm forced to continue my search elsewhere. I pay for my jeans and wander around the shopping centre looking for other options. Three shops and seven failed shirt-fittings later, I'm losing the will to live. I don't understand how people find any enjoyment in clothes shopping.

With my initial enthusiasm spent, I eventually stumble across a department store. I know that they only stock branded shirts that cost a small fortune, but I'm past caring now, so I begrudgingly enter the store.

I discover a section with shirts that appear to have a more generous cut. I select a black one, similar to the first one I tried on, and head to the changing rooms with my fingers crossed. Five minutes later, I triumphantly emerge with a shirt that fits. My triumph is tempered when I look at the price tag, but if I'm going to impress Tessa it's a price worth paying.

I take the shirt to the nearest till where a woman is in a heated discussion with the shop assistant. I wait patiently and my eyes drift around the store, looking at nothing in particular. It's then I spot somebody familiar, examining a rail of clothes about twenty-five yards away. It's bloody Marcus. Shit.

I stand like a rabbit caught in headlights. There is nowhere for me to hide, so all I can do is watch him, and hope he doesn't look my way. Thankfully, his attention remains fixed on the clothes rail in front of him. I keep my head lowered, but my eyes fixed on Marcus as he pulls a jacket off the rail and turns to show it to a young guy stood beside him. The guy smiles back at Marcus, his sharp jawline shaded with dark stubble. The two men appear to discuss the jacket for a moment, but they're too far away to be heard. Marcus then takes the jacket off the hanger and holds it out like a valet as the young man slips it over his white t-shirt. Marcus stands back and inspects his companion who, judging by his broad smile, seems happy with the jacket. The guy takes the jacket off, hands it back to Marcus before planting a kiss on his cheek. I assume the young guy must be Marcus's son, out on a shopping trip with his dad. For his sake, I hope Marcus is a better father than he is a sales director.

"Can I help you, sir?" a voice says tersely.

The shop assistant has rid herself of the bothersome woman, her patience obviously worn thin. I turn to her and hand over my shirt. She scans it, then unceremoniously dumps it into a fancy bag. I pay with a credit card and she pushes the bag across the counter with a disingenuous smile.

"Have a nice afternoon, sir."

I offer an equally weak smile back, and look across the store to check Marcus hasn't spotted me. Thankfully, he's now heading off in the opposite direction. With clothing acquired, I hurry back to the car park and spend fifteen minutes searching across several identical floors before I locate the Mazda.

I drive back to work, sneak in the back door, and head straight to my office before any of the staff spot me with my shopping bags. It would have been the perfect crime had Lucy not been coming out of the staff room at the precise moment I creep past.

"There you are. Geoff said you'd popped out to see if they'd added any new lines at the supermarket."

"Right, yeah, I did," I reply sheepishly.

Lucy's eyes drop to the store bags I'm clutching.

"That journey wouldn't have involved a slight detour to the new shopping centre by chance?"

Rumbled. A wry smile crosses Lucy's face.

"Okay, you got me. Thought I'd treat myself to some new clothes for this bloody reunion tomorrow."

"Let's have a look then," she orders.

Feeling just a little awkward, I pull the shirt from the bag and hold it aloft for Lucy's inspection.

"Very nice, try it on for me then."

"What? No, I don't think you need to see it on," I protest.

Lucy pushes out her bottom lip and scrunches her face in a show of fake indignation.

"Don't be shy, Craig. How am I supposed to give you an honest opinion if I don't see you wearing it?"

She stares at me with her opal-green eyes and my defences crumble.

"Okay, give me a few minutes and I'll see you in my office."

I traipse to my office and close the door. I strip off my work shirt and slip the new one on. I'm still fastening the last few buttons when there's a knock at the door.

"Are you decent?"

It's a subjective question, but I tell Lucy she can safely enter. She closes the door and stands a few feet in front of me, arms folded across her chest.

She nods her head.

"Almost perfect. One small alteration if I may?"

Without waiting for my response, Lucy unfolds her arms and steps forward. She grasps the material either side of my love handles and pulls it out, so it's no longer tucked into my trousers. She then grabs the hem and pulls it down, to straighten the shirt.

"There, much better untucked don't you think?"

I cast my eyes downward and examine Lucy's work. With the shirt now hanging loose, the prospect of an errant button pinging off is greatly reduced, and my bulging stomach isn't quite so obvious.

"Okay I concede, it looks better. Thank you."

Happy with her work, Lucy smiles and turns to leave. She stops, pauses for a moment, and turns back to face me.

"Do you mind if I say something?"

"Course not, fire away."

Lucy stares awkwardly at her feet before returning her eyes to mine.

"Are you happy?"

Not the sort of question I was expecting. I shoot her a puzzled look.

"I care about you, Craig," she says, "and it seems...I dunno, like you're carrying the weight of the world on your shoulders. I get the feeling that something is wrong."

"Where's this coming from?" I ask.

"Buying new clothes is supposed to make you feel good about yourself, but your face says the complete opposite. Then there's your mood over the last few days. Actually, if I'm honest, it's your mood over the last few weeks. I've known you long enough to tell when there's something wrong. You know you can talk to me, Craig, don't you?"

It's typical of Lucy to notice things that most people, including my own wife, either don't see, or choose to ignore.

"I'm okay, just a lot going on at the moment."

"But you didn't answer my question. Are you happy?"

I look to the ceiling and exhale a deep breath.

"Not really Lucy, no."

She steps forward and puts her hand on my arm.

"Talk to me, please."

I spend the next fifteen minutes unloading to Lucy. Everything from my woeful marriage through to my terrible relationship with my father. I explain my feelings of inadequacy about what I've achieved in life. I tell her about Marcus and his apparent vendetta against me, but I stop short of telling her about the possibility of the branch being shut down. I let everything out as Lucy sits patiently and listens.

By the time I finish, I feel slightly embarrassed, but also hugely relieved. I can't remember the last time I managed to get so much off my chest. My mum is too fragile these days and has her own problems to cope with. I never talk to Megan because she's usually unsympathetic and judgemental. I definitely can't talk to Dave, as he'd laugh and tell me to 'man up'.

"I'm sorry Lucy, you shouldn't have had to listen to that. I'm just feeling a bit sorry for myself, just ignore me."

"You're my friend, you should be able to talk to me. God, you've heard enough about my problems over the years, haven't you?"

I nod, and we smile at one another before a more serious look falls on Lucy's face.

"Tell me to mind my own business, but it seems like a lot of your unhappiness stems from your home life. If your marriage is so awful why don't you end it? It can't be doing either of you any good."

The million dollar question. Why?

"It's complicated. I know that our marriage is a car crash, but if Megan wants to end it, that would be her call, not mine."

"But what if she never ends it? Are you going to spend the rest of your life in an unhappy marriage just because you feel obliged to?"

It was a valid question, with an answer I had begrudgingly come to accept. Of all my shortcomings, I had a deep sense of loyalty passed down from my mum. While we never discussed it, I often wondered how she put up with my dad for so long. Was it love or was it a sense of duty? Either way, her blind loyalty was both a blessing and a curse I'd inherited.

"I guess I am," I sigh.

Lucy frowns at my reply, her eyes carrying a message I can't interpret. With nothing left to be said, she makes an excuse about needing to be somewhere else, and stands to leave. As Lucy reaches the door, she holds it ajar and turns to face me.

"You're a good man, Craig. I hope things change for you one day, you deserve it."

Although the words are said with a smile, they're delivered with a hint of sadness.

3

It's Megan's day off today, so I tip-toe around the bedroom, trying to get ready for work without waking her. She rarely shows me the same consideration when it's my day off, but best let sleeping dogs lie. I sneak another look at my new shirt and jeans for tonight's reunion, and satisfied my investment was a wise one, I quietly close the wardrobe door. I creep down the stairs and decide I can't be bothered to set up the coffee percolator. Megan will be pissed-off she'll have to start her day with instant coffee, but I'll be well out of earshot by that time.

I leave the house, jump in the Mazda and switch on the radio. A few hundred yards down the road, the fan belt makes an unhealthy screeching noise. I guess I'll have to change it tomorrow, hangover or otherwise. It doesn't matter. I'm determined not to let anything dampen my mood, because in around eleven hours, I'll be seeing Tessa for the first time in almost thirty years. So against a backdrop of cloudless blue sky, I drive onwards, serenaded by the sound of a screeching fan belt and Salt n Peppa on the radio, the latter repeatedly suggesting I should "Push it real good". If I knew what it was they wanted pushing, I'd gladly do it this morning.

Saturday is the busiest day of the week, and the morning flashes by with a steady flow of customers demanding assistance. My spirits are so high, I even manage to spend an entire hour helping a technophobic pensioner with his laptop, without wishing him dead even once. While I might be in an unusually good mood, Lucy is the opposite of her happy-go-lucky self. She spends most of the morning stomping around angrily and rolling her eyes whenever anyone asks her anything. Not like her at all. After several failed attempts to corner her, I get the feeling she might be avoiding me. She finishes at lunchtime on a Saturday, so whatever it is she's sulking about, any conversation will have to wait until Monday.

While the morning passed quickly enough, the afternoon drags slower than a tectonic plate. It's an afternoon for shorts and t-shirts, for paddling pools and barbecues, for pub gardens and iced cider. It certainly isn't an afternoon for browsing electrical goods. As the flow of customers decreases, the temperature in the store steadily increases to a stifling level — our ancient air-conditioning system merely wafting the humid air around. The few customers who venture in are sweaty and lethargic, much like the staff tasked with serving them. When closing time finally arrives, it's with blessed relief.

I lock up in record time and squint at the early evening sunshine as I walk across the staff car park. The Mazda has been sat in direct sunlight all day so when I open the door, I'm struck by a wave of broiled air, tinged with the smell of super-heated vinyl. I drop into the driver's seat and open all the windows to cool the oven-like atmosphere. I switch the air-conditioning to maximum, but it seems to have taken solidarity with its compatriot in the store, and just blows warm air in my face. With sweat pouring from places I didn't know it was even possible to sweat from, I exit the car park with the windows still open — allowing me to appreciate the squealing of the fan belt at maximum volume. I can now look forward to spending the next ten minutes being deafened or gently roasted.

After a tortuous drive home, I pull into the bay outside our house. My clothes cling to my clammy body, and my light blue shirt is heavily dappled with dark patches of sweat. I unlock the front door, wander through to the kitchen, and pull a microwave lasagna from the fridge. I'm not particularly hungry, but I need something to line my stomach for later. I stab the cellophane lid with a fork and throw it in the microwave. While I wait for the lasagna to cook, I casually stare out of the kitchen window. Megan is sat on a lounger in our tiny garden, reading a magazine, and seemingly uninterested in welcoming her husband home. I think back to my chat with Lucy and contemplate if I really can spend the rest of my days living with Megan. Much like my diet, it's something I'll address another day.

My thoughts are interrupted by the microwave beeping away. I stand in the kitchen and take unenthusiastic mouthfuls of the sloppy, anaemic gruel that looks nothing like the appealing picture on the packaging. I manage to eat half of it before nervous excitement snuffs out the final remnants of my appetite. I drop the plastic tray in the bin and head upstairs for a final, paranoid check of my outfit, and a much-needed shower. Half an hour later, I look, feel and smell significantly better. I head back downstairs and book a taxi into town. Although it's only a twenty-minute walk, the evening air is still muggy, and I don't think even the liberal amounts of deodorant I've applied are up to that challenge.

The taxi arrives, and with Megan still sat in the garden, I leave the house without a farewell. The air-conditioned interior of the taxi almost justifies the exorbitant charge for the short journey, as I reach the town centre without breaking into a single bead of sweat.

I've arranged to meet Dave at a strategically located pub, which is far enough from the reunion venue to avoid bumping into any former schoolmates, but close enough we can still walk there. I pay the taxi driver, and push open the door to the pub where, to my utter astonishment, I find Dave at the bar with two full pints of beer at the ready.

"Thought I'd break the habit of a lifetime and get the first round in," Dave says with a grin.

I grab one of the glasses and take a large gulp of the cold beer.

"You have no idea how much I've been looking forward to that," I say.

"Nice shirt," Dave says.

I don't know if he's being sincere or taking the piss, so I ignore his comment. Either way, I feel a tad inadequate compared to Dave. Judging by his bronzed skin, he's obviously spent the day sat in the garden, and he's wearing a tight white t-shirt which is cut low at the front to reveal the defined pectoral muscles at the top of his chest. Despite there being only a few months difference in age between us, Dave looks at least a decade younger than me — something that many, many people will no doubt point out this evening.

We grab our pints and head for the beer garden where we secure a table in the corner.

"So, on a scale of one to ten, how much are you shitting yourself about seeing Tessa then?" Dave asks.

"Probably somewhere between eleven and eighteen."

I'm actually so nervous I could happily stay sat where I am all evening.

"You do realise that your brief encounter thirty-odd years ago is unlikely to be grounds for a repeat performance, don't you?"

"I'm not a fucking idiot, Dave. Firstly, I'm married, and secondly, I only want to see her to clear the air about a few things."

"Just saying, mate, don't want you to have unrealistic expectations."

While Dave's comment was tongue-in-cheek, perhaps a tiny part of me still harbours feelings for Tessa. And while I genuinely have no expectations, I can't ignore the fact that Tessa was the girl who took my virginity. Like the first record you bought, the first car you owned, or your first job, nobody forgets the moment they lost their virginity, or who broke it.

One hour and three pints later, we're just about in the fashionably late zone, so we leave the pub and take the ten-minute walk to the reunion venue. Bolstered by alcohol and laddish bravado, my nerves have settled, perhaps to the point where I might have dropped a few points on the shitting-myself scale. We round the final corner and the venue is ahead of us. It's a bland municipal building that typically hosts wedding receptions and jumble sales. The front of the building is whitewashed brick, with a set of double doors in the centre below a weather-beaten sign that reads 'Memorial Hall'. Pairs of matching blue balloons, printed with the number thirty, are fixed to the woodwork either side of the doors, and I can just make out the faint hum of music from within.

We approach the doors and Dave drapes a muscly arm around my shoulder.

"You ready for this, matey?"

"Nope, but what the hell," I reply, as I push open one of the double doors.

We enter a reception area with doors to the toilets on one side, a cloakroom area opposite, and a set of solid double doors straight ahead. The volume of the music is now loud enough to determine the track — that established floor-filler, 'Sledgehammer' by Peter Gabriel. Apparently all the music this evening will be from the 1980s, so I expect it to be nostalgic and tragic in equal measure. As we approach the double doors that lead into the main hall, they burst open, filling the reception area with noise and the frumpy frame of Helen Robinson, the reunion organiser.

"Hello gentlemen," she shrieks, her voice only marginally louder than the yellow dress she's wearing.

As the door swings shut behind her, Helen consults her clipboard and asks for our names, which we duly provide.

"Oh David, you look amazing. You must give me your secret," she coos as she presses a sticky name label to Dave's sculpted chest, letting her fingers linger just a little too long.

"Um, Craig, yes. Lovely to see you," she says with significantly less enthusiasm, as she hands me my name label.

"We've nearly got a full house which is wonderful. Go on in and introduce yourselves to everyone. The bar is at the back of the hall on the left. We must catch up later, but I've got to run, lots to do, and I need to encourage a few people on to the dance floor."

Helen then tucks her clipboard under her flabby arm and disappears back through the door, into the hall. Dave looks across at me and shakes his head.

"What the fuck was that?"

Now furnished with name labels, we tentatively enter the hall and stand for a moment to survey the scene. With the lights switched off, and the blinds drawn, the only light in the hall is coming from the mobile disco rig and the bar area at the rear. Tables and chairs are set out, but unused, with most of our former schoolmates preferring to stand in small groups either side of the hall. It seems that many of the school cliques have withstood the test of time. I scan the room to see if I can spot Tessa, but its near-impossible to identify individuals at distance in the dim light.

Dave taps my shoulder and points towards the back of the hall, suggesting our first priority is to acquire beer. I nod in agreement, and we make our way through the middle of the hall. The twenty-yard walk to the bar feels much longer as dozens of heads turn to inspect us as we pass. I catch several women nudging one another and ogling in our general direction, presumably to eye up Dave, rather than in admiration of my new shirt. We reach the bar area, and I follow in Dave's wake as he bulldozers his way through the crowd to the front. More heads turn in Dave's direction, but as the bar crowd is primarily male, the looks are begrudging rather than admiring.

We order two pints of generic lager and find a quiet corner as far away from Helen as possible.

"No sign of Tessa then?" Dave asks.

"No. Are you sure your informant is reliable?"

"Yeah, he was positive she was coming. She doesn't live round here anymore so maybe she's missed her train or something."

If Tessa fails to show, this would turn-out to be the utter waste of time that I'd envisaged.

"On the upside though, I haven't seen Marcus either," Dave adds.

"True. If he was here, we'd certainly know about it."

As we toy with the idea of going back to the pub, two men approach us.

"Alright Craig, Dave. How's it going?"

Barry Walker and Ross Glavin were part of our small circle of friends at school, but I haven't seen either of them in years. Barry, the shorter of the two, is wearing a creased white shirt and brown cords. His curly black hair is tinged with grey at the temples, and he's now sporting a pair of red spectacles. Ross obviously misunderstood the casual dress code, and is wearing a navy blazer, white dress shirt and beige chinos. His blond hair is slicked across his head, with a severe side parting. Both men could not look more middle-aged if they tried.

We shake hands and spend ten tedious minutes updating one another on our humdrum lives. Both Barry and Ross have travelled down the same predictable path of marriage, kids, suburban house and mundane careers. But unlike me, they both seem happy with their lot in life. The tedium continues as mobile phones are pulled from pockets to proudly show-off pictures of gurning offspring and vanilla wives, all greeted with feigned interest.

It transpires that Barry works for an engineering company that produces aircraft components, while Ross is a pensions advisor. Both men wrongly assume we'd like to hear about their careers in more detail. Until this point, I never knew it was possible for boredom to induce actual pain. As they drone on relentlessly, and we nod politely, I gaze across to the dance floor where Helen has cajoled a handful of women to join her. The

DJ sees this as an opportunity to ratchet things up a level and plays 'Venus' by Bananarama. The six women, possibly fuelled with too much Prosecco, shuffle around the dance floor while waving their arms around like they're trying to swat a wasp.

Ross pulls my attention back to our little circle.

"Have you made any pension provisions, Craig?"

I glance across at Dave, who has taken a few steps backwards beyond the sight line of Ross and Barry. He mouths the word 'bar' and sneaks off, leaving me to deal with the boredom brothers on my own.

"No, I haven't," I reply with obvious lack of interest.

My eyes move back to the dance floor where Helen and her dance troupe are now reaching a state of sweaty hysteria. Barry picks up on Ross's pension question and asks him a question of his own.

"Could I pick your brains about an annuity?" he asks.

Ross doesn't need asking twice as he launches into a spiel about his dealings with annuities. With both men engaged in a conversation so mind-numbingly boring I actually feel slightly sick, I decide enough is enough. I'm just about to excuse myself when I feel a tap on my shoulder. I spin around and stood before me is a dark-haired woman with caramel eyes.

"Hello you," she says with a smile.

4

"Tessa, Hi. You look amazing," I splutter — and she does.

She's wearing a shoulderless white dress that contrasts with her tanned skin. Her hair is longer, and there are a few faint lines at the corners of her eyes, but apart from that, she looks precisely like the picture I've carried in my mind for the last three decades. She leans in and kisses me on the cheek. I take the chance to inhale the sweet smell of her perfume. No hint of Opal Fruits, something a little more sophisticated these days.

"It's really lovely to see you, Craig. Fancy grabbing a seat and having a catch-up?"

Brian and Ross are engrossed in their annuity discussion, so I don't bother excusing myself. Tessa and I leave them to it, and we take a seat at a table as far away from the dance floor as possible.

We go through the motions of updating one another about what we've been up to for the last thirty years. Tessa tells me she's now a director for a digital marketing company in London and has her own apartment in Chiswick, overlooking the river. She talks enthusiastically about her times living in Rome, Paris and San Francisco. About the amazing things she's seen, and the incredible people she's met. It sounds like an extraordinary and fulfilling life, completely removed from mine. I feel a pang of shame when I compare what Tessa has achieved to my stagnant existence.

Fifteen minutes into our conversation and one thing is clear — if Tessa was out of my league in school, she's now Champions League while I'm Sunday Pub League, such is the gulf in our respective lives. Then Tessa smacks the final nail into my coffin of unrealistic hopes.

"Have you heard of a band called Jessico?" she asks.

My knowledge of modern music is limited to the Radio 2 playlist, and even then I'd struggle to name many bands.

"No, can't say I have."

"They've had a few top-40 hits in the UK, but they're massive in Europe and had number-one singles in France, Germany and Holland."

I nod politely, unsure why this is relevant to anything.

"Anyway, the rather scrummy lead singer is a guy called Harry Parker, and guess what?"

I look at her blankly.

"We're getting married at Christmas, I'm just so excited," she squeals.

I can't say I'm surprised. Tessa marrying the lead singer of a semi-famous band makes perfect sense. Tessa harbouring feelings for the chubby manager of an electrical store makes absolutely no sense.

"Congratulations Tessa, I'm really pleased for you," I smile through gritted teeth.

Tessa continues to tell me about the plans for her dream wedding, but I don't listen to a word of it. Noting my apparent lack of interest, she stops mid-way through a sentence.

"You okay, Craig?" she asks sympathetically.

I smile back at her.

"Yeah, sure. Just been a long day that's all."

"Sorry, my bad. I know you boys find wedding stuff boring. Harry is already sick and tired of hearing about it. Let's consider that subject closed shall we?"

Before I can reply, a more serious expression crosses her face.

"Actually Craig, there is something else I wanted to talk to you about."

I give her a quizzical look.

"It's a bit awkward really, but something I've thought about a lot."

"I'm listening, go on."

"That afternoon in my bedroom, after you fixed Kevin's computer, I behaved appallingly. You probably never gave it another thought, and I'm going to embarrass myself here, but I feel I need to apologise."

I almost choke on her assumption I never gave that afternoon another thought. If only she knew.

"There's really no need, Tessa. If anyone should apologise, it's me. It wasn't my finest hour."

"No, it was selfish and inconsiderate of me, but I appreciate your understanding. I honestly didn't set out to use you Craig, but I was pretty messed-up back then."

Tessa sits back in her chair and brushes a strand of hair from her face. She takes a large gulp of her drink and drops a bombshell.

"Did you know I was only fourteen when I lost my virginity?" she asks.

"Christ, no I didn't," I reply with genuine surprise.

"To make matters worse, the arsehole dumped me afterwards. Things started to go downhill from that point. I tried to redress the balance by screwing around with boys, both emotionally and literally, I'm afraid. By the time I reached sixteen, I must have slept with...well, let's just say it was too many lads. It was a reckless way to behave, but I thought sex was an easy way to get things I wanted, and in your case, a way to repay a debt."

Her final words were delivered in such a throwaway manner, I thought I'd misheard her.

"Sorry, debt? What debt did you have to me?"

"You helped my brother to fix his computer of course," she casually replies.

A cold dagger of realisation stabs me in the chest.

"You had sex with me because I helped your brother to load a computer game?" I ask, almost in disbelief.

She eyes me with confusion.

"Sorry Craig, I always assumed that you knew. It sounds stupid now, but at the time I thought I was doing you a favour. I thought it was what you wanted."

"Are you serious? You took my virginity Tessa, and you're now telling me it was a charity shag?"

I slump back in my chair and try to process Tessa's revelation. Now she's said it, everything makes sense. I can't believe I didn't see it before now.

"Shit, this isn't what I wanted to get into. I honestly thought you understood why we got together that afternoon. What did you think I was apologising for if not for that?"

I feel stupid. Stupid and angry.

"You realise your favour pretty much destroyed my life, don't you?"

Her stance changes, the apologetic face takes on a more indignant look.

"Come on, let's get some perspective here. We were both kids, and if I recall correctly, you were a willing participant. I am sorry for the part I played, but you could have stopped it at any point — but you wanted me, so you didn't, did you? I admit my motives were screwed up, but I didn't have the emotional maturity to think about it any other way. And please don't play the victim because my life was pretty fucked-up back then too."

We sit in silence as I let Tessa's retort sink in. She makes a compelling argument, and if I'm honest, it never crossed my mind that maybe Tessa was carrying baggage of her own from our teenage years. I look into her puppy-dog eyes and see nothing other than sincerity.

My anger slips away, but the stupidity remains. While that afternoon was the catalyst, every subsequent turn in my life was my fault, and my fault alone. I chose to wallow in self-pity rather than deal with my emotions. I chose to obey my father and not re-sit my exams. I chose to stick in a dead-end job for years. I chose to marry Megan through duty, rather than love. I chose to work in a bloody electrical store for most of my life. Tessa had been kicked much harder than I was, and at a much younger age, yet she hadn't let that define her. She'd forged an impressive career, an enviable life, and found happiness with somebody she loved.

My shit decisions, my shit life. Tessa wasn't to blame.

"You're right Tessa, I'm sorry."

She gives me that killer smile.

"Still friends?"

I nod.

"Yep, still friends."

With Tessa having absolved herself, I get the impression our conversation is nearing its end. We make small talk for a few minutes, both waiting for the other to make an excuse and leave the table. Then just as the situation becomes a little awkward, a third person joins us.

"Thought I might find you two together. Planning a more intimate reunion of your own for later are we?" Marcus sneers.

I shoot a glance at Tessa. Her eyes are shut and her lips pursed as if she's been caught with her hand in the cookie jar.

"What the hell are you on about, Marcus?" I reply with beer-fuelled bluster.

"Oh Pelling, did Tessa not mention she told me about your little soirée back in the day?"

I feel sick. Tessa agreed that we wouldn't tell anyone about our afternoon together. And of all the people she could have told, Marcus would be the last person I'd want to know.

"You told him, Tessa? Why?" I snap.

Her cheeks turn red, possibly with anger, possibly with embarrassment, likely both. Tessa then gets up and stands a few feet in front of Marcus. She's at least a foot shorter than him, but that doesn't appear to phase her as she unleashes a stinging response to his comment.

"Listen you pathetic little man, I'm not in the slightest bit intimidated by you. I may have been once, but that girl is long gone. So, I suggest you take your snide comments, and fuck right off."

Marcus is clearly taken aback at Tessa's outburst, but can't be seen to lose face.

"Calm down darling, time of the month is it?" he retaliates, then looks around to see if anyone caught his witty retort. With the music blaring, nobody is paying us any attention.

Marcus turns to me.

"I wouldn't consider yourself too special anyway, Pelling. She'll probably work her way through most of the men in here by the end of the evening. Old habits die hard, don't they Tessa?"

It appears Marcus has lit a fuse, and Tessa blows.

"Well, if I do decide to fuck every man in here, I'm fairly sure every single one of them will be able to get an erection; something you failed miserably to do if I recall. Now, if you don't get out of my face this second, I'll go up to the stage, grab the microphone and tell everyone in this hall how Marcus Morrison couldn't get his tiny penis hard for the hottest girl in school."

The twisted smirk on Marcus's face fades in an instant. His lips move, as if he's about to say something, but the words don't come. His face contorts, he mumbles something unintelligible, then storms off.

Tessa watches him depart, her face still like thunder.

"Don't suppose you care to tell me what the hell just happened?" I ask.

She regains her seat and her composure.

"God Craig, I don't know where to start."

"Maybe at the part where you broke your promise by telling Marcus about us?" I suggest.

She takes another large swig of her drink and sits forward.

"It's not like you think Craig. I told him about us, but it wasn't exactly an honest account."

"What do you mean?"

"Long story short. A few weeks after you and I had our afternoon together, I did something incredibly stupid. You know what Marcus was like at school, he was manipulative and controlling. Anyway, he'd been pestering me to hook up with him for months, and he finally persuaded me to go over to his house one afternoon. As you probably just gathered, it didn't go well as Marcus couldn't get it up, so nothing happened."

I couldn't help but smile to myself at this revelation, but it didn't answer my question.

"As amusing as it is, I don't see why Marcus's erectile dysfunction meant you had to tell him about us?"

"I'm coming to that. Just before I left his house, he said that if I told anyone about his inability to perform, he'd make Kevin's life hell. I was livid that Marcus was threatening my little brother, so I sort of told him you'd screwed me senseless a few weeks earlier. I probably went a bit too far and said you were the best shag I'd ever had. I knew it would be a major dent to his ego to hear that the school computer nerd could satisfy me when he couldn't even get an erection. Please understand that I wanted to hurt Marcus, not you."

A dozen tiny switches suddenly flick, and a glowing light of realisation shines. This is why Marcus acts like such a über-arsehole towards me. Those obscure comments he made at the end of our meeting on Wednesday now make perfect sense. His threat to close our branch is just Marcus's petty and vindictive retribution for being humiliated thirty years ago.

"Did you know that Marcus is now my boss?"

A look of horror passes across Tessa's face.

"Oh god, I had no idea. If I'd known I wouldn't have said anything. I'm so sorry."

"To be honest, I'm relieved you never told him what actually happened. I may not have a job next week, but at least I'll still have a modicum of dignity left."

"Thank you for being so understanding."

Tessa reaches across the table and puts her hand on mine.

"I will never let people like Marcus have control over me, and neither should you. You're ten times the man he is, remember that."

We stand and Tessa gives me another kiss on the cheek. Then with a token promise to stay in touch, she flutters off to chat with her former classmates.

Part of me wants to leave and go home. The only reason I was here at all was because of Tessa, but with that part of my life firmly put to bed, there seems precious little point in hanging around. Another part of me wants to get blind drunk. I decide to find Dave and go with the blind drunk option, but not before I make yet another trip to the toilets.

I make my way back through the double doors into the reception area and push open the door to the gents' toilets. There are four empty urinals on the wall to my right, and two cubicles at the rear, one of which is occupied, judging by the grunts from within. I approach the nearest urinal and fumble with the stiff buttons on my new jeans as the cubicle occupant empties his bowels. A foul stench wafts across the room, and just as I'm about to gag, the door to the reception area crashes open.

Marcus steps through the doorway and glowers at me. It takes just a second for his expression to change as his nose informs his brain that he's just walked into a wall of shit. Unperturbed, Marcus moves toward me.

"If you think you can hide behind that little whore then you're badly mistaken, Pelling. Come Monday morning, I'm going to move heaven and earth to ensure your poxy little store is closed for good. We'll see if you're still laughing once you're unemployed."

With Tessa's advice fresh in my mind, and sufficient alcohol in my bloodstream, I retaliate.

"Do you realise just how pathetic it is to still bear a grudge for something that happened thirty bloody years ago? Get over it, will you."

"Trust me, I'm over it. But as they say, Pelling, revenge is a dish best served cold."

"What the hell are you actually seeking revenge for?"

"You and that bitch humiliated me. Just how long were you laughing at me behind my back?" he spits.

"I didn't even know anything happened with you and Tessa until this evening."

"Bullshit! I know it was you who wrote that graffiti on my locker at school."

"Wait, what? I seriously have no idea what you're talking about."

But then I do.

During the final weeks of school, somebody defaced Marcus's locker by scrawling, 'Marcus has a tiny cock', on the door with a permanent marker pen. While it caused a few laughs, I don't recall it being regarded as anything other than a childish prank. The culprit was never identified, but after this evening's revelations, I'm guessing Tessa had the strongest motive.

"Do you have any idea how much stick I got over that? One of you two obviously wrote it, and seeing as it was in the boys' locker area, my money is on you," he snaps.

He's obviously made up his mind, so there seems precious little point in arguing with him.

"Look Marcus, for the record, it wasn't me. Even if it was, does it matter now?"

"To me it does. Nobody fucks with Marcus Morrison and gets away with it. Ever."

I'm stunned just how bloody-minded and melodramatic he's being. I'm wasting my time even trying to reason with him, so I do what anyone backed into a corner would do — I start laughing.

"You're unbelievable, Marcus, but hey, if putting me out of a job makes you feel better about your tiny cock, then fair enough."

In hindsight, I probably shouldn't have said that.

He storms forward, and before I can even flinch, his hand is around my throat, his momentum slamming me against the wall. Marcus is taller, fitter and stronger than me, so I'm helpless as he leans in, his hand crushing my windpipe.

"What the fuck did you say?" he snarls.

Even if I felt like repeating myself, I can barely breathe, let alone speak. As much as I want to push him away, he's standing too close for me to position my hands for leverage. All I can do while he throttles me is stare at his reddening face. For a moment, I wonder if he actually is trying to kill me. His lip is curled, and a deep furrow has formed on his usually pristine forehead. He'll need more botox after this, for sure. His eyes are now just narrow slits and he's breathing heavily. I'm barely breathing at all. The fucking psychopath might actually be trying to kill me.

As Marcus maintains the pressure on my throat, I hear a toilet flush and a lock slide open. I can't move my head, and most of my vision is full of Marcus's contorted face, but I flick my eyes just in time to catch a slight movement beyond his left shoulder. I feel light headed — he *is* trying to kill me. Seconds pass and a hand taps Marcus on the shoulder. As he turns his attention to the shoulder tapper, his grip on my throat loosens slightly and I gasp for air.

With Marcus's head now turned at ninety degrees, and his grip loosening, I manage to shift my position a fraction. I turn my head just in time to see the blurry motion of a fist as it swings through the air and connects perfectly with Marcus's jaw. Within a split second, his hand is gone from my throat, followed by the rest of his body as he flails backwards and violently crashes into the door behind him. The snarling expression is replaced with one of total shock, and I suspect, a fair amount of pain. His legs buckle and he falls to the floor where he stays, groaning.

"You alright, matey?" Dave asks.

I nod. Dave moves across the floor and stands over Marcus.

"That was for fucking with my Big Trak," Dave growls.

Marcus correctly decides not to question what he's talking about.

"If you've still got a problem with Craig, we can discuss it outside if you like?"

Marcus shakes his head, and I take solace seeing the fear in his eyes. Dave then nonchalantly turns to me.

"Your round I believe."

5

Karen Carpenter used the medium of music to complain about rainy days and Mondays. If she was still of this earth, then she'd certainly be down today, because it's a Monday, and it's pissing down. I gaze out of my office window at the gloomy skies above the puddled RolpheTech car park. The monotone scene is only broken by half-a-dozen coloured cars and a small stretch of grass at the far boundary. I close my eyes and try to ignore the thumping headache and queasy stomach, which are now into their second day. Coupled with the throbbing pain from my bruised throat after Marcus's throttling, I feel appalling.

My thoughts drift back to Saturday's reunion, and it's only now that the implications are coming home. Marcus made a swift exit after his encounter with Dave's fist, but knowing Marcus, retribution will head my way soon enough. Tessa stayed for another hour before I caught her fleeting and final goodbye. The rest of the evening is a bit of a blur. There was definitely tequila drunk, there may have been dancing, and I vaguely recollect Dave and I doing a rendition of, 'Livin' on a Prayer'. I cringe and push the hazy memories aside. I've got more important things to worry about, which is why I'm holed-up in my office.

Brian sent me a text message this morning saying he'd call at eleven o'clock. I've spent the last few hours building up to his call, trying to plot and plan for whatever news he delivers. However, after my altercation with Marcus on Saturday, it seems pretty clear my future at RolpheTech is looking bleak. I need to be realistic and make the best of a bad situation. If

Marcus has his way, and the branch is closed, the saving grace will be my redundancy package. With twenty-six years' service behind me, I'll be due a significant lump sum. It will be enough for me to live on while I find a new job — but the obvious downside to the branch being closed is my colleagues will lose their jobs.

But what if Marcus fails, and the branch is saved, where does that leave me? My colleagues would keep their jobs, but my position would no longer be tenable. I have no desire to hang around waiting for Marcus to enact his revenge, so what do I do? My mind whirls as I consider all the various permutations. Then the throbbing pain in my neck gives me an idea.

Of all the terrible decisions I've made in my life, attempting to blackmail my boss could turn out to be the worst. But desperate times call for desperate measures. Armed with photographic evidence of my badly bruised neck, I'll give Marcus a simple choice — he resigns, or I'll take the pictures to the board and report his assault. Surely if he's facing the threat of instant dismissal for gross misconduct, he'll have no choice but to leave RolpheTech? It's a ridiculous plan, but if the branch is saved, it's my only plan.

I'm pulled from my thoughts as my mobile phone trills on the desk. I snatch it up and accept the call.

"Morning, young man."

Brian's greeting is not delivered with the same enthusiasm as last week.

"Morning Brian. How did the game go?"

"I came last by four strokes, but I suspect that's not what you want to talk about?"

"I guess it's not. Dare I ask if you got anywhere?"

There is a brief pause, and I hear Brian exhale a deep breath.

"Well, things are certainly afoot behind the scenes at RolpheTech. Pull up a comfortable chair because there's a lot to tell you."

I heed Brian's advice and flop into my office chair.

"Right, where to begin? Six weeks ago, a mobile telecoms company called Randall Holdings purchased a small stake in RolpheTech. It was a precursor to a complete takeover of the company. By making that initial investment, they could get a look inside the business and if they found any significant problems, they could walk away with only a modest amount of money still invested. It's like putting a deposit down on a car before a test drive, a show of good faith I guess."

"Okay, I follow you," I reply.

"That initial investment came with a catch though. Randall Holdings wanted one of their own men on board, to see the business in operation first hand. His job was to take a thorough look at every aspect of the company, from the branches through to the management, and identify any hidden issues beyond what the accounts told them. After six weeks, and based upon this chap's findings, Randall Holdings would then decide if they wanted to complete the takeover. I'm sure you can guess who their man is?"

My already queasy stomach does a turn.

"Marcus Morrison?"

"You got it. From what I can gather, this Morrison chap has gone beyond his remit and has been throwing his weight around. The current board aren't happy with the way he's been operating, but they don't want to rock the boat. It looks like the takeover will go ahead within the next week or two, subject to the final report from Morrison, which came in this morning."

"I don't suppose you know what was in that report?" I ask.

"My guy on the board was kind enough to email me the highlights, which I've just received. It's not good reading, Craig. Morrison's recommendations are for the takeover to go ahead, but subject to a number of branch closures, including yours. I'm sorry young man, but it looks like it might be the end of the road for your branch."

Part of me is relieved that I won't have to enact my ridiculous blackmail plan, and at least I'll be able to walk away with my redundancy payment. Then a severe prick to my conscience reminds me that this isn't such good news for my colleagues.

"Do you think the board will follow through with Marcus's recommendations?"

"What you have to understand is that most of the current board members are approaching retirement age, and this is a chance to retire with a huge pay-off. They'll do whatever the buyers want to ensure their pay day happens, even if it means closing branches. Besides, the industry is changing, and RolpheTech badly needs new investment and fresh ideas — something the current board are unable, or unwilling, to provide. If this takeover doesn't happen, the fear is that the whole business could go under."

"Jesus, this will hit a lot of people hard. What would be your best guess at a timetable for the closures?"

"My contact thinks they're going to re-brand the stores, so they won't want the negative PR of branch closures to affect the launch of their new brand. My guess is that they'll want the branches closed down quickly. I'm afraid you're probably looking at a few weeks at most."

"That soon? It doesn't give the staff much time to look for new jobs. I need to tell them today then."

"Hold on a second, young man. It is imperative you tell no one about this. This information is highly sensitive, and I've gone out on a limb to get it for you. If even one person finds out, the news will spread, and that could have serious implications for the whole takeover. I want your word this goes no further."

"But my colleagues have a right to know," I plead.

"Maybe they do, but you cannot say a word until an official announcement is made by the board. If this leaks, fingers will point in my direction, and you'll be putting me in an incredibly difficult position. You tell no one, are we clear on that?"

I reluctantly promise I won't tell a soul, and with little left to say, Brian offers his apologies one final time before hanging up.

I return to the window and the bleak scene beyond. For some reason it sparks a memory of the relatives' room in the hospital where I stood all those years ago. Maybe it's the helplessness — life playing itself out while I spectate from the sidelines. The key difference is that when Megan was in hospital, everyone involved wanted to achieve the same goal, whereas now, everyone has their own selfish agenda. How can it be right that hundreds of loyal employees lose their jobs, while a dozen old bastards on the board get a six-figure pay off? The employees are nothing more than a series of digits on an Excel spreadsheet, deleted in an instant with the indiscriminate click of a mouse. But as unfair as it is, I have to face facts, and that means taking control of my own future. There is nothing else I can do now.

I sit back at my desk, wake the PC and open the Internet browser. I stare at the screen for a long while —

I feel conflicted. I don't really want to leave RolpheTech but perhaps this could be my last chance to do something constructive with my life. My redundancy package will give me options. I'll be able to forge a new career, to start again, and that does excite me a little. But while I plot my future with money and time on my side, my colleagues downstairs won't have either luxury. Lucy will get a reasonable pay-off for her ten years of service, but she has a mortgage to pay on her own, and a teenage daughter to provide for. Her redundancy pay will only cover her living costs for a few months, and then she'll be in trouble if she hasn't found another job. Then there's Geoff. He's only been with us for four years, so he won't get much, and he's approaching the point of becoming unemployable. Most of the other staff members have only worked here for a few years, so none of them will leave with a golden handshake either.

I have to remind myself that I can't do anything to change the situation for my colleagues. While I feel for them, I'm not the one responsible for their impending unemployment. I return my focus to the computer screen and the empty search box. It's been a long time since I had to look for a job and I'm not really sure where to start. I type 'start a new career' in the search box and hit 'Enter'. A page of results appears and I scour the links for something that might point me in the right direction. An advert at the top of the page catches my eye.

"Don't Start a Career, Start a Business - Search Our Franchise Opportunities."

It's an interesting proposition, and not one I would have considered. Could I actually run my own business? On reflection, the thought of spending the next twenty years working as a wage slave, possibly with another arsehole like Marcus for a boss, holds little appeal.

I click the link and I'm greeted with a list of franchise categories. I scan the list until one option leaps out at me — 'Computer Services'. I click that link, and yet another list appears with information about specific franchise opportunities in the computer services sector. I scroll down the page and spot a franchise that provides IT support to businesses. I move closer to the screen and study the information. The franchise fee is just under £10,000, they provide full training, and the earning potential is almost treble what RolpheTech pay me. There's a big green button pleading with me to 'Enquire Now'. I click it, and I'm directed to a page containing more information about the franchise, and an enquiry form. I complete the form and click the 'Submit' button.

I sit back in my chair and contemplate the prospect of working for myself. The more I think about it, the more it appeals. I won't have to put up with insufferable customers and their tedious questions about domestic appliances. I can work the hours I choose, which won't include every weekend, and I won't be answerable to anyone. This option makes sense on so many levels I wonder if perhaps fate is giving me a break for once. In a twisted irony, being made redundant will give me both the cash, and motivation, to build a better future.

Fuelled with a real sense of purpose, I'm just about to explore the franchise market in more depth when an email pings into my in-box. It's from Marcus, and the subject line simply says 'Urgent Meeting'. I open the email and read the two lines of text. Marcus is coming into the store on Wednesday morning for a meeting and my attendance is compulsory. I guess it must be to gloat that his plan has come to fruition, and our branch is closing. He must be wetting himself with excitement at the prospect of delivering his revenge. It's a pity for him I'm already one step ahead.

6

After a constructive afternoon spent researching the franchise market, I arrive home with a wad of reading material downloaded from the Internet. Megan is already home, and I can hear her stomping around upstairs. There's no sign of dinner being prepared, so it looks like I'll be ordering a Chinese takeaway as I'm not in the mood to cook tonight. I take my reading material to the sitting room and flop down in my armchair. Five minutes into my reading, Megan appears in the doorway. She's wearing a pair of tight black jeans and a low cut white blouse, her hair and makeup immaculate. The smell of a perfume I don't recognise drifts across the room, and I have to admit she looks good for a change.

Without acknowledging my presence, she clacks across the laminate wood floor in her high-heeled shoes. She then rummages through a drawer in our abysmally constructed flatpack sideboard.

"Since when have we started dressing for dinner?"

"Hilarious, Craig. You do what you like for dinner, I'm going out."

"Again?"

This is becoming an increasingly common occurrence and the third time Megan has been out in the last week alone.

"Why should it bother you? It's not as though we ever do anything, is it?" she spits.

I can't argue with that. Apart from the occasional trip to the supermarket, we haven't been anywhere in public together since the RolpheTech Christmas party last year. While I'm not the most romantically attuned man in the world, even I know a trip to Tesco doesn't constitute an evening out.

"Where are you going?"

"Do you actually care where I'm going? Don't wait up, I'll be home when I'm home."

She slams the drawer shut and struts out of the room. I watch her backside wiggle in the tight black jeans and begrudgingly admit to myself that it's still a fine arse. Perhaps I should have told her that once in a while.

The brief conversation with Megan has quashed my appetite for franchise research or Chinese food. I drop the wad of paper into the magazine rack and switch the TV on. The news is just starting, but I pay it little attention as a seed of troubled thought sprouts in my mind. Even the least perceptive of husbands couldn't fail to notice the recent changes in Megan's behaviour. Going out more, buying new clothes, making more of an effort with her appearance. This is the realm of newspaper agony aunts, where the answer is obvious to everyone, except the dumb spouse writing in. All evidence suggests that my wife could be having an affair.

I let the possibility of Megan's infidelity sink in, and much like the moral dilemma of the store closing, my feelings are torn. The initial feeling is one of relief. Could this be the catalyst that brings our sorry excuse for a marriage to an end? Then a more surprising feeling rises — jealousy. No matter how dysfunctional a marriage is, no husband wants to picture his wife screaming in ecstasy while another man screws her senseless. The more I try to cast that image aside, the more vividly it returns.

Another penny drops when I consider our sex life, or more accurately, our non-existent sex life. I cast my mind back, trying to recall the last time we had sex. I think it might have been after the RolpheTech Christmas party when we were both so drunk that our mutual resentment drowned in an alcohol-fuelled frenzy on the sofa. But apart from a few half-hearted attempts on my part since that night, there hasn't even been the slightest suggestion of sex, let alone the actual act. Perhaps Megan has found another, more appealing solution to her sexual needs?

Just as I toy with the idea of confronting Megan with my baseless accusations, I hear the front door slam shut. It looks like I'll have to spend the evening stewing in my negative thoughts instead. This is one of those situations where my overly analytical mind is a curse. A tiny, inconsequential thought can catch fire in my head, and before I know it, my pernicious imagination has created a gloomy plot for me to live out. I recall one such scenario when I was sixteen — I thought I was having a brain haemorrhage, and I got my worried mother to make an emergency appointment at the doctor's. As it transpired, the prognosis was a migraine, caused by staring at a computer screen for too many hours. There was nothing wrong with me apart from my wild imagination. I wish I could control it, but it seems to be the way my brain is wired.

I try to distract myself by steering the negative thoughts down a different path, one where my wife isn't currently sat in her car and about to fellate another man. I light another mental fire by considering the more practical aspects of our marriage ending.

We made our final mortgage payment on the house a few months ago, so we'd each have a large chunk of cash to buy our own place. However, my occasional glance at the property section of the local paper suggests that even a one-bedroom flat would be beyond my budget; therefore I'd need to borrow at least £30,000. This raises another problem as obtaining a mortgage without a job is a non-starter. Even if I start a business, I'll need at least a year's trading accounts before a mortgage company will consider a loan. My only option would be to rent for a year, which isn't ideal as its dead money, plus property prices seem to be on an upward curve.

I shake my head and curse the lunacy of my thinking. Within ten minutes of seeing my wife dressed up to go out, I had mentally ended our marriage and started making contingency plans for my living arrangements. Trying to shake the negative thoughts from my mind, I head into the kitchen and make myself a coffee.

I return to my armchair and flick between the myriad of channels on the TV. I think back to the days where there were just four. We didn't have the quantity of programmes back then, but I'm sure we had better quality. There is rarely anything on TV these days to pique my interest, and that's certainly the case tonight. Inevitably, I settle on a film I've already seen. The rest of the evening is spent watching mindless American comedy shows, and the occasional dip into my franchise research. By eleven o'clock there's no sign of Megan, so I take a shower and retire to bed.

After a fitful night's sleep, I wake up earlier than usual. I get ready for work and twenty minutes later, I open the front door to another wet, miserable morning, courtesy of our bipolar British weather. I don't know what time Megan came home last night and decided against asking her this morning. She was her usual moody self, which doesn't seem quite right for somebody in the exciting first throes of a new relationship, clandestine or otherwise. Maybe I've misread the signs. Truth be told, I've got enough to deal with at the moment without over-analysing problems that may not exist beyond my fucked-up mind. If there was ever a right time to bury my head in the proverbial sand, this is it.

I arrive at RolpheTech and head for my office via the staff room to make myself a coffee. I settle into my office chair and soak up the silence. This is how I've started my working day since I became manager, but everything is different today, everything is pointless. Daily sales targets, staff rotas, stock orders, training schedules, product promotions — the planning of tasks that will never come to fruition. Given the choice, I'd rather Marcus shut the damn place down today. It has to be better than watching my colleagues go about their jobs like it's just another working day. I flirt with the idea of telling them about their impending unemployment, but Brian's warning pings into my mind and quickly douses that thought. If the takeover fails for any reason, I can kiss goodbye to my redundancy, and RolpheTech will face an even more uncertain future.

I'm just about to check my emails when there's a knock on the office door.

"Morning Craig. I don't suppose you've got five minutes free? I need to have a chat with you," Lucy asks.

"Sure, grab a seat," I reply.

Judging by her body language, we won't be having the same sort of chat as the one last week. Considering she's been in a strange mood ever since, I'm just relieved she's actually talking to me at all.

Her eyes skip around the room for a moment before she notices the bruising on my neck.

"Jesus, Craig, what happened to your neck, are you okay?"

"Slight scuffle with somebody on Saturday night. It looks worse than it is, I'm fine."

I'm not sure she's convinced, but she pulls her attention back to the matter in hand.

"Right, I never thought I'd say this, and I've practised every way of saying it. All boils down to the same thing though, I'd like to hand in my notice."

I didn't see this coming.

"Really? Why?"

"I've been thinking about it for a while, but you know how it is, life just drifts by."

"I don't know what to say, Lucy. Where are you going?"

"The reason I've been thinking about it for a while is because my sister has been nagging me to move down her way."

Her sister owns a boutique hotel in Brighton, and I know that Lucy and her daughter spend the school holidays down there.

"What are you going to do for work?"

"Well, that's actually the reason for moving. Her business is going well, and she's just bought the adjoining house so she can expand the hotel. She needs help with the management side of things, and that's where I come in."

"But where are you going to live? Property prices in Brighton are ridiculously high, you know."

"I've got that covered. There's a detached annexe in the garden of the house Claire is buying, so I'm going to sell my place here and use the equity to buy it from her. It'll help her with cash for the renovations, and it gives us a nice place to live that we can afford."

This is both the best, and worst news I could have expected from our chat. The best news because it means that the branch closing won't affect Lucy, but the worst news because I'm losing one of my few true friends. Ordinarily, I'd move heaven and earth to change her mind, but that's not an option.

"When are you going?"

"I know my contract says I have to give four weeks' notice, but if you're able to do anything, I'd like to go as soon as possible. I've got a lot to organise, and there's already interest in my house from a few potential buyers."

Until this point, the prospect of our store closing was just words and thoughts. Nothing had actually happened, but the inevitability of it all has just crashed into my office alongside Lucy. Every fibre of my being wants to tell her to stay, but the reality is there's nothing for her to stay for.

"Leave it with me, Lucy, and I'll see what I can do," I sigh.

She'll have her answer soon enough, and it will be an answer that works in her favour. No notice period and an unexpected redundancy payment. At least she'll derive some benefit from the store closing.

As I slump back in my chair, Lucy pulls an envelope from her pocket and drops it onto my desk.

"I know you need my resignation in writing, so there you go."

I let the envelope sit where she dropped it, like picking it up would be a sign of acceptance. Lucy, perceptive as ever, spots that something is troubling me.

"Are you okay, Craig? Is there something you want to say?"

"No, not really, just a bit disappointed to know you're leaving, that's all."

"But do you think it's the right thing for me to do, leaving everything behind and moving on?"

She stares at me with expectant eyes, like I'm the right person to ask for career advice.

"I think you're doing the right thing, Lucy," I reluctantly confirm.

Her head drops.

"Okay, if you see no reason for me to stay, then I guess we're done here," she sighs.

Without another word, or even a glance in my direction, she gets up and leaves.

7

Yesterday afternoon brought better news than the morning. Once I'd got over the shock of Lucy's resignation, I made a few calls to franchise operators, and set up two meetings for next week. Both of them spoke enthusiastically about their respective opportunities and said I was just the sort of person they're looking to recruit. I don't know how much of that was sales spiel, but they left me with the impression I was about to embark on an exciting new career. But before I have any meetings with potential franchise suitors, I've got a more pressing meeting scheduled with Marcus this morning. At least I can take comfort that this will hopefully be the last time I have to see his sneering face.

I have to admit that even though I know what Marcus is going to say, I'm still a little nervous. There is just something about him that spikes anxiety in me. As a distraction, I've been in my office since I arrived this morning, surreptitiously wading through years of accumulated junk and sorting my personal possessions for their inevitable trip home in a cardboard box. Amongst the detritus in one of my desk drawers, I unearth a photo taken at a Christmas party a few years ago. I'm sat on a chair with a stupid grin on my face. Lucy is sat on my lap, with her arm draped around my shoulder and looking a little tipsy. It was a great night, and a reminder that there's a lot about this job I'll miss.

As I sit staring at the photo, Geoff charges in without knocking.

"Sorry boss, thought you'd want to know that Marcus has just pulled up in the car park."

I look up at the clock, it's only 9.40am. Marcus appears keen to have his moment.

"Thanks Geoff, tell him I'm up here."

Geoff nods and disappears. I put the photo in my jacket pocket and quickly tidy up, so it's not obvious that I'm already clearing out my desk. I then open a page of branch reports on the computer so it looks like I'm going about my job as usual. I take a long, deep breath and gather my thoughts. This is it.

Marcus appears in the doorway, looking dapper as ever in a navy blue suit, crisp white shirt, and lilac silk tie. There is no greeting offered as he closes the door behind him. He carefully lays his leather briefcase on my desk, placing his mobile phone and car keys on top. He then unbuttons his jacket, takes a seat, and casually crosses his legs.

"You're early," I say, just to break the uncomfortable silence.

"You know what they say, Pelling, early bird and all that. Let's get down to business shall we?"

I'm slightly surprised that he hasn't already launched into a tirade about Saturday night. His bottom lip looks a little swollen, and I'm sure I can see faint yellow bruising around his jawline. He also conveniently seems to have missed the hand-shaped, purple bruising around my neck. I guess it's all irrelevant now, anyway. I suspect his ego feels more bruised than his face, which is why he hasn't brought the subject up.

Marcus makes a slight adjustment to his tie and clears his throat.

"The reason I called this meeting is because I've been conducting a root and branch analysis of the business for the last six weeks, to identify ways we can improve profitability. I reported my conclusions to the board during a meeting on Monday, and part of my recommendations were for a limited amount of branch closures. I considered several factors when reaching my decision on which branches had to close, and I'm afraid to inform you that this branch is one of them."

As I listen, I feel slightly unsettled. Not by what Marcus is actually saying, but the way it's being delivered. His words sound scripted. After Saturday's events, I thought he'd be delivering this news with unbound joy. Something isn't right.

"God, that's terrible news," I reply, sounding just as wooden as Marcus.

"When will it close?"

"The last trading day will be Sunday. We'll need the staff to remain for another week to assist with the closure, and then they'll be free to seek other employment. The board have kindly agreed to pay them until the end of the month."

"Okay, understood. What about redundancy packages for the staff who've been here for a while?"

"Anyone with more than two years' service will receive a redundancy payment, together with their final pay at the end of the month."

Marcus sits back in his chair and locks his hands behind his head. Then for the first time since he walked into my office, he displays some emotion, as a smile creeps across his face.

"Sorry Pelling, let me clarify that last statement. Anyone with two year service will receive a redundancy payment...except you. You're going to resign, and you're going to do it now."

He doesn't say another word; he just sits there with an inane grin on his face. What the hell is he playing at?

"Why would I resign? If I do that, I forfeit my redundancy package. I'm not stupid and I'm certainly not going to resign."

He remains silent for a moment; then he slowly pulls an envelope from the inside pocket of his jacket, and drops it onto my desk. My name is printed on the front, and it's marked 'Private & Confidential'.

"What's that?" I snap.

"It's your letter of resignation, all ready for you to sign. Would you like to borrow my pen?"

"Forget it Marcus, I'm not resigning, so stop wasting your breath."

"Fair enough, but you might want to take a look at the supplementary documents in that envelope, before you make any hasty decisions."

I snatch the envelope from my desk and tear it open. There are three sheets of paper, the top one being my pre-prepared resignation letter, which I discard on the desk. The next sheet looks like a photocopied page from a RolpheTech job application form. The final sheet is a copy of my exam results from Heathland Secondary School. Noticing my puzzled expression, Marcus is more than happy to explain.

"I got chatting to a few people on Saturday evening at the reunion. Several of them remembered that you flunked your exams, which surprised them, considering what a studious little boffin you were. I have to admit I was puzzled why you were working here, rather than some software company with all the other nerds. Anyway, that got me thinking, so yesterday I managed to obtain a copy of your exam results, and I checked them against your original application form. You're looking at copies of both."

My mind flashes back to the moment twenty-six years ago, when I sat in this very room, completing my application form with Brian. After a few months of working at RolpheTech, I had assumed I'd got away with my falsified exam results, and my gamble had paid off.

"As you can see, there appears to be some discrepancy between the results you entered in the application form, and the results you actually achieved."

My pulse begins to race, but I try to play it cool.

"Well done, you found out I exaggerated my exam results. So what?"

"I'm surprised nobody picked up on it at the time, but to answer your question, if you care to check your contract of employment, section six, clause two, you'll see it clearly states that any deliberate falsification of information on the application form can result in immediate termination of your contract."

"This is bullshit. If I have breached the terms of my contract why aren't you sacking me? You're trying to trick me into resigning," I protest.

"It's a valid point, Pelling, and if I had my way, I'd sack you here and now. However, it appears you have some support on the board, and my recommendation to sack you wasn't well received after your long service to the company. Allowing you to resign is considered a fair compromise. Either way though, you leave without a penny in redundancy pay. If you don't believe me, I suggest you check with head office, they'll confirm everything."

I think back to my telephone conversation with Brian on Monday. He must have mentioned my name during his game of golf, so it might explain why a few board members were fighting my corner. But it makes no difference if I resign or I'm sacked — either way, my funding for the franchise is gone. I have no option now, other than to resort to my ludicrous backup plan.

I nervously pull my phone from my pocket and scroll through the image gallery to find the pictures of my bruised neck I took on Sunday morning. I place the phone on my desk and point at it.

"A few pictures of my neck after you attacked me on Saturday. Take a closer look," I order, trying to sound more confident than I feel.

Marcus doesn't even flinch, let alone look at the pictures. He just sits there, maintaining his smug expression.

"You say 'attacked'? Are you referring to the altercation we had, in which I was violently punched in the face?"

"You know damn well I am. I want you to talk to the board and change their minds about my redundancy pay. If you don't, I'll make a formal complaint about your assault. I think you'll find that's grounds for instant dismissal."

"So let me get this right, basically you're blackmailing me?"

"Call it what you will, but I'm not leaving without my redundancy pay. Sort it out, or it'll be your career on the line."

The smile on his face grows wider as he reaches across and picks up his mobile phone, still sat on top of his briefcase on my desk. He flicks his finger across the screen a few times and then holds the phone aloft. Distant voices echo from the phone speaker, clear enough for me to recognise my own voice.

"I have dozens of meetings every week, and to accurately recall the key discussion points, I record every meeting as a matter of course. Unfortunately for you, Pelling, I've also recorded your crude blackmail attempt, and your admission you punched me."

"Wait, what? I never said I punched you. You know it was Dave," I protest.

Marcus swipes his finger back across the screen and plays the part of our conversation where I acknowledged a punch being thrown. I never mentioned that it was actually Dave who punched him.

"Notwithstanding the crude blackmail attempt, which in itself is a criminal act, your failure to mention the Neanderthal's name would suggest that you and I argued, and you punched me. Purely in self-defence, I had no option but to restrain you. The bruising to your neck occurred during that restraint. It's all here, Pelling, plain as day. But if you'd rather implicate your friend, and make this a legal issue, be my guest."

Checkmate. Even if forging my exam results wasn't a sackable offence, I had gifted Marcus a bullet-proof failsafe. I can't believe I've been so stupid. What the fuck was I thinking?

Noting my horrified expression, Marcus leans forward and withdraws a pen from his jacket pocket. He carefully places it on top of the resignation letter and sits back in his chair.

"I'll give you thirty seconds to sign the letter. If you don't sign it, I'll head straight to the nearest police station. I'm sure they'd be very interested to hear my recording. If you think it'll be tough getting a job now, just think how much harder it will be with a criminal record for attempted blackmail."

My mind furiously explores every avenue of escape from my current plight. None of them lead anywhere good. If I sign the letter, I kiss goodbye to my redundancy pay, but if I don't, Marcus now has enough ammunition to seriously undermine my future career prospects, and maybe even my liberty.

"Twenty seconds, Pelling. Sign it."

I pick up the pen which is probably worth more than my car. One signature and it's all over. Twenty-six years of service, and I walk away with nothing.

"Ten seconds."

Shit. Shit. Shit. I don't make great decisions even when I've time to think them through. This is too big a decision to make on the spur of the moment.

"Five, four, three..."

I sign the letter.

Marcus snatches the signed letter, folds it up, and slips it back in his jacket pocket. A sickly feeling rises in my stomach as the finality of my action sinks in.

"Now we've got that out of the way, I'll give you five minutes to get your belongings together. I'll then escort you off the premises. If any of the staff ask, tell them you're not feeling well and you're going home, but I think it would be better for all concerned if you avoid speaking to anyone."

There is no emotion in Marcus's voice, which remains calm and businesslike. I wonder if he's still recording the conversation, not that it makes a shred of difference now.

"You want me to leave now?" I reply in surprise.

"Don't panic, Pelling. You'll be paid until the end of the month, but I don't want you here, stirring things up. Think of it as gardening leave."

"But who'll tell the staff about the branch closure?"

"Not that it's any longer your concern but I'll tell them at the end of the day. Somebody from head office will arrive tomorrow to oversee the final trading days, and the closure process."

Marcus stands up, opens his briefcase, and rifles through some papers. I continue to sit in my chair, bewildered.

"Come on, Pelling, get your act together will you. I've got things to do, and I want you out of here. Now."

After my preparations earlier, it only takes a few minutes to get my sorry box of possessions together. Marcus takes a cursory glance in the box to check I haven't stolen any RolpheTech property before demanding I hand over the store keys and the code for the alarm system.

As I follow Marcus from my office and down the stairs, I feel like a death row prisoner, taking his final walk to the chair. Mercifully, we don't bump into any of the staff, and twenty seconds later, I'm stood at the door to the staff car park. Marcus pushes it open and ushers me out. I don't know why, but as I cross the threshold into the car park, I stop for a moment, and stare across the tarmac vista. I must look a forlorn figure, stood there clutching my cardboard box. I expect to hear the door slam behind me, but Marcus can't resist having the final word.

"Remember what I said last week, Pelling? What goes around, comes around. It may have taken thirty years, but you mess with Marcus Morrison and there will only ever be one winner."

I turn to face him. I can feel tears welling in the corner of my eyes, and a lump dances in my throat. I'm about to lose it, but with my last ounce of resistance, I clear my throat and muster a reply.

"A winner, with a tiny cock."

He slams the door shut.

8

The alarm clock shrills at 7.20am. I nudge Megan awake and continue my search for the sanctuary of sleep. I toss and turn for half an hour, but I'm constantly dragged back to consciousness as Megan bangs and slams her way around the house. I told her about my new employment status when she came home from work yesterday. Considering she's been nagging me for years to find a better job, I assumed that she might see the positive side of leaving RolpheTech. I was wrong, and she went ballistic. I touched on the idea we could re-mortgage the house to invest in the franchise, but she shot that down immediately, and made it clear she wasn't willing to risk her half of our home to solve a problem I'd created. Her mood this morning hasn't improved.

Megan eventually leaves the house and silence is temporarily returned, only to be broken once more when the neighbour's fucking dog starts yapping. With the prospect of sleep looking unlikely, I get up, visit the bathroom and plod down to the kitchen. I fill the kettle and pull a mug from the cupboard. As the kettle rumbles away, I spoon coffee granules and sugar into the mug. It's the same routine I've enacted every morning for years, although at this time of the morning I'm usually stood in the RolpheTech staff room. But not today, or ever again. I fill the mug with boiling water, give it a perfunctory stir, and take it into the sitting room.

I drop into my armchair and draw a sip of coffee, trying to get my thoughts into some order. I pluck my mobile phone from the coffee table and open the calendar app. I count back the days to last Tuesday, when my life was mundane, but comfortable. Nine days. It has taken just nine days for everything to collapse around me. The shock of yesterday has now given way to cold realisation. I've made some lousy decisions, and now I've got to fix them. It's a daunting task, and I don't even know where to begin. In lieu of any real answers, a series of alternate scenarios play out in my mind. What if I hadn't attended the reunion? What if I hadn't tried that stupid blackmail stunt on Marcus? What if I had made more effort in my marriage? The first two questions invoke more regret than the last, but it's all part of the same core problem — I can't do right for doing wrong.

My mind drifts further back, trying to unravel the threads of my life before they all tangled together into my current noose: Tessa, my exams, Video City, Megan, the baby, RolpheTech, Marcus. There are so many ways that my life could have played out if I'd made a different decision at any point. But did I make bad decisions, or did bad things just happen to me? Was I unlucky, or simply an idiot? Perhaps it wasn't the decisions I made, but the way I dealt with the consequences of those decisions? The more I think about it, the more it gives me a headache, and the pointlessness of the exercise becomes all too apparent. I need to concentrate on finding solutions to my immediate problems, rather than over-analysing the reasons I have them.

I open the web browser on my mobile phone, and as I'm about to search for retail management jobs, a message pings up to remind me I'm due at my parents' house this afternoon to clear out my old bedroom. Great, an afternoon wading through boxes of junk. I consider calling the old man and postponing, but the chore won't go away and he'll only pester me daily until they move.

Then another thought crosses my mind. It's not a thought I really want to explore, but given I'm fresh out of alternatives, I need to consider it. As my parents are selling their house and buying a cheaper property, they'll have some free capital soon. Perhaps I can persuade them to lend me the ten grand I need to buy the franchise. I'm fairly sure Mum would be willing, but the old man is not renowned for his philanthropic generosity. It's at least worth asking.

I return to my job search and spend the next hour scouring various websites, but my heart really isn't in it. Not only are most of the jobs advertised poorly paid or require formal qualifications, but I've all but convinced myself that I don't want to spend the next twenty years of my life as an employee. While the opportunity to work for myself is not without risk, the prospect of continuing a retail management career now fills me with dread. I never wanted a retail career in the first place, and it was only circumstances that pushed me in that direction. If I've learnt anything over the last week, it's that I need to get a grip on my destiny, rather than standing by and letting it happen.

Clutching at my new-found hope I head upstairs, take a shower, and get dressed. I then head back to the kitchen and fill a bowl with bland cereal before I take a seat in front of the TV to eat. I endure twenty minutes of daytime TV before my will to live is completely eroded. I switch the TV off and pick up my mobile phone. I contemplate calling Lucy, but think better of it. I do feel guilty that I wasn't able to tell the staff about the branch closure as I doubt that Marcus would have been particularly empathetic. But what does any of that matter now? I'm actually worse off than many of them, and Lucy can start her new life with an unexpected redundancy payment. I need to look forward, to think about myself.

After wasting another hour mindlessly browsing the Internet, I leave the house and make the short journey across town to my parents' house. With most residents at work, their street is less crowded with parked cars. I pull into the parking space at the front of the house and take a deep breath before ringing the doorbell. Seconds pass and the old man opens the door with his usual sour expression.

"Morning Dad."

He mumbles a complaint that I'm early and shuffles back into the sitting room. I follow him in and give Mum a kiss before taking a seat on the sofa. As Dad lowers himself into his armchair, he looks at me with a frown.

"You forgotten where your bedroom is? You won't get much done sat on your fat arse down here."

"Actually Dad, there was something I wanted to have a chat with you about before I get started."

"If this is about your bloody marriage, we don't want to hear about it, do we Janet?"

Mum offers a faint smile, but keeps quiet.

"No, it's nothing to do with my marriage Dad. It's to do with my career."

Dad eyes me with suspicion as I give him a highly edited version of what happened at RolpheTech, and then a textbook pitch about the opportunity to work for myself.

"So Dad, I need about ten grand to invest in a franchise I've been looking at."

The ticking of the carriage clock fills the silence as the old man slowly rubs his chin with a gnarled hand. I look across at Mum, but she's now staring out of the window, lost in her own world. There will be no support from that corner of the room. I know that Dad knows what my next question will be. He won't make this easy and obviously wants me to ask it.

"I was wondering if there is any way you could lend me that money? I'll get a proper loan agreement and repayment schedule drawn up, so it's all above board. If I had any other option, I wouldn't ask, but no bank will touch me now I'm out of work."

The old man leans over and pulls a large brown envelope from the side of his armchair. He extracts a ream of paperwork and thumbs through the pages, eventually finding what he's looking for. He holds it out for me to take.

"Those are the service charges for the flat we're moving into. Have a good read."

I reach over and grab the wad of paperwork, unsure how this answers my question. The page contains a table with three columns labelled *Standard Care*, *Enhanced Care* and *Total Care*. There is a list of services running down the left side of the page, and each cell in the table contains a cross or a tick. I scan the page, without knowing what I'm looking at.

"Because me and your mum aren't in the best of health we've gone for the *Total Care* package."

My eyes move to the bottom of the page and then water when I see the monthly charge of £450.

"£450 a month?" I say in disbelief.

"That's why you're begging in the wrong place. Once we've paid for the flat, we're investing all the remaining equity into a pension fund which should cover the service charges for as long as we're both still around."

"And this pension fund will swallow every penny of your equity?"

"Yes it will. I want to ensure we have a decent quality of life for our remaining years."

"So you can't help me then?" I sigh. "You do realise I've got no other options?"

"Why don't you do what I did? Get a bloody job and save up. That's the problem with your generation, you want everything now, and don't have the discipline to wait. It's no surprise the country is in such a bloody mess when everyone is borrowing money left, right, and centre."

He then begins ranting about the state of the country before I interrupt.

"Dad, if you're not able to lend me the money, I need to get on," I snap. "I'll deal with the bloody bedroom and then I have to sort out my life."

Before he can reply, I storm out of the room and stomp up the stairs to my old bedroom, slamming the door behind me. I lean against the door and close my eyes for a moment. Fuck. What do I do now?

I pad across the room and sit on the edge of my old single bed to think. The bed where my mum held me as I cried over Tessa. The bed where Megan and I first consummated our relationship. The bed that hosted my teenage dreams about being a computer programmer. I gaze around the room and feel an overwhelming sense of regret. Every object in the room holds a memory from a time when I had hope. When I had a future. If the objects could talk, I wonder what they'd say about the forlorn figure sat before them today? Would they ask what happened to the intelligent, ambitious young boy who spent countless hours beavering away at his computer? I stare up at a faded poster of The Pet Shop Boys, fixed to the pale blue wall with drawing pins. The enigmatic duo stare down on me with a look that could be construed as disappointment. I remember putting the poster up not long after I first heard 'West End Girls'. It was the first pop song that truly resonated with me, and I played it to death in this very room.

As I sit and wallow in reflective self-pity, it dawns on me that in a few weeks' time this shrine to my youth will be no more. Reduced to an empty shell with every memory stripped away. Maybe the new owners will have a child, and this will be their room, their little den of dreams. A fresh, blank canvas, ready for some lucky child to create their own visions, their own memories. I hope they create something worthwhile, because I sure as hell haven't, and for that, I feel guilty, I feel angry — most of all though, I feel sorry for myself.

I accept there's little to be gained by dwelling on what might have been. For now, this is still Craig Pelling's bedroom, and it won't sort itself out.

9

I reluctantly get to my feet and survey the room, looking for the easiest place to begin my task. It's not a huge room, maybe just about a double, and it feels much smaller now than it did when I was a child. A fitted bedroom unit stretches the length of one wall, comprising a double wardrobe, a chest of drawers and two large storage cupboards. A friend of my dad's built it not long after we moved here, and I'm amazed it's still standing, such was the sub-standard quality of both the materials, and the workmanship. I suspect the first thing the new owners of the house will do is rip the damn thing down.

Apart from my bed, the room also houses a pine bedside cupboard, a narrow bookcase, and a desk covered by a dust sheet. Despite Mum's poor mobility, she has always included my bedroom in her limited housework regime. I wonder how many hours she's wasted over the years, cleaning a room I had no intention of ever occupying again, and why she'd go to the trouble. I guess it must be hard for a mother when their one-and-only child leaves home, particularly if that mother is left to live with someone like my dad. Maybe Mum sits in this room occasionally and thinks back to my childhood when she was the centre of my universe. A time when her life had purpose, other than waiting on my dad. Maybe clearing out my room would be like purging the last remnants of motherhood. I'll never ask her.

I wander over to the window and stare out across the poorly maintained garden, and the houses beyond. The dark blue curtains smell strongly of fabric conditioner from a recent wash. It's the same brand of fabric conditioner Mum has used for decades, and it jolts a memory of freshly laundered school jumpers, cotton bedsheets and denim dungarees. I stand for a few minutes, content to wallow in the nostalgic scent of my childhood and the temporary sense of comfort it bears. Sadly, the comfort is fleeting as a screaming child in the neighbour's garden pulls me back to reality, and the tedious job ahead of me.

I decide to tackle the wardrobe first and pull open the wonky door. Apart from a few wire coat hangers, the hanging space is empty. The bottom, however, is full of random junk I'd chosen to be out of sight, and therefore out of mind. It's unlikely there will be anything in here I wish to salvage. After a few minutes of delving through old school books, empty boxes, and discarded items of clothing, my suspicions are confirmed. I close the wardrobe door and move on to the four drawers alongside.

The first drawer produces more school books, my old pencil case, several plastic rulers, and various odds-and-ends. On initial inspection, drawer two looks equally uninteresting, but a quick delve beneath the pile of computer magazines unearths my teenage porn stash. It's a fairly meagre collection, comprising three copies of 'Escort', a single copy of 'Penthouse', and a Dutch magazine called 'Blue Climax', which I smuggled-back from a school trip to Bruges.

I pick up the copy of 'Penthouse' and scan through the pages, reacquainting myself with the delights of Amber, Christy, Candy and Electra. Huge perms, bright lipstick, lurid blusher, and the bushy pubic hair no longer favoured in modern pornography. I turn my attention to my preferred masturbation material of the time, 'Blue Climax', and thumb through the tatty pages. Unlike the highly staged shots of solo girls in 'Penthouse', 'Blue Climax' contains pictures of couples having sex. Every page is a feast of mustachioed studs doing all sort of unspeakable things with obliging continental women. I spent many a happy evening under my duvet in the company of Lars & Sabine from page eight.

I tear off a black sack from a roll that Mum has left on the bed and drop the magazines into it. Not because I have any use for them, but because I still don't want my mum to find them. The rest of the drawers fail to deliver much of interest, unless I can find a market for a dozen blank C90 cassettes, a battered Sony Walkman, a half-dismantled Rubik's Cube, or scores of depleted batteries. However, one of the two large storage cupboards finally delivers something that might be worth keeping — my old Commodore 64 computer. A few months after starting work at Video City, I replaced the antiquated computer with a cutting-edge Nintendo games console. The ability to load a game simply by inserting a cartridge was a revelation, compared to the temperamental and tediously slow cassettes used with the Commodore. No longer of use, I boxed the computer up and placed it in this cupboard, where it has sat for thirty-odd years.

I carefully lift the box from the cupboard, place it on the bed and open it up. I give a nod to my teenage self for so meticulously packing it away. Everything is exactly where it should be and carefully wrapped in the original cellophane packaging. Even the box itself is in perfect condition. I pull my mobile phone from my pocket and search for a website to get an idea of retro computer prices. I find a page of Commodore machines, most of which aren't boxed or look in as good a condition as mine. Looking at the prices being asked, I guess mine must be worth about £150, especially as I've also got the original cassette player still in its box. It's a tiny step towards my ten grand target, but it's something. However, this modest windfall depends on whether the computer still works or not.

For a few moments, I consider taking the computer home to test it, but I doubt I'll be able to connect a thirty year-old computer to a modern TV, so I'd also have to lug my worthless old portable TV with me. With little else in my schedule for the rest of the day, I decide to set up the computer here. I pull the dust sheet away to reveal the black ash desk beneath. Sat proudly on top of the desk is my old 14-inch Ferguson portable TV. I never quite understood why we used to refer to small televisions as 'portable'. It weighs more than a hod of house bricks and getting a half-decent picture involved dozens of miniscule adjustments to the feeble aerial. Once you'd achieved a reasonable picture, the last thing you dared do was move it.

I unpack the computer and place it on the desk in front of the TV. I then position the cassette player next to it and connect all the cables. I plug the transformer and TV power cables into a double socket behind the desk and then check all the connections. Satisfied I've remembered everything, I nervously flick the switches on the wall socket. Nothing explodes, which is a good start. The red LED light above the keyboard is brightly lit, indicating the computer has power. The light is an encouraging sign, and with a twinge of excitement, I push the power button on the TV.

For a few seconds nothing seems to happen. Then I smell burning dust and the TV makes a slight hissing noise as the screen flickers into life. With my more immediate problems put to one side, I take a seat on a foldaway plastic chair in front of the desk. Although the screen is awake, it's only displaying static, so I pull open a panel on the front of the TV and try to recall which of the preset tuners I used for the computer. I press the top one and I'm met with a slightly different array of static. The second button displays a faint, ghostly picture of a lunchtime TV programme. Buttons three and four only produce more screens full of static. I press the fifth button and the static is finally replaced with a vibrant blue screen, displaying the once-familiar pale blue text...

**** COMMODORE 64 BASIC V2 ****
64K RAM SYSTEM 38911 BASIC BYTES FREE

While those two lines offer some assurance the computer is working, they should be followed by the word 'Ready' and a blinking cursor — neither are present. Instead, there's a single line of text I've never seen before...

PATH CORRUPTION ERROR. RESTORE? Y/N

I find the operating manual in the top drawer of the desk, and flick through the pages until I reach the section on error messages. I scan the list of standard system messages, looking for the solution to my particular fault, but there's no reference to it, let alone a solution. I grab my mobile phone and conduct a web search for the error message. I scan through the first four pages of results, but there is nothing even remotely relevant to my query. I sit back in the chair and stare at the screen. If there is an error, it makes sense to restore the system. However, if that restore fails, I'll be left with a worthless block of retro plastic.

My finger hovers over the keyboard, floating up and down between the 'Y' and 'N' keys. Based upon years of making wrong decisions, I go against my instincts, and hit the 'Y' key. Another message pings up on the screen...

INPUT PATH RESTORE DATE:

Another check in the operating manual draws a blank, so I can only assume I need to enter a date to reset the computer back to. Initially, this seems an impossible request, but there is one infamous date from my teenage years I'll never forget — Saturday 17th May 1986. I distinctly recall working on a bug in one of my self-coded games that morning, as I tried to keep myself busy before visiting Tessa's house. I know the computer was working perfectly that morning. I enter the date and hit the 'Enter' key. Another message appears...

RESTORE DURATION (1-48):

Any initial excitement I had about tinkering with my old computer is now being replaced with frustration. I refer to the operating manual again, more in hope than expectation. Unsurprisingly, there is no reference to this message either. I drum my fingers on the desk and wrack my brain, trying to recall if I'd ever seen a reference to 'Restore Duration'. Nothing comes to mind, so I need to work it out with simple logic. Patently 'duration' refers to time, but do the numbers 1-48 refer to seconds, hours, days or even weeks? I scrub that line of thought as with no other point of reference, the numbers could mean anything, so there's precious little point in procrastinating over it. I input the maximum number, '48', and strike the 'Enter' key again. I shake my head as yet another message appears...

CONFIRM PATH RESTORE? Y/N

I hit the 'Y' key with more force than is necessary. Nothing immediately happens. With frustration mounting, I'm just about to unplug the damn thing when the screen turns from blue to red. A message appears in the centre of the screen, in large yellow letters...

RESTORING CORRUPTED PATH - PLEASE WAIT...

I stare at the text as it blinks on and off, every second. On, off, on, off, on, off. I'm not sure if the text is getting a tiny bit bigger every time it reappears. I move my face closer to the screen and inspect the text in greater detail as it continues to blink rhythmically. For a split second, I could swear the message changes, but it blinks off again in a heartbeat. I move closer again, so my face is now only a foot away from the screen. The blinking appears to be more rapid. Again, I'm sure a different message pings up, but with the increased speed of the blinking, maybe it's just my eyes playing tricks on me.

And then the blinking stops, the text holds for a moment, and disappears. I can still see the ghostly outline of the letters as I flick my eyes across the screen.

I hold my position for a few seconds, but the screen remains blank. Just as I'm about to sit back in my chair, a tiny white square appears in the centre of the screen.

Suddenly, the square rotates ninety degrees in a clunky movement. It seems an odd way for the computer to restore, and I stare at the square with increasing curiosity. Then it rotates another ninety degrees. A few seconds pass and the same thing happens. The clunky rotations gradually become faster, and more fluid, until the square is rotating like the sweeping second hand on an expensive watch. I watch it rotate through mesmerized eyes as it grows marginally larger on each rotation, eventually becoming so large that the corners are almost touching the edge of the screen.

Then the restore process gets weird. Worryingly weird.

It's barely perceptible at first, but after a minute, I become acutely aware that my peripheral vision is tinged scarlet red. I try to move my eyes, but something compels me to keep focussed on the rotating square. The redness encroaches further across my line of sight, becoming increasingly vibrant. Panicky seconds pass until it feels like I'm looking at the square through a pair of red-tinted binoculars. The blanket of scarlet red continues to dominate my entire field of vision when, all of a sudden, the square starts to shrink slowly until all I can see is a tiny square, rotating against a solid red backdrop. My initial curiosity gives way to mild terror, and my brain instructs my legs to stand and walk away. The message is sent, but not received, and my position remains fixed. The panic mounts and further efforts to move away from the screen prove futile.

Then the square disappears, and a message in yellow letters appears...

PATH RESTORED. GOOD LUCK PROFESSOR.

The message fades out, but the solid red backdrop remains. My mind struggles to process what the message means as a slow throbbing sensation develops at the back of my eyes. It doesn't bring pain, just unadulterated fear as it spreads quickly until it feels like my entire head is beating. The throbbing intensifies, the beats coming faster and deeper. It spreads down my neck and engulfs my chest, syncing in time with my rapidly beating heart. It may have been within seconds, it may have been within minutes, but at some point my entire body pulses.

As the throbbing approaches a crescendo, the blanket of red slowly fades to white. A kaleidoscope of colourful, indeterminate shapes zoom from the centre of my vision, and the throbbing is accompanied by sense of weightlessness, like being in an aircraft during turbulence. I feel like I'm falling faster and faster, as the coloured shapes spin past me at an increasing pace. A metallic tang hits the back of my throat, and I try to cough it back, but my body and my mind are now separate entities with no communication between the two. The assault on my senses is completed when static crackles in my ears. The throbbing is now so intense that it's become a constant humming sensation, penetrating every limb, every muscle, every nerve. There is nothing for my mind to cling to, other than the thought I must be dying. Did I have a heart attack, and this is my journey to the afterlife? I feel such terror I'd happily embrace the calm waters of death in lieu of this.

Then I feel nothing. There is just darkness and silence.

PART THREE

1

I've had some epic hangovers in my life. The kind of hangover where you feel so intolerably awful that sleep is the only way out. The kind of hangover where you can only recall vague fragments of what occurred the night before. This is worse. I try to pull my thoughts together, but even the slightest concentration pounds a sickening ache across my skull. I clear my mind and focus on my breathing. Slow, deep breaths. Three seconds to inhale, three seconds to exhale. I subconsciously disengage every sense, so nothing can divert my attention back to the pain, to the nausea, to the fragmented memories. I want to sleep, and eventually, my mind relaxes enough that I do.

I sleep for maybe minutes, maybe hours, maybe days. I don't know how long I sleep, but I do feel marginally better when I come around. Thoughts start to order themselves. Where am I? How did I get here? What the fuck was I drinking last night? My tender head is on a pillow, and I'm cocooned in a duvet, so I know part of the first question; I'm in a bed. I cautiously open my dry, gritty eyes and squeeze several exaggerated blinks to encourage moisture back. The mist clears from my vision and I can see the outline of vaguely familiar shapes, but wherever I am, the light is too dim to see much. Despite the darkness, I know that this isn't my bed at home; the pillow is too thick and the mattress too hard. I draw a breath through my nose and instantly recognise the smell of a certain brand of fabric conditioner from the bed linen. The dots join up, and I realise that I must be in bed at my parents' house. I don't know why, nor do I know why I'm naked.

Every answer seems to raise more questions. Why am I lying in bed at my parents' house, naked and seemingly at some stage, incredibly drunk? I pull my arm from beneath the duvet and raise a hand to my temple, massaging it to encourage answers. As my hand moves around my temple, it brushes something. I stop and cautiously inch my hand towards my forehead. Again, I feel it brush something. What the hell is that? I probe a little further with the tips of my fingers and they also make contact with the mystery foreign object. It's hair, my hair apparently. Most people wouldn't be too alarmed to feel their own fringe — unless that fringe receded a decade ago. I pat my head, and rather than the large expanse of bare skin I expect to find at the top of my forehead, I feel thick hair. Was I so drunk last night that somebody glued a merkin to my head? I gently pull a few strands, but there is no resistance. This thing is well and truly stuck down.

I roll onto my back and stare at the dark expanse of ceiling. I concentrate more intensely to recover some memories, but there's nothing there. It feels like I'm wandering around a field in a claustrophobic, impenetrable fog. I need to find a stimulus, a sign to point my mind in the right direction, but I won't find it lying here in the dark. I cautiously raise my upper body, so I'm sat-up, and swing my legs ninety degrees to the left, placing my feet on the carpeted floor. Something doesn't feel right, but I put it down to residual alcohol that must still be in my system. Trying to ignore my confused thoughts, I focus on confirming my location, and shedding some light on the situation, literally and figuratively.

Assuming I am in my old bedroom, I should be facing the window, which is only a few feet from my position on the edge of the bed. I lean forward and slowly reach out with my right hand until my fingers touch the curtains. I brush my fingertips across the fabric until I find the thick vertical hem, securing it tightly between my thumb and forefinger. I delicately pull the fabric towards me. A shard of daylight bursts from an inch-wide gap between the curtains, prickling my heavily dilated pupils. I quickly turn my head back to the darkness. I squint as my eyes readjust to the tepid light, and after a few seconds, I can clearly see the pine bedside cupboard, and the jaunty angles of a black office lamp sat upon it. In one fluid motion, I reach out with my left hand and flick the switch on the lamp, while releasing the curtain from my right hand. My eyes welcome the transition to the soft glow of a forty-watt bulb. If I had any lingering doubts as to my whereabouts, they are quickly dispelled, as the soft light illuminates my old bedroom, and my naked body. My naked, and unbelievably skinny body.

Losing weight is damn hard, especially for somebody with my lack of self-discipline. I simply love beer and cake too much. Not together, obviously. I'm sure I'm not the first man to have wished I could wake one morning to find my beer belly, love handles and b-cup moobs had magically disappeared overnight. As much as I may have wished for such an impossible intervention, the reality of sitting on a bed, staring at a body that is several stones lighter than when you last looked at it, is a truly terrifying experience.

I stare down at my genitals like I've never seen them before, which isn't too far from the truth as they've lived in the shadow of my pot belly for years. My once-chunky thighs are now like those of a marathon runner, and my moobs replaced with a table-flat chest. This is not right, this is not right at all. The only vaguely plausible explanation my addled brain can muster is that maybe I'm not suffering a hangover, but I've been in a coma and fed intravenously for months. In isolation, it might just about be a credible notion, but when combined with everything else about my situation, it doesn't make a whole heap of sense.

If my miracle weight loss was not perplexing enough, my eyes are drawn beyond my genitals, to something strewn across the floor that defies explanation. I lean forward and stare at it with disbelieving eyes. The item in question is a distinctive, blue and orange dressing gown, which looks identical to the one I owned as a teenager. Of the many things I currently don't know, I certainly do know I consigned this dressing gown to the dustbin, sometime in 1986 after Mum burned it with the iron.

I tentatively pick the dressing gown up and inspect it for scald marks. I check the front, the back, and then both sides again to be sure. There are definitely no scald marks. How can this garment be here? I distinctly recall mum showing me the burn mark, and I put it in the bin myself. Truth be told, I never liked the dressing gown and was glad to see the back of it. Yet despite all logic, I'm now holding it in my hands.

While the dressing gown adds yet another unanswerable question to the growing list, it solves the immediate problem of my nakedness. I stand up on shaky legs and slip it on, fastening the cord around my inexplicably slim waist. I pause for a few seconds to ensure my woozy head can coordinate my movements, and shuffle forward to the window. Hoping some fresh air might help to clear my mind, I pull back the curtains and push the window open as far as it will go. Squinting at the bright daylight, I lean on the ledge as my stomach tries to return its contents. I swallow hard to keep it contained, my gut growling angrily in protest. I close my eyes, lean forward and draw several deep breaths. The dizziness ebbs away enough for me to dare to open my eyes again.

I'm greeted with the view of my parents' garden, but it looks completely different to how it looked when I peered out of this window earlier. Under the care of Dad's seemingly incompetent gardener, the garden I saw earlier was a far cry from how it looked when Dad used to tend it, and remarkably, the way it now looks. The lawn is impeccably manicured against large slate slabs that form a path down the centre. The lawn is separated from the boundary fences with neatly trimmed borders, which are stocked with orderly rows of plants and shrubs. At the end of the lawn is a small potting shed, shielded by a wooden trellis, itself partially hidden beneath a climbing plant interspersed with delicate white flowers. Directly beneath me on the patio, there are three wooden tubs, all bursting with an array of brightly coloured flowers.

As I stand and absorb the view, a flicker of motion near the potting shed catches my eye. I cast my gaze to the rear of the garden, just in time to see the door to the potting shed swinging back and forth. A figure then appears from behind the door, carrying a tray of plants. He's only about thirty yards away, so I can clearly see he's wearing dark brown trousers and a chequered red shirt. From my first-floor vantage point, his face is hidden below the peak of a flat cap as he looks down towards the tray in his hands. He stands for a few moments as if inspecting the plants. Both the man's clothing and posture seem eerily familiar, but not recent familiar; distant familiar. The man then bends over and places the tray on the ground. He scratches his head through his flat cap and looks up the garden towards the patio. For the first time since he left the potting shed, I can clearly see his face. It's the middle-aged face of Colin Pelling. My dad.

My legs buckle and I stumble backwards, dropping onto the bed behind me. I struggle to find any air in my lungs as my heart pounds like a pneumatic drill. I cannot have seen what I just saw, surely? I was only just downstairs talking to the wizened, arthritic old man. A man who can barely walk without the aid of a stick, let alone carry trays of plants around a garden. I'm either mistaken, or I'm going insane. Either way, this makes absolutely no sense. Another thought fights for attention in my confused mind — it's just a dream, the only rational explanation.

I decide to test my theory. I stumble across the floor to the wardrobe and pull open the door. I stand before the mirror, fixed to the inside of the door, and slap my face so hard that it brings tears to my eyes. Real tears, real pain. Through my teary eyes, I stare at the reflection before me. I can't accept what I see, so I move closer until I'm just a foot away. The reduced distance only serves to confirm that this is no hallucination. No wrinkles, no receding hairline, spotty chin, rake-thin body. I'm looking at a photograph of my teenage self, but it's not a photograph because as my mouth drops open, so does the image before me.

I perform a series of random movements, trying to trick my reflection into revealing itself as a fake. I press my hand up against the mirror, and my teenage doppelgänger meets my hand on the cold glass. I drop my hand and tug at the cord holding the dressing gown around my waist. It falls open to reveal a skinny, post-pubescent body. I feel mildly perverted as I run my fingertips across the flat chest. But it's really my chest, isn't it? I can feel my hand brush across my skin, and I can see the action reflected on the man-boy in the mirror, precisely in unison. I comb my fingers through the thick mop of hair and grab a tuft at the forehead. I pull it left, then right, then straight up. I examine my scalp as I tug the tuft around, and conclude it's no wig, this is my hair. I step back a few feet, while maintaining eye-contact with the reflection in the mirror. Whatever, or whoever I'm looking at, it definitely isn't a figment of a preposterous dream.

I re-fasten the cord around my dressing gown and slam the wardrobe door shut. I need answers and they aren't to be found in there. I survey the room, searching for a clue that might unlock this schizophrenic nightmare — and then I spot something that ignites a spark, deep in a recess of my mind. Sat upon the desk, in the far corner of the room, is my Commodore 64 computer and the Ferguson portable TV. The screen on the TV is as black as night, apart from a tiny white blob in the centre. I scurry across the room and collapse on to the plastic chair. I lean forward to examine the blob which, on closer inspection, is actually a single line of miniscule white text...

PATH RESTORATION: 17/05/86 - DURATION: 39H:48M.

As I stare at the screen, the '48M' changes to '47M'. I study the words and suddenly, the initial spark in my brain ignites a firestorm of memories. The rotating square, the psychedelic colours and the sense of falling.

As I stare at the screen and try to process the barrage of memories flooding my mind, the text changes again. '47M' becomes '46M'. The numbers are decreasing, and logic suggests that the 'M' signifies minutes, and therefore, the 'H' must be hours.

I focus intently to recall the text I entered into the computer before the madness ensued. I'm sure the duration option was 1-48, and I entered '48'. A potential connection dawns on me, and I raise my eyes to the top of the TV where a small digital clock displays the time at 8.14am. I do some quick maths in my head. If I take the original 48 hours that I set for the 'duration', and subtract the 39 hours and 46 minutes currently displayed, I'm left with 8 hours and 14 minutes — the current time. Working backwards, the 'duration' countdown must have begun at midnight.

While I now know what the duration is, I have no idea what it is I'm set to endure for the remaining 39 hours and 46 minutes, or what happened to the other 8 hours and 14 minutes since midnight. I think back to the intense pain in my head when I first woke up. I remember breathing deeply while counting the time of every breath. I remember I needed sleep to escape the pain. I must have fallen asleep, and that would explain the missing time. But it doesn't explain why I'm currently residing in my teenage body, or how my dad apparently discovered the fountain of youth while tending his shrubs.

It's clear that the computer has more answers than it's willing to share, so the obvious course of action is to fathom-out what it's doing. I hit the 'Enter' key. Nothing happens. I work my way across the keyboard, striking every key with increased frustration, but the computer stubbornly ignores me. What if I just switch it off? Will it end this nightmare, or will it send me into a computer-generated purgatory? I flick the power switch. The computer remains on, the LED light shining brightly, and the text still on the TV screen. Shit. I lean down behind the desk and hit the switch on the power socket. I turn back to the screen, but absolutely nothing has changed. Just to underline the impotence of my efforts, the duration timer drops another minute.

I slump back in the chair and close my eyes. This is too weird, too unfathomable, too unbelievable. This is too much.

2

When people approach middle-age, you'll inevitably hear them chirp, "On the inside, I still feel like a teenager." Translate that, and it basically means that while their body is a car crash, they still buy clothes from Superdry and know the lyrics of at least one Ed Sheeran song. My problem is the reverse. I'm a middle-aged man trapped in a teenage body — and I do literally mean trapped, as in I cannot see any way out of this. I need to formulate a plan, but to do that, I need to establish some facts. So far, all I know for sure is that my body has lost thirty years, and at least as many pounds of flab. I know that a man who looks exactly like my middle-aged father is currently muttering profanities in the garden, which itself has undergone some sort of miracle transformation. That is all I know, and I desperately need more information.

With some sense of purpose, I get up from the plastic chair and begin my fact-finding mission. I stand and think back to how the room looked earlier when I was clearing it out. It looks and feels different now. It feels lived in. A pair of battered Gola trainers sit by the door, the laundry basket is full, as is the rubbish bin to the side of the desk. For the first time, I also notice the smell; that distinctive, and unpleasant smell of a teenager's bedroom. If this is an elaborate prank, the perpetrator has absolutely nailed the ambiance of my teenage bedroom. Trying to ignore the smell, I continue my visual inspection of the room. I cast my eye towards the bookcase near the door, and in particular, the shelf on which my old Saisho stereo sits.

I approach the bookcase and wistfully stroke the gloss-black plastic casing. The stereo was a birthday present, maybe my 14th or 15th. It came with me when I moved to the studio flat with Megan, but it eventually met its end at the local tip years ago. I can't remember the last time I saw it, but I do remember that the soundtrack to my teenage years played through these speakers. The seminal moment I first heard 'West End Girls' by the Pet Shop Boys. The tortuous sessions listening to 'Now 6' post-Tessa. Randy Crawford serenading my first sexual liaison with Megan. Just a few of the hundreds of memories immortalised in music from this device.

Distracted from more pressing tasks, I press the power button and the gentle hum of electricity emanates from the speakers. I turn the volume down to a lower setting and nudge the output switch from 'Tape' to 'FM'. The sound of a distant piano, accompanied by low bass notes, fills the room. I know the song — George Michael's, 'A Different Corner'. The vocals begin and I stand motionless, listening to the words, with a particular line from the fourth verse triggering an itch deep in my mind. The lyrics mention being *taken back in time* and *turning a different corner* so a lover is never met.

As the track plays out, and I try to scratch the itch in my mind, the DJ cuts across the closing bars…

"That was 'A Different Corner', the former number one by George Michael. You're listening to Peter Powell this Saturday morning here on Radio 1. Next up is a chart climber from Falco. This is 'Rock Me Amadeus'."

I hit the power button, and the room is quiet, unlike my mind, which is screaming with more confused thoughts. I distinctly remember the Falco track, not least because somewhere in the second verse he appears to say the word 'cunt'. A few years ago, I discovered he actually says 'könnt', the German word for 'can'. It was a disappointing revelation. However, it isn't Falco's lyrics that perturb me. Firstly, Peter Powell is now of pension age, and hasn't been on the radio for decades. It seems unlikely that Powell has resurrected his career on the youth-obsessed radio station that is today's Radio 1. And secondly, I'm positive he said 'chart climber'. Unless Falco has just died, and news of his demise has created a temporary spike in downloads, I fail to see how his track could be climbing the charts again.

Far from finding answers, all I've done so far is spawn more unanswerable questions.

The frustration sharpens the dull ache in my head. I raise my hand and place my palm on my forehead, offering me an unsettling reminder of my restored hairline. I draw a deep breath and slowly exhale, willing the pain to leave with it. The aching eases, but I feel dizzy again, so I slump back down on the plastic chair at the desk. In lieu of any other options, I investigate the contents of the desk, and pull open the top drawer. It's a disorganised mess. Scraps of used paper, the operating manual for the computer, sweet wrappers, a few empty cassette cases, and some loose change. I slam it shut and open the second drawer, which contains only two items: a C90 cassette, and an A4 jotter pad with a single line of text written on the front in marker pen...

AFTERPATH PROJECT by Craig Pelling

I pull it from the drawer, sit back in my chair and hold the pad in front of me with both hands. Memories of the long-forgotten 'Afterpath' game I created flood back. I spent hundreds of hours on it as a teenager, meticulously planning and coding the complex set of scenarios the lead character, whose name escapes me, could find himself in. It was an ambitious project, and I'd nearly completed it before an impenetrable bug, and my post-Tessa depression, brought the curtain down on it for good.

I open the pad and study the first page. Paragraphs of neat handwriting, reminding me what the world was like before every form of communication became digital. As I read the text, it seems hard to believe that I am actually responsible for the words on the page. Not just because the handwriting is a world apart from the few words I write today, but the almost palpable enthusiasm they convey. These are words written by an intelligent and creative young man.

As I digest more of the content, I feel an odd sense of appreciation for the cleverly constructed premise of the game. Odd, because I actually wrote it myself, albeit thirty years ago. However, my appreciation is also tinged with disappointment I never fulfilled the obvious potential demonstrated in these pages. I turn to the second page, titled 'Characters', and the first line sends a cold shiver down my spine...

MAIN CHARACTER: Professor Lance Gilgrip

The word 'professor' connects with another memory. The final words on the screen before my hallucinogenic episode, 'PATH RESTORED - GOOD LUCK PROFESSOR'. I flick back to the first page and desperately scan for a line which initially caught my eye...

"Time, both current and past is called a 'path' due to its linear nature. By restoring the path, the main character is able to go back in time to the start of that path (the path restore date) and has to determine at which point he deviates to create a different path, and a different future."

The term 'path restore date' sets my pulse racing. It's the same term I entered when I was trying to get the computer working earlier. No, it's too ridiculous to even contemplate. But then again, it would explain an awful lot about my current situation. I let this new information sink in, and wonder if I'm going crazy. Do crazy people actually know they're crazy? Maybe this isn't real at all, and somewhere back in the real world I'm lying in a hospital bed being pumped full of drugs. Maybe Megan and my parents are solemnly sat at my bedside, wondering how I got there, blaming themselves for not spotting the signs of my impending mental breakdown.

I read the first page of the jotter again. The core plot of the game surrounds the professor going back in time to change a series of decisions he made — decisions which led to his wife being killed in a bungled kidnap rescue. He could have booked a different restaurant that night. He could have called a cab rather than suggesting they walk back to the hotel. He could have paid the ransom without informing the police. Dozens of different decisions he could have made that would have taken him on a different path and changed the events which led to his wife's death. Even now, I have to admit it was a clever concept for a game.

As I stare at the page, an obvious conclusion strikes me — perhaps the professor shouldn't have gone on holiday in the first place. Patently, that wouldn't have made for a particularly interesting game, but his problem would have never have been a problem if he'd reversed one fundamental decision.

Those George Michael lyrics suddenly slam back into my mind.

The itch is scratched. Unlike the game where the professor had to unpick a whole series of decisions, my future was more easily fixed. If only I'd walked past Patels' Newsagent on that Friday afternoon after school. I wouldn't have met Tessa waiting in the queue, and it wouldn't have set off the chain of events which screwed my life up. Different corner, different outcome.

I drop the pad on the desk and stare at the TV screen. The timer has continued its countdown and now reads 39 hours and 29 minutes. My eyes move across the line of text to the date, 17/05/86, and I'm aware of the significance. In just over four hours time, I'm due at Tessa's house for some extremely brief, and unrewarding sex. Or am I? I consider the parallels with the 'Afterpath' game, and how my own future is determined by what happens this afternoon. What if I don't go to Tessa's house? I won't break my virginity, or suffer the emotional turmoil afterwards. That would mean I pass my exams and go to college, so I never work at Video City, or meet Megan — and if I don't work at Video City, I don't end up at RolpheTech, and Marcus Morrison becomes an irrelevance.

As I think about it, a slow realisation dawns that maybe this is my 'Afterpath moment'. The timeline is changed and the single, yet critical event which forged an unwanted future is removed. The professor cancels his holiday and I don't have sex with Tessa. If this isn't real then the consequences of anything I do are surely moot? I can play the game and see where it takes me, or I can give in to the madness, and sit here watching the timer on the TV screen drop minute by minute.

My previous thought about having a mental breakdown gains validity as I chuckle away to myself. Here I am, considering the ridiculous notion that my feeble Commodore 64 computer has spent thirty years in a box, autonomously working on the bug within my game, to the point where it's created a real-world version. There's science fiction, and then there's science fantasy. This firmly falls into the latter genre. But despite how ludicrous the theory might be, the reality is I appear to be sat in my teenage bedroom, inside my teenage body, and seemingly hours away from re-breaking my virginity in 1986. This feels just as real as when I stood here earlier, reminiscing about my porn collection.

The countdown timer drops another minute. Counting down to an unknown end. Do I wake up in a hospital bed surrounded by my family, or do I wake up in a new future? In 39 hours and 28 minutes *something* happens, but what?

I decide I'll play this like a game. I'm going to spend the next 39 hours and 28 minutes living, no, reliving my teenage life. But I won't make the same mistakes. I'm going to avenge my stupid teenage self. If this is, as I suspect, some psychotic episode, then it won't matter what I do. As unlikely as it seems, if it is real, maybe I'll wake up to a new future, one where I fulfilled my early promise. A future where I don't waste years of my life in a loveless marriage, or in a dead-end career. A new path where Craig Pelling is the head of a successful IT business, maybe living in a fabulous home, with a loving wife and doting children. A life without Megan, without

Video City, without RolpheTech or Marcus fucking Morrison.

Even if this isn't real, I think it's a game I'd like to play.

3

As the countdown continues and I reluctantly accept my ludicrous situation, I decide that I need to get organised, and reacquainted with my teenage life. As any right-minded teenager would do, I spend a few minutes searching the bedroom for my mobile phone, before the obvious dawns on me. Even if my phone had made the journey here with me, the mobile phones in 1986 are almost as unportable as my Ferguson TV, and the current infrastructure is unlikely to support an iPhone. Besides, a mobile phone without access to a yet-invented Internet, would be nothing more than a glorified calculator. No Google, no Facebook, no Twitter, and not even email. Perhaps no bad thing.

The lack of technology gets me thinking. All I have to do is invent something commonplace in twenty-first century life, and I'd wake up a billionaire. I immediately dismiss the idea as I doubt I'll be able to convince anyone of my futuristic ideas within 39-odd hours. How the hell do you sell the idea of Facebook to somebody who doesn't even know what the Internet is? More shortcuts to wealth are considered and quickly dismissed. Gambling? I don't have any stake money, and as I've never been into sport, I have no idea who will win anything this weekend. Shares? Again, where does a sixteen year-old get sufficient money to invest, and can you even buy shares over a weekend, especially without the Internet? Perhaps I could approach a record company with a song that's a huge hit in the future and sell it to them? No, I wouldn't have a clue where to start.

I conclude there aren't any paths to instant wealth I can take in the here and now. But what if I write instructions and leave them for my teenage self to implement? Would my notes still be here once the timer reaches zero, or would they disappear with me? Even if the notes survive, would a teenage Craig have the wherewithal to follow through on my instructions, or would he file them in the bin? Truth is, I have no idea. It seems there aren't any practical, or foolproof shortcuts to creating easy money for my future self. I'll have to do this the hard way.

I'm punched from my thoughts by a knock on the bedroom door that nearly invokes an involuntary bowel movement.

"Are you awake yet, love? I'm starting breakfast in a minute."

Holy shit, my mum. But it's not the frail voice of my septuagenarian mother, rather the sprightly voice of a much younger woman.

What do I do? What do I say? My heart pounds. Keep it together Craig.

"Yeah, I'll be down in a minute," I croak.

Hearing Mum's youthful voice is almost as unsettling as hearing my own. It seems to have increased by several octaves since the last time I used it.

"Okay love," she replies, before I hear her potter back down the stairs.

Sitting in my teenage bedroom is mind-bending enough, but the reality of interacting with actual people from my distant past is just insane. The obvious problem is that while I might look and sound like the teenage me, forty-six years of life experience have shaped everything in my head. My vocabulary, my persona, my mannerisms, all so far removed from those of my sixteen year-old self I might as well be a different person. The only realistic option is to adopt the default teenager setting; sulky and uncommunicative. I can only hope my parents put my odd behaviour down to hormonal changes, but I suspect my dad won't even notice.

I need to get dressed so I go back to the wardrobe, avoiding the door with the mirror, and inspect the contents. The hanging space, which was definitely empty earlier, is now full of clothes on wire coat hangers. I sort through the first dozen garments: two navy blue school jumpers, a black tank top, a blue polo shirt, two pairs of jeans, three t-shirts of various designs, a pair of grey tracksuit bottoms, and a khaki green Parker jacket. The final item is a burgundy shirt. I reach up, pull the hanger off the rail, and lay the shirt on the bed. I run my hand over the soft material. It's the same shirt I wore to Tessa's house on that fateful afternoon in 1986, and will wear again this afternoon. It invoked so many bad memories I never wore it again, and a few months later it left the house in a carrier bag of clothes destined for the local charity shop. I leave the shirt on the bed and pull one of the t-shirts and the tracksuit bottoms from the wardrobe. I slip the dressing gown off and get dressed.

My mouth feels like something has died in it, so my first foray from the bedroom has to be to the bathroom to brush my teeth. I tentatively open the bedroom door and step out onto the landing. Even though I've visited my parents' house hundreds of times since I moved out, the ambience is now markedly different from their twenty-first century home. Dad used to be a heavy smoker until his early sixties, and he would smoke in the house with no thought to the damage his habit inflicted on our health. As bad as the odour in my bedroom smelt, the pungent stench of cigarette smoke on the landing is far worse. Coupled with the underlying smell of fried food coming from the kitchen, it reminds me of the saloon bar at the Fox & Hounds before smoking in public places was banned.

I sneak across the landing and close the bathroom door behind me. The stench of cigarette smoke is replaced with a cocktail of coal tar soap, medicated shampoo, and pine disinfectant. Memories of my once-a-week childhood bath night. I survey the small bathroom and I'm immediately struck by how little is in here. Not that I recall, but ablutions in this era apparently require little more than a bar of soap, shampoo, and a flannel. My bathroom at home looks like a supermarket shelf, stocked with a variety of shampoos, conditioners, exfoliators, cleansers, and moisturisers. I pad across the linoleum and stand at the avocado-coloured basin. The last time I used this bathroom the basin was white, the avocado suite replaced at least a decade ago after coloured bathroom suites fell from fashion.

Beside the sink sits a ceramic cup containing a tube of Colgate toothpaste and three coloured toothbrushes. I remember that red is Mum's and blue is Dad's, so I grab my yellow toothbrush and examine the bristles, which are flattened into a centre parting. With little faith in my own oral hygiene, I turn on the hot tap, wait until the water steams, and hold the head of my toothbrush under the flow. Satisfied most of the bacteria on the brush should now be dead, or at least lightly steamed, I squeeze a line of the toothpaste onto the brush and set about trying to remove the filthy taste from my mouth. I can't recall the last time I brushed my teeth with anything other than an electric toothbrush, and I'd forgotten what a chore it is to manoeuvre a blunt piece of plastic around your mouth. The chalky toothpaste tastes like shit, but I tolerate it long enough to give my teeth a cursory scrub. I run the tip my tongue across my teeth. Not great, but better than a few minutes ago.

I'm just about to leave the bathroom when it dawns on me I should take a leak. It's been a long time since I slept for over eight hours without getting up to empty my bladder at least once in the night. It's not something I usually need to remind myself about. As I stand and wait for my bladder to empty, I become more conscious of my teenage body. Now the pain in my head has subsided, there's a void which would typically be filled with the pain of aching muscles and stiff joints. Not this morning.

The other noticeable difference is just how nimble this body feels compared to its middle-aged counterpart.

The sensation reminds me of the time I had to attend a god-awful Outward Bound course, which all RolpheTech managers had to complete. It was four days of absolute hell, spent traipsing across the Brecon Beacons in the pissing rain, and camping in tents we had to transport in our rucksacks. We spent every miserable day shuffling mile after mile across muddy terrain, following maps nobody could read. When we reached each camp, the simple act of removing the rucksack was heavenly. Unbridled by thirty pounds of sodden kit, I felt as light and nimble as a ballet dancer. But that was only a fleeting illusion whereas it's the reality in this body. As disconcerting as it initially felt, I now quite like it.

I wash my hands with a bar of coal tar soap and draw a deep breath as I prepare myself for the first of the many challenges coming my way — breakfast as a teenager. I leave the bathroom and head back across the stinking landing. As I descend the stairs, the smoky fog intensifies with every step. How did we ever live in this? At the bottom of the stairs, I open the door to the sitting room and cautiously enter. Neither parent is present, and it's quiet, apart from the ticking of the carriage clock. Little appears to have changed over the years although the chintzy two-seater sofa looks in much better condition than when I last sat on it.

I move across to the window and pull back the net curtain. Dad's maroon Mark II Vauxhall Cavalier is sat on the tarmac driveway. Apart from our house, the car represented the single biggest purchase Dad ever made, and it was his pride and joy. Whenever I was privileged enough to ride in it, I was under strict instructions to wash my hands, and ensure my shoes were clean. I never liked the car. The spongy suspension always made me feel sick, and after one close call, Dad made me carry a plastic bucket on my lap for any journey of more than a few miles. Even then, he'd spend a worrying amount of time staring intently in his rear-view mirror, checking I wasn't about to projectile vomit across his velour upholstery.

Beyond our driveway, the street is quiet, and free from the scores of cars cluttered along the kerb I'd expect to see on a typical Saturday morning in my time. The scene looks more orderly, tidier. Front lawns are neatly cut, driveways are uncluttered, and there's a distinct absence of rubbish anywhere. It's a shame that the obvious sense of civic pride amongst the homeowners has diminished over the years. The still scene is interrupted as a gate beside a house across the street swings open. A young kid pushes his bike out of the side passage, and I recognise the striking blue and yellow colours of a Raleigh Burner BMX, with its distinctive five-spoke plastic wheels.

When the BMX craze was at its peak in the early 1980s, I begged my parents for a Burner. One Christmas morning, I recall excitedly unwrapping what I assumed was the Raleigh Burner I craved. It turned out to be a red and grey Falcon BMX, with normal spoked wheels. My disappointment turned to humiliation when my pre-pubescent friends later pointed out that my new bike was from Woolworths. They accordingly mocked my budget BMX for months.

I watch the kid wobble down the street with no helmet, no hi-viz tabard, and probably no parental concern for his safety. We must be at least a decade away from the dawn of the over-protective, health & safety obsessed society that killed childhood adventure. I wonder if we've made things better for them.

I let the net curtain fall back to the window and switch into moody teenager mode. With my nerves jangling, I slowly shuffle across the sitting room and open the door to the kitchen. The smell of frying bacon sets my mouth watering in an instant. Mum is stood at the hob, busying herself between pans, while the old man is sat at our dining table on the opposite side of the room, his copy of the Daily Express raised in front of him. I plant my eyes to the floor and take a seat at the table opposite Dad. I raise my head just enough to read the headline on the front of the newspaper…

'MAGGIE: YES I DO CARE - New Tax-Cut Pledge'

I assume it refers to the Prime Minister, Maggie Thatcher, unless former Swap Shop presenter, Maggie Philbin, is now Chancellor of the Exchequer in this fucked-up version of my life. I'm past taking anything for granted.

The old man suddenly lowers his paper and looks directly at me before I have the chance to drop my eyes.

I try not to soil my tracksuit bottoms as I stare at the steely face of my forty-something father. There are no happy memories triggered by that face. No learning to ride a bike in the park. No trips to the zoo. No impromptu games of football in the garden — and it was only after I left home I discovered that Mum had paid for every one of my birthday and Christmas presents. She had a part-time job in a cafe, and would put a tenner aside every week so she could afford to buy me a decent gift. The old man was never happy about this and complained about how spoilt I was. I think it might have been because Mum felt guilty that I had no siblings. What good is a football, or Monopoly if there's nobody to play with? I realised all the expensive gifts I'd acquired over the years were things I could use on my own. The computer, the stereo, the portable TV, the expensive trainers, even the sodding Falcon BMX. They were all gifts for a solitary child.

My gaze meets the cold eyes of my father and I squeak the least cheerful "Morning" I can muster. If there is any residue shock on my face, he fails to notice it and returns a barely perceptible nod. He then looks across the kitchen to where Mum is still stood at the hob, with her back to us.

"How's that tea coming along? I'm bloody parched," he grumbles.

Mum replies over her shoulder.

"One minute dear, it's just brewing."

The old man rolls his eyes before returning to his newspaper. A tiny part of me wants to tell the lazy bastard to get his own tea, but I've always been just as subservient to him as Mum. At least I eventually escaped his tyrannical ways. I don't understand how Mum tolerated him for so long.

I return my stare to the green chequered tablecloth and continue my best impression of a sulky teenager. Mum approaches the table and I can't resist the overwhelming compulsion to look up. The brooding resentment towards my father is immediately replaced with a warm glow as my eyes absorb the figure before me. Mum is stood with a stainless steel teapot in one hand, and a small milk jug in the other. Her ever-present apron covers a light blue dress, dotted with tiny yellow flowers. She places the teapot and milk jug on the table, and then ruffles my hair with her hand.

"Sleep well, sweetheart?"

I smile and nod. I desperately want to leap from my chair and throw my arms around the cuddly frame of my childhood mother, but I resist. She looks down at me with her kindly green eyes, her sandy hair tied back into a pony tail, and a rosy glow to her cheeks. I think about the mother from my future and I'm suddenly slapped by an irrational feeling of betrayal. Irrational, because it's the same woman, only it's not.

When I left home to move in with Megan, the mother I left behind slowly ebbed away, devoid of purpose and anchored to my cantankerous father. With no maternal duties to perform, she became a mother in name only. Once again she was solely the wife of Colin Pelling, not a duty I'd wish on anyone, but she did it with steadfast resolve. Maybe I should have made more effort. I should have visited more often, taken her out to lunch now and again. But I didn't. I let our bond wither away, until Mum only had the most fragile of threads to cling to. As crap a husband as my dad might be, in hindsight, I wasn't a much better son.

Seeing the bubbly, cheerful mother in front of me makes me realise what I lost.

4

Maybe it's a nostalgic illusion, but I'm convinced everything tasted so much better when I was a kid. I suspect it's because nobody seemed to care what went into our food, or worried if it was actually bad for us. Sugar always tasted better than sucralose, butter always tasted better than polyunsaturated margarine, and anything fried in lard always tasted better than just about everything. We went through an unhealthy amount of lard in our house, particularly on Saturdays. Sunday to Friday we ate cereal and toast for breakfast, but Saturday brought the 'Full English'.

Mum delivers two plates to the table, each laden with two pork sausages, three rashers of streaky bacon, fried slice, black pudding, tinned tomatoes, beans, button mushrooms, and two fried eggs with runny yolks. No matter how many times I have tried to recreate this gloriously unhealthy meal over the years, it's always ended in disaster. There were too many components that needed to be cooked at specific times to coincide with the final serving. My efforts inevitably ended up with either partially raw sausages, cremated bacon, or vulcanised eggs, sometimes all together in one inedible disappointment. Mum has it down to a fine art and everything looks cooked to perfection.

My stomach rumbles as I salivate over the plate in front of me. I try to recall when I last ate. It must have been yesterday morning and the bowl of bland, high fibre cereal. I tuck in to the breakfast like a ravenous dog, every sumptuous mouthful sparking a delicious memory of Mum's cooking. It's one of the things I really missed when I moved out. Megan's culinary ineptitude meant that by default I became responsible for the cooking in our home. But as bad as Megan's few attempts at cooking were, I wasn't much better. For the first few months we lived on a diet of chicken nuggets, crispy pancakes, and fish fingers. Whenever we went food shopping, we had one simple rule; if something couldn't be cooked by simply throwing it in the oven, or microwave, it stayed on the shelf. We did exclude tinned foods from our rule, but never anything more exotic than peas, beans, or spaghetti hoops.

As Dad and I tuck in to our breakfasts, Mum joins us at the table and sets about her equally generous breakfast. The silence is only broken by the chinking of cutlery on ceramic and the occasional slurp of muddy tea. From the outside, we must look like the typical nuclear family, sat together eating breakfast. All very civilised, all very normal. Beneath the surface I feel anything but normal. I look up at the clock on the kitchen wall and calculate that I've been living this life for about forty-five minutes. I'm actually surprised how well I've coped. Here I am chewing on a sausage when I could have just as easily been running around like a demented lunatic, screaming at my parents that I'm actually a middle-aged man trapped in a living nightmare. On further reflection I understand why I'm not currently being taken away by men in white coats. I'm simply doing what I always do in life, and that's treading the path of least resistance. Just go with the flow, accept the status quo. No ambition to change anything, no stomach for conflict. A sad man accepting whatever life throws at him, good or bad, but generally bad.

Mum's voice breaks the silence and my reflective thoughts.

"So what have you got planned for the day, sweetheart?"

"Not much, going to see a friend at lunchtime," I reply, still conscious of my awkward teenage voice.

"That's nice. Will you be back for tea?" she asks.

"Yep."

"Good. It's toasted crumpets tonight, and I've made some of that Battenberg cake you like," she smiles.

My mind floods with a surging sense of déjà vu. It's not the first time in my life I've experienced it, and I'm aware that it's a trick of the mind; a false memory of a situation that never happened. But this isn't déjà vu because I know for sure I've lived this moment before. I know for sure that the Battenberg never gets eaten because when I return from Tessa's house, I lock myself in my bedroom for the evening. We quickly forget the mundane moments in our lives, but those that trigger strong emotions always live on. The Battenberg might be mundane, but the connection to my impending emotional turmoil saved it from the memory recycle bin.

We finish our breakfast in silence. The old man clears his plate and heads straight out to the garden without a word of thanks. Riled by my father's lack of manners, I pick up my plate and take it over to the sink. I stare at the cupboard below, trying to recall if we ever had a dishwasher, but it seems unlikely so I turn on the hot water tap and rinse my plate off. Mum approaches me from behind.

"What are you doing, sweetheart?" she asks with a puzzled voice.

"Just rinsing my plate off. If you wash, I'll dry," I smile.

One simple, innocent gesture, but judging by the look on my mother's face, I don't think this is typical of my teenage behaviour.

"Have you done something wrong, young man? You're not in trouble at school are you?" she asks with a stern expression.

"What? No, course I'm not. Just trying to be helpful," I reply, a little too defensively.

Mum tilts her head slightly and stares at me through narrow eyes before a smile breaks across her face.

"Okay, thank you. It's sweet of you to help."

I grab a plate from the drainer and dry it with a gingham tea towel. With the plate dry, I turn to the array of white laminate cupboards on the wall and realise I don't have a clue where anything goes. This was not a good idea. Spotting my hesitancy at putting the plate away, Mum comes to my rescue.

"Shows how often you help with the washing-up. Second cupboard from the end," she laughs.

"Why don't we swap? You wash and I'll dry," she suggests, much to my relief.

Washing-up is not a skill, it's a simple process we refine to maximise efficiency. As such, I prefer to rinse everything off before filling the bowl with hot water and washing-up liquid. With all the food debris rinsed-away, I can then get through it quickly. These little idiosyncrasies usually go unnoticed, but not today. My washing-up technique is clearly an affront to my mother's domestic principles.

"What are you doing, Craig? You're wasting an awful lot of water doing that."

"I'm rinsing the grease off so the water in the bowl doesn't need to be changed half way through."

"Why would you change the water half way through? That's Fairy Liquid in there you know, good for an entire dinner service," she replies, nodding towards the bowl.

Christ, no wonder I never helped the first time around.

I revert to my mother's inefficient washing-up method and after a few uneasy moments of silence, she switches on a portable radio sat on the window sill. The feeble speaker emits a piece of classical music which Mum happily hums along to. I pull the last remaining items of cutlery from the soupy water and give them a quick wipe with a bacteria-ridden cloth. I drop the cutlery onto the drainer with a clatter, making a mental note to wash my knife and fork before I use them later.

Washing-up completed, Mum thanks me, although I'm not sure she'll be calling upon my services in the future. At least I tried. I return to my bedroom and lie on the bed, bloated. I've still got over three hours before I'm supposed to be at Tessa's, if I go. That's my first dilemma. The obvious decision would be not to turn up, and then I could spend the weekend wallowing in nostalgic pointlessness before returning to my new and improved future. However, two things trouble me about that plan.

Firstly, there's Kevin, Tessa's younger brother, and his inability to get his computer working. I'll never forget his reaction when I showed him how to load a game, and the thought of him sat there staring at a blank screen day after day makes me feel particularly uncomfortable. I don't want to let him down.

Then there's Tessa herself. While cancelling our brief liaison is unlikely to make any difference to her future, in a few weeks she's due to encounter Marcus and his erection issues. I think back to our conversation at the reunion and how she described herself as "fucked-up" in her teenage years. Perhaps this is an opportunity to point her in the right direction and save her from years of grief? The problem is that I don't know what happened to Tessa after we left school and any interference is just as likely to do harm as it is good. She seemed really happy with her life so whatever twists and turns she encountered, things seem to have worked out well in the end.

I think through the options and decide that I shouldn't mess around with things I don't understand. It's one thing trying to change my future, but a completely different matter when it comes to people whose lives I don't know enough about. For all I know, my interference could create a future for Tessa where she ends up as a crack-addled prostitute, or an estate agent. No, I'll head over there, sort out Kevin's computer and make some excuse about needing to be somewhere else. I will leave with my virginity intact so when this is over, my teenage self will pick up his life like nothing has happened.

I snigger at my reference, 'his life', like teenage Craig is a different person. Then another thought strikes me — what will the teenage version of Craig remember from this weekend? When he wakes up on Monday morning, will he recollect everything I've done as if he'd done it himself? Surely he won't just have an empty void where his memories should be, like a particularly brutal stag weekend in Amsterdam? It's a paradox I can't begin to unravel, but I guess I'll find out when the timer completes its countdown.

I turn my attention to how I'll fill the hours before my trip to Tessa's house. I could go downstairs and watch one of the four available TV channels. I could read a book. I could listen to the radio. None of these options appeal and the alternatives lead me down a blind alley, with an Internet-sized hole at the end. We've become so reliant on the Internet for information, for entertainment, and for communication, we only really appreciate how embedded in our lives it's become when it's no longer there. However, a more interesting, and more obvious option slaps me around the face. I should go and explore 1986. I could be the only human to have ever revisited a bygone era so who needs the Internet? Idiot.

I head back to the bathroom and indulge in a retro bowel movement, complete with translucent single-ply toilet paper. I grab a towel from the airing cupboard and strip off my t-shirt and tracksuit bottoms. We don't have a shower cubicle, or even a shower for that matter. What we have is a five-foot hose with a shower head at one end and two rubber cups at the other. These cups have to be pushed onto the hot and cold taps with sufficient force they don't detach when the taps are turned on.

I climb into the bath and force the cups onto the taps. Three turns of each tap and a disappointing jet of water spouts from the shower head. One thing I haven't forgotten is the 'Goldilocks Game' we had to play before any showering could take place. This game involved numerous miniscule adjustments to each tap, followed by a cautious hand being placed in the jet of water to see if it was too hot, too cold or just right. For added spice, once you'd found the right temperature and commenced showering, another tap being turned on anywhere in the house reset the game. You could be rinsing a head full of suds when, without warning, you'd be showered with freezing cold or scalding hot water.

On the positive side, it was good for the environment as nobody dared spend more time in the shower than was necessary. I conclude my shower within two minutes.

I hop out of the bath, dry myself off, and then wrap the towel around my skinny waist. I open the bathroom cabinet in search of my limited toiletry collection: a can of Lynx deodorant, a pot of toxic-green hair gel, and a bottle of Jazz aftershave. I grab the can of Lynx and spray it liberally under my arms and across my hairless chest. Although you can still buy Lynx in my time, its reputation as the deodorant de rigueur amongst teenage boys puts it strictly out of bounds for any self-respecting adult male. For me, it's the smell of school changing rooms after PE, and getting ready for youth club on a Friday night. I guess things probably haven't changed much.

Now I smell like a teenager, I shuffle across the landing back to my bedroom. I open and close several drawers before I remember that my socks and underwear are kept in a drawer in the bedside cupboard. I open the wardrobe and pull a pair of jeans from a hanger, noting with some shame that the waist size is ten inches smaller than the pair I purchased for the reunion. I grab the burgundy shirt, which is still lying on the bed, slip it on and button it up. The finishing touch is a pair of Nike trainers from their box at the bottom of the wardrobe.

Fully dressed, I stand and stare at myself in the mirror. My hair is a mess and I look like a teenage kid trying too hard, which is exactly what I was when I thought this was a good look. I ditch the burgundy shirt and slip on a plain black t-shirt. I head back to the bathroom and run a dollop of green gel through my hair. I'm well out of practice in the art of hair styling, but I eventually fashion a style that is almost certainly thirty years ahead of its time.

I head back to my bedroom, take one final glance in the mirror, and grab my Casio digital watch from beside my bed. I instinctively pat the pockets of my jeans to check I've got my mobile phone and wallet. For a millisecond I panic that neither are present before my brain reminds me I don't own either a mobile phone or a wallet in this time. Panic over, I head downstairs and back to the kitchen where Mum is sat at the table flicking through a magazine.

"I'm going out a bit earlier than I thought, Mum, should be back in a few hours."

"Okay love. I'm heading into town shortly so don't forget your key as your Dad will probably be in the garden all afternoon."

Out of habit, I lean over and kiss her on the forehead. The shocked look on her face tells me I've stepped beyond my normal teenage behaviour again. I offer an embarrassed smile and bolt from the kitchen before my mother can question why I'm acting so out of character.

In the quiet sanctuary of the hallway I pluck my key from a hook near the front door and drop it into my pocket. A quick check of my watch, 10.40am. Time to head out and see what 1986 has to offer.

5

As I wander up our street, I yet again curse my decision not to wear a jacket. While the sun sits high in the sky, my nimble body doesn't provide much insulation against the chilly breeze compared to its later counterpart. I up my pace and slowly some warmth builds. With no specific plan or route in mind, I meander through our estate, paying particular attention to the cars on the driveways. Much like my Dad's maroon Cavalier, many of the cars I spot are rarely seen on the road in my time. I stop and admire a few of them, in particular a nearly new Escort XR3i, a Toyota MR2, and a Rover SD1, which I seem to recall was particularly popular with the police and nicknamed, 'the jam sandwich'. As much as I'd love to spend all day staring at retro cars, my loitering attracts attention from homeowners who probably think I'm either a vandal or a car thief. I quickly move on.

I reach the edge of the estate and head in the general direction of Tessa's house. The scenery becomes more urban as I stroll along a busy road which eventually leads into the town centre. I stop every few hundred yards and absorb the view. There's dozens of independent shops that won't survive much beyond the millennium. Trucks pass by with liveries of High Street retailers that will befall the same fate: Rumbelows, C&A, Radio Rentals, Index, John Farmer Shoes, and Courts Furniture — all gone in my day. Everything feels familiar, but also slightly alien. It's like the first time you visit a foreign country on holiday. You see shops, people and vehicles which are all recognisable for what they are, but they're not quite the same as those you see every day. It's a little disconcerting.

Now and then I stumble across a shop that makes me stop and gaze in the window. Big Breakers is one such shop and sells CB radio equipment. Judging by the lack of customers in the shop and the dejected expression of the guy behind the counter, I guess we're probably at the tail-end of the CB craze by now. Next door is the record shop, Solid Sounds. I think it was part of a small chain of stores. It didn't survive much beyond the late-90s once their customers realised that downloading music from the Internet was cheaper and easier. I'm tempted to enter, but change my mind when I hear the muffled sound of a Duran Duran track playing inside.

A few doors along from the record shop is The Rendezvous Cafe; a sight that makes me smile. The cafe is long gone in my day; I think it's now a bookmaker. In this era, it's where my mum has worked for the last nine years, alongside my Aunt Judy, who isn't actually my Aunt, and Fat Derek, the affable owner. Mum worked a lunchtime shift during the week, and I'd often pop in for an ice cream float or a milkshake during the school holidays. Unshackled from the domineering presence of my father, it was a place where Mum could be herself. It was a place always filled with laughter.

I slowly shuffle past, trying to look inconspicuous as I stare through the plate-glass window at the dozen or so tables, all laid with red polythene tablecloths. I look down on an empty table near the window. Amongst the condiments sat on the table, there's also a straw holder, a ketchup bottle shaped like a tomato, and a house brick. If I recall, Fat Derek got fed up with his ashtrays being stolen so he replaced them with house bricks. It was a crude, yet effective solution. I cast my eyes towards the counter at the rear where the conspicuous figure of my Aunt Judy, wearing a luminous pink headscarf, is fumbling with the coffee machine. Beyond the counter, Fat Derek is stood over the griddle in the kitchen, bedecked in his grubby chef's tunic. For a second I consider going in and saying hello, but if I recall correctly, Aunt Judy's pink headscarf is a sign that her aura is absorbing negative energy. Her delusional, new-age beliefs are a little too much for me to handle this morning.

I walk on and the street becomes a little busier with pedestrians as I get closer to the town centre. Every stretch of pavement sparks more memories as I pass long-forgotten shops, buildings and landmarks. It actually becomes a little overwhelming and I really wish I could share this experience with somebody. That's the thing about memories I guess — it's lovely to hold them in your head, but the real joy is in sharing them. This feels a bit like looking through an old photograph album on your own. I want to point at things and say, "Hey, remember that?", but with my sanity already in question, an excited public conversation with myself is probably not advisable.

The one thing that I hadn't noticed at home, but is now very obvious, is how people are dressed. My parents were never exactly at the cutting-edge of fashion, favouring a look one might describe as 'timeless'. Out on the streets though, people seem to be dressed as if they're off to a Ukranian nightclub. Garishly coloured leisurewear seems particularly popular amongst the men, while the women favour equally garish ruffled skirts and baggy tops. The one fashion statement shared by both sexes is an obvious fondness for the fuller hairstyle. I catch a glimpse of my own hair, reflected in a shop window, and immediately feel a little self-conscious. I've gone for a hipster-inspired side parting with a neatly gelled comb-over; something considered vaguely fashionable in my day. Unfortunately in this era, it's a style more likely to be favoured by retired Librarians.

A few hundred yards further along the road and I stop outside a branch of Tandy, another name consigned to the High Street graveyard. I've reached the periphery of the town centre and need to decide whether to venture further, or make my way to Tessa's house. It's only just gone midday and as I ponder the options, I casually look up and down the road. Then I spot something that really gets me excited — a blue neon sign for Astro Arcade. I dash across the street and just avoid being run over by a putrid-green Austen Allegro. The elderly man at the wheel angrily waves his fist at me before the car lurches down the street, puffing clouds of grey smoke in its wake.

There was quite a buzz around school when Astro Arcade first opened in 1982, and it used to be packed with kids in the afternoons and at weekends. It's a place I spent an unhealthy amount of time, and money. Sadly, its popularity waned as more games consoles became available and home computers could handle more sophisticated games. It eventually closed down in the mid-90s and became a mobile phone store.

Flushed with excitement, I push open the glass door to my childhood Eden. Within the dimly lit arcade, I'm hit with a barrage of electronic sounds as I stand in nostalgic awe. The space is about forty feet long and gaming machines are lined up along the walls to the left and right, with two further lines of machines stood back-to-back, running down the centre of the room. There must be over fifty machines in total and most of them are being played by pale, glassy-eyed kids. I take a slow walk up the left-hand aisle, studying the distinctive graphics on each game cabinet. My excitement mounts as I read the names on back-lit panels above each screen: Pac-Land, Defender, Galaxians, Scramble, Frogger, Pole Position, and my personal nemesis, Gorf.

Truth be told, there are now dedicated websites for retro gaming where you can download fairly accurate simulations of these games and I've played most of them on my laptop within the last year. While the game-play, graphics and sound might be similar, the simulations will never recapture the experience of dropping a hard-earned 10p piece into a slot and grasping a sweaty joystick. Knowing you only had one life remaining, and empty pockets, added a real sense of jeopardy to the experience. You'd enter the arcade with 50p and if you were on your game, you could make that last a couple of hours. But if you were having a bad day, you'd be done within thirty minutes. Every visit to Astro Arcade was either thrilling or galling; there was rarely any middle ground.

I reach the end of the room and take a right turn, back down the parallel aisle. More games, more names: Joust, Tron, Paperboy, Track & Field, Spy Hunter, and Cosmic Guerrilla. I'm gutted that I hadn't had the foresight to bring any money with me, so all I can do is peer over the shoulders of kids playing the games, an action that irritated me when I was the one playing. I watch for a few minutes before the player notices my presence and shoots me an angry glance. After thirty minutes of video game voyeurism, I'm on the verge of being asked to leave by the management, or being attacked by a gang of pre-pubescent teenagers. Neither appeals so I reluctantly leave Astro Arcade.

I squint at the bright daylight bathing the street and take a glance at my watch. 12.40pm. Tessa's house is only a ten-minute walk away, but if I drag my heels a little, I should only be a few minutes early. I swerve down a side street past a row of Victorian terraced houses, the noise of the main road ebbing away behind me. I turn left at the end of the street and duck down an alleyway which leads out behind the railway station. I plod up the steps of the footbridge which crosses the line and stand at the top for a few minutes to kill time. The platform is about fifty yards beyond the bridge and I watch as a man in a dark suit appears from the ticket office. He hurries across the platform to one of the blue and white British Rail carriages, pulls open the door and slams it behind him with a loud clunk. A whistle sounds and the train pulls away. Seconds tick by as the train disappears into the distance and the station is silent once more.

I'm not sure why, but I've always had a fascination with trains. I've never had to commute to work by rail, so most of the journeys I embarked upon were for pleasure. Some of my earliest memories were of Mum and I taking trips to visit relatives, or an occasional day out to the coast. As I hit my teens, I became a little more independent, and together with my small band of friends, we'd make a monthly foray into a neighbouring town by train. It was never really about the destination, the excitement was always in the journey.

My reminiscing is brought to an abrupt halt as a chill wind whips across the bridge. I check my watch and realise five minutes have passed. Time to move on. I pad down the steps and cross the road. I pass a red phone box and I'm tempted to inspect it further, but time is against me. I stroll down anonymous streets, lined with equally anonymous houses. If it were not for the cars parked along the kerb, there wouldn't be any obvious signs I'm anywhere but the present day. Although when I look closer, it's not the things that are present which suggest a difference, it's the things that are missing. There are no satellite dishes bolted to the walls of the houses. There's no collection of coloured wheelie bins stood outside each house, and despite the impending World Cup in Mexico, there are no England flags draped out of bedroom windows.

I eventually turn the corner into Tessa's street and glance at my watch. 12.57pm. Close enough. I approach the gravel driveway and compose myself. Unlike the last time I visited this house, I don't feel nervous, just a little apprehensive maybe. This should be perfectly straightforward — get in, sort out Kevin's computer, exchange a few pleasantries and leave. How difficult can that be? I'm forty-six years of age and Tessa is a sixteen year-old schoolgirl for gods-sake. I'm in control this time and I need to keep reminding myself of that fact. Stick to the plan and within twenty minutes, I'll be back outside with my virginity and emotional faculties both fully preserved. Easy.

I crunch across the driveway and rap the brass knocker on the front door. Seconds pass, the door swings open, and there stands Tessa in her white jeans and cropped yellow t-shirt.

"You're the early bird aren't you? Come on in."

She looks every bit as delicious as I remember. Maybe this won't be as easy as I'd envisaged.

6

One common thread that ran through all my school reports was the phrase, "quiet and polite nature". Beyond my small group of friends, I was a solitary, shy teenager. I was the type of kid that would pass under the radar, anonymous. At the time I always considered it to be a curse, but as I stand in the grand hallway of Tessa's house, I can now see how it might be an advantage. Tessa has no idea what I'm really like, what personality lurks beneath my bland facade. The only words I think she's ever heard me say, beyond our brief conversation in the newsagents, is my name in registration. I don't have to worry about her thinking I'm acting out of character, because she doesn't even know I have a character.

"Afternoon Tessa," I smile confidently.

She invites me upstairs and I follow her up, averting my eyes from her backside this time. We cross the landing and she raps on Kevin's door before opening it. I follow Tessa in and she introduces me to Kevin. I say hello and Tessa disappears from the room. So far everything is panning-out as I remember. I consider bypassing the chore of asking Kevin to show me what the problem with his computer is, but I want to keep everything as close to the original timeline as possible. Kevin eventually types his incorrect command and I go through the motions of asking him for the operating manual which I open and stare at blankly for a few moments. I put the manual down, type the correct command, hit the play button on the tape recorder, and then the 'Enter' key.

As the loading graphic appears, Kevin's face breaks into a grin as he launches into his clapping and whooping routine. I stand back and watch him for a few moments. I never knew it at the time, but clearly Kevin is autistic. I've seen a few TV programmes about kids with the condition, but my knowledge doesn't stretch much further than a layman's understanding. I consider raising the subject with Tessa, but it could attract some difficult questions to which I have no answers. At least I've helped him sort out his computer, and that's as much as I can do for him.

On cue, Tessa returns to the bedroom and suddenly she's got me in an embrace, hugging me tightly. There wasn't much I could do to evade the hug so I go with it. Then something more troubling becomes apparent. The mind itself might be forty-six years old, but the physiology of everything else in my head is most definitely that of a teenage male. Hormones rush and messages are received; prepare for engagement. I feel a stirring in my groin and break from Tessa's embrace. She looks at me oddly, but quickly turns her attention to Kevin. Words are exchanged and I allay his concerns about loading other games. He leaps from his chair and throws his arms around me.

"Thank you friend," he grins.

I smile back at him. The unrecognisable feeling returns but I now know what it is. Empathy. Kevin might well have siblings, but whatever world he's locked into, I can imagine it's a lonely place. He breaks from our hug and darts off, leaving me alone with Tessa.

"Got any plans for the rest of the afternoon?" she asks.

I take an exaggerated glance at my watch, without actually looking at the time.

"Yeah sorry, I've got to be somewhere at two o'clock," I reply with mock reluctance.

"Great. You can spare half-an-hour then. Let's go to my room."

Bugger. Why did I say two o'clock? Still, it's nowhere near enough time for a repeat of our first liaison.

"Sure, but I really have to shoot in half-an-hour."

Tessa smiles and leads me across the landing to her bedroom. I hear the front door slam in the hallway as her mum and Kevin leave the house.

We enter Tessa's pink lair, and she takes a seat on the bed. She pats the duvet with her hand to suggest I join her. I'm letting this get out of control and I need to stand my ground.

"Actually Tessa, I should get going. I don't want to be late."

She looks up at me with steely determination in her eyes. She stands back up and positions herself less than two feet away from me.

"Don't be such a square, Craig. Sit down, I'll be back in a minute with a little surprise that might change your mind."

Before I can say a word, she gives me a knowing smile, turns and leaves the room. I hear another door open and close on the landing. I assume she's gone into the bathroom. Time for subtlety is over, I've got to get out of here. I sneak across the landing and tip-toe down the stairs, the squeaky floorboards signalling my escape. I cross the hallway and twist the knob on the front door, but it doesn't budge. I twist it again with more force, but there is absolutely no give. Panic rises as I squat down to inspect it and immediately spot the keyhole in the centre. It's locked. Fuck.

Beyond the fact I'm now locked in the house with a predatory teenage girl, the other concern is that this doesn't fit with the original timeline — I was able to leave the house unhindered the first time. What's changed? I glance at my watch. 1.17pm. I think back over the last twenty minutes, trying to determine what I might have done differently that would result in the door now being locked. For all my social inadequacies, one thing I'm blessed with is an acutely analytical mind. The reason I was so good at writing computer code is that I can look at a page of data and instinctively spot an anomaly. This skill is also useful in other situations and my mind quickly determines the anomaly between the two timelines — I arrived three minutes earlier this time. Maybe last time Tessa's mum was in a hurry and forgot to lock the door. Maybe those three extra minutes were just enough for her not to feel rushed. Whatever theories I consider, the fact remains I can't leave the house without a key.

I sneak back up the stairs and sit down on Tessa's bed. This is the sort of situation it's easy to excuse yourself from in the future. You say you've received a text or an email and have to be somewhere urgently. Sadly, not an option open to me in 1986. My mind contemplates other escape routes including the big window across the room. I'm about to check the viability of that option when Tessa saunters back into the room and closes the door behind her. The white jeans and yellow cropped t-shirt are gone, and she's now wearing her silky pink dressing gown. This isn't going to plan. Maybe fate is predetermined, and no matter what I do, some things in life are simply inevitable. Has fate decreed that I absolutely must suffer forty seconds of unsatisfactory sex with Tessa? I shake that thought from my head. Just because there is a very attractive, near-naked, and sexually charged young woman stood before me, I don't have to do anything about it. Do I?

As Tessa edges towards me I curse myself. Why did I put myself in this position? All I had to do was sort out the bloody computer and leave. Coming into this room was a huge mistake and all that has changed is that we've lost the twenty minutes of small talk and some clumsy dancing. The actual part of the afternoon that destroyed my life looks set to take place just like it did before. To emphasise my lack of control, Tessa steps forward, so she's only a few feet in front of me. I know what happens next. Right on cue, she teases the cord undone and the dressing gown falls open. As much as I want to look, it feels so wrong. I raise my eyes to meet the sultry expression on Tessa's face. With a glint in her eye, she sweeps the dressing gown from her shoulder and it falls to the floor. Apart from the odd visit to a strip joint, the only naked female body I've come this close to in the last few decades is Megan's. The pert, nubile body in front of me is slightly more enticing than that of my middle-aged wife. My penis agrees.

At this point, any self-respecting man of my years would kindly, but firmly, tell the young woman that this should stop. He would pick up the dressing gown and cover her modesty. He would reassuringly say that while she is beautiful, it would be morally wrong for a man of his years to take advantage of an impressionable girl. I'm ashamed to say that my thoughts are heading off on a different tangent. It's a feeble defence, but when you're starving, it doesn't matter how forbidden the fruit might be. I haven't had so much as a grape in months.

I'm not proud to admit it, but I'm actually trying to justify other ways I could work this situation. While my mind is that of a middle-aged man, I am physically and legally a sixteen year old boy. We are both over the age of consent so I wouldn't really be doing anything wrong, would I? It's tempting, and that temptation is being fuelled by one egotistical justification — I'm not a virgin now, at least not mentally. There will not be a repeat of my original woeful performance because this time I can call upon all that sexual experience gained from my years of marriage.

Like most couples, Megan and I went through the three traditional phases of sexual congress. There were those awkward first months where you're conscious of being naked in front of a virtual stranger or acting like a deviant. You tend to be fairly conservative but the sex is exciting because it's with somebody new. During the second phase, you overcome any shyness and start to be a little more adventurous. You learn from your mistakes and while the frequency of sex might decline from phase one, the quality and variety is usually better. The third phase is the golden years. This is the period when you perfect the skills learnt in phase two. Boundaries are pushed, inhibitions are lost and you become finely attuned to the needs of your partner. The frequency is down to just once or twice a month but when it happens, it's usually exceptional. Unfortunately, I have discovered there is a fourth phase — angry, resentful wanking in the bathroom.

My eyes fall from Tessa's face and I savour the sight of her naked body. The temptation to pull her onto the bed and demonstrate all those years of experience is now overwhelming. There would be no humiliating re-run of the first time, nor the crushing emotional turmoil afterwards. Maybe this is an opportunity to create a different path where I have a future with Tessa. Surely if we have mind-blowing sex, the last thing she'll want to do on Monday morning is chuck me? Perhaps we'll start dating and I'll pass my exams with flying colours. Perhaps I'll go on to university and have the career I yearned for, with Tessa stood by my side. And if I'm dating her, she won't have that awkward afternoon with Marcus in a few weeks' time. It does seem a viable alternative to the scenario where I run away.

Of course, this alternative plan is formulated in a split second and I haven't thought it through. This amazing, improbable, inexplicable opportunity to rewrite my history is too precious to treat with such reckless flippancy. But with hormones raging through my body and an erect penis desperate to escape my jeans, all sense of logic and reasoning are quickly quashed. I need clear thinking but my mind is stifled by Tessa's sweet, fruity perfume filling my nostrils and her perfect naked body filling my vision. I can't help myself.

I get up from the bed and stand directly in front of Tessa. Our eyes lock and I give her a confident smile. I place my index finger on her shoulder and slowly draw it across her smooth skin, delicately meandering the tip over her breasts and along her stomach, dropping further and skirting the top of her abdominal area. She closes her eyes and purrs. I trace my finger towards her taut buttocks as I shift a step to my right, then forwards, deftly turning around so I'm stood behind her. The entire manoeuvre happens in a split second, and before Tessa knows it, I'm gently kissing the nape of her neck. I return a hand to her stomach and tease my finger up and down. Her purr becomes louder and I can't help feeling just a little smug. I am a love god.

I am totally in the zone as I run the tip of my tongue from her neck to the top of her back. My hands move in unison to cup her pert breasts, fingertips teasing her nipples. Tessa's purr becomes a gentle groan as I bend my knees slightly and run my tongue down her spine. I drop lower until I'm kissing the sensitive spot just between the lower back and buttocks. This used to drive Megan crazy and I assume it has the same effect on Tessa as her legs tremble, her approval becoming increasingly vocal.

I give it a few moments and then fall to my knees, my hands dropping from her breasts to her hips. I run my tongue further south, passing over her buttocks and down the back of her thighs. Slow, deliberate strokes of my wet tongue gliding over her delicate skin. She shuffles her feet a few inches further apart, an invitation for my tongue to move towards her inner thighs, getting closer to where she wants me. All in good time Tessa.

My seduction is working like a dream, unlike the nightmare of embarrassed fumbling the first time round. I plan my next move — to get her lying on the bed so I can ratchet things up a notch. I want to deploy every weapon in my sexual armoury. I want to do more than merely satisfy Tessa, I want to blow her mind, to leave her lying on the bed, drenched in sweat and quivering with orgasmic exhaustion. I want her to feel like she's never felt before, or ever likely to again.

But as I move my tongue back up her body, something on Tessa's bed catches my eye, causing me to freeze.

7

Propped up against the wall at the end of the bed is a pink teddy bear, about ten inches tall with a sparkly red bow around its neck. I don't recall noticing it the first time I was here, but why would I? It's just a teddy bear, although in this instance it isn't just a teddy bear — it's a harbinger of shame, staring at me through judgemental beady eyes. A muffled voice in my head tries to speak, but I really don't want to hear what it has to say. Whether it's the teddy bear, or just my conscience talking, I've had enough craziness for one day and a schizophrenic episode is the last thing I need. I try to stifle the voice and return my attention to Tessa's naked body, but an inevitable question breaks through.

"What do you think you're doing, Craig?"

My tongue is still hanging from my mouth and pressed against Tessa's shoulder. I regain my composure. I'm not going to stop just because a pink teddy bear has the temerity to question my motives. I continue to move my tongue across Tessa's shoulder as I fire an answer back across my mind.

"I'm seducing an attractive young woman, although for some inexplicable reason I also appear to be talking to you, teddy."

"Actually, my name is Cuthbert, but that's beside the point. She's not a young woman is she, Craig? She's just a kid, you pervert."

"Well, legally she's an adult, and how am I a pervert if I'm the same age as her?"

"You're forty-six years of age for crying out loud! You're taking advantage of her because you want to prove that you're not a pathetic sexual failure."

I nibble on Tessa's earlobe as I become annoyed at the voice interrupting my seduction.

"What the hell do you know about anything?"

"You forget I was here the first time, Craig. I witnessed the whole pitiful, embarrassing episode. What you're about to do is driven by your own selfish need to prove yourself. You don't give a toss about Tessa, or the consequences for her. You're a self-serving shit."

"She seems to be enjoying it, and to be honest with you, Cuthbert, it's been a while for me. Please shut up, or I'll wipe my dick on you when I'm done."

"Fine, do what you like. But if you think this will fix your future, you're more deluded than I thought. She isn't the problem, you are."

"Stop being so melodramatic. Tessa will be fine and so will my future."

"You're kidding yourself but don't worry, I'll still be here for her tonight when she cries herself to sleep, much like she does most nights. She's a fucked-up kid, but you already know that, don't you?"

I turn my head away from Tessa and stare at the potty-mouthed teddy bear. Whether it's Cuthbert or my conscience talking, the words cut right through me. I shouldn't be doing this. What the hell was I thinking?

I gently place my hands on Tessa's shoulders and manoeuvre her around so she's facing me. I bend down, pick up her dressing gown and drape it over her naked shoulders. I grab the ends of the cord and loop them into a makeshift knot. She looks up at me, clearly frustrated.

"What are you doing, Craig? I was enjoying that!"

"So was I, but it's not right is it?"

Before she can answer, I move away and sit on the bed.

"Come and sit down for a minute and I'll explain."

She pulls her dressing gown on properly and sits next to me on the bed, her arms crossed. Her expression has changed from puzzlement to sulky frustration. Her body language that of a stroppy teenager not getting what they want, which sort of vindicates my decision to stop.

"Look Tessa, I really fancy you, but I don't think you feel the same, do you? Let's be honest, you don't know anything about me."

"What are you on about, Craig? I know you fancy me, you stare at me in class like a lovesick puppy. I don't understand why we're sat here talking when we could be shagging. Don't you want to shag me?"

"That's irrelevant. I'm more curious why you want to have sex with me? Be honest, Tessa."

She shoots me a fierce glance but doesn't reply. She unfolds her arms and sits forward, staring at the pink carpet. Moments pass and I can feel a bubble of tension growing.

"Well?" I ask again.

She turns to me and the bubble bursts.

"What do you want me to say, Craig? That I'm doing this because I feel like I should?" she yells. "You fix Kevin's computer, and I let you shag me. You don't want to hear that, do you? It's just sex, what's the big deal?"

Her outburst would have stung if I hadn't already known her motivation. I decide not to say anything as she rests her elbows on her thighs and lets her head drop to her hands. The room is deathly quiet for a minute.

"Sorry, I shouldn't have said that," she whispers.

"It's the truth though, isn't it?"

"Yes," she sighs.

I place my hand on her shoulder.

"Look at me, Tessa."

After a few seconds, she lifts her head and turns to face me. Light from the window glints off her moist eyes, those beautiful caramel eyes.

"You don't have to apologise and you certainly don't have to have sex with me just because I did you a favour. I'd have been happy with a bag of Maltesers."

Tessa lets out a slight chuckle and runs a sleeve under her sniffly nose. For the first time this afternoon, I see her for what she really is. There are no remnants of sexual bravado, just the confused face of a kid trying to make sense of her life. Seeing her like this makes me feel like an utter bastard for taking advantage. My sixteen year-old self didn't know any better, but I've got no excuse.

"For what it's worth Tessa, I'm sorry too. I shouldn't have let things get as far as they did. I promise you, I only came here to help Kevin with his computer, not to end up in bed with you."

"But sex is all you boys care about though, isn't it? Seems that if you want something in life and god has given you the tools why not use them?"

"Sex is not a bargaining tool, Tessa. It's what people do when they're in a relationship, you know, when they care for each other. Every time you have sex with somebody you don't care about, you're giving away another slice of your self-respect. You keep giving it away and eventually there won't be anything left. Do you understand?"

She drops her head and slowly nods. Perhaps I've overstepped the mark with my advice. I need to bring this back to more relevant matters.

"The reason I'm saying this stuff is that I've heard a few rumours at school. Rumours about you and Marcus Morrison."

On hearing his name she sits up and glares at me defensively.

"What rumours?" she snaps.

"You know what Marcus is like, always bragging about stuff. I heard he's been telling his mates he's going to get you into bed."

"What! He's been flirty with me lately but nothing more than that."

"At the moment maybe, but boys like Marcus eventually find a way to get what they want. All I'm saying is be careful. If you end up in bed with him, you'll regret it for the rest of your life. The guy is toxic, and I'd hate to see you caught up with him."

I look her in the eye and let my final words sink in. She pauses for a moment and finds some resolve.

"You don't need to worry about me, Craig. There's no way that creep is getting anywhere near me, and that's a promise."

I give her a reassuring smile, conscious I don't say too much more. It's tempting to give her the further benefit of my wisdom but there's every chance I could send her life spinning off in a direction that doesn't end as happily as her current one. I also need to remember that to her I'm just a classmate, a kid. She probably thinks I'm a bit preachy already so any further counsel might freak her out. I've done my bit by warning her about Marcus, and more importantly, I managed not to have sex with her. An unusual but productive afternoon's work.

I get up from the bed and take another exaggerated glance at my watch.

"So I guess you're not going to finish what you started then?" she asks with a wry smile.

"As much as I'd love to, Tessa, I've got to be somewhere else I'm afraid. Besides, I don't think Cuthbert would approve."

She laughs and picks up the teddy bear.

"How did you know his name?"

"He introduced himself, wanted to know my intentions," I smile.

She stands and playfully punches me on the arm.

"You're a funny guy, Craig."

I'm not sure if she means funny weird or funny hilarious. I'd take either over the way she felt about me when I left her bedroom the first time.

Tessa gives me a goodbye hug and I breathe in her delicious scent one final time. She then leads me downstairs to the hallway and plucks a set of keys from a hook on the wall, about three feet from the door. I ruefully smile as she unlocks the front door. Given the choice, I'm glad I wasn't able to escape before I had the chance to talk to her about Marcus, even though my testicles are now throbbing. I may need to reacquaint myself with Lars & Sabine when I get home.

"I'll see you at registration on Monday then," she says as I step out of the door.

"Yes you will. Don't be too freaked if I seem a little distant at school. Got a lot of studying to cram in so my head might be all over the place."

"You're such a nerd," she says with a wink.

I turn and crunch across the driveway. I get halfway when Tessa calls out to me.

"Craig, just one thing. Where did you learn those...err...bedroom moves?"

I turn to face her.

"PornHub.com"

A final, fleeting glance at her confused face and I walk away.

I stroll along Tessa's road, the sun finally gaining a little warmth, heightening my contented mood. All things considered, that went pretty well, if you overlook the impromptu foreplay and talking teddy bear. I actually feel quite proud of myself because for once in my life, I decided not to take the easy option. It would have been so much simpler, and more gratifying, if I'd just gone along with Tessa's seduction. But I chose to do what was right rather than what was easy. It's just a shame it's taken me forty-six years to realise that the path of least resistance isn't always the right path.

As I cross the footbridge and head back towards the main road, my thoughts turn to the schizophrenic conversation with Cuthbert. I don't know if I was conversing with a teddy bear or my subconscious mind, but the points raised remain valid. I may have changed one fundamental aspect of my future, but it won't make much difference to the person I become. I may avoid the post-virgin crisis and pass my exams, but I'll still have all the negative traits that held me back throughout my life. I need to confront a few other demons I've let fester for far too long. Demons I should have dealt with when I was originally sixteen. Maybe if I had, I wouldn't be living the wholly vapid existence that is my future life.

I pass the arcade, the shops, and the cafe, carefully plotting what I need to do to ensure that I don't return to a future tarnished with the same hangups. By the time I reach the edge of the estate, I think I've got some semblance of a plan. Whether I have the fortitude to follow it through is another matter. I guess one potent motivator is that I've only got about thirty-four hours left here before I'm thrown back to my middle-age. What a catastrophe it would be if I return to find the only thing that's changed is that I've got a drawer full of exam certificates. It would be like your numbers coming up on the lottery in a week where you've forgotten to buy a ticket. The thought makes me feel a little sick. However daunting it might be to fix my past, it can't possibly be as bad as the way I'd feel if I blow this opportunity.

I wander through the estate and turn into our road. I can see Dad's car sat on the drive so he's almost certainly still at home. Every step closer to our front door is a step closer to my next challenge. Butterflies flutter in my stomach and my mouth is bone dry. I pull my key from my pocket and unlock the front door to silence. The thick stench of stale cigarette smoke invades my nostrils and I hold the door open for a few seconds to acclimatize. I take a final deep breath of clean air and pull the door closed. The first thing I have to do is confirm that Mum isn't home so I call her name up the stairs. No reply. I wander through the sitting room and into the kitchen. Mum isn't home, which is good.

I open the fridge looking for something to drink but there's no beer, no wine, nothing. I could kill for something alcoholic about now. Not just for refreshment but a little Dutch courage. I have to settle for a carton of Um Bongo, which I slurp through a plastic straw. Thirst sated, I cross the kitchen to the door which leads out to the garden. I take a deep breath and open the door.

Here goes nothing.

8

I hate gardening, always have done. Actually, that's not strictly true. I'm hopeless at gardening, always have been. Every plant I've ever had to take responsibility for has died within weeks. If society treated plant life like human life, I'd be on some sort of register by now, or locked away in horticultural prison for crimes against geraniums. I can just about push a mower across our tiny lawn at home but that's as far as the green in my fingers extends. However, that's not to say I can't appreciate a nice garden when I see one, and the one in front of me is particularly nice. Beyond the aesthetics, the smell of freshly cut grass and tubs of sweet-smelling flowers provides a welcome relief from the sickly stench of cigarettes inside the house.

But I'm not here to complement my father on his gardening skills.

The old man is nowhere to be seen so I wander down the slate path towards the centre of the garden. I rarely came out here as a child because it wasn't somewhere to play. This was strictly Dad's space and woe betide anyone who messed with it. I lost count of how many errant footballs came over the fence from our neighbour's garden, only to be punctured with a garden fork and tossed back. He was never a man willing to engage in reasoned discussion, which is why I'm not in a rush to find him now.

I edge down the path in ponderous steps, inspecting the beds either side of me in more detail. The old man is clearly off-the-scale obsessive about every detail. The borders are straight as a rod and so neatly manicured I suspect scissors were used. Beyond the clinically trimmed borders, the dark soil beds contain a wide variety of plants that look lovely, but are all totally alien to me. Maybe someone with knowledge of such things could truly appreciate the meticulous placement of carefully selected plants, but that person isn't me.

As I watch a bee lazily float from flower to flower, the serenity is spoilt by a waft of cigarette smoke and the sound of a throaty cough. I turn to face the potting shed, just as another plume of cigarette smoke drifts from the open door. My foe is obviously in residence so I stride towards the shed, trying not to let my nerves get the better of me. My analytical mind delivers a crumb of comfort by reminding me that my dad is actually my junior by a few years. It's a minor psychological advantage, but as this could be the most difficult conversation I've ever had, I'll take it.

I stand in the doorway of the shed and let my eyes adjust to the relative gloom. The shed is about eight foot square, and the only light is provided by two grimy windows either side of the door. The still air is heavy with cigarette smoke, and tinged with an undertone of creosote, compost, and sweat. Shelves run the entire length of the back wall, laden with plastic bottles, metal cans, hand tools, and an assortment of gardening paraphernalia. A bright orange hover mower is sat on the floor below the shelves, next to a wheelbarrow, and two large cylindrical tubs. The opposite side of the shed is given over to a wooden workbench, covered with packets of seeds and white polystyrene trays. Stood at the bench, with his arm buried to the elbow in a bag of compost, is the old man.

Judging by his startled expression at seeing me, I suspect he doesn't entertain many guests down here.

That expression only stays on his face for a second as his default frown returns.

"What do you want?" he snaps, the cigarette in his mouth flicking up and down in time to his words.

I let the question hang for a moment as I fuel my resolve by mentally picturing my dreary future. This is a one-shot deal. I have to push through with this, as otherwise I'm consigning myself to the exact same future as before.

"Just thought I'd pop down and see what you're up to," I nonchalantly reply.

He says something under his breath I don't catch and returns his attention to a tray of plants on the bench.

"Are they Delphiniums?" I casually enquire.

Fate has played into my hands on this occasion as I've just won the flower lottery. From my own failed efforts to grow anything in our garden, I recognise the distinctive spiky Delphiniums because I'd purchased some from the local garden centre last year, and subsequently murdered them within three weeks.

"How do you know what they are?"

"Let's just say I'm more worldly wise than you give me credit for. You'd be amazed what I know."

He doesn't reply. He turns away and continues to scoop handfuls of compost into a tray. Maybe he thinks I'll go away if he ignores me, but I press on.

"I know, for example, that those twinges you get in your knees from time to time will eventually become arthritis."

He bellows cigarette smoke from his nostrils like an irritated dragon, but still doesn't say a word.

"And I know that it's Mum who pays for all my Christmas and birthday presents."

His frown deepens and I can tell he's becoming increasingly annoyed at my presence. He's going to snap any moment, so I get to my point.

"And I know that you're not really my dad."

He freezes for a second, his face reddens, and tiny twitches ripple in his cheeks. He removes the cigarette from his lips and crushes it into an ashtray on the bench.

"What the hell are you on about, boy?" he barks without warning, causing me to flinch.

I regain my composure.

"You see, it's things like calling me 'boy' that give it away. That, and the way you've treated me over the years."

Actually, his behaviour was just a series of clues — a DNA testing kit, purchased online last year, provided me with the categorical proof. I don't know what I hoped to achieve by finding out but it was something that niggled away at me for years. When I opened the envelope from the testing company and read the results, it wasn't any great surprise, and it changed nothing. As terrible a job as he'd done, he's the only father I've ever known, and I'm stuck with him. I never shared my revelation with anyone. Too much water had passed under the bridge and true to form, I buried it away.

"How dare you say such a thing. Get out of here before I do something we'll both regret," he bellows, his face full of apoplectic rage.

My heart is now pounding in my chest and I'm thinking this wasn't such a great idea. Too late, the genie is now out of the bottle. I have to stand my ground and follow this through.

"I'm not listening to your threats any more. You either tell me the truth and we deal with this now, or I'll ask Mum the minute she gets back. Your choice, but I'm not going to let this go."

I see something in his eyes I've never seen before — panic. He doesn't respond, which suggests he's still hoping I'll just fuck off, or he doesn't know what to say. I can see him scrambling for the appropriate reaction, but nothing comes.

I don't want to lose my momentum, so I continue.

"You don't want me to tell Mum I know, do you? Shall I tell you why I think that?"

He rests his hands on the workbench and stares straight ahead at the panelled wooden wall. He takes long, heavy breaths through his nose, as if he's trying to control his anger. As his anger subsides, I can feel mine rising.

"The only reason Mum puts up with your attitude is because she's afraid I'll find out the truth. She puts up with you to protect me. But if I know the truth, you no longer have any hold over her."

During a management training session a few years back, I recall the course leader telling us that the greatest tool in negotiation is silence. Once you've shown your hand, keep your mouth shut and your adversary will eventually feel compelled to fill the silence. It's one of the few things I've ever learnt on a course that has been useful beyond the shop floor. It's a strategy I deploy with brutal efficiency now, as we stand in complete silence.

He eventually breaks.

"You can't say anything to her," he mutters.

For the first time in my life, I don't feel like the old man is in control. It's a liberating feeling and I take full advantage, releasing years of pent-up anger.

"Why can't I say anything to her? Because if I do, she'll have her bags packed and we'll be out of here in a heartbeat? You'll have nobody to cook your meals, nobody to clean the house, to do your washing, iron your shirts, run your errands. You'll just be a sad, angry man, living out the rest of your days on your own."

I keep quiet again. It takes roughly ten seconds before he feels compelled to say something.

"All right, all right. What do you want?"

Stripped of his power he sounds broken. I almost feel sorry for him. Almost. I take a step forward and prepare to conclude the negotiation by offering him a way out on my terms.

"I'll do a deal with you. I'll give you my word I won't say anything to Mum, but in return, I want something from you."

He turns to face me.

"What?" he grunts.

"Firstly, you need to treat us with a little respect, Mum in particular. Secondly, I want to know how your name ended up on my birth certificate."

He shakes his head and swears under his breath.

"You're opening a can of worms here, boy, but if you insist," he huffs, the reluctance in his voice obvious.

I can almost see him physically deflating. He gestures towards the two large cylindrical tubs sat on the floor opposite us.

"Sit down, my knees are killing me."

We both grasp a container each and drag them across the wooden floorboards, a comfortable distance apart. The old man drops down, with obvious relief, and runs a hand through his thinning hair.

"Before you ask, I don't know who your real father is. Your mum never told me and I never asked. Whoever he was, he wasn't on the scene when we began courting."

He pauses, perhaps hoping I've now got the answer I want. I haven't.

"Carry on."

"She was a typist in the office where I worked. We got to know each other because I worked in the payroll department and she needed some advice, something to do with her hours, I can't remember exactly what. I eventually plucked up the courage to ask her out on a date, and she just broke down in tears. It was only then she told me she was pregnant. Anyway, she said the father wasn't around any longer but she wanted to keep the baby. I think she assumed I'd run a mile when she told me, and I probably should have."

"But you didn't."

"Obviously not, I'd already fallen for her by that point. We talked about it for a while and I persuaded her we could make a go of it, and I'd be willing to bring you up as my own. She hadn't told a soul she was pregnant so everyone assumed I was your father. It all happened so quickly, but it made sense all round."

"And at what stage did you realise that bringing up somebody else's child wasn't quite what you'd hoped?"

His head drops, and he draws a deep breath.

"I thought we'd have kids together, and when we did, we'd feel more like a family. We tried for years but it didn't happen. Your mum kept nagging me to see the doctor, but I never did. What would have been the point? And all along, there was this constant little reminder that some other bloke had managed to do something I couldn't."

"Me, you mean?"

"I'm not expecting you to understand but yes, you. It's no excuse but the more time that went by, the more resentful I became. I was angry at myself and started taking it out on you and your mother. It started with just the odd snappy comment but the less your mother reacted, the more I pushed it. I know it's wrong, but I justified it by telling myself that I'd given you both a nice home and looked after you. I'm not proud of the way I've treated either of you, but I didn't know any other way to cope with the jealousy, the resentment. It ate me up."

Silence descends on the gloomy shed. I'm not sure how I feel about what I've just heard. I want to be angry, I really do, but it's just not there. Can I honestly say I would have felt any different in those circumstances? It certainly answers a few questions about my upbringing and Dad's lack of involvement. Whichever way you cut it, none of us have come out of this particularly well, Dad included.

"You okay, boy?"

"Fine, and stop calling me that," I murmur.

"So where do we go from here?"

There is something unfamiliar in the tone of his voice. I wonder if its relief. Perhaps he's become so trapped in his own, angry little world, he's just relieved to be offered a way out.

"That depends on you. You've already fucked up the first sixteen years of my life so I'm not going to let you ruin the rest of it, or Mum's for that matter."

His expression suggests he's about to chastise me for swearing, but he thinks better of it and poses a question of his own.

"Where has all this come from? This isn't like you, has something happened?"

246

"Let's just say I've had a long time to think about it."

He doesn't press me any further.

"So what do you want from me then?" he asks.

It's a good question.

"Honestly? I want you to be happy, Dad. I want us to be happy, you know, like a normal family. I'm sick of living in fear you're about to lose your rag over something and nothing. I'm sick of you never giving a damn about anything I do. I'm sick of your constant complaining about stuff that doesn't matter. I want a Dad, not a distant stranger who just pays the bills and stomps around like he hates the world."

He closes his eyes and rubs his fingertips over his temples in circular motions. He eventually opens his eyes and looks down at the floor.

"I knew this would happen one day. I've carried on the legacy my old man left behind. He was a terrible father too, so I learnt from the best."

"Perhaps you should have known better then."

"For what it's worth, I am sorry you know. I can't make any promises I'll change overnight, but I can promise you I'll give it a go. I know you've got no reason to believe me but I do want to be happy, it's all I ever wanted, really."

There is enough sincerity in his voice for me to believe him. I guess I won't know just how successful this brief conversation has been until I return to my timeline, but I've done what I can.

"Okay, we have a deal then? I'll give you my word I won't tell Mum I know, and I want your word that things will change."

He pauses for a moment as if he's still thinking of another way out of this, but he eventually leans forward and offers me his hand.

"All right, deal."

"And just so we're clear, Dad, I'll pretend this conversation never happened. I'm going to act exactly as I always have, so the onus is on you to make this work. I don't want to tell Mum I know anything, so don't let me down and I won't have to."

He looks me in the eye and nods. I think I believe him.

At this point I'm reminded of those Hollywood films where everyone wears their heart on their sleeve. If this was such a movie, we'd now embrace one another, with tears and apologies flowing. As this isn't Hollywood, we both just stand and endure a moment of excruciating awkwardness. The old man thankfully breaks the silence.

"I need to finish up in here so I'll see you a bit later."

"Okay, I'm going to my room."

"Right...off to listen to the hit parade eh?" he says with an uncomfortable smile.

I want to tell him he's just uttered the lamest sentence I've ever heard, but he's making an effort, so I don't.

"Yeah, I am. I'll see you at teatime, Dad."

9

Seven hours. Ridiculous. As I lie on my bed, I can barely believe it was only seven hours ago that I awoke to this madness. For the first time since my day began, I can pause and take stock of all that's happened. I'm not sure how I feel. I should feel elated because I've been so uncharacteristically decisive, but there are other emotions swimming around my mind that take the gloss off the elation.

The old man's confession has stirred feelings about my own childless existence. The child we lost, and I'm yet to create, would be in their mid-twenties in my timeline and maybe they'd have brothers or sisters. Would my life have been so much different if I'd been a father? Judging by how it had affected the old man, maybe it's not a question I want to explore too deeply. All hypothetical anyway — by sticking with Megan I had willingly consigned fatherhood to a wish-list that would never be fulfilled. Different situations, but neither Dad nor I got the chance to see our own child grow up. While I can't excuse his behaviour towards me, I can at least now understand it, even empathise with him I suppose.

Trying to shake thoughts of fatherhood from my head, I think about what I'm going to do for the rest of the day, and tomorrow. There are still a few loose ends I'd like to tie up while I've got the chance, and while they might not necessarily make much difference to how I hope my future pans out, I'm keen to exercise my newfound assertiveness. But right now, I'm tired. The day has been mentally exhausting and I could do with a nap. I set the alarm on my watch to go off in an hour and close my eyes.

I spend the next twenty minutes tossing and turning, but sleep doesn't come. Too many thoughts and too much latent emotion. With time to kill before tea, I do what any bored teenager would do in such circumstances, and review my porn collection.

My earlier dalliance with Tessa brings a premature end to my 'duvet time'. Barely ten minutes later, and after a nervous dart to the bathroom, I'm back on my bed listening to the tail end of the American Chart Show on Radio 1.

The top 10 of this week is a mixed-bag that predictably includes Madonna, Janet Jackson and Whitney Houston. I guess the audience is revelling in this fresh, new music, but having had to listen to it for thirty years, it's now irritating white noise. Thankfully the top 10 is saved by the presence of OMD, Mike & The Mechanics and much to my delight, The Pet Shop Boys at number four with 'West End Girls'. There's even the rare gem and one-hit-wonder, 'I Can't Wait' by Nu Shooz, one of my personal 80s favourites.

For reasons best known to themselves, our American Cousins have decreed that Whitney Houston's 'Greatest Love of All' should be number one this week. It's with great relief that thirty seconds into it, Mum knocks on my door to tell me tea is ready. I turn the stereo off and hope Whitney's lyrics aren't stuck in my head for the next five hours.

I visit the bathroom to wash my hands before heading down to the kitchen where Mum is predictably busy, preparing tea. Also predictably, the old man is sat at the table reading the newspaper — did he listen to a word I said? The stainless steel teapot is already on the table, along with three china cups and accompanying saucers. I pour myself a cup of tea, sit down and take a sip.

"I hope the tea is okay, your Dad made it," Mum chuckles across the kitchen.

I almost spit a mouthful of tea across the table in surprise.

"It's not bad, for an amateur."

I look across the table at the old man. His eyes lift from the paper and the faintest hint of a smile surfaces on his craggy face. The slight nod I return betrays the significance of what just happened. Forcing him to change his ways through blackmail alone would never work in the long term. He had to realise that our conversation was a desperate act by a desperate kid, and that his destructive behaviour had to end, for him as much as us. Maybe it was just a slight smile and a cup of tea, but those simple gestures represent so much more. He made an effort, and that gives me a sliver of hope for the future.

As I contemplate the old man's progress, Mum delivers a plate to the table, piled-high with toasted crumpets. She then heads over to the fridge and returns with a ceramic butter dish she places next to the crumpet mountain.

"Tuck in then," she orders.

I grab a still-warm crumpet and drop it onto my plate. I scrape a knob of butter onto my knife and spread it over the crispy surface. The creamy butter slowly melts, saturating the floury innards of the crumpet and oozing onto the plate below. I lift it to my mouth and take a large bite, warm butter dribbling down my chin. I can't remember the last time I ate a crumpet, and I'd forgotten just how moreish they are. Five crumpets later and I no longer need reminding. Despite my gluttonous assault on the crumpet mountain, there's still just enough room for two large slices of Battenberg cake. I wash it all down with the dregs of my tea and slump back in my chair, defeated by Saturday tea.

"Thanks Mum, that was lovely."

"Yes, thank you, Janet," Dad adds awkwardly.

She pats me on the hand and gives Dad a lingering smile.

"You're both welcome."

To his credit, Dad offered to clear the table but Mum ushered him out of the kitchen. With the benefit of witnessing my earlier efforts, Mum also declines my assistance with the washing-up. I help her clear the table while we swap small talk.

"Anything planned for this evening, sweetheart?"

"Not sure yet."

"There's a good film with Robert Urich on BBC1 later if you fancy it?"

Notwithstanding the fact I have no idea who Robert Urich is, I suspect my mother's definition of a good film differs greatly from mine.

"Maybe. I might go up to the arcade though."

"That's nice. Your dad is taking me out for a drink," she says casually.

Such is my surprise, I almost drop the butter dish on my way to the fridge.

"Really? That's...good."

For as long as I can remember, the old man has ritually spent every Saturday evening playing snooker at the British Legion Club. Whether it was a birthday party, a wedding reception or a family barbecue, if it landed on a Saturday night then Mum and I would always attend with an abashed apology for the old man's absence.

As Mum continues with the washing-up, Dad pokes his head around the kitchen door.

"I'm just going upstairs to freshen up."

"Okay darling. I'll finish in here and I'll be up to get ready," Mum replies.

I know the old man said he'd make an effort, but this is beyond anything I had expected. I dread to think what his 'freshening up' is likely to entail but one thing is for sure, I won't be touching that flannel in the bathroom anytime soon.

With the kitchen spick and span, Mum disappears upstairs like a giddy teenager on prom night. I head into the sitting room and slump down on the sofa. I grab Dad's newspaper from the magazine rack and study tonight's TV schedule. It's not an altogether unexpected disappointment. Maybe there might be some nostalgic entertainment to be gleaned from the adverts so I scan the room looking for the TV remote control. There is no TV remote control.

I get up from the sofa and cross the room to our archaic TV set. As was the fashion in TV manufacturing, the bulky unit is bedecked in a fake oak veneer, with a vast plastic casing at the rear to house the cathode ray tube within. Beside the bulbous twenty-one inch screen is a plastic panel that contains the on/off button, four push buttons for the channel selection, and dials for the volume, brightness and colour.

I poke the 'on' button and wait while the TV splutters into life. I'm greeted with a sepia-tinted scene of a car chase, involving an American Police Cruiser and The General Lee. I was never a fan of 'The Dukes of Hazzard', although one of the earliest entries into my fledgling porn collection was a magazine cut-out of Daisy Duke in her tight white vest and denim shorts.

With the enticing prospect of seeing Ms. Duke again, I return to the sofa and make myself comfortable. I watch the final eight minutes before the closing titles and disappointment roll. Just a fleeting glimpse of Daisy Duke. I instinctively pat the cushion next to me in search of the remote control. Christ, no wonder people were fitter in this day, all that marching back and forth to change the channel. I'm too full of crumpets and Battenberg to be bothered, so it looks like I'll be watching BBC 1 for a while.

The stiff BBC announcer informs me that the next program is 'The Keith Harris Show'. Kill me now. I pick up the paper and scan the pages while trying to ignore the TV. I manage ten minutes. If Keith Harris and his insufferable green duck weren't bad enough, cockney duo Chas & Dave are wheeled out. Enough is enough. Just as I'm about to get up and switch the TV off, my parents enter the sitting room, their arrival announced by the overpowering fragrance of Old Spice and Tweed. Despite smelling like a prostitute's handbag, they do look quite the dapper couple. They actually look happy.

"We're off now sweetheart, we won't be too late," Mum smiles.

"Okay, have a nice time."

The old man shuffles around while attempting to pull something from the pocket of his beige slacks.

"Your Mum says you're off to the arcade. Here."

He hands me a pound coin and I catch his expression which seems to imply that the coin is in no way payment for my silence.

"Cheers, Dad."

Mum plants a lipsticked kiss on my cheek and they leave the house. All is quiet apart from the ticking carriage clock and the grating voice of Keith Harris on the TV. I shudder and switch it off.

I trot up the stairs and put my trainers back on. Knowing it will be the final time I ever visit Astro Arcade, I want to ensure I'm sufficiently financed for a lengthy session. While the pound Dad gave me is symbolically priceless, I suspect my gaming skills will be rusty so I'll need more than just a quid. I scan the bedroom and locate my Darth Vader money box, which I empty. I put on my jacket, and just as I close the bedroom door behind me, the doorbell chimes downstairs.

I pad back down the stairs and cautiously open the front door. For once, I'm hoping it's somebody selling tat on the doorstep, rather than somebody I know. Unfortunately, it is somebody I know and my heart sinks when I open the door to Ross Glavin, the future pension adviser. I could really do without a conversation with, if I recall correctly, one of my more immature schoolmates.

"All right Craig? You coming out?"

He stands there with a wide grin, his hair heavy with gel and his pale face dotted with angry spots. I stare at him for a moment while I consider the quickest way to end this impromptu meeting.

"Earth to Craig. Hello, did you hear me?"

"Sorry Ross, I was miles away," I reply, wishing I was.

"Watcha doing?"

"Um, I'm meeting my parents for dinner in a minute."

As excuses go, it's a poor one. I don't recall ever going out for dinner with my parents on a Saturday evening.

"You saddo! I'm meeting Barry at the skate park, he's got his hands on a few bottles of cider. Why don't you blow-out your parents and come along?"

For a nanosecond, the prospect of consuming alcohol clouds my judgement, and I actually consider his invitation. Do I want to spend the next few hours sitting in a concrete bowl, drinking cheap cider and listening to Barry and Ross brag about which girls they've allegedly fingered?

"Think I'll pass mate. My folks won't be happy if I don't turn up."

"Suit yourself. More booze for me then."

A few seconds of silence pass, and just as I think he's about to go away, he continues.

"Oh, do you know Charlotte Pike?"

"No, don't think so."

"Yes you do. She's in our physics class."

I don't know why he felt it necessary to ask me a question to which he already knew my answer.

"Oh, yeah. What about her?"

"I titted her up last night."

Ross lets his revelation hang in the air, his grin widening. I don't know what reaction I'm supposed to have to his claim, or indeed what's involved in a girl being 'titted up'.

"Right, well done you," I offer.

"Yeah, probably gonna shag her next week if she's lucky. Anyway, seeing as you're being boring, I'd better get going before that greedy sod drinks all the booze."

"Good luck with that. I'll see you at school on Monday."

"Okay, seeya mate."

As I watch Ross jog away, I can't help wonder why I ever hung around with him. The naivety of youth I suspect.

I wait five minutes for Ross to clear the area, and armed with £3.80 in loose change, I head out into the evening sun towards the arcade.

Compared to modern amusement arcades where the games are incredibly sophisticated and a quid a go, every machine in Astro Arcade requires a single ten-pence piece to play. I stretch my £3.80 budget to almost three hours, losing my final life on Gorf just minutes before the arcade is due to close. It's almost ten o'clock when I emerge onto the quiet street, penniless, but contented with my evening of retro gaming. I stroll home under dark skies, the scenery bathed in a phosphorous orange glow from the street lights. I pass a chip-shop, which is doing good business even at this late hour. The mouth-watering aroma of freshly cooked chips hits me, triggering regret I've blown all my money.

I arrive home to find the house in complete darkness, and a space on the drive that would usually be occupied by Dad's car. This bodes well. They're obviously still having a good time at the pub as Mum is usually tucked up in bed by now — either that, or they've gone dogging up on the heath. I admit the latter isn't likely, I'm not sure dogging even existed in 1986. I let myself in and spend a few minutes blindly patting the walls in search of a light switch. With light eventually shed, I head into the sitting room, slump down on the sofa and stretch my legs out in front of me. A deep yawn reminds me how long today has been. Long, yet constructive. Constructive, yet challenging. I can say with all certainty it has been the most extraordinary day of my life, possibly anyone's life.

With no other distractions in the silent room, my ears fix on the unabating tick-tock of the carriage clock. My eyelids grow heavier with every passing second until I can no longer resist. I close my eyes. Sleep isn't far away, the rhythmic beats of the clock enticing me to move closer. Tick. Tock. Tick. Tock. I drift slowly from reality until I fall into the blissful abyss of sleep.

I could have slept where I sat for hours, but the slamming of a car door outside the sitting room window puts paid to that. For a few seconds I struggle to comprehend where I am. Once I establish the *where*, the dawning realisation of the *when* eventually follows. I quickly acclimatize back into my role and through bleary eyes, I consult my watch. 11.25pm. The sound of the front door opening is accompanied by laughter. My parents, or at least two people I assume to be my parents, waltz into the sitting room. It's difficult to tell if they're deliriously happy or just drunk. Maybe a little of both, but I've never seen them like this before.

"Hello sweetheart. We thought you'd be in bed by now," Mum literally shouts.

She wobbles across the room and plants a sloppy kiss on my forehead, the smell of Cinzano Bianco heavy on her breath.

"You had a good evening I assume?"

"We had a lovely time, didn't we Colin?"

"Magic dear," the old man slurs, clearly quite pissed.

I'm just about to launch into a sermon about the perils of drink-driving when I remind myself that this is a different era. As enlightened as 80s society thinks it is, there isn't anywhere near the same social stigma attached to drink-driving as there is in the present day. My parents are of a generation where it's considered no more a crime than speeding. Everyone does it, and that's fine as long as you don't get caught.

"Did you have a nice time at the arcade, sweetheart?" Mum asks.

"Yeah, not bad thanks," I reply wearily.

"You should be in bed, young man, you look beat."

"I am. I was just about to head up when you came in."

"Okay. We're heading up to bed now, aren't we darling?" Mum says suggestively as she nudges the old man in the ribs.

"Yes we are," he replies with a little too much enthusiasm.

Mum gives me another kiss on the forehead and wishes me good night. She disappears up the stairs, leaving me with the old man. I'm just about to get up when he strides across the room and flops down next to me. He turns and places his shovel of a hand on my knee. I wish I'd gone straight up to bed when I came in. This is beyond awkward.

"I've had a few drinks, so I'll say this now because I don't think I could if I were sober."

"Okay," I reply nervously.

"Thank you, son."

"Err, you're welcome. I'm not sure what for though."

"I forgot how lucky I am. Our little chat earlier helped me to remember."

He's right about one thing. I cannot imagine those words leaving a sober mouth.

"I'm pleased Dad. You just have to keep reminding yourself, every day. I guess it's easy to take what we have for granted."

"You're not wrong, son."

He gives me a drunken smile and staggers off to bed, leaving me to reflect on the hypocrisy of my advice.

I sit and wait until I hear my parents' bedroom door close and drag myself upstairs, collapsing onto my bed. I strip off my jeans and lie on top of the duvet, waiting for sleep to return. That prospect diminishes as the muffled sound of giggling passes through the paper-thin wall of my parents' bedroom. A few minutes pass, and all is quiet once more.

Then it's not.

It starts with the faint groaning of a single voice, barely audible. Then another voice joins in with the groaning, raising the combined sound a few decibels. It grows louder, interspersed with an occasional shriek and several heavy grunts.

I leap off the bed and frantically rummage through the drawers opposite. I find my Sony Walkman in the third drawer. I place the padded headphones over my ears and flick the output switch to radio, the volume to maximum. A jazz track bursts through the headphones. I've got an eclectic taste in music, but I detest jazz with a passion. However, anything is preferable to the sound of my parents having sex. What horrors have I unleashed?

As I return to my bed, I pray the Walkman batteries last longer than the old man.

PART FOUR

1

One of the many criticisms Megan levied at me during our twenty-five years of marriage, was my inability to show spontaneous affection. This was such a problem for her she even went to the trouble of giving it the acronym of SAD — Spousal Affection Deficiency. Despite Megan's prognosis, it was something that I just couldn't change. As I saw it, the act of being spontaneously affectionate needed to be exactly that; spontaneous. But how can something be spontaneous if you have to consciously make an effort to do it? After a decade of trying to fix my SAD, she gave up and accepted that I would never be as affectionate as she wanted me to be.

I always blamed the old man for my inability to show affection. Mum was always very demonstrative but I don't recall receiving even a handshake from him. As for any affection shown by the old man towards his wife, it was perfunctory at best. A peck on the cheek as he left for work, and maybe one on his return if his day hadn't been too stressful.

So as I sit in the kitchen munching on a slice of toast, it's a little disconcerting watching the old man stood behind Mum at the kitchen sink, his arms wrapped around her waist. While I don't know the specifics of what occurred in their bedroom last night, nor do I wish to think about it too deeply, it seems to have had a profound effect on the old man. It's no bad thing, I'd just rather not pay witness to their public groping. Hopefully this will calm down in time and they'll find a happy balance, otherwise I might have just inflicted years of late night Dizzie Gillespie on my teenage self.

I finish my breakfast and leave the lovebirds to it. I head upstairs to the bathroom for a ninety second shower, and with a towel wrapped around my waist, I dart across the landing to my bedroom. It's just gone 10.00am and the countdown timer on the computer shows I've got a little under fourteen hours remaining before it reaches zero. Unfortunately, I have to fit at least an hour into my schedule for Sunday lunch where my presence is mandatory. I've now got a three-hour window to complete the first of my planned tasks. This is a task born of pure principle. It probably won't make a difference to my revised timeline but I'm hopeful it will prove beneficial for the teenager who wakes up tomorrow. I'm not sure the consequences will be so positive for the other individual involved, but I don't care.

Bedecked in a clean pair of jeans, a dark blue polo shirt and my Nike trainers, I scour the bedroom looking for loose change. I've already rued two occasions where I've not had any money in my pocket — the lack of easy access to cash is something I'm finding a real annoyance. In my time, I leave the house with a contactless debit card, three credit cards, and a payment app on my phone. Cash is becoming increasingly redundant in my life, but here it's still king. I wonder what a teenager of this era would make of our burgeoning cashless society? It would be quite something to see their shocked face as they watch you pay for a coffee, simply by waving a piece of plastic or a mobile phone over a small terminal. Saying that, they'd probably be more shocked that you're willing to pay four quid for a cup of coffee.

Having wasted ten minutes searching every drawer in the room, I manage to scrape £1.08 together. I drop the meagre funds into my pocket and head back down the stairs. I cautiously open the kitchen door, fearful I might find the old man rodgering my mother up against the fridge-freezer. It's with some relief I find them both sat at the table, reading the Sunday papers.

"I'm just going out for a while. Be back in time for lunch."

"Okay sweetheart, see you later."

"Bye son," the old man cheerfully adds.

I give them both a smile and leave the house, destined for what is likely to be the first of several interesting encounters today.

Unlike my initial foray into 1986 yesterday, it's much warmer today and there's little breeze. The streets echo to the sound of lawn mowers and dozens of cars are being washed on driveways. The smell of cut grass lingers in the air, occasionally joined by a trace of frying bacon. If you wanted to capture the quintessential essence of a suburban Sunday morning, today would be the day to do it. The scene is only fractionally marred as I pass a dowdy woman, stood watching her Labrador take a shit on the pavement. I hurry my pace to avoid the rancid stench. After a few seconds I turn to see both the dog and his owner cross the street, the mound of shit left where dispatched. It seems we haven't reached the point where dog owners are obliged to scoop their pets' faeces into a thin plastic bag and carry it home like a stinking fairground goldfish.

It takes less than ten minutes to reach the far side of the estate, but another five minutes to navigate my way through the confusing network of cul-de-sacs. I seldom had reason to venture into this part of the estate unless I was making a delivery to the house I'm about to visit. The goods being delivered were my computer games, and the recipient was a young Marcus Morrison. It wasn't something I did through choice. Marcus would overhear me mention a new game during computer club and then suggest I lend it to him. And by *lend*, I mean deliver it to his house that evening and immediately rescind ownership. When it dawned on me that I would never see the games Marcus borrowed again, I made copies using the tape-to-tape recording facility on my stereo. I ended up with about a dozen bootleg copies of games I'd actually bought and paid for. It didn't seem fair, but in Marcus's intimidating style, he demanded and I always obliged.

Now I'm stood at the junction of Orchard Gardens, there is no fear, just simmering anger and determination. I'm here to reclaim my computer games and more importantly, my self-respect. Physically I might be a teenager, but my middle-aged mind won't let a spoilt teenage brat win this particular battle. I have the psychological advantage and thirty years of pent up angst to call upon. And one thing I do know is that despite Marcus's threats in school, he never once had the guts to follow through on any of them. Sure, he could intimidate because he was taller than most of the kids, but when it came to inflicting physical harm, he was strictly third division compared to some of the psychopaths in our school. His only weapon was fear, but if he sees I'm no longer afraid of him, I'm confident he'll back down. At least that's what I hope.

As I enter Orchard Gardens I focus on a picture in my head. It's a picture of Marcus's future where he's sat on a toilet floor with terror in his eyes. One punch from Dave and he goes down, he stays down. I wish I'd been the one to deliver that punch, but that's an irrelevance now because my actions yesterday should ensure that

I'm never in the same toilet as Marcus, and certainly never in a position where he can destroy my career. However, this isn't about Marcus, this is about giving my teenage self the chance to be a better, stronger person. What I hope to achieve in the next ten minutes is to remove the fear and the self-doubt that blighted my life. I just need to show Marcus that I'm not scared of him any more.

Marcus's house is situated at the end of Orchard Gardens; a leafy cul-de-sac of seven imposing mock-Tudor houses. Compared to our modest semi-detached house, these homes are more like mansions. Nobody here is washing their car or mowing their lawn, probably because the residents would rather pay somebody else to complete such menial chores. With no reason for anyone to be outside, it's eerily quiet, just the sound of birdsong and my trainers scuffing across the tarmac pavement as I approach No. 4. Despite the presence of a double garage, there are two cars sat on a paved driveway outside Marcus's house. A dark green Jaguar XJS and a silver VW Golf. Both are less than a year old and I suspect the Jaguar is worth more than my dad earns in a year. Mr & Mrs Morrison are clearly wealthy people, which would go some way to explaining Marcus's indulged upbringing.

As I take a few steps along the path to the front door, I hear something. Shouting? I stop and turn around, but there's nobody else in the cul-de-sac. Whatever it was, I can't hear it now. I shrug my shoulders and continue along the path. Barely four steps later and I hear it again. Definitely shouting, from Marcus's house. The double glazing is doing a fine job of dampening the voices so I can't hear what's being said. Maybe I should come back another time. I'm only fifteen feet from the front door so if I'm going to abort, I need to do it now. I'd rather avoid being embroiled in a family argument. Seconds tick by as I stand motionless, feeling exposed. I need to make a decision, but then my mind is made up for me.

At the very second I shift my weight onto my right foot to turn and walk away, the front door opens. I freeze, and my initial confidence drains in an instant as I stare straight at Marcus and his crimson face. He does a brief double-take when he sees me, but quickly finds his angry face again. He steps from the doorway and strides towards me. I instinctively raise my hands, palms outward, in a pathetic show of surrender. With less than six feet between us, my mouth drops open as I try to find some words. I can just about mutter Marcus's name, but it's pointless — his eyes are fixed firmly ahead and he brushes straight past me into the cul-de-sac.

As I turn and watch Marcus march into the distance, I realise my hands are still in the air. I drop them and try to comprehend what just happened. This was definitely not the right time to confront him and it feels like I've dodged a bullet. Whatever pissed him off, he didn't appear to be in the mood for discussing computer games. I let out a breath I may have been holding for too long and decide it's time to head home. I take barely three steps before a voice booms from behind me.

"Who are you?"

I slowly turn around to face a giant of a man filling the doorway. My eyes move up his frame, meeting his rocky face sat beneath a crown of close-cropped black hair. His dark eyes are barely visible in the shadow of his prominent brow, and a bushy moustache twitches above his mouth. There's something about him that suggests he once had a career in the military.

"Craig," I reply meekly.

"What are you doing here?" the giant bellows.

"I...err...just came to see Marcus."

A deep crease develops in his brow.

"Speak up, boy," he barks.

"I came to see Marcus," I splutter.

He eyes me with lingering contempt.

"You a poof?"

"What?"

"A poof. You know, a faggot, a bender," he spits.

"Sorry, I don't know what you're talking about."

Without warning, he lurches off the step towards me, stopping a few feet away. I almost soil my pants. He raises one of his orangutan arms and points at me, his face now twisted with fury.

"I'll say this only once, I don't want your sort around here. If I see you or your perverted bum-chums anywhere near my house again, I'll rip your fucking head off. Clear?"

I have no idea why I'm being subjected to his homophobic tirade, and to be honest, I don't really care. I just want to get away from this unhinged lunatic so I nod enough times to make it clear I understand although I don't. Having made his point, he throws me a look of disgust and stomps back inside the house. The door is slammed shut and I slowly walk backwards up the path, keeping my eyes fixed on the door in case he changes his mind and decides he'd rather rip my head off on this visit.

My trainers barely touch the pavement as I scoot out of the cul-de-sac. I run for a few minutes until I feel I'm a safe distance from Marcus's house, coming to a stop near the skate park on the edge of the estate. With the majority of teenage skaters likely to be in bed until lunchtime, there isn't a soul around and the park is quiet.

I lean against a chain-link fence while I catch my breath and try to make sense of what just happened. Unlike yesterday, my hopes for this morning's task could not have been more savagely dashed. I begin to feel annoyed with myself for pushing my luck. In hindsight this was a badly planned and reckless idea that wasn't worth the risk. I suppose I can take solace from the fact I avoided a confrontation with Marcus, although that creates another problem. Once he calms down, he'll want to know why I was as his house. In about thirteen hours' time, I won't be here to answer him, least not this version of me.

The positivity I had when I left the house fizzles away. I've made a problem for myself that I have to fix within the next thirteen-odd hours, but I don't even know where to start. I need to talk to Marcus, but there's no way I'm going back to his house. My immediate thoughts turn to social media and contacting him via Facebook or Snapchat. Obviously not an option. How did we survive as a species without the ability to communicate with one another every second of every day? What are the alternatives? I wander around aimlessly all day in the hope I bump into him? I find his phone number and hope the psychopathic giant doesn't answer when I call? Both totally impractical and I've got nothing else.

I push myself off the fence and head home, with the faint hope Marcus will be curious enough about my visit to come and find me.

I trudge alongside the perimeter fence of the skate park and turn into the road which runs along the rear boundary. A grass embankment extends for about fifty yards along the road, acting as a noise barrier between the park and the nearby houses. There are three wooden benches sat at even intervals at the top of the embankment. The nearest two are empty, but the one at the far end is occupied by a solitary figure. I get halfway along the road, and as the figure gets closer, my heart beats a little faster. I quicken my pace until I'm only fifteen yards away and able to confirm the identity of the lone benchwarmer. This could be incredibly good luck, or incredibly bad luck — I'll know which within the next few minutes.

2

I've been on the receiving end of a punch twice in my life. I was only a ten year-old when it first happened and the assailant was my eleven year-old cousin, Darren. He claimed I was cheating at Battleships and decided to avenge my deceit by punching me squarely on the nose. It bled for about ten minutes while Darren received a slippering from his father as punishment. Darren and I never spoke again. Twenty years later, I was on a stag night in Newcastle when I received my second punch. At the end of an all-day drinking session, I had entered that stage of drunkenness where I believed I was invincible. Turns out it was just an illusion and I probably shouldn't have tried to jump the queue at the taxi rank. I awoke the next morning with hazy memories and a vivid purple blotch around my left eye.

I've just received my third punch, courtesy of Marcus Morrison. As he swung wildly at me, I tried to back-peddle and lost my balance so his fist only glanced my cheek. However, I'm now sat on my arse at the top of a grass embankment, with Marcus looking down upon me.

"Say that again, Pelling and I'll fucking kill you."

I scuttle back a few feet and reassess my strategy, which clearly hasn't gone according to plan. My opening gambit to Marcus was, in hindsight, maybe a little too direct. I hoped my shocking revelation would unnerve him. It didn't, it enraged him. I need to adopt a different strategy, and quickly. I'm gambling everything on my experience prevailing over Marcus's youthful, but uncontrolled, aggression. If I get it right, I can gain control of the situation. If I'm wrong, I look set to receive punch number four, then five, and possibly six.

As we grow older, it's inevitable that the amount of information we absorb becomes deeper and broader. Most of this fairly useless information is stored away in the deepest recesses of the mind, waiting for the moment where it might prove its worth. For example, things like knowing that the capital city of Uganda is Kampala, or that the distinctive smell in the air after it rains is called 'petrichor'. Information of no value beyond a pub quiz. However, amongst all that trivia, some of the information stored in your head can occasionally provide a practical use. This might be one such an occasion.

I've picked up this information by reading dozens of books centred around an outcast-type hero. Books where a former military loaner arrives in an American backwater and stumbles across some dark secret amongst the townsfolk. Before he rights all the wrongs, our hero will take part in several fight scenes where he kicks the shit out of the bad guys. Such is the author's attention to detail in these books, my brain has absorbed a lot of the tactics used by the hero during those fight scenes. If that information turns out to be written with poetic licence, I'm in trouble. But if it's vaguely accurate, it could prove invaluable for my own impending fight scene.

There is about eight feet of space between where Marcus is stood and my position on the ground. I need to appear subservient, which I guess is what he expects. Surprise will be my ally. I climb to my feet, adjusting my stance so my left foot is planted forward of my right with about twenty inches of space between them. I have to keep my centre of gravity low for this to work so I bend my knees slightly. I lean forward a fraction, keeping my eyes fixed on Marcus. My right shoulder is tensed and my hand balled into a fist. I raise my left hand as if to show surrender, and to focus his attention away from my fist.

Time to repeat the line that provoked Marcus's initial punch, and will undoubtedly trigger the second.

"Marcus, I want to talk about your homosexuality."

I wasn't 100% sure he was gay, but his father's outburst was the tin lid on a box of clues stretching back over the months since Marcus started at RolpheTech. It was the only viable answer to a lot of questions. My theory was that Marcus would be so shocked that I know his secret, he would beg me not to say anything. I hoped we could have a civilised conversation and reach an agreement where he'd leave me alone, in return for my silence. Turns out my theory was wrong and I've now got to do this the hard way.

Repeating my initial statement only serves to enrage Marcus further. It doesn't appear he's in the mood for a civilised conversation as he prepares to dispatch his second punch. This time I'm ready for him.

His first mistake is that he draws his arm so far backwards, there is no element of surprise. The second mistake is that he swings wildly while still moving forward so he can't control his momentum. The third mistake is that his feet are only a few inches apart so his balance is compromised. All three mistakes play right into my hands. I keep my entire focus on the travel of his fist as it takes an age to arc through the air towards my head. My timing needs to be perfect. Move too soon and he might adjust the course of his fist or abort the punch. Move too late and some part of his haymaker will connect with my head.

If I could repeat it a hundred times, I doubt my timing could be any more precise. I bend my knees and stoop at the exact moment Marcus's arm reaches the point of no return. His fist passes through air previously occupied by my head, and with nothing to stop its momentum, continues its trajectory. As his body twists to follow his flailing arm, the entire right side of his torso is open to attack. The window of opportunity is now open to implement the second move borrowed from fiction. Using every joule of kinetic energy in my body, I uncoil like a loaded spring and deliver a measured, but devastating punch to Marcus's rib cage. Such is the force of the impact, pain streaks across my knuckles and travels up my wrist like forks of lightning. If my punch hasn't debilitated Marcus sufficiently, I'm in trouble because I doubt my fist will withstand a repeat performance.

As it transpires, I don't have to worry about Marcus retaliating because he's lying on the floor, holding his ribs, and groaning between irregular breaths. I take a few seconds to shake the pain from my hand before I step across to his crumpled body and stand over him. I'm not a violent man, and ordinarily I can't stand seeing anyone in distress, but I'd be lying if I said there wasn't a tiny part of me gleefully savouring Marcus's discomfort. I squat down in front of him and his eyes dart around as if he's trying to evaluate his limited options for escape. He knows he's helpless. If the pain in my hand is anything to go by, I suspect he might have a cracked rib or two so I doubt he can get up and run. I could kick seven shades of shit out of him now and there would be nothing he could do. I could unleash years of pent-up anger. It would be the sweetest revenge.

As tempting as it is, I don't enact this kicking because when I look at his face, all the arrogance, the narcissism and the sneering attitude are buried beneath a pained expression. Almost to my annoyance, my glee dissolves.

"Don't worry Marcus, I'm done here. Okay?"

He nods his head as he tries to choke back tears. I suppose I should be gracious in victory.

"Can you get up?"

He unfurls his body and rolls onto his back. He gingerly raises his knees and props his torso up by extending his arms behind him. Certain movements are accompanied by a gasp of air through gritted teeth. Slowly, but surely, he sits upright.

"Do you think you can make it over to the bench?"

"Think so," he mumbles.

I stand up and hold my arm out. He grasps it with one hand, keeping the other held to his rib cage. I take a step backwards and help him to his feet. It's an action that clearly hurts, judging by the way his face contorts. I guide him over to the bench and he cautiously lowers himself down, his hand steadfastly fixed to his side. I take a seat at the other end of the bench, and for a few minutes, neither of us say anything. I suspect we're both equally stunned at what just happened, although for very different reasons.

Marcus eventually feels compelled to speak.

"How did you learn to fight like that?"

"My Uncle Jack used to be in the military police. He taught me."

A lie, but more believable than the truth.

"I could report you to the police, you know. That was bloody GBH," he whines.

I detect a hint of the real Marcus rising to the surface. His pride has been as badly damaged as his ribs so he wants to regain the upper hand. I've come too far to let that happen.

"Shut up, Marcus. You tell the police and it'll be all around school by lunchtime tomorrow that I kicked your arse. You really want that?"

He lets out a sigh and shakes his head.

"No, thought not."

Silence falls again and I suspect Marcus is considering a way to turn this situation around. Time to return to plan A.

"Are we just going to sit here and pretend I never said anything about you being gay?" I ask.

He twists to face me, but immediately regrets it as a jolt of pain reminds him of his injury.

"I don't know what the hell you're talking about," he hisses.

I ignore his protestation.

"I assume the fearsome giant at your house was your Dad?"

"Yeah, so?"

"Well, he hid it well, but I sort of got the impression he's not keen on gay folk?"

"What did he say?"

"He seemed to think I was gay, and he made it clear I wasn't welcome. Why would he think that?"

"Dunno, ask him if you've got the balls."

"No, you're okay. It seems odd though, don't you think? You were arguing about something when I arrived and then you ran out of the house. I then had to listen to your dad's homophobic threats, presumably because he thought I was gay. I'm guessing your dad knows about your sexuality and isn't too happy about it. Would that be about right?"

He doesn't answer me. An ice cream van appears on the road at the far side of the park, and the chimed melody of 'Mr Softee' fills the air, somewhat ironically.

"I need to go home," he says, before delicately lifting his body off the bench.

"Are you not going to answer me? Is your dad giving you grief because you're gay?"

"Just stay the fuck out of my business, will you," he blasts.

He obviously isn't keen on discussing his relationship with his father so I change the subject.

"What are you going to tell your parents about your injury?"

"Don't panic, Pelling, I'll tell them I fell off a mate's skateboard. Besides, If I tell my Dad a skinny runt like you did this, I'll never hear the end of it."

"Less of the insults Marcus. This skinny runt can add a couple of black eyes to your injury list if you like."

He avoids eye contact and shuffles away. He gets five or six yards when I call after him.

"Oh, one other thing before you go. This plan of yours to get Tessa Lawrence into bed. Can I suggest you drop that idea because it won't end well for either of you?"

He stops abruptly.

"What? Who told you that?"

"Doesn't matter. You need to accept your sexuality, Marcus. Besides the fact you probably don't want to have sex with her, it won't change who you are. And whether you're trying to kid yourself or your dad, it's not fair to use Tessa like that."

"Even if any of this shit was true, which it isn't, why is it any of your business?"

"Sit back down and I'll tell you."

Marcus turns his head and surveys the skate park. Still too early for anyone to be out there, so for now we've got the park to ourselves. Seconds pass and it appears he's weighing up his options. It doesn't matter what he does now, I've done enough to keep him off my back for the foreseeable future. But it feels like I've only done half a job, and while I might have eased the symptoms, I haven't cured the problem. For that I need a willing patient.

"If you're worried I'll say anything to anyone, then you needn't be. Anyway, who'd believe me? It's my word against yours."

"I'm not admitting to anything, but if you wanna talk I'll listen," he begrudgingly replies.

He edges over to the bench, and with one hand on the armrest for support, he lowers himself back down.

"I'll tell you why it's my business, Marcus, it's because you're an arsehole. I don't think it's your fault you're an arsehole, but just because your old man has issues with you, doesn't make it fair you vent your frustration at the kids in school. And I include myself in that."

He doesn't react, or give the slightest indication what's going on in his head. He changes the subject though.

"What were you doing at my house, anyway?"

"I wanted to get my computer games back. You know, the ones you borrowed and never returned?"

"Oh yeah, those. Shit games anyway," he sniggers.

My patience frays.

"It's not funny. You keep treating people like you do and I won't be the last one who retaliates — and maybe the next guy you piss-off will do a lot more than just punch you in the ribs."

The grin on his face fades away and he chooses not to respond. Void of threats and snide remarks, it's clear he doesn't have much else to offer in the conversation department. I'll give him one last chance to grasp the olive branch.

"There are people you can talk to about what you're going through. People who can help you."

"I don't need any help," he snaps.

"I think you do, and you're not doing yourself any good by ignoring it. It's not like a cold, it won't suddenly clear up. If you're gay, then that's it, you're gay."

"I'm not bloody gay."

"Whatever. I know you are, and you know you are. Keep kidding yourself and you'll make things worse in the long run, I promise you."

I sense I'm wasting my time here. I can't help him if he's not prepared to accept the truth. Maybe he really does think it's just a phase, and his plan to sleep with Tessa will somehow cure him. But I know what humiliation awaits him. If Tessa ignores my advice and they end up in bed, it will only make matters worse for the both of them.

Though in all likelihood, I suspect the reason he's in denial is the era in which we currently live.

This is not a time where gay men and women can marry, adopt children or enjoy equal rights. Nor is it a time where, on the whole, homophobic bile is silenced by hate crime laws. This is an era where the spectre of AIDS looms large. Where fear and intolerance are fuelled by newspapers and their jaundiced headlines about the 'gay plague'. This is an era where it's illegal for a sixteen year-old to even engage in consensual sex with another man. Would I want to come out as gay in this era? Would I embrace my sexuality in a time where it's not unusual for people to decline a handshake with a gay man in ignorant fear of catching AIDS? No, 1986 isn't even close to mainstream tolerance of homosexuality, let alone acceptance or celebration.

In truth, I'd do exactly what Marcus is doing. I would remain in vehement denial.

"Look Marcus, you have my word I won't tell a living soul about what happened this morning, or anything we've said. You don't have to justify yourself to me, or anyone else for that matter, but can you at least accept a few words of advice?"

He looks at me, rolls his eyes and eventually nods.

"Only you know how crap it must feel to have your old man treat you the way he does. But you can't keep treating other people the same way. If you don't want to become a small-minded, spiteful man like him, you need to deal with things differently. You need to be making friends, Marcus, not enemies."

"Why do you even care? It's not as though we're mates or anything."

"Well, maybe we could be friends?"

"That's the gayest thing I've ever heard, Pelling."

There was no malice in his statement and I guess most sixteen-year-olds would consider it a fairly lame thing to say.

"Fair point. But can I assume that neither of us want a re-run of this?"

"Not really, no," he sighs.

"Good. Come tomorrow, I'll go about my life like this never happened. You keep out of my way, and I'll keep out of yours. There's not long left until the end of term so we won't have to avoid one another for long."

My work here is done. Maybe it didn't go quite as I'd hoped, but considering how bleak the outlook was when I left Marcus's house, it's not a bad result. Whether he accepts any of my advice remains to be seen, but I won't be around to find out, at least not for three decades. Maybe he'll come to terms with his sexuality sooner than he would have done, or maybe he'll just bury it deeper so nobody else can discover his secret. Not my problem.

"Are you going to be okay getting home?"

I suspect whatever remains of his pride will only allow him to answer my question one way. He stands up and takes a couple of tentative steps away from the bench.

"I'm fine, you didn't hit me that hard, Pelling. I'll be right as rain come tomorrow."

"Okay, I'll see you around."

He nods and ambles away towards the far end of the embankment and the gentler slope leading down to the road. His gait suggests he's still in pain, but he's trying hard not to show it.

I stand and watch him shuffle down the road. If all goes according to plan, it will be the last time I ever see Marcus Morrison.

3

For all the benefits of the Internet, it has ruined nostalgia. Toys, fashion, music, TV shows — every childhood memory digitalised and regurgitated through social media, to the point where there are no more forgotten moments. I remember once watching an episode of 'Roobarb & Custard' on a VHS cassette at a friend's house, several years before the Internet invaded our lives. The picture was grainy, and the sound terrible, but it didn't matter. It had been over twenty years since I'd last seen my favourite childhood cartoon, and it was a magical moment. Now I can open YouTube on my phone and watch every episode of 'Roobarb & Custard', or 'Mr Ben', or 'Captain Pugwash', or 'Hong Kong Phooey'. Nostalgic memories should deliver surprise and delight, but thanks to the Internet, they're now so ubiquitous that there's no surprise, and therefore no delight.

With Marcus sorted and an hour to spare before I'm due home for Sunday lunch, I've decided to indulge in some tangible nostalgia. After a ten minute stroll and a visit to Patels' Newsagent, I now possess a Texan Bar and a can of Quatro; two of my favourite childhood treats that are long-gone from the shop shelves in my day.

I find a bench a few hundred yards from the shop and sit down to indulge in my retro brunch. I open the can of Quatro and take a hesitant sip. The whole shtick behind the Quatro name was that it combined four fruit flavours: pineapple, orange, passion fruit and grapefruit. All I can taste is a sickly, sugary brew of chemicals that bears little resemblance to actual fruit. I put the can down on the bench and take a large bite of my Texan Bar. Stripped of its childhood allure, I'm left with some extremely chewy toffee and an aching jaw. I can't help feeling somewhat underwhelmed. That's the problem with childhood memories I guess — everything is tinged with a fuzzy hue of sentimentality, clouding the reality. At the end of the day, it's just junk food.

With the nostalgic illusion broken, I head home, dropping the nearly full can of Quatro and the Texan Bar into a bin on the way.

I arrive home about fifteen minutes before lunch is due to be served. I unlock the front door, and rather than the stench of cigarette smoke, I'm greeted by the aroma of roast beef and Yorkshire puddings. I kick my trainers off and head straight to the kitchen where my mum is carving the joint, and my dead grandmother is stirring a pan on the hob. My equally dead grandfather is sat at the kitchen table, reading the newspaper.

For a few seconds my brain can't process what I'm seeing. My maternal grandparents died over two decades ago, but now they're a few feet away from me, living and breathing. In the last twenty-four hours I've focused so much on fixing my life, it never crossed my mind that there are people here, in my past, who are long-gone from my future. It's as much as I can do to stand on jelly legs and stare, my mouth agape, while the kitchen walls close in on me.

I never knew my dad's parents, not that they were really my biological grandparents, anyway. His father died before I was born, and his mother when I was only three. George and Alice are the only grandparents I've ever had in my life, and we were exceptionally close. My gran was everything my mother was, and my granddad everything my dad wasn't. The day they died was by far the worst of my life. I don't know if I should feel ashamed for feeling it, but it was far worse than hearing Megan had lost our unborn baby. These were real people who had been part of my life for as long as I could remember, and suddenly they were gone, for good.

Looking back, it was my first real experience of bereavement, and I don't think I ever came to terms with their deaths, not properly. For weeks, months and even years after they died, I still had moments when, without warning, the stark reality they had gone would hit me. A moment when you wanted to share, to talk, or just to sit with them. A moment you needed a hug, a kindly word, or just a smile. Gone. Eventually you do adjust, and in some way it's easier, less painful, to bury the memories. I hadn't forgotten my grandparents, but I'd locked them away in a distant part of my mind where their memory couldn't hurt me. Maybe it's a cowardly thing to do, but it was pure self-preservation, a way to stop the hurt turning up unannounced. They were always there, just never close enough to encroach upon my conscious day-to-day thoughts.

Now, stood motionless in the doorway of our kitchen, I can feel twenty-two years of bottled-up emotion about to be uncorked. My shield of self-preservation isn't designed to withstand a reality where I sit down to Sunday lunch with my grandparents once more. Why would it?

"You've forgotten, haven't you sweetheart?"

Mum's voice breaks through the noise in my head but my mouth won't function. The best I can do is let my face convey my confusion.

"You've forgotten your grandparents were coming for lunch — I told you on Friday when you got home from school. What are we going to do with you, eh?"

My Gran turns away from the hob and wipes her hands on a tea towel.

"Don't be standing there like a lemon, young man. Come and give me a hug."

Somehow my brain sends a message to my legs and I shuffle forward towards the tiny frame of my gran. Growing impatient at my hesitancy, Gran takes a few steps forward and suddenly we're stood in front of one another in the centre of the kitchen. The cork pops and I fling my arms around my gran, burying my head in her shoulder. Her curly grey hair brushes my cheek as I inhale lilac and cotton. The times I have wished, begged for this moment again. Hundreds, thousands of times, knowing it could never be. Any effort to maintain constraint is futile and tears stream. I become oblivious to my surroundings, to the people stood watching a teenage boy smothering his grandmother, who herself must be bewildered by my emotional outburst.

Gran eventually unpeels herself from my embrace because I can't let go. She lifts her hand to my cheek, sweeping a tear away with her thumb. As she looks up at me, her green eyes dart across my face.

"Darling, what's the matter?"

My granddad has left his chair at the table and is now stood a few feet to my side, seemingly just as puzzled by my behaviour as everyone else in the room. I now feel incredibly self-conscious as my mum, and both grandparents, stare at me with some concern.

"I...I...err, had a bad dream last night. I thought you and Granddad had died," I stutter.

Considering the circumstances, it's a better explanation than I would have credited myself for. If I'd been a forty-six-year old man standing here, blubbering away because of a bad dream, it's an excuse that would

285

never have washed. As a hormonal teenager, I think it's just about plausible.

My granddad drapes a reassuring arm across my shoulder.

"You've nowt to worry about lad, we're not planning on going anywhere for a while yet, are we love?"

Just hearing his broad Yorkshire accent again almost brings more tears. He left the county of his birth over forty years ago, to build a life with my gran, but his accent remains a badge of honour. For years after his death, I would turn the TV over if I heard anyone talking with a Yorkshire dialect. I couldn't bear to hear it. Now it's the sweetest sound.

"Course we're not, silly," Gran smiles at me.

"See, your gran and I are in fine fettle, least we will be once we've got some lunch in us. Come sit down and we'll have a catch up."

He guides me over to the table and we sit down. I try to compose myself, at least externally. My inner turbulence shows no sign of abating.

I sit in a trance while Granddad natters away. It's all I can do to offer an occasional mumbled reply or a nod. Mum and Gran are busying themselves preparing lunch, accompanied on the radio by the Country & Western crooner Jim Reeves. The normality of a typical Sunday lunch, no different to millions of families across the land. Well, maybe slightly different inasmuch that I'm about to dine with two dead grandparents, sat beside a mother and father who are currently both younger than me. Perfectly normal.

I need to take five minutes to get my head together.

"Sorry Granddad, just need to pop to the loo."

"Okay lad, don't forget to wash those hands."

I get up from the table, give him a nod and head upstairs.

I close the bathroom door behind me and lean against the sink for a few moments, drawing deep breaths. The shock of seeing my grandparents is ebbing away, but not before it kicked open the door to memories I had safely locked away — and behind that door is nothing but hurt. This should be a special moment; who hasn't dreamt of spending just a few more hours with somebody taken from them? Nobody ever gets to live that dream but I do. So why can't I see beyond the pain which is welling inside me? Why can't I take this blessing and be happy for a few hours?

Because my pain is fuelled by anger. Unresolved, latent anger.

People die. Mothers, fathers, brothers, sisters, grandparents. It's the only certainty in life. My grandparents were in their mid-seventies when they died so it shouldn't have been such a huge shock. However, most couples their age aren't taken together in one cruel moment. They float away slowly, one first, then the other. You can't bear it, but you can just about accept it. Maybe you get to say goodbye to them. Maybe they tell you they're happy to have lived such a long and fulfilling life. Maybe they tell you not to grieve because they're ready to go. I was never afforded any such words to take comfort from. I was in the car park at RolpheTech when my not-altogether sensitive father told me my grandparents were dead. I will never forget that day.

Tuesday 13th September 1994.

A man by the name of John Williamson is driving his thirty-two ton truck along a dual carriageway when he reaches for his pack of cigarettes. The pack slips and falls to the floor of the cab, so Williamson scans the floor to locate it. He takes his eyes off the road for no more than five seconds, but it's sufficient time for his truck to travel over one hundred and thirty yards. Locating the pack, Williamson plucks it from the floor and looks up just in time to see the brake lights of my grandparents' stationary Ford Orion in the lane ahead of him. He slams his foot down hard on the brake pedal but the momentum of the huge truck carries it a further sixty yards until it strikes the rear end of my grandparents' car with unimaginable force. Sandwiched between the rear end of a National Express coach and Williamson's oncoming truck, the Orion is obliterated beyond recognition. My grandparents are killed instantly, along with three people on the coach. A further nine people are left with life-changing injuries. Williamson escapes with a broken collarbone and mild lacerations to his face.

He served three years of a five year prison sentence before alcoholism and guilt pushed him under a train eight months later. Those five seconds in that truck eventually claimed the lives of six people and left an indelible scar on countless others. No matter what I achieve this weekend that one cataclysmic event in 1994 will still happen. I can't let my grandparents leave like that again. I won't carry that anger or that pain again. I won't sit and watch my poor mother fall to pieces. Whatever pain I went through, it was far worse for her. She came close to a complete mental breakdown. It took nearly a year to gain anything of her old self back, but even then she still carried the deepest scars.

I have to find a way to stop my grandparents being on that road on that day.

My mind churns with analytical fury. In an ideal world I'd track down John Williamson and happily kill him. One life for five seems a fair exchange, but it's not possible within my limited time, even if I believed I was capable of killing a man. No, my solution will need to be simple and I need to implement it within the next few hours.

I splash my face with cold water and let the cogs continue to turn. Ideas are seeded, then quickly dismissed. Think Craig, think. I could just tell my grandparents not to get in their car on that day, but it's such a ridiculous request and even if they happened to remember my prophetic advice in eight years' time, I doubt they'd heed it. Shit, this is impossible. How on earth do you convince somebody you know the exact date and circumstances in which they'll die? If somebody claimed that they knew when I was due to clock-out, I'd assume they were a charlatan, or a lunatic. I'd treat their warning with the same contempt as an email from an exiled Nigerian Finance Minister, offering to drop a few million dollars into my bank account for a modest processing fee. The fact of the matter is that it's just totally unbelievable. The only possible way such a statement would be credible is if the words came from a Priest or...

An idea.

I turn it over for a while and consider any flaws. Maybe one or two, but they can be addressed. I dry my face on a towel and push the idea further. Could it really work? It's got as good a chance as anything else I've considered. I look at my youthful face in the bathroom mirror and concur with my reflection that our idea is workable.

Now I have something to work with, I need to pull myself together so I can enjoy the next few hours. It pains me to accept it, but even if my plan works, it's unlikely my grandparents will still be alive in my future. They'd both be a few years short of a century by then, way past the average age most people live to. The only certainty I have is that we're together now, and for what remains of the afternoon. Tomorrow might be uncertain, but today is a gift. Time to unwrap it.

4

Religion, politics and sex. Worthy subjects for a discussion in a pub with friends, but not ideal for a family lunch. Mercifully, Gran has never sought my mother's opinion on the reverse cowgirl position, and as we're all cut from the same religious cloth, it's not a subject to prompt serious debate. However, when it comes to politics, the old man and Granddad have polar opposite alliances, and views to match.

To look at my Granddad, you'd think he'd just stepped off the set of a Werther's Original advert. His portly frame is decked in a navy cardigan over a checked shirt, mustard-coloured cords, and tan leather brogues. His head of white hair caps a kindly face, with rosy cheeks and twinkling blue eyes. But beneath that genial veneer lurks some militant left-wing views. He grew up in a Yorkshire mining town that was hit hard when the pit closed by order of Thatcher's Government. Conversely, the old man is a staunch Conservative and Thatcher is his hero. As long as I can remember, our Sunday lunches have descended into both men squabbling over their political differences.

Not today it would seem.

It's clear within a few minutes of sitting down for lunch that Granddad is ready to commence battle. He stabs a whole roast potato with his fork and waves it around while delivering his opening salvo about the strong Labour results in last month's local elections. I look across at the old man and it's clear he's trying desperately not to retaliate, to keep up his good behaviour. He smiles politely through gritted teeth while

Granddad continues to push his agenda. I do feel for the old man and decide to interject.

"Granddad, what do you think of this new M25 motorway opening?"

While trying to ignore Keith Harris on the TV yesterday, I read an article in the paper about the M25. It's due to be officially opened later this year, and the article contained a timeline of the project history, together with some useful facts I could use to steer the conversation away from politics.

"A white elephant if you ask me. What's wrong with the current inner ring road? It's just another example of this Tory government wasting taxpayers' money."

"But wasn't the project first endorsed back in the 1960s by the Greater London Council, under Labour leadership?"

I didn't mean to undermine him but I couldn't help myself. He fumbles for an answer while a mile-wide grin spreads across the old man's face. For a second I catch his eye. He shoots me a look I can honestly say I've never seen before; a look of pride. As pleasing as it is to gain the old man's approval, I need to put Granddad out of his misery so I move the conversation along.

"Anyway, you don't think it's a worthwhile project then, Granddad?"

"No I don't. Mark my words lad, twenty years' time and they'll be ripping it up. No bugger will use it."

I offer a sage nod as if to agree with him. He couldn't be more wrong but I let him have the final word.

With Granddad seemingly not keen to engage in any further political discussion, we finish our lunch with nothing more than banal small talk. The roast is followed by a homemade trifle for pudding, which we annihilate with gusto. Mum and Gran then chat away about cake recipes while they do the dishes. Granddad and the old man retire to the garden to bore one another witless on the subject of perennial plants. I offer to make the tea as it's preferable to joining in with either conversation.

Mum and Gran make light work of the untidy kitchen while I fill the teapot with boiling water and assemble the cups and saucers on a tray. Once the kitchen is shipshape, and the tea is brewing, the three of us head out to the garden. I place the tray down on a small patio table and everyone takes a seat while I pour the stewed tea. It's been a long time since I made tea in a pot with proper leaves and I've clearly underestimated the water to leaf ratio. Keen not to dampen my enthusiasm for helping out with such chores, nobody complains.

We spend the next few hours sat in the garden chatting away. I'd usually avoid this part of my grandparents' visit and retreat to my bedroom, but that's not going to happen today. I want to make the most of every minute of their company. My only frustration is that I have to play the part of my sixteen year-old self. There are moments of my life I desperately want to share with them, and several times throughout the afternoon I almost blurt out something yet to happen. There is so much to say, to catch up on, but so little I can actually talk about. In the end, I spend most of our time together sat quietly listening to my grandparents chatter away. But it's more than enough for me, and no matter what comes of this weekend, it's a few hours I will savour for the rest of my days.

Before I know it, four o'clock rolls around and it's time for them to depart. Granddad plays bowls every Sunday and kick-off, or whatever it is they do to start a bowls match, is in an hour's time. The five of us stand on the driveway next to the old man's Cavalier. Parked across the road is a silver, nearly new Ford Orion — destined to carry my grandparents on their final journey when they leave this life for the next. I'm surprised I never spotted it when I arrived home earlier, but it's such a common, unremarkable car, it's easy to miss — particularly if you happen to be driving a thirty-two ton truck.

Mum and Dad say their goodbyes before Gran steps forward and gives me a hug. The last hug I'll ever receive from her. This is the goodbye I never got to say before, and I struggle to keep my emotions in check. Tears begin to well and I draw in huge gulps of air to quell the convulsions brewing in my stomach. I summon just enough composure to whisper a few words.

"Love you Gran."

"And I love you too sweetie, so very much," she whispers back, as she tightens her grip on me.

I bite down hard on my bottom lip, the pain a distraction from the hollow ache in my chest. I reluctantly break our embrace, which has already passed the point of being socially acceptable. As Gran steps away, Granddad moves in and puts his arms around me, his hand on the back of my head. I rest my chin on his shoulder and breath in the subtle traces of patchouli and sandalwood from his favoured aftershave.

"Don't worry about us lad, it was just a silly dream. We'll see you as usual in a few weeks' time, I promise you that."

He's right that he will see me, just not this version of me. In a few weeks' time, I'll be thirty years away and I doubt he'll be there. He pats me on the back and we break apart. With a final goodbye, they set off across the street to their car. Mum and Dad give them a wave and head back inside. I stand and watch their silver Ford Orion make its way down our road until they're out of sight. I head straight up to my bedroom and collapse on the bed. I'm glad my parents are in the garden and can't hear me crying.

It takes me almost thirty minutes to pull myself together and focus on what I've got to do in the next seven hours and twenty-five minutes. My plans for the afternoon have been completely shot due to my grandparents' unexpected visit. Couple that with the additional task I've now got to complete and I need to get my backside in gear. The time I have left is precious, and I can't afford to waste any more of it on self-pity. I dash to the bathroom, take a leak, and wash my tear-stained face. I hurry downstairs and poke my head around the door to the garden, where my parents are still sat.

"I've got to sort out some homework with Dave. Do you mind if I skip tea?"

"That's all right love, we were thinking about going out for a drive, anyway. Come back whenever you're ready and I'll make you a sandwich," Mum replies.

I skip the kiss this time and leave them to it.

I break into a slight jog as I make my way through the estate. It's such a liberating experience travelling in a fit young body, yet to be wrecked by excessive alcohol and fast food consumption. When it's this easy, I can almost see why people enjoy jogging. From the one-and-only attempt I've made to get fit in recent years, I can vouch that it's not so much fun when you're an overweight, uncoordinated, wheezing lump. Such is the irony of exercise — those who need it the most are the least capable of performing it.

I lie to myself that maybe I'll try again when I return to the future.

I reach the edge of the estate in just a few minutes, and dart across the main road towards the shops. My destination is a small terraced house situated in a back street not far from the Rendezvous Cafe. It was in the cafe nine years ago that my mum first met Aunt Judy, although she was just plain Judy back then. I was about seven years old when Judy received her 'aunt' status. She had all the hallmarks of becoming a spinster, so Mum thought that being allocated a nephew by proxy would make her feel better about her childless existence. I've always thought she was a bit of a loon, but for the purposes of my plan to save my grandparents, she's the perfect stooge.

Two minutes later, I'm stood outside Aunt Judy's tatty terraced house and knock on the weather-beaten front door. A wind-chime above my head catches a breeze and clangs random metallic notes as if to signal my arrival. As I wait for the door to be opened, I run through my plan one more time to ensure I've got every base covered. I have to admit, it's a long shot and not without its risks, but with no other options open to me, I've got little other choice than to try.

The door opens, no going back now.

"Hello darling, what a lovely surprise," Aunt Judy beams.

She's dressed in a style best described as Bohemian bag lady. Today's outfit is a psychedelic patterned skirt, and sage-green blouse layered beneath a crocheted pink cardigan. Although she's only a few years older than my mum, Aunt Judy's fondness for cigarettes and stubborn refusal to use skincare products have jointly taken their toll on her face. It would better fit a woman ten years her senior. Her long hair, once jet black, is now the colour of clouds, and her blue eyes have long-since lost their youthful lustre.

Such is the extent of Aunt Judy's oddball nature, she developed Alzheimer's disease in 2007 and nobody noticed for almost a year. At this moment in time, if I recall, she would best be described as mildly eccentric. In fairness, she has never shown me anything other than kindness, but as I got older, I realised her eccentricities were a symptom of some fairly delusional beliefs. I guess if you live your life with a completely open mind, at some point it becomes a little overcrowded, a little noisy.

"Hi Aunt Judy. Sorry to drop by unannounced, but I was wondering if I could have a chat with you about something?"

"Of course you can, come on in."

She leads me through a cramped, dingy hallway to her front room. The air is thick with the smell of spiced incense and possibly marijuana although I don't see any physical evidence to suggest Aunt Judy is a pot head. It might explain a lot though. Her taste for interior design is as disjointed as her fashion sense. The walls of the room are painted in a deep shade of purple and the ceiling duck-egg blue. A huge Matisse print dominates the space above the tiled fireplace while the other walls hold shelves laden with books, and pieces of low-budget art. Hippy-chic meets Victorian brothel.

We sit down on a threadbare sofa and I decline Aunt Judy's offer of herbal tea. The springs below the thin cushion jab at my buttocks as I twist to face her. She asks me a few polite questions about how things are going at school before getting to the point.

"So what is it you wanted to chat about?"

"Well, it's a little awkward, really. It's not something I can talk to Mum or Dad about, but I know you've got more of an open mind."

"This isn't about...you know, bedroom stuff, is it Craig?" she asks with a concerned frown.

"God, no. It's about a dream I had."

"That's a relief. I'm the last person you want to discuss that sort of thing with."

"Right...well, err, about this dream."

"Sorry darling, go on."

"You might think I'm crazy, but I had this dream last night, and I saw my grandparents die in a road accident. It was so real and so detailed that I think it was more than just a dream. Is that possible?"

It's a leading question. Aunt Judy is a true believer, which is why I'm here. She is obsessed with tarot cards, ouija boards, fortune telling, astrology, clairvoyance and just about anything you could label as otherworldly. She is so passionate about such things that sometimes her views seem almost plausible. My hope is that I can convince her my dream was real and she'll then deliver that information to my mother. Mum has always been fairly open-minded to Aunt Judy's views and I think she'll believe her. She is far more likely to heed a prophetic warning from Aunt Judy than me that's for sure.

She casually replies to my question.

"Sure, it's possible for some gifted people to see future events in their dreams, but it's very rare Craig, very rare indeed. What those people see is more of a prophecy than a dream. I suspect that what you experienced was nothing more than a vivid nightmare. I'd just forget about it if I were you. I'm positive your grandparents will be just fine."

Aunt Judy smiles at me, seemingly happy she's allayed my fears. Fuck, she didn't take the bait. I thought she'd jump on this and my plan would drop into place with very little effort on my part. I now have to revert to a strategy I really didn't want to adopt, but she's left me with no other choice.

"Actually, the bit about my grandparents, it's only half the dream."

She drapes an arm across the back of the sofa and moves a fraction closer to me.

"Okay, I'm intrigued. What was the other half of your dream about?"

"That was about you. You were in my dream too."

"Oh, really? And what was I doing in this dream of yours?"

"You were running away."

"And what was I running away from, darling?"

Judging by her sympathetic smile and the breezy nature of her questioning, I get the feeling she's humouring me. She isn't making the connection I want her to make. I need to be a little more blatant.

"A man in dirty green overalls was chasing you."

The smile disappears from her face almost as quickly as the colour in her cheeks. She gulps down hard and stares at me with wide-eyed horror.

"What did you say?" she says slowly.

"In my dream, you were running. A man in green overalls was chasing you. I think you locked yourself in a room, a dark room, to hide from him."

I hate myself for doing this, but there is no other way.

5

Aunt Judy gets up from the sofa and stumbles across the room to the fireplace. Her hands reach for the mantelpiece and she slides a metal tin from behind a picture frame and opens it. She takes out a hand-rolled cigarette and lifts it to her lips with a shaky hand. The same shaky hand then takes a match and strikes it against a matchbox. She lifts it towards the tip of the cigarette and pulls a large drag. A plume of smoke spreads across the room and judging by the smell, I suspect there's more than tobacco wrapped in that cigarette paper. Whatever she's smoking, it has the desired calming effect, and she turns back to me.

"Do you remember anything else, Craig? It's important."

What I remember is that in the mid-90s, a scandal involving the local girls' school was uncovered. For almost two decades between 1950 and 1969, the caretaker, a piece of work called Harold Duffy, was accused of systematically abusing girls in the school. The abuse was only brought to light when a former pupil died and her husband read her childhood diaries. Extracts from those diaries made it to the national papers and before long, dozens of other women came forward to share their horrific tales of abuse at the hands of Duffy. One of those women was my Aunt Judy.

Like many predatory paedophiles, Harold Duffy was calculating and controlling when it came to hiding his abuse. Girls were threatened with all manner of unpalatable consequences if they told a soul about what he'd done to them. He made it clear he would watch them forever, long beyond their schooldays, to ensure they kept their silence. Duffy was a truly evil piece of shit.

Fortunately for Duffy but not so for the justice system, he died in 1992, a few years before his vile crimes hit the headlines. However, anyone and everyone who had any association with the school during his years of paedophilia was brought to account. Teachers, governors, support staff; everyone who was still alive was tarnished by association, just because they worked in the school at the same time as Duffy. Such was the frustration at the inability to punish the perpetrator, the whole thing descended into a witch-hunt in the national media and within the education system. How could he have conducted his vile acts for so long without anyone knowing? Did he have any accomplices? Were allegations made at the time but swept under the carpet? The sordid, accusatory dialogue continued in the newspapers for months, impossible to forget for those of us looking on, let alone the poor souls who had their wounds reopened.

And this is my shameful last resort. As I sit here in 1986, Harold Duffy is still very much alive and the only people aware of his dirty secret are his victims, and me. It's an odious hand to play but the only feasible way I can convince Aunt Judy that my dream was really prophetic and not just the vivid imagination of a teenage boy.

"I remember there were other girls in the room with you, I think. It's difficult to remember clearly. The man in the green overalls, he was balding and had a small moustache. I can still see his chubby face and round glasses, like John Lennon wore."

Duffy's distinctive face wasn't easy to forget. Like the bearded face of The Yorkshire Ripper in the 70s, it was everywhere in the media and they always used a photo of Duffy from the period when his crimes were committed, rather than an image of him in later years. I guess it was considered more emotive to view the face of a man in the midst of his abominable crimes rather than a sad old man who could pass for someone's grandfather.

Aunt Judy takes another deep drag on her cigarette and sits back down on the edge of the sofa.

"Listen to me carefully, Craig, I don't think it was a dream. I think you may have some insight into things that not even I understand. I don't want you to be scared but we need to get as much detail about your dream as we can. Can you do that for me?"

I spend the next twenty minutes telling her about my grandparents' accident, trying not to dwell too much about what happened at the school.

"You see why I couldn't discuss this with my parents? There is no way they'd believe me."

"I see that now. You did the right thing coming to see me but I need you to do something. I need you to promise you will never discuss the part of your dream about the man in overalls with anyone...ever. Make that promise for me and I promise I'll convince your mum she needs to keep her parents off the road on that date."

"How will you do that?"

Aunt Judy looks towards the ceiling and closes her eyes as if trying to calm whatever turmoil I've unleashed. She takes deep, deliberate breaths before opening her eyes and turning to face me.

"I'll invite her for a tarot card reading. Your mum has an open mind on these things and with all the details you've given me, I'm sure I can convince her I've seen what will happen to your grandparents."

Clearly still shaken, she repeats her offer of herbal tea but doesn't wait for a reply. She disappears from the room and returns five minutes later with two white mugs which she places on a small coffee table. Her eyes look puffy and the colour still hasn't returned to her cheeks. I just want to get out of here but it seems unfair to drop this bombshell and casually walk away from the carnage. I pick up one of the mugs and take a sip of the tea which has a peculiar green hue. It tastes every bit as bad as it looks. Aunt Judy sits back down on the sofa with her elbows resting on her thighs, holding her mug in both hands and staring blankly into space. The silence in the room is excruciating.

She seems almost oblivious to my presence as I sit and wonder what horrors I've disturbed in her already fragile mind. Or maybe her mind is fragile because of those horrors. Either way, I really didn't think through the full implications of this plan.

"Are you okay, Aunt Judy?"

She nods with a weak smile. She clearly isn't okay, I need to do some damage limitation.

"The man in my dream, you know who it is?"

She stares back into nothing.

"Aunt Judy?"

"Yes," she murmurs.

"There might be something else, something I've just remembered about him in my dream."

She stares at me with a look somewhere between curiosity and panic.

"It must have been one of the last things I dreamt before I woke up but the man, he wasn't chasing you. He was the one in the dark room and he was much older. He looked broken, pathetic, all hunched up like he was in constant pain."

Duffy would be in his early eighties by now and even if there was any substance to his threats, I seriously doubt he's in any fit state to follow through on them. I need her to forget the man who abused her and concentrate on the feeble octogenarian enjoying his liberty somewhere.

"And you were stood outside the room with a group of girls. You all seemed to be happy, smiling. I remember that too."

A flash of hope crosses Aunt Judy's face.

"What was the room like? Can you describe it?"

"It's difficult; it was dark so I couldn't make out much detail. I guess it was a bit like a prison cell."

She sits back in the chair and seems to process my revelation. I need her to make the connection, to realise that Duffy is no longer a threat and there is still time for him to face justice before he dies. Whatever he did to her and those other poor girls, now is the time to let her voice be heard. I know for sure that in ten years' time when she finds the resolve to tell the police about her abuse, Duffy will be dead, along with her final chance of closure.

"You said the man looked really old?"

"Yeah, really old, and his overalls had changed colour too. They were a light grey colour."

"And there were other girls outside the room?"

"Lots of them."

She lifts her hand and strokes her chin for a moment, deep in thought.

"His name is Harold Duffy, the man in your dream."

I feign surprise.

"Really? So who is he?"

"Let's just say he's a man I'd rather have forgotten about. He's a bad person, Craig."

"I got that impression when I first saw his face. But at the end of the dream he didn't look that bad, he looked old and scared, properly terrified. Is he old like that now, like in my dream?"

"I guess he would be. I'm not sure how old but your description could be about right, I suppose."

"And do you think that room could be a prison cell?"

The slightest upward movement of her left eyebrow suggests that she is considering my vision as a possible reality. For decades she's been running scared from the middle-aged version of Harold Duffy, but that man is long gone.

"Maybe it could be, darling, maybe."

I can only hope I've done enough to push her over the line.

Much to my relief, the change in Aunt Judy's demeanour from when I first shared my prophecy is obvious. Maybe I have inadvertently helped her to deal with her past and finally seek solace. Or more likely, maybe I'm just trying to justify my actions so I can cleanse my conscience of guilt. I don't know if I've done her any favours but I guess it could have turned out much worse, such is her unpredictable personality. Even if all I've done is sown a few seeds of hope, surely Aunt Judy is in a better place now than when I arrived? Most importantly though, there is now some hope that my grandparents won't be meeting the front end of John Williamson's truck in eight years' time. Whatever dormant fears I may have released in Aunt Judy's mind, I have to weigh that up against the premature death of my grandparents and the anguish that awaits my family, and my future self. I have to believe I've done the right thing.

We sit for a few more minutes and I politely sip my herbal tea, hoping the slight grimace on my face isn't obvious. I get the distinct feeling Aunt Judy wants to be on her own so I oblige and she sees me to the front door.

"Thank you for coming by, and for trusting me with this. I won't let you down."

"Thanks Aunt Judy. Are you okay though? I didn't mean to upset you."

"I'm fine, just a few things on my mind I've been putting off for far too long."

"Can I ask one other thing?"

She nods hesitantly. Her face bears a look that suggests she doesn't want to hear any more of my revelations or questions.

"I was thinking that maybe it's better if we don't discuss this ever again. Obviously it's painful for you, and to be honest, the dream scared the hell out of me so the sooner I forget about it, the better."

She smiles, perhaps relieved.

"I think that would be very sensible indeed, darling. You have my word I'll never mention it again, not to you, not to anyone."

"But you'll definitely tell Mum about my grandparents?"

"Of course. Don't worry about her, I've got that covered."

She gives me a pat on the arm and stands at the door while I walk away. After twenty yards I turn around but she's gone back inside. She still has over thirty years left on this planet so maybe there is time for her to heal her wounds and move forward. I assume that she'll still have passed away when I return to my timeline, but I hope I discover that Aunt Judy and her fellow victims finally managed to bring Duffy to account. Selfishly though, my greater hope is that I find my grandparents were never killed in a horrific road accident. I've done my part — it's now all down to Aunt Judy.

6

In around ten months from now, a man from Radio Rentals will deliver and install a video cassette recorder in our home. A silver box the size of a small suitcase and more complicated to program than the Hubble Space Telescope. Still, it revolutionised the way we watched films and TV. I remember the day with such excitement, not least because it meant I could bring home films to watch from my job at Video City. Joining the revolution in home entertainment came at a price though. I was too young to sign a rental agreement so the old man had reluctantly agreed to sign it on the strict understanding I paid the monthly rental every month, or I faced eviction from the family home. However, when I think back to how many films I watched for free, it was a small price to pay.

As I stroll along Eton Drive towards my destination, I have yet to take delivery of that video player or start my job at Video City. With the tampering of my timeline over the course of this weekend, it should be a certainty I never will work at Video City. That doesn't mean I can't do a favour for one of my former, or is that future employers? Either way, it's a man who gave me a lifeline when I was at absolute rock-bottom. As terrible as my life might have seemed post-Tessa, it would have been a lot worse if Malcolm Franklin hadn't offered me a job. I owe him one.

I have to admit that I've only given this part of my day the minimum of thought. In the big scheme of things it doesn't make one jot of difference to me. There isn't anything to be lost if my makeshift plan doesn't work. The encounters I've had with Tessa, my dad, Marcus, my grandparents and Aunt Judy have taken their toll and I don't think I can handle any more conflict or emotional turmoil. My work here is done so whatever happens from this point onwards is inconsequential; at least I assume it is.

I reach Video City a little before six o'clock and stand outside for a moment. This was my place of work for over four years and as jobs go, it was pretty cushy with little pressure, no ambitious colleagues and no career-driven boss overseeing my every move. Perhaps I spent too long working at Video City for my own good. Did I really do everything I could to find a better job? Possibly, but I'm not sure.

I push the door open, step into the store and do a quick scan of my surroundings. A guy in his early twenties is browsing the videos in the sci-fi section off to my left and a woman with a young child is stood waiting impatiently at the counter. Little ever changed in all the time I worked here and the only obvious sign that this is the version of Video City before my employment is the lack of a computer on the counter. There's no sign of Malcolm so I assume he's out the back trying to locate a video with the aid of his antiquated card system.

I need to catch Malcolm on his own so I saunter over to the left side of the store and peruse the videos in the comedy section while I wait for both the customers to leave. Within a minute, the guy browsing the sci-fi section huffs a sigh, and seemingly disappointed with the videos on offer, leaves the store empty-handed. I continue to browse the meagre pickings in the comedy section when I hear Malcolm's wheezy voice as he returns from the back of the store to deal with the woman at the counter. It's a voice I haven't heard in a long, long time.

After he sold the store, Malcolm became a lost soul. While he had money in the bank from the sale of the store, he'd lost the two things that provided any purpose to his life. He apparently had no appetite to start his Star Wars collection again, and with little chance of employment, he fell into an apathetic malaise. Then one day, eighteen months after he sold Video City, he met Mali Surat at a car boot sale.

She was thirty years his junior and a Thai national in desperate need of a British husband, or more accurately, a British passport. It was obvious to Megan and me that Mari was playing Malcolm to secure citizenship but he was smitten and wouldn't listen to our warnings. They married within four months but then to everyone's surprise, the Home Office declined Mali's application for a visa. We suspected it was because of something dodgy in her past but again, our concerns fell upon deaf ears. She was given a few weeks to leave the country, at which point Malcolm announced he was selling his flat and moving to Pattaya in Thailand where they intended to buy a bar together. It was one of those situations where everyone looking on could see that Malcolm was being taken for a ride, but he was so happy, so in love, that logic and common sense never came into the equation.

True to his word, Malcolm left the UK within three weeks, having sold his flat for significantly less than it was worth to secure a quick sale. With a healthy bank balance and Mali on his arm, Malcolm waved goodbye to Megan and me as we stood outside the terminal at Heathrow airport. We would never see him again.

For the first few months, Malcolm would write to us every week but as the months went by, the letters became less frequent and the content strangely curt. It was almost as if the words on the page were being dictated by somebody whose first language wasn't English. Just beyond the first anniversary of his move, the letters stopped altogether. As our concerns grew, we discussed what we could do to establish if Malcolm was okay. Those discussions came to an abrupt halt the day we received a visit from Megan's parents. They solemnly informed Megan that her Uncle Malcolm had died of a suspected heart attack.

Malcolm Franklin was buried in Thailand in an unmarked grave; the only mourner being Mali Surat, with her new status as a comparatively rich widow and bar owner. She robbed us of any potential inheritance and even a chance of saying a final goodbye to Malcolm. The post-mortem stated that Malcolm had died of a heart attack, and that his excessive weight was a contributory factor. He was far from a healthy weight when he left the UK but according to the post-mortem report, Malcolm had added another eighty pounds of bulk in the year leading up to his death. I'm fairly sure Mali Surat fed Malcolm to death.

It was a tragically sad end to the life of a decent man.

My reason for being here this afternoon is not to tell Malcolm to avoid Thai women, or Thai food for that matter, but to steer him along a path where neither will be the death of him.

From the corner of my eye I watch the woman grab her child by the hand and leave the store. Now it's just Malcolm and me, time to go to work. I approach the counter where Malcolm is frowning at a messy heap of index cards laid out before him. He finally looks up.

"Yes young man."

When you've known somebody for so long, it's a disconcerting feeling to look them in the eye without the lights of recognition shining back at you. The only time I've experienced such a feeling was in the last few months of Aunt Judy's life when I visited her in the care home, by which time Alzheimer's disease had stolen her memories of me. Now Malcolm is staring at me with the same vacant expression. It takes a monumental effort to maintain my composure as I stand before my old, long-since deceased, friend.

"Are you the owner?" I gulp.

"Yes I am, unless you've got a complaint," he chuckles.

"No, it's something else. I think your store is going to be burgled."

Malcolm drops the cards to the counter and folds his chubby arms. He looks at me with a doubtful expression.

"Oh really?"

"Yes, in a few weeks' time," I lied.

It will be a few years before Malcolm needs to worry about his unwanted guests but my claim will have absolutely no credibility if I tell him that.

"And how do you know?"

"I heard two blokes talking in a pub," I reply sheepishly.

This isn't sounding plausible.

"Well, all of our videos are embossed with a security seal with the store name and a message which states they are for rental only, so I doubt they'd have much value to anyone thinking of stealing them. I can honestly say I've never heard of a video store being burgled because there isn't much point."

Malcolm unfolds his arms and returns his attention to the pile of index cards.

"I don't think they're after your videos, they mentioned something about a 'collection'."

He eyes me suspiciously.

"I don't know what you're on about, son, and I'm a busy man."

"Look, I could only pick up a few words from their conversation as the pub was noisy, but I definitely heard two blokes planning to burgle this place and steal some sort of collection. But if you're a busy man, I won't waste any more of your time."

I turn to leave and manage a few steps towards the door before Malcolm calls me back.

"One second, young man."

I turn back to him and give my best impression of a teenager not giving a shit.

"I thought I was doing you a favour but if you don't believe me, I've got better things to do with my time."

We reach a stand-off before Malcolm relents.

"I'm sorry if you thought I wasn't taking you seriously. Tell me everything you heard and I promise I'll keep an open mind."

I wander back to the counter and tell Malcolm how I was sat in a pub waiting for a mate when two middle-aged men, whose improvised description might have been based upon the Chuckle Brothers, sat at the table next to me. I give him the basics of what I supposedly overheard, careful not to mention anything specific about his Star Wars memorabilia. I need to give him just enough information to realise the threat is real without saying so much I might undermine my story.

"So why come here and not go straight to the police with this?" Malcolm asks.

"Because I'm only sixteen and I was drinking illegally with a fake ID."

Malcolm nods and seems to be pondering what he can do with this information.

"You say they mentioned the lack of an alarm system here?"

"Yes. Again, I only heard bits and pieces but they seemed confident that there was no alarm system or much in the way of security."

"And they definitely mentioned a collection?"

This is becoming painstaking.

"Yes, and something about signatures if that means anything?"

It appears the penny has dropped with Malcolm finally realising that the target for the break-in is his beloved Star Wars collection and not the videos. He assumes that nobody knows about his valuable memorabilia but clearly somebody at some point will find out.

"Right, thank you. I appreciate you telling me about this. I think it might be time for me to install some security measures."

He holds out a pudgy hand and we shake, his palms as clammy as I remember.

"Just to say thank you, how about I give you ten free video rentals?"

"Thanks, but we don't have a video machine," I reply.

"Ah, okay. Let me give you something to show my gratitude though."

Before I can answer, Malcolm turns and disappears through the archway towards his office. I take the opportunity to gaze around the store for one final time. Of all the uncertainties surrounding my new future, one thing is for sure; video stores like this one will still become obsolete and eventually disappear altogether. I hope Malcolm retires before that happens.

"Are you being looked after?"

A voice so recognisable, but so unexpected, rips me from my thoughts. I spin around and stare straight into the eyes of a sixteen year-old version of my wife, although in this moment she isn't my wife, she isn't even my girlfriend. I was sure she only worked on Saturdays, and if I'd known she was here, there's no way I'd have dropped in. I didn't want to see her, let alone have any kind of interaction with her.

"Yes...yes, I am," I splutter.

Megan smiles at me, the same smile she gave me when we first met in the office at the back of the store. I feel an overwhelming yet irrational urge to jump over the counter and pull her into my arms. Considering she hasn't a clue who I am, it's not a good idea. She's wearing her trademark baggy orange t-shirt and her blonde hair is as tightly permed as I remember it. This is the girl who will eventually confess her love for me. But because of my meddling in this timeline, she'll never fall in, or out of love with me.

A torrent of conflicted feelings rain down on me. This is what I wanted, isn't it, to remove my time at Video City and therefore Megan from my life? I wanted to pass my exams, to go to college, to university. I wanted a proper career and a wife who loved me as much as I loved her. And yes, I probably wanted to be a father. But fate had decreed that none of those things were possible for Megan and me together. To be happy, we had to have different paths, different lives. Until this point I've convinced myself that my motivations weren't purely selfish and changing our future was in Megan's best interests too. If we don't get together, she won't become the girl burdened with the loss of an unborn baby or have the chance of motherhood stolen because of the miscarriage. She'll remain untainted by my presence in her life, ready to start college and embark upon a bright future, without me. Surely that has to be better for both of us than wasting twenty-five years in a sham of a marriage?

But as I stand here, I can't pretend that this doesn't feel like I've just signed my divorce papers. No matter how bad a marriage is, that act is surely always tinged with some level of regret, isn't it? It's not what I expected but a feeling of lament for the life I've now lost rises to the surface. While Megan is currently looking at me in a state of blissful ignorance, I'm trying desperately to keep myself together; to act like our twenty-five years of marriage never happened. I try to focus on just how bad our marriage became in the end but my mind will only let me remember the good times. It doesn't matter now; my actions have ensured that there will be no shared times between Megan and me, good or bad.

Noticing my dazed expression, Megan steps from behind the counter.

"Are you okay? You look like you're going to faint."

"I'm okay...just had a dizzy spell, sorry," I stammer.

She tilts her head and a look of concern spreads across her face.

"Are you sure? Can I get you a glass of water, or a chair?"

I don't want her to be nice to me. I want to remember the moody, contemptuous version of Megan who might be having an affair. I want to see the spite and the bitterness that bolstered my decision to change my future. I don't want to see a cute, thoughtful girl with a smiley face and caring eyes. I definitely don't want a glass of water or a chair, I want to get out of there and as far away from Megan as possible.

"No, thanks. I've got to go. Sorry."

Avoiding any further eye contact I keep my head low, spin around and bolt out of the store. I sprint along the street and in the vague direction of the estate until the burning in my lungs becomes unbearable. I stop and lean against a wall while I catch my breath. The burning in my lungs subsides but the regret at deciding to visit Video City remains resolute. What was I thinking? Idiot. No matter what challenges I've overcome this weekend, no matter how I may have shaped my future for the better, seeing Megan would never end well. Was it really worth the risk just so Malcolm could be sent on a different path and inevitably find another way to fuck up his life? Now all I have is a head full of doubts.

I wait until my breathing returns to normal and push myself off the wall. With my hands buried deep in my jean pockets, I slope homewards, all the while trying to banish thoughts of the teenage Megan.

7

By the time I arrive back home, Mum and Dad have finished their tea and are sat in the lounge listening to some god-awful Country & Western album on our antiquated music centre. Mum offers to make me a sandwich but I've lost my appetite so I decline her offer and head up to my bedroom. I kick my trainers off and slump down on the bed, exhausted both mentally and physically. I'd forgotten what life was like before I could drive and had to walk everywhere. On the plus side, at least I got plenty of exercise, unlike my future where I clamber into my crappy Mazda every time I need something from the local shop. Laziness again.

Beyond my exhaustion, I'm still annoyed with myself for visiting Video City. I need to find a distraction from my thoughts of Megan so I clamber off the bed and turn the stereo on. Another check of the clock on the computer — five hours and fourteen minutes remaining. As I lie back down on the bed, the voice of Bruno Brookes chirps from the speakers as he introduces 'Lessons in Love' by Level 42 as a non-mover in this week's charts. I close my eyes and immerse myself in the deep notes thumping from Mark King's bass guitar.

Before I can make a conscious decision not to, I fall fast asleep.

Considering what I've been through over the last few days, it's no surprise that my sleep is disturbed by a vexing dream. It's so vivid that I wake with a start and spend a few seconds trying to separate aspects of the dream from reality.

I was being chased through the streets, slowly it must be said, by a milk float. John Williamson was at the wheel, sat next to Harold Duffy who was laughing maniacally. I escaped their plodding pursuit and found sanctuary back at my parents' house. For some inexplicable reason I was completely indifferent to the fact that Tessa and Megan were operating a topless car wash on the driveway. I nonchalantly entered the house without a second glance at their soapy exploits. I walked into the lounge where two coffins were sat on the floor. I distinctly recall the terror of that sight and I ran straight into the garden only to find the old man pushing Marcus around the garden in a wheelbarrow. They were both naked, and singing 'It's Raining Men', badly.

However, the most troubling aspect of the dream is that at some point, I appear to have ejaculated into my underwear. Wet dreams were a common occurrence throughout my adolescent years and resulted in many a covert trip to the bathroom to rinse my jizz-stained underwear in the sink. However, it's been close to thirty years since I last awoke to sticky pants and it's not an aspect of my youth I would have chosen to relive.

I gingerly get up from the bed and pad across the landing to the bathroom, double-checking I've locked the door behind me. I hop in the bath and use the shower attachment to rinse both my genitals and the soiled pants. This is not a task any self-respecting middle-aged man should have to endure.

Feeling a little sheepish, I wrap a towel around my waist before darting back to my bedroom, holding the pair of sodden underpants in front of me like a trophy of shame. I get dressed and hide the pants on the window ledge behind a curtain, where I'm hoping they'll dry before the next washing cycle is due.

I get dressed and glance at my watch. 8.53pm. Shit, two hours lost. I suppose I should be grateful my ejaculation woke me when it did. I head downstairs and into the kitchen where Mum is just finishing her weekly baking marathon. The aroma drifting around the kitchen is beyond mouth-watering. Every Sunday evening she bakes bread, cakes and pies for consumption over the following seven days. Some baked goods are destined for the dinner table and some destined for lunchboxes, mine specifically.

"I wondered when you'd make an appearance. Did you hear me scraping the bowl?" Mum smiles.

I assume she's referring to my childhood penchant for licking remnants of raw cake mix or icing from the bowl. I'm not sure when I grew out of the habit but it's not something that particularly appeals at this precise moment.

"I'm okay thanks, Mum."

She looks at me with a raised eyebrow.

"Well, that's a first."

Trying to change the subject I ask her if she wants a cup of tea. My motivations are purely selfish as my post-nap mouth feels like the bottom of a sewer. She accepts my offer, and I put the kettle on while Mum clears up the kitchen.

"Where's Dad?" I ask.

"Oh, I told him to go down the Legion for a few hours while I do the weekly bake. He can't be trusted to keep his hands off my muffins while I'm busy in the kitchen," she says innocently.

It takes a superhuman effort not to snigger. I tell myself to grow up, which I'm certainly going to do in about three hours' time.

I pour the tea as Mum takes on the bowl licking duties herself. Using a plastic spatula, she scrapes icing from one of the bowls and then licks it clean before repeating the process.

"This is lovely. Sure you don't want some?"

I shake my head, a little perturbed at the amount of icing she's consuming with scant regard for the huge amounts of sugar it contains. Each laden spatula must contain the maximum daily sugar allowance on its own, and she's already returned to the bowl with her spatula three times. I know my mum has a sweet tooth but I also know where that will eventually lead her.

"Have you ever heard of type-2 diabetes?" I casually ask her.

"I think so. Isn't that where somebody has to inject themselves every day?"

"That's type-1 diabetes and can't be prevented. Type-2 usually happens to people when they reach middle-age and have high cholesterol or high blood pressure due to a poor diet."

"It's not a serious condition though, is it? I'm sure it's not much fun having to inject yourself every day, but it won't kill you."

"No Mum, that's not how it works with type-2 diabetes. And I think it can kill you, or at least it can do some serious damage to your body. Did you know it can cause blindness and in some cases, sufferers have limbs amputated? It's a nasty condition."

The ever-present smile on Mum's face fades, and she subconsciously drops the spatula into the bowl.

"You seem to know an awful lot about it," she says grimly.

"We've been studying it in biology."

"So how do you avoid getting it then?"

"I think it's mainly down to diet. If you eat too much sugar, salt, and fat over a prolonged period, that sort of thing."

She forces the smile back on her face.

"Well, I feel absolutely fine, sweetheart, so there's nothing to worry about."

I think she's missed the point. I brought the subject up because I want her to be worried, or at least to think about the consequences of her eating habits.

"I'm sure you're right, Mum. Might be worth keeping it in mind though. I think you'll have trouble working in the cafe after having a foot amputated."

She glares at me for a second. Perhaps I've offended her but sometimes you have to use a little tough love to get your point across. I hope this brief conversation will stick in her mind and her ignorance of the condition won't become her downfall. Maybe it's advice I should consider myself but it's always easier to preach than to practise.

I down the dregs of my tea as Mum finishes the washing-up. There isn't much in the way of conversation and I think it would be a good idea to retreat to my bedroom.

"Think I might get an early night, got a long day tomorrow."

"Okay, I'll see you in the morning," she replies with a little frostiness in her voice.

Sadly I won't be seeing her in the morning. The next time I see her she'll be an old woman but hopefully not the same old woman I left behind. I hope she takes on board my warning about the diabetes, and if the old man manages to maintain his personality change, she won't have to suffer a further thirty years of marriage to a cantankerous bastard. If my tinkering with their lives has the desired results, I should return to find both my parents have enjoyed a long, happy marriage.

With little thought to keeping up the pretence of being a teenager, I step towards her.

"Don't suppose I could have a hug?"

Mum isn't the sort of woman who can let negative feelings stew and her frown falls away. If she's still annoyed with me it's well hidden as she delivers the sort of reassuring hug only a mother can.

I give her a final kiss on the forehead and turn to leave, but not before one final thought crosses my mind.

"Do you mind if I make a quick phone call?"

"Who are you calling this time of night?"

"Just an old friend. It'll only take a minute, promise."

"Okay, just a minute, mind. You know what your dad is like checking the phone bills."

Indeed I do.

I wander through to the hallway and take a seat on the telephone bench. I pull the phone directory from a shelf below and flick through the pages until I reach the one I'm looking for. I run my finger down the column of surnames and spot who I'm after...

WADDOCK G, MR.

There is only one other Waddock listed, and that's a Mrs, so the first entry must be my former RolpheTech colleague Geoff. I pick up the receiver and dial the number using the tediously slow rotational dialler on our phone. I glance at my watch; it's now 9.28pm. Maybe a little late for an unsolicited call but I'm doing Geoff a favour so I'm sure he won't mind in the long run.

"Hello," a male voice grunts.

"Hi, is that Geoff?"

"Yeah, who's this?"

"I'm, err, Steve, I got your number from a friend of a friend."

"What friend? And you know it's late?" he snaps.

"Look Geoff, I'm on a pay phone and I haven't got any more coins so I don't have time to explain. Just listen to what I say and when I hang up, it's up to you if you act on my advice or not. There's nothing in it for me, I'm just doing a favour for a friend of a friend. Okay?"

"All right, go on," he grumbles.

"I've heard a whisper you're considering buying shares in the banking sector. Don't."

"What? I dunno where you got your information from but I'm not thinking of buying any shares."

"Maybe not soon but you might do in a few years' time. All I want to stress is that if you decide to buy shares, don't invest in the banking sector. Again, hypothetical, but if you buy any shares, buy into a company called Apple."

"The record company?"

"No, the computer company."

"Can't say I've heard of them."

"You will, and you'll be glad you brought their shares. I guarantee it."

"Right, thanks, I guess. What did you say your name was?"

"My money is running out Geoff, I've got to go."

"But you haven't told me..."

I hang up before Geoff can ask more questions I can't answer. I could have warned him about how his company will collapse or that he really shouldn't offer personal guarantees on company loans, but there is no way I could make that conversation plausible. I've given him a helping hand so hopefully he might have something left over for his retirement. It won't stop him losing his business, his home or his wife but it's the best I can do.

Satisfied that I've ended the day on a high after the incident with Megan, I clamber up the stairs and close the door of my teenage bedroom behind me for the last time. I lean back against the door and exhale a deep breath. What a fucking day that was. I shuffle over to the computer and note the countdown timer — two hours and twenty-one minutes remaining. I sit down on the plastic chair and ponder what I'm going to do to fill the time. My immediate and obvious thoughts turn to another spell of 'duvet time' with Lars and Sabine, but my wet dream earlier has somewhat sated my appetite. I think I should probably do something constructive, anyway.

After ten minutes of considering several impractical or risky options, I open the desk drawer, pull out the jotter pad I originally used for my 'Afterpath' project notes, and find a blank page at the back of the pad. I scour the drawer for a pen and find a biro with barely any ink remaining. I put my feet up on the desk and rest the jotter pad on my legs, pen poised. I've decided I'm going to write down everything I've done over the last two days so it sticks in my head. It would be a reckless waste of an impossible opportunity to let any part of this experience slip from my mind. In the last two days I've learnt more about myself, and what I'm capable of, than I managed in my previous forty-six years. It needs to be written down, to be implanted in my mind for future reference.

I start at the moment I sat down for breakfast yesterday and go through the day hour by hour. Every word I said, every response, every action. I think about how I handled situations, what went well and why, and what mistakes I made. The fact I did anything at all is remarkable, such is my usual reluctance to stray anywhere beyond my comfort zone. It's both a constructive and therapeutic exercise. I have no idea if I'll remember any of it or what will happen when the timer reaches zero, but it's better than sitting here fretting about every negative aspect of what has taken place and what is to come. Even if I do wake up in a hospital bed to discover this has all been a hallucinogenic episode from the depths of a comatose mind, I hope some of this experience sticks, real or otherwise.

As I flip to a new page to make notes from the start of today, there's a rap on my bedroom door and it slowly creaks open. I turn in my chair to see the old man's head poking around the door. He decides against coming into the room, possibly because it smells like a teenage boy's bedroom although I no longer notice it.

"Just wanted to say good night."

"Night Dad," I smile.

He hesitates for a few seconds, his awkwardness with the new dynamic in our relationship still obvious.

"Everything all right?" he asks.

"Everything is fine, Dad. And you?"

"I'm getting there."

"Good to hear. Night then."

We swap reassuring nods and he closes the door behind him.

I suspect he'll struggle to maintain such a dramatic change in his character in the long term. In time he'll probably settle on some middle ground where he's more comfortable. That's fine by me. I don't expect him to be perfect, just better. It's too late to undo the damage to my childhood but for Mum's sake I hope he truly has turned over a new leaf so her future won't be blighted by his tyrannical ways. And maybe he'll be more receptive if I ever need to borrow money. We'll see, but I hope I'm never in that position again.

I continue working on my notes from today and then go back over both days to check I haven't missed anything. I mentally relive every moment as I read through my notes, concentrating specifically on the parts where I strayed furthest from my comfort zone and what positives could be taken from each foray. Satisfied I've covered everything, I tear the pages from the jotter, fold them up, and tuck them into my pocket. I let out a satisfied sigh and glance at the countdown timer. Twenty-six minutes remain.

My fate is now out of my hands. Decisions made, actions taken. Too late to change anything, too early to know if those decisions and actions were the right ones. I know I've achieved an awful lot this weekend, but I'd be lying if I said I wasn't feeling apprehensive about what might lie ahead for Craig Pelling. Theories are one thing; it won't be long before I discover the reality.

8

On our tenth wedding anniversary, Megan decided that we needed to be more grown-up, more civilised. Her first act of this new lifestyle was to purchase tickets for the local theatre production of Antony & Cleopatra. She thought it would be a romantic way to spend the evening of our anniversary. There are many words I could use to describe that evening but 'romantic' would not be one of them. Within the first thirty minutes I was bored witless. I spent the remaining hours gazing at my watch, the hands creeping around the dial at such an excruciatingly slow pace it had to be faulty. Shakespeare is not for me, I'm afraid.

I'm reminded of that evening as I watch the digits on the countdown timer pass from fifteen minutes to fourteen minutes. That single minute felt like a lifetime. However, there is one key difference between the tedious minutes of Antony & Cleopatra and the minutes I'm losing now. As I sit on my plastic chair and stare at the screen, every declining minute increases my heart rate as anxiety builds. Every declining minute takes me closer to an unknown future.

To distract myself I try to synchronise the countdown timer on my digital watch with the numbers on the screen. The only reason for doing this is that the timer on the screen doesn't display seconds, which I suspect is one reason every minute feels so long. After a few attempts I get both timers perfectly synchronised and waste a few more minutes in the process. I get up and pace around the bedroom. I'm tempted to turn the stereo on but it's nearly midnight and the last thing I want to do is encourage an angry parent into my bedroom to see why I'm playing music at such a late hour. So all I can do is endure a silence so still all I can hear is my own heart pounding away in my chest.

It soon becomes obvious that my frantic pacing around the room is not helping my anxiety levels so I slump back down on the plastic chair and focus on my breathing. The calm satisfaction I was basking in while distracted by my note-taking dissipates with every passing minute. I now feel like a nervous flyer about to board a plane under thunderous skies. I glance up at the screen and my stomach flips as the counter reaches single digits. Nine minutes to go.

Whatever my meddling in 1986 has achieved, I'm now only minutes from discovering the outcome. Surely it has to be better than what I left behind? It dawns on me that my growing anxiety is actually fear of the unknown. I'm going back to a life I never really lived, founded on thousands of decisions I can never change. Thirty years is a long time so even though I may have fixed some of the issues that blighted my teenage years, it's a drop in the ocean compared to all the subsequent life I would have lived. What if I made worse decisions in my twenties or thirties? I could be in prison, I could be homeless, I could be married to Katie Hopkins. There's no way of knowing and that thought scares the hell out of me.

The only certainty I have is contained within the next nine minutes. I know who I am. I know where I am. I know what I am. I am sixteen years of age although my mind holds forty-six years of knowledge about what has passed and what is to come. I am a miracle. As an idea barges its way to the front of my mind, I realise I'm also an idiot. I kick the idea around for a moment. Why had I not considered it before? Is it even possible? Suddenly I feel rushed, pressurised. It's a ludicrous idea, but it has to be worth a try. I'd never consider making such a monumental decision with so little thought, but time is not a luxury I have. It's now or never.

The timer drops to eight minutes at the exact moment I reach my decision. I don't want to go back. I want to stay here as a sixteen year-old.

No matter what positive changes I've made to my future, I'll still be going back to a life where my best years are probably behind me. If I've had a fulfilling and happy life, I'll have some great memories but that's all they'll ever be; memories. My body, even if I've managed to look after it in my new future, will still be past its best. Then there's the years I spent as a teenager in my former life — job, girlfriend, flat, miscarriage, marriage. I should have spent those years enjoying myself, not tied to one girl, one job and a tenancy agreement. If I changed my life so those things never happened then I want to experience the alternative myself. I want my youth ahead of me, not behind me.

Seven minutes.

And what if I've had children? I'll still miss out on their birth, their first steps, their first words, their first day at school. All those moments that make parenthood so special will be nothing more than hazy memories. At best, I'll be entering the life of a stroppy teenager whom I don't know, or possibly like very much. Then there's that perfect marriage I've fashioned for my future self. Our first date, the proposal, our wedding day, our honeymoon, buying our first home — I can never relive any of that.

Six minutes.

From a practical perspective, can I live this life again? School and my impending exams will be a problem as I can't remember a damn thing about any of my coursework. But with all the knowledge in my head why would I need formal qualifications? I'd be able to set up my own business in any one of a dozen fledgling sectors and make a fortune. I could open a mobile phone store just before the industry explodes in popularity, going from one store to hundreds in just a few years. And when I'm done there, I could get involved in the Internet before most people even know what it is. I could create Facebook before Mark Zuckerberg. I could create Amazon before Jeff Bezos. I could be an Internet billionaire simply by replicating websites that I already know are hugely popular. No, qualifications won't be a problem, that's for sure.

Five minutes.

As sure as I am that I want to stay here, can it be done though? How do I escape the return leg of this impossible journey? There isn't a single clue to guide me, let alone enough time to let my analytical mind research a solution. The most obvious, and only conclusion I can draw is that I must not be sat at the computer when the timer hits zero. I have no idea if that's even important but I've got sod-all else to go on. Or maybe I could just destroy the computer? Would that work? Will the timer stop or will I end up floating between the two timelines forever more? I dismiss the idea. Too risky.

Four minutes.

I force my feet into my trainers with the laces still tied and pull open the bedroom door. I creep down the stairs as quickly as I dare. If I wake my parents or trip over in the dark, it's game over. I turn the lock, open the door and step outside into the chilly night air. I gently pull the door closed until I hear the lock click before checking my watch. Just over three minutes remain. This might be utterly pointless but as I don't have any better ideas, I've got to try it. All I can do is assume, hope even, that if I'm not sat at the computer when the timer hits zero, I'll avoid the hallucinogenic episode that triggered my journey here.

So I run.

I don't know why it should make any difference but I want to put as much distance as possible between myself and the computer before the timer reaches zero. It's a pretty weak theory but I've got nothing else. I run as fast as I can through the dark streets, my thumping heart and vinyl soles slapping tarmac the only sounds to accompany me. I don't know where I'm going, nor does it matter I suppose, I just need to keep moving. More seconds are lost, my lungs sting and lactic acid burns through every muscle in my legs. I push past the pain and focus on nothing but the few yards of tarmac ahead of me. More seconds pass, more tarmac, more pain. I must keep moving.

I glance down at my watch as I pass a street lamp. Fifty-one seconds.

I round a corner onto an unlit road. Every muscle in my body is now screaming at me to stop. I do the opposite and push harder. I can't see more than a few yards in front of me now but it doesn't matter, I have to keep going. I summon every ounce of resolve I have left to fuel my faltering legs. Another glance at the watch but it's too dark to see the display now. I can barely catch my breath as my body demands more oxygen than my lungs can process. The pain is now all-encompassing and every single stride is a victory for willpower over biology. Not even the chill night breeze can prevent beads of sweat running from my forehead and stinging my eyes. Every part of me hurts now.

Like a newborn giraffe, there is no rhythm or control in my steps. It's more stumbling than running. My arms flounder in the air to aid my balance as I eke out whatever is left in me. There's not much, maybe enough for a few more ungainly strides. Even if I could see my watch, I no longer have the energy to steady my arm long enough to confirm how many seconds remain. It doesn't matter.

Beep beep. Beep beep. Beep beep.

The forward motion of my left leg is abruptly arrested. All I can do is force it down to the tarmac and adjust my balance so my right leg swings forward and carries my momentum. It doesn't. A force pushes in the opposite direction, like I'm trying to wade through a swimming pool of syrup. I drop my right leg and try to lift my left. Same result. My upper body should still be moving forward towards a fall but whatever force is preventing my legs from moving, it's also keeping my body upright. It feels like I'm moving in slow motion but with no reference point in the darkness; I could be wrong.

Just as I come to a juddering halt in the middle of the road, the redness arrives.

I know what it means. The future is coming for me and there isn't a thing I can do about it. If my heart wasn't pounding so violently, I'm sure I'd feel it slump to my stomach. The only crumb of comfort I can take is that I'm no longer running and all I can feel in my legs is a deep throbbing sensation. The last traces of adrenalin subside and the throbbing works its way through my body. There is no option other than to succumb.

As the redness closes in around me, it doesn't bring quite the same level of fear as before. Maybe because it's so tinged with disappointment. My makeshift plan has failed and I won't be staying here. I won't get the chance to relive my life the way I wanted to. Whatever I'm going back to, it seems that it's an inevitability I could never change. Maybe it's my new way of thinking, of finding the positive from a negative experience, but I resign myself to my fate. All I can do is hope that I've done enough this weekend to make a difference.

I take my last glimpse of 1986 as the redness engulfs my field of vision. The pulsing in my body reaches a crescendo before the redness fades into a calming white canvas. I think I'm ready now. I let the fear go, it's time to head home. The kaleidoscope of indeterminate shapes return and I feel myself falling. I adjust my perception so I'm not in a terrifying descent. I'm flying now, passing through a cloud of colourful shapes. Faster and faster, but in control, like I'm sat in the cockpit of a supersonic jet. The humming sensation now feels like a massage, purging my body of the pain from my attempted escape. I don't fight any of it. I let it embrace me, carry me.

Then everything stops. The humming, the shapes, the flying sensation. For a second I'm suspended in a perfectly still darkness. This didn't happen before, I'm sure of it. I can't hear anything. I can't see anything. I can't feel anything.

Then I feel something. I really feel something. Bright white light burns my eyes and a searing pain racks my entire body. Pain like I have never felt before. It feels like my bones are being crushed, my muscles ripped from their tendons. An agony of medieval torture proportions, like my body is being turned inside-out. It's a pain that no human could possibly endure for more than a few seconds.

Mercifully my seconds pass and everything fades away until there is nothing.

9

The pain is so intense I'm actually scared to open my eyes. It doesn't matter though as even when I do, I'm in complete darkness. All I can hear is a ringing in my ears. My head is pounding and I'm beyond nauseous. This is far worse than when I first arrived in 1986. I so badly want to investigate, to establish where and who I am, but it's impossible. Even the thought of moving hurts. I now know this feeling was never a hangover; it feels far, far worse. Whatever happened on the return journey, this older version of my body is less able to deal with the consequences than its youthful predecessor. I want to die.

I turn my head a fraction and immediately regret it. I move my right leg and a stabbing pain shoots up my thigh and across my groin. If I could scream I would, but it feels like an invisible elephant is sat on my chest. Blue light strobes in the corner of my eyes. I can't do this. I focus on my breathing and count. Three seconds to inhale, three seconds to exhale. Slow, deliberate breaths that will pull my mind away from the pain and guide me to sleep. I slip away.

Hours pass and I sleep so deeply that no dreams can reach me. Hour after hour of nothing. Then something.

I'm lying on my back in a bed, head on a pillow. I tentatively open my eyes and the darkness has been replaced with muted light. I let my eyes slowly scan from left to right, up and down, trying to convert the shapes into something that might spark a memory. I recognise nothing. This is not a room I've been in before. I draw the obvious conclusion that as I'm in a bed, this must be a bedroom but the scale is different to any bedroom I've ever occupied. The ceiling is impossibly high and the white walls are an unusual distance from the bed. Directly ahead of me there is a ceramic sink fixed to the far wall, next to a chair and a small table with a jug and stack of paper cups sat on top. The source of the dim lighting in the room is a window to my left, hidden behind dark blue vertical blinds that are closed. There is a door to my right but very little else to give any clue to my whereabouts.

Except the smell.

Difficult to describe but a distinctive enough smell that anyone would recognise it within seconds of their first sniff. It's the smell of a hospital. Suddenly a cold realisation sweeps across me. I raise a stiff arm and pat my forehead to find too much skin and not enough hair. I let my arm drop down to my chest and towards my stomach. My podgy, bloated stomach. I close my eyes and curse under my breath. Please, this can't be. My memory scrambles to recall the last two days. Little by little it all comes back, with one stinging memory more vivid than any other. The memory of when I first arrived in my teenage bedroom. I distinctly recall my theory that wherever I was, it wasn't real, and that I was actually lying in a hospital bed being pumped full of drugs.

That moment seemed just as real as everything else that happened but here I am — a chubby middle-aged man with receding hair, just as I was before my psychotic weekend in 1986 began. Did I really have a nervous breakdown? Maybe I had a heart attack. The latter seems more likely with my high blood pressure and unhealthy cholesterol levels. Either way, I've obviously been ill; otherwise why would I be here? The logic is hard to ignore and my analytical mind won't allow me to.

I feel sick to my stomach. How could those two days have been a figment of my imagination? It was too real. The feel of Tessa's naked body, the taste of Mum's Battenburg cake, the smell of my Granddad's aftershave. How could any imagination conjure up such realistic hallucinations? It's not possible, it can't be possible. Yet here I am, as I predicted, in hospital. Everything I did to change my life was just a charade, a cruel and pointless game played out in my own broken mind. There is no reinvented future — I'm still married to Megan, I'm still unemployed, I still have an arsehole for a father and worst of all, my grandparents were still killed.

As the stark realisation of my situation dawns it awakens a sense of bereavement. Mourning for a future that died the moment I awoke in this bed. If my memories of the weekend were only a figment of my imagination why does the pain feel so real? Why am I grieving the loss of what was never mine to begin with? I close my eyes and search every corner of my mind for a way out. Every path I want to take leads down a blind alley and the only exit is acceptance of this reality. Jesus fucking Christ.

As my mind tortuously unpicks everything it created over the weekend, I hear a door swing open. I open my eyes as a nurse bustles past the end of the bed towards the window where she makes a slight adjustment to the blinds, letting more mottled light seep into the room. She moves towards the end of the bed and grabs a clipboard before shuffling up alongside me. She shoots a perfunctory smile in my direction before her attention switches to the clipboard in her hands. She remains silent while she studies whatever awful information is contained on the page. I try to work out her age but the light is still too dim and her uniform too shapeless. She then turns to me and finally speaks, voice low, her accent nondescript.

"I'm Nurse Henley. How are you feeling?"

My mouth is dry as sand so the words leave as a whisper.

"I ache everywhere, particularly my head."

Noticing my difficulty speaking, the nurse trots over to the table and fills a paper cup with water. She returns to my side and holds it out for me. I lift my chubby arm, take the cup and down the tepid water in one gulp.

"Apparently you took a bang on the head, which is why you were unconscious when you came in, but it's nothing serious. A few aspirins should sort that out. Do you have any significant pain anywhere else?"

"No, I just ache."

"Any problems with your vision? Nausea?"

"I felt sick earlier but my vision is okay."

"We'll keep an eye on that but there's nothing broken or any obvious problems it seems. The doctor will be doing his rounds shortly so he'll pop in and check you over."

"How long have I been here?"

She scans the clipboard and checks her watch.

"About six hours."

As she turns to leave, I still have one fundamental question that needs answering.

"What's wrong with me?"

She hooks the clipboard back on the bed and stares at me.

"In medical terms, it's a condition we refer to as 'hung over'. Apart from that, I don't think there's anything wrong with you."

Her blunt answer hangs in the air for a few seconds after she leaves the room.

Alone again, the stillness is a stark contrast to the commotion in my head as I try to piece together the little information I have into something that makes any sense. How could I have been drunk? I don't recall having anything to drink since the reunion, let alone being so paralytic I required an overnight stay in hospital. Another memory crashes in. When I first awoke in my hallucinogenic weekend, I was convinced I was suffering a hangover. Is that connected to my current predicament? I press my balled fists into my temples, trying to force my thoughts into order. But nothing fits. The answers found only spawn more questions.

I close my eyes and try to clear my mind. There is nothing to be gained by going over and over the same questions. There simply isn't enough information to draw any conclusions. My only option is to wait for the doctor and hope he can fill in the blanks. I focus on my breathing but I doubt sleep will come. All I can do is doze sufficiently to find respite from the barrage of questions pummelling my bruised mind.

I drift on the cusp of consciousness for some time. I'm not sure how long, but I'm dragged back to reality as the door opens again. I open my eyes to find a man stood at my bedside. Mid-thirties, average height and build. He's wearing a cheap blue suit, white shirt with no tie. Untidy blonde hair and tired eyes. He doesn't fit my mental image of a doctor.

He speaks with a South London accent.

"How you doing?"

I shuffle into a more upright position and cough to encourage moisture back to my dry mouth.

"Okay, I think."

The man nods and slides his hand inside his jacket, pulling out a black wallet. He flicks it open to reveal a badge and an ID card I can't read.

"Detective Constable Evans. Mind if I take a seat?"

He doesn't wait for an answer as he strides over to the far side of the room and drags a chair across to my bedside. He slumps down on the chair and returns a hand to his jacket pocket, pulling out a notebook and pen.

"If you're up to it, I'd like to ask a few questions. Can we start with your name?"

"Craig Pelling."

"Right, Mr Pelling. That's more than we knew when you arrived here so it's a good start."

He scribbles in his notebook and looks up again.

"Address and date of birth?"

I quote my details as he returns to his scribbling before he closes the notebook. He tucks it back inside his jacket and sits forward on the chair.

"Do you mind if I call you Craig?"

I shrug my shoulders which he takes as a yes.

"Craig, do you want to tell me about last night? What was it? A stag-night prank that went wrong?"

I don't have the first clue what he's on about.

"Sorry, you've lost me."

"You don't remember?"

I shake my head and hope his detection skills are honed enough to see I'm not lying.

"Okay, let me fill in a few blanks for you, see if we can nudge a few memories. That all right?"

I doubt I have much choice but nod, anyway.

"At 12.11am we received reports of a man lying in the middle of Alexander Road. A unit was dispatched and our officers found the man unconscious, and naked. Despite the efforts of our officers to revive him, the man remained in a state similar to somebody heavily intoxicated. As they couldn't question him and were concerned for his safety, he was brought here for examination, still unconscious. I'm sure you can guess who that man is?"

I stare back at the detective with a mixture of confusion and horror.

"Me?"

"We're getting somewhere. Now we know the details, care to explain how you ended up in such a state?"

My mind is now approaching a cataclysmic meltdown. I have no memories, no answers. I want to curl up in a ball and hide from the world, pretend none of this is happening. Such is my need to find stability, safety, a few involuntary words leave my mouth.

"I need to see my wife."

The detective lets out a deep sigh and rummages in his jacket pocket. Judging by his expression I suspect he wants to be here even less than I do. An open-and-shut case of a pissed, middle-aged idiot found naked after a stag do. Not worth the ink on the paperwork.

"Fine. I'll make a few calls and we'll fetch your wife. What's her name?"

"Megan."

"Once your wife is here, we need to get some answers so I can close the file. I can assure you I've got better things to do than investigate your drunken pranks. Jesus, you're old enough to know better. Are we clear?"

I nod and he mutters something before stomping out of the room.

I wait for maybe twenty minutes and decide I can't lie in the bed any longer. I'm past caring if there is anything physically wrong with me. I drag the heavy blanket off my body and look down on the faded gown I was somehow dressed in when I arrived here. I swing my legs around and place my feet in the floor. With so little energy at my disposal, it takes a monumental effort. I catch my breath and wait for the dizziness to fade. I steady myself by planting my hands on the bed and then I push myself up. It's a mistake. I lurch forward, my legs buckle and I collapse in a heap. This just gets worse. I pause for a moment and check nothing more than my dignity is damaged. With a strained effort, I reach across to the chair still sat by the bed and pull it towards me. After a few attempts, I manage to hoist myself up, twist my plump body around and fall onto the chair.

The only consolation of my tumble is that my thoughts are temporarily dragged away from the myriad of questions buzzing around my head. I take a few deep breaths and try to work out my next move. It seems anything beyond sitting down is impossible. I need to get my energy levels back, I need food. The thought actually makes me want to heave. I have no appetite, least not for hospital food, but I can't do a thing until my body is properly fuelled.

I turn and press the button beside the bed to hail the nurse. While I wait for her to arrive, I sit and stare at my plump body which I'm now able to view in its full glory. I'm not sure why it would be any different to how it was before my psychotic episode but it feels twice the size now, like one of those inflatable fat suits people wear to fancy dress parties. I hate it more than I ever thought possible.

The door opens and Nurse Henley marches in.

"You're up I see. What do you want?"

"Can I have some food please?"

She eyes my partially clothed body with disdain. It's clear I'm not going to die of malnutrition any time soon.

"They'll be around with breakfast shortly," she snaps.

She spins on her heels and leaves before I can ask how long 'shortly' is.

I wonder if the detective told her about my alleged drunken antics? It would explain why she seems so unsympathetic, and who could blame her? Why should I be taking up a valuable bed when there are people with genuine health issues waiting for it?

Minutes pass but without a watch or clock anywhere I can only guess how many. Thirty? Forty? Maybe longer? I've got no idea. All I can do is sit in my uncomfortable chair and stare at the walls. Just to add to my depressed thoughts, the room sparks memories of the one Megan was in after she lost the baby. A million years ago but hard to forget. Is it fair to drag Megan back to a room that might remind her of the worst moment of her life? Maybe not, but for the first time in decades I need her support right now. And if I'm honest, I have little choice.

I continue to stare at the walls, lost in my thoughts, when the door crashes open and Detective Constable Evans storms in. He stands a few feet in front of me and judging by his expression, he's not a happy man. His words are delivered with obvious frustration.

"I don't have the patience for your antics. I'll ask you one more time and I want the truth — what's your name?"

10

I stare at the detective for a moment. I heard what he said but I'm not sure I understand why he said it.

"What? I told you. It's Craig Pelling."

He pulls his notebook from his pocket and studies the page. He then holds it out, a foot from my face.

"And that is definitely your correct address?"

I squint at his atrocious handwriting and convert the scribbles into letters that form my correct address.

"Yes, definitely."

He puts his notepad back in his pocket and stares at the ceiling for a moment.

"Right. The problem we have is that Craig Pelling doesn't live at that address."

"Eh? That's not right. I've lived there for over twenty years."

"I've checked the electoral roll for the last twenty years and no Craig Pelling has ever lived at that address."

Before I can say anything in reply, he squats down and lowers his voice.

"In fact, there is no record of a Craig Pelling having lived anywhere in this town within the last twenty years."

This guy is starting to rile me. I know any computer system is only as good as the person who inputs the data and somebody has clearly made an error.

"Did you find my wife? I want to see her," I snap.

"Well, that might be possible — if she existed. But unsurprisingly, there's no record of a Megan Pelling at that address either. Or anywhere else for that matter."

"This has to be a computer error. We've lived at that house for over twenty years, I'm telling you straight."

"Could have been a computer error, but I'm a diligent detective so I called the current occupants of the address you gave me. Turned out to be a very helpful couple called Mr & Mrs Emberson, who've lived there for twenty-two years. They bought the house from a Mr Curtis who purchased it from new. Two owners, neither of them you, or your mystery wife."

The detective stands back up and folds his arms. His eyes burn into me and his brow creases.

"Whatever trouble you think you're in, it's gonna get a lot worse if you keep lying to me."

I bow my head.

"I'm telling you the truth."

It appears that the detective's patience is at breaking point.

"You know what? I think you're involved in some sort of stupid prank and for reasons only known to you, even now you're keeping it up."

"It's not a prank," I protest.

"I don't believe you. And I'm telling you, it ends here and now."

"My name is Craig Pelling and my wife's name is Megan."

Detective Evans considers his next move. He pauses for a moment before pulling a mobile phone from his pocket. He swipes the screen a few times and hands it to me.

"If this isn't a twisted prank, explain that."

I take hold of the phone. After my apparent sabbatical from mobile phones it almost feels strange holding one again. I stare at the screen, which displays a website. It looks like the front page of our local newspaper and I can just about read the tiny headline text...

"TEENAGER KILLED IN TRAGIC HIT & RUN"

I double-tap the screen so that the story text is large enough to read...

"Police are seeking witnesses to a tragic hit-and-run incident that occurred around midnight on Sunday. The teenage victim, so far unnamed, was struck by a white van and fatally injured at the junction of Alexander Road and Eton Drive. Emergency services arrived within minutes but the victim was pronounced dead at the scene. According to a witness, the victim was standing motionless in the middle of Alexander Road as a van rounded the corner from Eton Drive. The van then struck the victim at speed before driving off. In a police statement, Detective Inspector Mark Perry asked the public for any information regarding the whereabouts of the vehicle which is thought to have suffered significant damage to the front end."

I drop the phone to my lap.

"That's awful, but what has it got to do with me?"

"The junction of Alexander Road and Eton Drive. Ring any bells?"

"No, why should it?"

"It's where my colleagues found you last night, around midnight ironically."

"Sorry, I don't understand where you're going with this. Shouldn't you be trying to find my wife?"

He rolls his eyes and presses his hand to his temple, seemingly now at the end of his tether. He steps towards the bed and perches himself on the edge, only a few feet from my position on the chair.

"Your date of birth makes you forty-six years of age. Correct?"

I nod, unsure why my age is relevant to anything.

"I pegged you for at least fifty, no offence. I don't suppose you're lying about your age as well as your name?"

"No, no. I gave you my correct date of birth."

He drums his fingers on his chin for a moment.

"They never found him, you know."

"Found who?"

"The van driver. Somebody killed that kid and just drove away, like nothing happened. Terrible really."

He doesn't add anything else, content to let me endure the silence and absorb his words. Maybe he thinks I'll feel pressurised to say something. I know to keep quiet.

"Do you know how I found that newspaper article?"

"No I don't," I sigh, wishing he would just fuck off and leave me alone.

"When I couldn't find the name, 'Craig Pelling' on the electoral roll, I searched on the Internet. That's where I found the article you just read. There were several other articles about the incident too. A couple of them included the kid's name once it was released to the public."

I look at him with a vacant expression.

"That poor kid hit by the van — his name was Craig Pelling."

Both my stomach and mind simultaneously churn. The detective presses on.

"He died over thirty years ago, which is why his name didn't appear in our original search. That website page was from the local newspaper archive for May 1986."

He leans towards me, his eyes narrow.

"So, whoever you are, why are you using the name of a kid who was killed thirty years ago? Is there something you want to get off your chest?"

My analytical mind had already finished its work before the detective finished his sentence. Just as well because it then collapses into a ball of impenetrable fear. Pure, unadulterated fear. The only time I can recall such terror is when my body was wracked with pain — a moment I was beginning to think never happened. But it did, and the memories cascade. The countdown timer, running through the streets, burning lungs, the dark road, the redness, my legs seizing. And then that pain.

Sweet Jesus. What have I done?

I can barely say the words but if I'm to believe them, I have to. They eventually fall from my mouth.

"It's…my…fault."

The obvious, devastating conclusion is finally drawn. I ran from my bedroom and put my teenage self in front of that van. I killed him and the universe has corrected itself by dumping my fat carcass back where it belongs in the here and now. And that's all I am now, a carcass, an empty shell of a human being. Craig Pelling died in 1986 because I left him in the middle of the road. Far from fixing anything, I've broken everything. I've deleted my own existence — I'm now a John Doe, the prime suspect behind my own demise.

The detective gets to his feet and moves closer to me, barely a few feet away. I stare into space, numb now. Too much emotion for any human to endure. My mind shuts down. The words he utters next are meaningless. I hear them but it's too late for them to be processed.

"I am arresting you on suspicion of causing death by dangerous driving. You do not have to say anything but it may harm your defence if you do not mention when questioned something you later rely on in court. Anything you say may be given in evidence."

The blackness returns and I welcome it. The room spins and the last thing I hear is a muffled voice. I feel like I'm falling.

Then I'm gone.

TEN MONTHS LATER...

19th May

It may not be a prison but I'm not allowed to leave until they say I'm well enough. It's not that bad though. I have my own room, and after ten months and sixteen days, I've almost come to think of it as home. I like the routine here, it's comforting. It was probably the routine that saved my fragile mind when I first arrived here. I remember little about those first few weeks. I think my mind just shut down, unable to determine what was real any more. I do remember the conversation with Detective Evans, and his suspicion I killed Craig Pelling back in 1986. I am guilty, but not in any way the detective could prove, which is why I'm currently residing in a secure hospital rather than a prison.

I wanted to tell them the truth, I really did, but they would have thrown away the key. What happened to me was so implausible that I barely believe it myself some days. Without the truth, they're struggling to work out what's wrong with me. I've undergone so many tests I gave up counting a long time ago. At first they thought I was suffering from acute amnesia until I underwent a few sessions of cognitive hypnotherapy. I dread to think what they dredged from my fucked mind but whatever it was, they quickly decided that a lost memory wasn't the problem. They've narrowed down my condition to some form of delusional schizophrenia although I know they're wrong. Still, I have to play the game.

By the fourth week of my incarceration here, I was mentally stable enough to self-diagnose my condition and determine if I really was suffering a delusional breakdown. It wasn't difficult. We have a small library which contains four archaic computers. Although we can access the Internet, our usage is monitored and extremely limited in terms of the websites we're permitted to visit. We're not allowed to create social media or email accounts — we can look out on the world but we can't engage with it. It doesn't matter as there's nobody for me to communicate with. Besides, all I needed to test my sanity was Google Street View.

It took less than fifteen minutes for me to determine I wasn't suffering a mental illness. The first address I searched was my marital home. I dropped the marker right outside our home and zoomed-in on the boxy, terraced house as close as I could. So much was different. The front door was dark blue, not red. The wooden windows had been replaced with those horrible plastic PVC frames, and the tiny front garden was paved, now a parking space. Then I searched the name of a small retail park on the edge of town. I dropped the marker on the boundary road so I could clearly see the RolpheTech store. It was still a RolpheTech store and appeared to be still trading. Finally, and with some trepidation, I searched for my parents' address.

The differences were subtle. There were no net curtains and the small decorative plate on the front of the house which once displayed the house number, was gone. There were weeds sprouting around the edge of the driveway; something my old man would never have tolerated. Most telling though, were two small pairs of wellington boots sat by the front door, one pair pink, one pair red — children's wellington boots. It was no longer my parents' home, but I had no way of telling how long it had been since they moved away, or even if they were still alive. Perhaps they moved, as they planned, to the retirement flat. Maybe they couldn't live in that house after my death and sold up years ago. I can't access any website that might tell me where they went.

When I'm not thinking about my parents, or Megan, or Lucy, or Dave, or anyone else who was once in my life, I keep myself busy. Actually, I keep myself busy so I don't think about them. To my parents, Craig Pelling is now a distant memory; a long-dead son. To Megan and Lucy, Craig Pelling is nobody; I was never part of their lives. I only use that name in my head now as I was told I couldn't use it when I arrived here because it was considered inappropriate. I chose the surname 'Wilson', my mother's maiden name. Craig Pelling doesn't exist. He's not on any database, anywhere. He's never worked, never paid taxes, never passed a driving test, never married, never had children, never registered on the electoral roll. So now I am Craig Wilson although I only exist in this place. Besides a short journey here in an ambulance, Craig Wilson has never stepped foot in the real world.

I forget, keeping busy. I read, a lot, sometimes five books a week. I love the escape, my mind drifting beyond these walls as I lose myself in a fictional world for hours on end. When I'm not reading, I'm exercising in the modest gym we have here. It was a promise I made to myself, well, to Lucy really. She'll never see the results but I think she'd be proud of me. I started on a treadmill, walking a few mindless miles as I stared at the blank wall ahead of me. Then I discovered 'happy pain'. I pushed my body, and it hurt, but the pain served as a distraction from my reality and the boredom. The more I pushed myself, the more I became addicted to the rush of endorphins. As the months passed, and coupled with my inability to consume fast food or alcohol, my weight plummeted. I now weigh seventy pounds less than I did when I was Craig Pelling and my body is unrecognisable. It's not like Dave's muscled physique; I'm lean, toned, my muscles defined but not bulging. It's the body I always wanted but I'm not able to share my success with anyone who really cares.

My case officer tells me I'll be able to leave soon, maybe next month. They're waiting for accommodation to become available. When I leave here, it will be for a small flat in a block managed by social services. That will be my home for up to a year, while I rebuild my life and reintegrate with society. Then I'm on my own. As part of the reintegration process, they've organised a part-time job in a charity shop for me, if I want it. They say it will help to prove that I'm not a danger to myself and I can function as a normal human being. I'm going to try. Craig Wilson's CV is looking a little sparse so it will be a start.

The hardest part of my transition will be living a life as sparse as my CV. I'll be starting from scratch with no real home, no real job, no family, no wife, and no friends — a clean slate. In some ways, I've got what I wanted. I'm fit, healthy, and I'm no longer stuck in a dead-end job or a loveless marriage. It's what I wanted, but not this way. I miss too many people, particularly my mum and Lucy. I feel alone, scared if I'm honest. I have to decide if I can live with that, or if I need to find answers. I honestly don't know. Can I forge a new life knowing there might be a chance, no matter how improbable, to undo the damage I caused?

It's a good question.

THE END (or is it?)

Want to know what happens next?

Well, that was 'The '86 Fix' — I really hope you enjoyed it. If you did, you might want to read the follow-up, 'Beyond Broadhall', which is now available on Amazon.

I promise you there is an awful lot more in store for Craig Pelling, and a definitive ending to his story.

Now, can I beg a favour?

Writing a book is hard, especially the first one. And once it's written, getting people to actually read it is even harder. I don't have an agent or a publisher so I'm reliant on good people like you to help me share the word.

If you enjoyed reading this book and have a few minutes spare, I would be eternally grateful if you could leave a review on Amazon. I know it's a pain, but for fledgling authors like me, it's the only way we can gain traction for our books (which allows us to write more books).

You'd make this budding author very happy indeed if you're able to say something nice in the Amazon reviews.

Just before you go...

For more information about me and to sign-up for emails on new releases, pop-over to my website...

www.keithapearson.co.uk

I'd like to thank Simon Brooks, Keith Randall and Julia Perry for their kind help reviewing, and providing honest feedback. And finally, a dedication if I may — for Jean Pearson, my mum. Always in my heart.

Printed in Great Britain
by Amazon